REBECCAH GILTROW is
Suffolk. She escaped f ⌐olchester,
Essex, where she achie ⌐.A. (hons) English
Language and Literature, and M.A. Literature: Creative
Writing from University of Essex.

She has published a collection of Christmas short stories, but *Lexa Wright's Dating Sights* is her first full length novel.

For more information about Rebeccah and her writing, please visit her blog - http://rebeccahgiltrow.blogspot.co.uk

ALSO BY REBECCAH GILTROW

12 Days of Krista May Rose

Lexa Wright's Dating Sights

Rebeccah Giltrow

First published in England in 2012 by Createspace for Amazon

Text copyright © Rebeccah Giltrow 2012
Author image (back cover) copyright © Di Humphrey 2012

All Rights Reserved
No part of this publication may be reproduced or transmitted in any form or by any means, electronic or mechanical, including photocopy, recording, or any information storage and retrieval system, without prior consent and permission in writing from the author.

The author asserts the moral right under the Copyright, Designs and Patents Act 1988 to be identified as the author of this work.

This is a work of fiction. Names, characters, businesses, places, events, and incidents are either the products of the author's imagination or used in a fictitious manner. Any resemblance to actual persons, living or dead, or actual events is purely coincidental.

ISBN-13: 978-1482350593

ISBN-10: 1482350599

For Mum and Dad (and Lily)

1

The clock on the wall in my study isn't working. It's not that it's broken; it just needs a new battery but I can't be bothered to change it. I'll do it later. According to this clock it's nearly ten past eleven. I watch the motionless hands as I start up my computer. The familiar dah-dah-dah-dah tune belts out of my speakers. I sing along. The screen flickers and wakes up. A drowsy eye opens to reveal a full screen desktop background of a photo montage of Beryl, my shih-tzu, at various stages throughout her three human year, twenty-one dog year, life. The real life Beryl pads her way across the carpet and jumps onto the armchair by the window. She pushes the cushion off with a shove of a paw and makes herself comfortable. She knows she's going to be there a while. She scratches and claws at the material before pulling the hand-knitted throw from the head rest and wrapping it around her freshly coiffured body. She stretches, yawns and falls asleep.

I turn back to my computer. I open the document that I started yesterday, imaginatively entitled book. It is here that I will write my masterpiece. It's going to be a semi-fictional account of my life. I haven't done many exciting things in my thirty human year, two-hundred-and-ten dog year life, but I've always been told to write what I know, and what do I know better than my own life? A little bit of exaggeration here and there won't hurt. I mean, that's what autobiographies are anyway, right? I'll just omit all the school bullying, adult heartbreak, and general death, destruction and decay, and replace it with, well, something nicer.

The page is blank. The erect, black curser winks at me, flirtatiously. 'Come on, write something, make me ... dirty,' it says. It licks its lips and winks some more. I pull my hair back into a ponytail, flex my fingers and hover them over the keyboard.

I can't write anything until I've chosen the font. The font is very important when writing a book. It can't be too silly but it also can't be too severe. I scroll down the list, pondering the swirly, ye olde Englishe, Shakespearian-looking font. It's so pretty. I type my name. I can't read it. I enlarge it. I still can't read it, and I know what's written there. I reluctantly return to the pre-set font that appears whenever you open a document. I suppose that will do for now.

Page numbers. A book isn't a book without page numbers. I click the tab to insert page numbers. Like with the fonts, there is so much choice; too much if you ask me. Do I want the numbers on the left, in the middle or on the right? Do I want them as digits or as words? Do I want them at the top or the bottom of the page? Bold? Bracketed? Underlined? Under dots? I settle on a clear Page 1 of 1, at the bottom, in the middle of the page.

I glance at the clock. It's still nearly ten past eleven. Beryl is quietly snoring. I open facebase and scroll through the list of banal status updates. Jenny is bored. Nicola wants a bacon sandwich. Chris loves Lisa lots and lots and lots and lots and lots. Bleurgh. Marie is off to the dentist this afternoon. Since when have I ever cared about these things? Social networking for the anti-social. I scroll down. Max dont no wot 2 do wiv myself 2day so board. Why do I stay friends with these people? Bastian kommer aldrig att få sin avhandling klar. I should really learn Swedish. Torsten braucht einen Urlaub. And German. I'll do that later.

I check my e-mails before I start seriously writing. I don't want to be distracted by those later on, when I'm in the zone. I have one-thousand-one-hundred-and-forty-two unread messages. It's not that I'm super popular; it's that I never read them and I never delete them. I scroll down the first page of e-mails and quickly scan the subject lines. It's your last chance to grab a bargain in various clothes shop sales. You really should treat yourself to something from your bookshop wishlist; you know you want to. I do want to but I could spend hours window shopping and I'd never get anything done. Bank Holiday gig listings in your area. Hello friend. I know it's going to be spam but I click on it anyway. Considering that I'm a white, English woman, from an ancestral line of white, English people, I apparently have an extremely rich Nigerian relative who has just recently died. I guess we must be related through marriage. I am their last living relative and I am set to inherit one million dollars (USD $1,000,000). That's right, one million dollars (USD $1,000,000). My rich Nigerian relative's lawyer has searched the whole world and has managed to locate me and e-mail me with this tragic but also awesome news. All I have to do in order to receive the money is send him my name, address, age, date of birth, bank details, shoe size, favourite brand of shampoo and the number of marshmallows I can fit in my mouth at once, and he will transfer the funds into my bank account immediately. Seems legitimate. I click the red X in the corner of the e-mail. It disappears. One down, one-thousand-one-hundred-and-forty-one to go. My eyes have become immune to the penis enlargement and male sex aid tablet e-mails and messages from sexy singles in my area that want to meet me.

The red light flashes on my phone like an angry Cyclops. I unlock the screen and it lights up with an alert bubble. I have three missed calls from Louise and a text message from Louise. I open the message. Why do you always have your phone on silent? Anyway, no can do for drinks tonight, got another date. Will text you later if I need you to be my get-out-call. Make sure your phone's turned on! Love you bye. Great. I turn and look at Beryl.

"It's just you and me again tonight, Beryl," I say.

She raises an eyelid in annoyance. I click the arrow at the bottom of the computer screen and move to page two. More junk and sales and scams. Louise has invited you ... curiosity compels my finger to click open this e-mail ... to join MatesDates.com. She's been nagging me for ages to join, but, I don't know, it just seems weird. Our conversations are always the same, word for word. *You'll never bump into the man of your dreams in a supermarket* she'll nag. I do all my shopping online anyway. *Even more reason to step into the world of online dating. It's not like Deb, the Russian shot putter delivery driver, is going to turn into a hunky man, is it?* she'll say. You never know. *Come into the twentieth century. Internet dating is the way of the future* she'll nag. Twenty-first century. *Whatever.*

MatesDates is a safe and secure site where you can meet the partner of your dreams, date to your heart's content, or just meet and make new friends. Whatever your relationship needs, MatesDates is the site for you. Every day, thousands of people throughout the world use MatesDates to make contact with people, flirt, chat and date. Your perfect partner is out there somewhere and they could be right here on MatesDates waiting for you. So what are you waiting for? Sign up today, FREE! I move the mouse towards the red X in the corner of the e-mail. I'm happy being single. No I'm not. Yes I am. I'm an independent woman with my own home and my own money. I don't need a man. Yes I do. No I don't. I might not need one, but I'd quite like to have one. No I wouldn't. They make life complicated. I've got Beryl and my writing. My life is complete. No it's not. I hate my life. I don't really hate it. But having a man would give my life another dimension. My finger doesn't click the button to delete the e-mail. In fact, my mouse moves back down the screen and sits on the large JOIN NOW button. I click. Curiosity is going to kill me, I just know it.

A new page opens. A scrolling bar along the top of the website shows an array of happy couples partaking in various couply activities; walking along the beach, laughing in a restaurant, pointing at a giraffe at the zoo, eating breadsticks on a checked blanket in a park, picking grapes in a vineyard, salsa dancing, rowing a boat. It's free. Where's the harm. I scroll down. I am a … I click the drop down box … woman, looking for a … I click the drop down box … man, aged between … I click the drop down box. I have a rule that I will never date anyone who is young enough to be my son (I don't have one of those) or old enough to be my dad (I do have one of those). So that gives me a sixteen human year, one-hundred-and-twelve dog year window, either way. I am a woman looking for a man aged between fourteen, wait, hang on, no, that's wrong on so many levels. The list of ages doesn't even go down that young. I don't want to meet someone too young. I don't want to be labelled a cougar just yet. I am a woman looking for a man aged between … I click the drop down box … 26 and … I click the drop down box … 46. I guess I'll be able to change it later if I need to.

Username. I hate these things. Every time I sign up to something, the username I've chosen has already been taken, and then I have to have a strange concoction of numbers and letters that I can never decipher. I type in my name and immediately delete it. There are some right weirdos on the internet and I'm sure Louise has been on dates with all of them. I don't want to give away too much to start with just in case I get my very own stalker, although I have often wondered what it would be like to have a stalker. One of those nice ones who sends you flowers and pays for your parking ticket fines. Not one of those creepy ones who sends you boxes of human toes and has plastic surgery on their face so they look like you.

I need something subtle with a bit of mystique to it. Something unique and catchy. Something that encapsulates me in every essence. I think, but as usual, my creativity is always stumped when it comes to making up names.

I open a new web page and do a search for 'username generators'. Pages and pages of sites appear but I can't be bothered to search through them all. I click on the first page. It looks straightforward enough.

Generate a random username with randomusernamegenerator.com ... these guys are clearly as creative as I am when coming up with names for things. But there are still so many decisions. Do I want a two-word, three-word, four-word username? Do I want it to contain numbers? And I have to choose various topics that I want my two-, three-, or four-word username to come from. As three is a magic number, I choose a three-word username that will consist of one emotion word, one colour word and one animal word, and no numbers. Animal usernames are always cute. I click on the GENERATE button and a list of about twenty names appear on the screen. HappyPurpleLobster. No. SadBlackCat. No. AngryPinkBear. Still no. ScaredBlueFerret. This isn't as easy as I initially thought it would be.

I look inside the coffee mug sitting on the table next to my desk. It's empty. I get up. Beryl lifts her head but doesn't follow me. I walk into the kitchen, flick the kettle's on switch and lean against the worktop. I look around the room for username inspiration; breadbin, fridge, washing up liquid, knife block, mixing bowl, colander, ladle, scary painting of a headless woman dragging a boat through a forest. No inspiration here. The kettle steams and clicks to let me know it's ready. I have no idea why I turned the kettle on; I don't even like hot drinks. I open the fridge, take out a carton and fill my coffee mug with juice. I check to see what else is in the fridge; eggs, cheese, yoghurt, leftover shepherd's pie, dog food, milk, beef tomatoes, lemonade, an expired credit card in an old cream cheese tub, no, it's still in date so it's going to stay in the fridge, mayonnaise, but no usernames. I close the door and walk back to my study.

Beryl is in the same position she was when I left the room. I put my face close to hers to make sure she's still breathing. She opens her eyes wide and jerks her head backwards. I kiss her nose and she growls at me. I don't mind; at least she's alive. My screensaver drags itself past my eyes. In bold pink lettering, the words STOP PROCRASTINATING, START WRITING scroll by. I'd completely forgotten that I was supposed to be writing. I jiggle the mouse and the dating website greets me. I minimise that and stare at the white page, tainted only by Page 1 of 1 at the bottom in the centre.

I hold down Ctrl on my keyboard and hit BU in quick succession. I type Chapter 1, and it appears at the top left of the page in bold type and underlined. I hold down the Ctrl key again and press E. The text jumps to the centre of the page. I don't like it there. It looks like a school essay. I hold down the Ctrl key and press L to send it back to its original position.

I look at the clock. It's still nearly ten past eleven. My eye is drawn to the dating website that is resting at the bottom of my screen. I wake it up and type TheProcrastinator into the username box, and my e-mail address into the box beneath it. I squint my eyes and click the CREATE PROFILE button. Flashing red text informs me that I have not completed all the compulsory fields, and a red asterisk drags my eye to the date of birth box. I do as

I'm told. My username is taken, but some other suggestions are TheProcrastinator378, TheProcrastinator941, TheProcrastinator667. No. I always feel that a number detracts from the strength of a username.

I spin my chair around and notice that Beryl is no longer lying in the armchair. I didn't even hear her get up. I call her name and look for her. She's sitting by the back door. I look at the clock in the hall. This clock works, even if it's a bit slow. It's quarter to one. Where did the morning go? I open the back door and Beryl runs outside. She does her business and bounds around the garden like a lamb. I notice a peg on the ground. I pick it up and clip it to the washing line.

It starts to rain. I quickly walk inside and call Beryl in. She doesn't move. Some days she hates the rain and won't take a step outside and other days she loves the rain and would gladly spend hours under the clouds. Today is one of those days.

"Fine," I say. "You can stay out there."

I move to close the door and she comes bounding towards me. She smells like wet dog. She finds her towel and pulls it out from under the kitchen table. She contorts herself and rubs her wet body over the fabric. I give her a hand and dry her as much as I can. I put a couple of slices of bread in the toaster and wander into the living room. I switch on the television and Beryl makes herself comfortable on the sofa. For such a small dog, she manages to stretch herself over all three seats. The toaster pops. I walk back into the kitchen and take the toast out of the toaster. I smother the toast with peanut butter, crunchy of course, and take it back into the living room.

The television depresses me but I can't be bothered to get up to get the remote control. A woman is yelling at her ex-boyfriend because he slept with both her and her mother, and now they're both pregnant. He has about three teeth and a large tattoo of a panther on his face, starting just above his eyebrow and crawling down to his jaw. This is why I'm single. I can't risk finding someone like this. I guess the internet isn't the only place to find weirdos. They're on chat shows too. The man doesn't seem to be able to pronounce consonants. I assume this has something to do with his lack of teeth.

"I laah yeh yeh naa I laah yeh yeh meh girh I caah liih wowh yeh," he says.

I'm sure my ears started bleeding. The women are equally as classy. The daughter is wearing a leopard print, skin tight dress, at least four sizes too small, and she clearly hasn't heard of shampoo.

"I laah yeh tooh buuh aas maah muuh," the daughter replies.

She points across the stage to a woman with no teeth, wearing another inappropriate dress.

"Yaah neeh a reeh wuuhmaah," the mother coherently interjects, rubbing her hands down her body.

At this point I think my eyes start bleeding too. I don't want to live on this planet anymore. Beryl sits at my feet for her corner of toast. I get up and switch off the television before I smash it. The postman comes. Beryl sniffs the envelopes and walks off. If it's not food, she's not interested. To be honest, if it's not food, I'm not really interested. I notice a leaflet for a new curry place in town. That's food; I'm interested. Free delivery. Bonus. I stick it to the fridge with a London bus magnet. The rest can wait until later. I put the other envelopes on the pile of yesterday's envelopes on the kitchen table. It falls over. I guess it's not just yesterday's post there.

I open the dishwasher, take out the clean cutlery and shove it into a bulging drawer. It won't close. I pull it out. It's chaos in there. I make a space on the kitchen table and drop the drawer there. A few things bounce out; a chop stick, a stack of Post-it notes and a pipette I used for feeding Beryl when she was ill as a puppy. I take out all the knives, forks and spoons; the things you would expect to find in a cutlery drawer, and put them on the worktop. I'm left with a stapler, seven chopsticks, a stack of Post-it notes, a puppy feeding pipette, two medicine spoons, a pair of glow in the dark eyebrow tweezers, a crumpled up page with one of my poems on one side and a recipe for beef stroganoff on the other, three dog poo bags, eighteen hair clips, a comb, a floppy disk, a packet of prawn cocktail flavour crisps, a china swan figurine, a black bootlace, a black shoelace, a small jar of oregano, a box of matches, a lone gold hoop earring which isn't mine, an instruction manual for the sandwich toaster, four bunches of keys, eleven squashed cupcake cases, a bottle opener, a jelly mould in the shape of a teddy bear, and a lot of crumbs. I tip the crumbs into the bin and put the drawer on the draining board, ready to wash it. I'll do it later.

I put a huge jumper on over all my clothes. It's purple and comes down to my knees. I could probably fit three people in here without too much trouble. The sky is still grey but at least it's stopped raining. Beryl has resumed her position on the armchair in my study. My screensaver yells at me for the second time today. I sit down and type words. Random words. Anything just to get rid of the abrasive whiteness of the blank page. The random words turn into a poem. Not a very good poem, but a poem nonetheless. I click File then Save As and type poem and hit the Enter key on my keyboard. I return to the book. My masterpiece. I write a page about a young girl's first day at school. Her first day at school is surprisingly similar to my first day of school; floods of tears, rivers of glue, storms of glitter, fields of dressing up clothes, and mountains of potatoes and seas of multi-coloured paint for potato stamp printing. I'm pleased with the progress so I give myself a break.

I go back to the dating site. If they don't have TheProcrastinator for me to use, how about TheProcrastinatress? Username accepted. Brilliant.

Password. Oh you've got to be joking. I can't be thinking up something that no-one else will guess, because I always forget those number letter underscore star hash hash letter number passwords. I type in my name. That's one word I will always remember. Password not secure enough. I add 123 to the end. Password accepted.

Now to start building my profile. It seems they've started with the scariest bit; choosing a profile picture. A profile picture guarantees you will receive more interest from other MatesDates users. Whoever wrote that clearly hasn't seen my photo albums. I click the BROWSE button and scroll through an array of unsuitable shots. It's not that I'm naked. It's that I don't photograph very well at all. I could use one of me dancing in a club. It shows that I like having fun and that I'm social, but it also shows me sweating like a pig, with red, puffy cheeks and eyes that have rolled back into my head. I could use the one of me on holiday with Louise and Marie, sitting under a parasol on a Spanish beach. Again, I'm sociable, I like to travel, I like having fun, and I'm also the worst looking girl in the photo. Why did I pick such attractive friends? And why did I pick friends who tan, whereas I burn, peel and go white again? How about an obligatory cheesy Christmas photo with the family? It shows I love my family, but it also shows how much of a mess my house is and I don't know how to cut my drunk uncle, who's wearing a blonde wig and lipstick, out of the picture. I take a picture with my phone there and then. No. Definitely no to that one. I'll have to find a photo later. I move on to the next section.

Hobbies and interests. I think for a minute. I have hobbies and interests, surely. What do I enjoy doing? I like shouting at idiots on the television. No, I can't put that. That'll make me sound like a crazy lady, which isn't too far from the truth. I take photos of street signs and house numbers, and lightbulbs at odd angles, and close-ups of the patterns made by peeling paint on wooden doors, and Beryl.

Again, not really helping me seem sane. But photography, that's a hobby. I type photography. Well writing, obviously. I write. I click open my document again. I minimise it quickly. I have written. I type writing. I look around my study. Piles of books prop up piles of books. They could really do with some sort of alphabetising or organising by genre. I'll do it later. I like to read. I type reading, without being specific about what my literary tastes are, as I'm still not really sure myself.

I notice a book with a bookmark sticking out, about a third of the way through. I gingerly pull the book out, while another ten tomes balance precariously on top of it. I steady the wobbling tower with my hip and flick through the first few pages. I don't remember reading this. I don't even recognise the front cover, the title or the author. I hold the book open at the bookmarked page. The bookmark is an old Chinese takeaway menu. I open it up. It all looks so good. I turn to the back page. RECOMMENDED SET MEALS. A - for one person: Chicken Chop Suey, Sweet & Sour Pork, Egg Fried Rice. Yum, but I'm really hungry. B - for two persons: Beef Chop Suey, Sweet & Sour Chicken, King Prawn with Mushrooms, Yeung Chow Fried Rice. That's more like it. I pick up my phone and punch in the phone number on the front of the menu. I place my order and ask for it to be delivered. The voice tells me it will be half an hour to forty-five minutes. That'll give me enough time to get this stupid MatesDates profile finished.

I take the menu to the kitchen and stick it to the fridge with an inspirational magnet that Mum bought me; something about daughters being like flowers or some other such slushy nonsense. I pick up the stack of Post-it notes from the kitchen table. Writers always need Post-it notes. I walk back into my study to find Beryl stretched out on the floor. I sit down next to her and she jumps into my lap. I pick up a book of nonsense poetry that has managed to find a hiding place under my desk.

***

The doorbell rings. Beryl is no longer on my lap. She is by the front door, barking. I grab my purse out of my handbag and run to the door. The delivery boy passes me my food and I put the bag on the floor while I root through old receipts, shopping lists, hair bands, pens and chocolate bar wrappers that line my purse. I find the correct change although he doesn't look too pleased when I sprinkle a cascade of five, two and one pence pieces into his hand. I thank him and close the door. Beryl happily chomps on a prawn cracker and doesn't notice me wander into the kitchen. I open the back door and Beryl saunters out into the garden to do her business. I take a clean plate out of the dishwasher and look for an empty space to put it down. I put it on the hob and open up the steaming food containers. Beryl comes back in and I lock the door and pull the curtain across. I pour out half of each container on to the plate and carry it into my study, picking up a fork and a set of chopsticks on the way. I know, I've been told never to eat where I work, but I'm a busy girl and I've got to finish the MatesDates profile and write some more to my first chapter. There's no time for a break.

I ponder my hobbies and interests as I wipe sweet and sour sauce from my chin. Foreign food, I like foreign food. I type foreign food and delete it. I can't write that; it makes me sound a bit racist. Exotic food. That's it, I like exotic food. I type exotic food. And culture. I know I haven't travelled as much as I would have liked, but I have been to Japan and I liked the culture when I was there. I type and culture. A mushroom escapes my chopsticks' grip and rolls across my keyboard. I stab it with one chopstick and make sure it gets into my mouth. I look at the screen to find that one of my hobbies is mkkmmmmmkkmmmmm. I think about leaving it in, as it could be some sort of Japanese delicacy but decide to delete it as I don't want to appear more stupid than I already do. That's got to be enough for now. I can add more later when I think of them.

Beryl drags the throw from the armchair and fights with it, shaking it in her teeth until it's dead. Once it's dead, she lays on it so it can't escape. I never realised my knitting could be so dangerous. Knitting. I like knitting. I type kni and then quickly delete it. I can imagine it now; 'Hello, would you like to date me? I know I'll get on well with your family, especially your grandma as we have the same hobbies. I like knitting and I collect cardigans.' I do like knitting and I do collect cardigans, but I think I'll leave that information with the other skeletons in my closet. Strangely enough I've never actually knitted a cardigan. Maybe I should put that on my 'to do' list.

I don't have a 'to do' list but now is as good a time as any to start one. I see a note pad poking out from under a pile of papers and envelopes on the table next to my desk. Some of the paper pile falls down behind my desk. I'll sort that out later. I pick a pen out of the peanut butter jar on my desk. It doesn't work. I put it back. I pick another. It doesn't work. I put it back. I pick out a pencil. I write To Do List at the top of the page and underline it with a squiggly line. I write 1) Make a 'to do' list. I tick that one off straight away. One hundred per cent of things done. I am so productive. I write 2) Write a masterpiece. That one will probably be there for a long time, but still needs to be done. I write 3) Finish the stupid MatesDates profile. I'm glad I'm writing this in pencil. I'll be able to rub it out when I get so frustrated with it that I throw my computer out of the window. I write 4). I tap the pencil against my lip. What else do I need to do? I look around my study. Nothing at the moment.

I look back at my 'to do' list. Number one is done. Number two; well that's an on-going project. I'll never get that finished right now, so I'll leave that for the time being. Number three, I can get that done now, and that'll be another thing ticked off the list. I look at the computer screen and click NEXT. I'm presented with a list of questions, otherwise known as The Basics. I'm single, 5'11", thin, Caucasian, with brown hair, hazel eyes. I don't smoke, I drink socially, I don't have children, but I do have a dog. I choke on a king prawn as I read the next question, and a blob of half chewed rice flies out of my mouth and lands on the computer screen. I wipe it off. How often do you exercise? I click the drop down box. Every day, 4-5 times a week, 2-3 times a week, once a week, less than once a week, never. I click never, but that will make me sound like a fat, lazy slob. I pop the last chicken ball into my mouth. Surely walking across the road to my car counts as exercise. Sometimes I have to run if there is a cyclist zooming along. And I take Beryl out for walkies every day, pretty much, when I remember and when I can be bothered. So I exercise ... I click the drop down box ... every day.

I type writer next to Profession even though I've not made a penny from my writing. But it makes me sound a bit more interesting, and unemployed would make me sound like a lazy, fat slob. I leave Income blank, which adds some mystery and intrigue. I could be an artist starving in my garret or I could be a millionaire, finalising my next movie deal with Hollywood.

I open the drawer next to me to see if I can find a napkin. My sleeve isn't up to the job anymore. I find a bottle of Electric Punk nail varnish. It's blue. I paint the nails on my left hand. I now can't do any typing until it's dried. I pick up my plate in my right hand, take it into the kitchen and put it into the sink. I notice my phone in the cutlery drawer on the draining board. I don't remember putting it in there. The angry Cyclops eye is winking at me again. I have three missed calls from Louise and a text message from Louise. I open the message. *Fat lot of good you are. I needed you to get me out of this date and where are you? How often do I ask you for something?* All the time, Louise.

All the time. I'm coming round. You'd better be there. At least I know you can't set your doorbell to 'silent'. Brilliant. Just what I need. An interruption when I'm working on my book. The doorbell rings.

2

I open the door. A dishevelled looking Louise is leaning against the wall, holding a pair of four inch heels in her hand.

"Good night?" I ask.

"You ... you ...,"she glares at me, as she pushes past, shoving her shoes into my chest.

She runs through the house to the bathroom, but doesn't shut the door as usual. Beryl pads about in the hallway.

"Drink?" I ask.

Louise looks at Beryl.

"Beryl, would you please tell your mother that I would like a hot chocolate, made with half hot water and half hot milk," she says.

Beryl looks at me.

"Beryl, would you please ask Aunty Louise if she would like marshmallows and whipped cream and chocolate sprinkles on the top," I say.

Beryl plods off into the living room. I go into the kitchen. I spoon some chocolate powder into a clean mug from the dishwasher, add water and milk and put it in the microwave. As I put the milk back into the fridge I notice the leftover shepherd's pie. I can have that for lunch tomorrow. I turn around and see the rest of my Chinese food sitting on the hob. I can have that for breakfast tomorrow.

I walk into the hall. Louise walks towards me.

"You had Chinese food for dinner?" she asks.

"Yeah," I reply, puzzled.

I look down and see a modern art splatter of brown sauce, rice and vegetables smeared across my front. I'm surprised Beryl hasn't eaten that. We walk into the kitchen. The microwave pings and Louise opens the door, barely missing my head with the swing.

"Thanks," she grunts, lifting the mug out.

She sips the drink and wanders into the living room. I follow her. She takes one of my cardigans from the back of a chair and curls up on the sofa.

"So what was wrong with this one?" I ask.

"What was right with him?" she snorts.

She pushes some magazines out of the way and puts her mug on the coffee table. She puts on the cardigan.

"To start with, when he said he was six foot five on his profile, he got the numbers the wrong way round. How much of an idiot did I feel wearing four inch heels, walking along next to a man whose head just about reached my shoulder?!" she says. Secondly, he kept calling me 'Lucy'. I don't know how many times I corrected him. Thirdly, whenever he laughed, he would touch his crotch and then lick his finger." She stood up and showed me. "And his laugh was all 'hur hur hur' and his shoulders juggled up and down it time with the noise coming out of his nose. It wasn't even like a laugh. It was a weird pig grunt snort thing. Thirdly…"

"Fourthly," I correct her.

"I shouldn't number the things wrong with this one. I don't think 'seventeethly' is even a word," she says, rolling her eyes.

"It's going to go up to seventeen?" I ask. "I think I'm

going to need some snacks."

I walk into the kitchen and pick up the prawn crackers and take a can of lemonade out of the fridge.

"You haven't got any cheese, have you?" yells Louise.

I pull a block of cheddar and a block of wensleydale out of the fridge.

"And a jar of pickle?" she yells again.

I haven't eaten pickle in ages. I'm not even sure if it's still in date. Yeah, it is, for another two months. I struggle my way back into the living room and dump it all on the sofa next to Louise.

"Anything else, oh master?" I ask, and bow.

"A spoon?" she asks.

"Use your fingers," I say.

She laughs, touches her crotch and then licks her finger. Beryl snatches a prawn cracker before I have a chance to pick them up again. Louise glances up at me.

"She's got a robust constitution," I say.

Louise opens the jar and shoves a chunk of cheese in the brown pickly goo.

"So," she continues, "So I walk up to the restaurant and he's waiting outside and it looks like he's just rocked up straight from, well, sitting around doing nothing. He's wearing jeans and scuffed trainers, not even nice trainers, you know. He was wearing those ugly white ones, the ones I hate! And it looked as though he'd had to fight off a dog to get his shirt back. It's all crumpled and dirty. He waves at me like he's waving to a nation of children on kids' telly. He grins and walks towards me, and as he's getting closer I see just how short he is. And that's when I understood why he's only put face pictures on his profile and not full body shots."

She takes a bite of cheese and pickle.

"He stands on his tip toes to give me a kiss on the cheek and I still have to bend down. He tells me that I look gorgeous, which I do. At least I'd put an effort in. He holds the door open when we go in, which I thought was very nice, and he holds the chair out so I can sit down. So I put the height thing and the clothes thing to the back of my mind. And then he started with the 'You look like you're a *dot dot dot* kind of girl' thing," she says.

I raise my eyebrow. Well I pull a strange face. I can't raise my eyebrow.

"I know!" she screams, spitting cheese all over herself. "The waiter hands me the drinks menu and Mike, that's the guy's name by the way, Mike says, 'You look like you're a red wine kind of girl.' I shake my head. He then says, 'Well, you look like you're a rosé kind of girl.' I shake my head again and tell him that I don't like wine. He doesn't get the hint at all, and says, 'You look like a gin and tonic kind of girl.' I calmly turn to the waiter and ask for something, anything, with vodka and fruit in it. Mike then says, 'That was going to be my next guess.' The waiter finds it really hard to stifle a laugh and I just want to go home, but I'm starving. He orders his drink and I think that it can't get much worse than this. So I pick up the menu and he starts talking to me, and you know how much I hate people talking to me when I'm trying to read something."

"But he wasn't to know," I say.

"I know, but it still bugged me, because we have to keep asking the waiter for another five minutes, and I could see he was getting annoyed with us. I try to move the conversation to the menu by saying that I couldn't decide what to have, and then he says, here it comes, and then he says, 'You look like a caramelised onion and goat cheese tart kind of girl.'

I laugh and dribble some lemonade down my chin.

"It's not funny," Louise whined. "The annoying thing was that I quite fancied that, but just to spite him, I chose the artichoke and asparagus soup, which was disgusting and looked like snot."

I laugh again. Louise hurls a cushion at me.

"Stop it," she whimpers. "It doesn't even stop there. I'm

about to ask the waiter for the sea bass and he says, 'You look like a sea bass kind of girl,' so I have to ask for some sort of herby crusted lamb thing."

"So he was right, you must have looked like a sea bass kind of girl," I say.

"That's not the point," she grumbles. "I don't like people assuming they know me, especially after a few e-mails and an awkward five minutes in a restaurant. I try to explain to him, once the waiter has gone to laugh about us in the kitchen, that I'm not an anything sort of girl as my tastes change all the time. 'Oh Lucy,' he says."

She takes a deep breath.

"'Oh Lucy,' he says. 'You're so interesting; there are so many levels to your character. I can't wait to find out more about you. Unravel the layers, as it were.' He winks. I laugh but I want to throw up. Especially as he has touched his crotch forty-six times up until now. The waiter comes up and asks if we would like to see the dessert menu. I want to leave but you know I can't pass up on a dessert. When the waiter brings the menus, he looks at Mike and says, 'She looks like a tiramisu kind of girl, doesn't she?' and winks at me."

I stifle a laugh. I don't want her to throw the pickle jar at me. Beryl jumps off the sofa and onto my lap. She doesn't like it when people get excited.

"Through gritted teeth I ask the waiter to give us five minutes and he obliges. Mike pipes up, 'I was going to say that you look like a crème brulée kind of girl.' I tell him that right now I'm a lemon cheesecake with raspberry coulis kind of girl. We order the desserts and I go to the toilet, and that's when I called you so you could call me back when I was at the table and I would have a reason to escape. But no, you've got more important things to do than help out your best friend. What on Earth was more important than saving me from a fate worse than death?"

"I've been writing," I say proudly.

"Ooh, finally. And how much have you done?" she asks.

"About seven pages," I fib.

"Is that seven dog pages?" she asks with an actual raise of an eyebrow.

She knows me well.

"Show me what you've done, let me have a read. I need a good laugh after the evening I've had," she says.

"It's not a comedy," I tell her.

"I know, but you're a terrible writer, so it'll be funny regardless," she winks.

I stab the television remote into my chest and feign death.

"It's on the computer in my study," I say.

She walks along the hall, hugging the jar of pickle and a chunk of cheese. I go into the kitchen to put the Chinese food into the fridge. The kitchen table is a mess with all the things from the cutlery drawer. I'll sort it out later. I walk into my study.

"What's this?" Louise guffaws.

"I told you, it's not a comedy," I answer.

"I'm not talking about your pathetic attempt at a page of ramblings about your childhood," she says, so kindly. "I'm talking about this."

She turns the computer screen towards me. I'm faced with my incomplete MatesDates profile. I try to lean over the desk to close it but Louise is too quick for me.

"I never thought you'd actually join," she smiles.

"I haven't joined!" I say, trying to snatch the mouse from her claw-like grip. "It's taken me all day just to get that far."

"I thought you'd been writing all day," smirks Louise.

"I have," I say. "I've been trying to write a stupid profile about myself. Do you know how difficult it is to write about yourself? I have no idea what to write, and it's about my favourite topic; me."

"I've had to rewrite mine a couple of times," she says. "But it wasn't that difficult to do the first one."

"It doesn't matter," I say, "I'm not going to bother with

it. Just shut it down."

"Fine," she says.

I'm tired and I just want to sleep.

"Is it ok if I stay over?" Louise asks.

"Of course, you know where everything is," I say.

She gets up from my desk and walks to the airing cupboard. She pulls a duvet down from the top shelf, covering the floor in towels.

"I'll clear that up tomorrow," she says.

I'm too tired to argue. She hugs me and kisses me on the cheek.

"By the way," I say. "How did this date with Mike end?"

"Brilliantly!" she grins.

"Eh?" I mumble.

"When Mike was in the toilet, the waiter gave me his number," she says. "We're going out on Friday."

3

I wake up to the sound of the front door slamming shut. My alarm clock tells me it's ten twenty-two. Beryl jumps up on the bed and paws at my hair. I climb out, pull the curtains open and wander to the kitchen. I pass a mirror and it looks like a truck has run over my head. I open the back door and Beryl saunters out into the garden to do her business. It's cold. I leave the door ajar and go to find a jumper. I stand in front of the mirror and try to flatten the growth of weeds that has sprung from my scalp. I find a chunk of prawn cracker at the back. I pull it out and throw it on the floor. Louise has folded the duvet and left it on the end of the sofa, along with my cardigan she was wearing last night. I pull that on and go back into the kitchen. I take the chop suey out of the fridge and a clean plate out of the dishwasher. I pour out the leftover vegetables and put the plate in the microwave. I press the Auto Reheat and Start buttons.

I look out the door. Beryl is chasing a pigeon and can't work out how it keeps getting away from her. I call her in. She runs towards me. I lock the cold day out. I take Beryl's food out of the fridge and slop it into her bowl. I mix in some biscuits and put it down on the floor. She scoffs it down as though she hasn't been fed for years.

The microwave beeps. I put on my Father Christmas oven glove and take the plate out of the microwave. I go into the living room and turn on the telly. A Post-it note falls off the remote control. Cheers for <u>part</u> of last night. Took some of your food. Laterz LX. I screw it up and throw it at the bin. It misses and bounces under the sofa. I'll tidy that up later.

A woman is screaming expletives at a man with a skull tattoo on his face. Not just on his face. It's covering his entire face. Again, more reason to be single if this is what men are doing to themselves nowadays. A banner across the bottom of the screen reads Get rid of your tattoo or I'll get rid of you. What is it with getting face tattoos? I'm all for self-expression, but not when it's all over your face.

The man yells, "You gotta love me for me, right? I'm still the same man on the inside."

The woman cries, "But you're an ugly ****** on the outside. I can't look at you anymore."

The man gets on his knees in front of the woman and holds his hands up, pleading, "I'll always love you, no matter what. You could get a tattoo of an **** on your face and I'd still love you."

She pushes him away and shouts, "An ****? A ******* ****? Why the **** would I want to get a ******* **** tattooed on my face? Are you ******* stupid?"

The host jumps in and tells her not to swear on his show. She goes to walk off. The host follows her. She sits on a sofa backstage.

The host pushes a microphone under her nose and asks, "How are you feeling?"

She's still crying, "How am I feeling? How do you think I'm ******* feeling?"

The host says, "No swearing please."

She apologises and continues, "It's so ugly. I can't stand

to look at him. Do you know how terrifying it is to wake up in the middle of the night and have that staring back at you from the darkness?"

The host shakes his head, feigning empathy.

"I'm scared for the kids. They're too young now to know anything, but what's going to happen when they wake up in the middle of the night, crying because they think a monster is in their room, and then that ******* monster goes in to comfort them?" She waves her hands around. "I don't want to put them through that. They're my world, you know. And what's it going to be like when they go to school?"

She drops her head into her hands. A woman comforts her.

The host goes back to the stage. The tattooed man sits on a chair.

The host asks him, "Do you know how this is affecting your girlfriend?"

He stands up, holds his arms out and says, "Come on, this tattoo is awesome. Who here doesn't like it?"

The whole audience boo him.

"Come on, there must be one person here who likes it," he shouts.

The room is silent.

"**** you!" he yells.

"One more swear word out of you and you'll be off the show, you hear me?" the host shouts.

The tattooed man sits down. His girlfriend comes out clutching a tissue to her face. She pulls the empty chair to the other end of the stage, away from her boyfriend.

"Babe, please, I love you," begs the man.

She turns away from him.

He stands up and throws his arms up in the air, and yells, "**** you *****. I slept with your sister," and walks off the stage.

My bladder can't cope with much more excitement. I turn off the television and go to the toilet.

Bleary eyed, I stumble into my study. There's a Post-it note on my computer screen. It reads I couldn't sleep last night so I finished your MatesDates profile and sent a few messages out to men who look your type. I've ticked it off your 'to do' list. You can thank me later. PTO. I sigh and turn the note over. You really shouldn't use your name as your password. Anyone could do anything ... LX. I turn on my computer and look at the clock on the wall. It's nearly ten past eleven. Curiosity is going to kill me, I know it. As soon as the screen flickers on I type Mat into the internet address bar and the website address drops down. I click on it and I'm taken to the same screen with the happy couples doing couply things. I type in my username and password and hold my breath, waiting for the profile written by Louise.

In the top left corner of the screen, a red envelope pulses, with a number five boldly poised in the middle. Does that mean I've got five messages? Who in their right mind would have sent me a message? I don't know what to look at first; the botch job of a profile that Louise wrote about me in her drunken, tired, cheese induced high state, or the messages. I shut my eyes in the hope it will all go away but it's still there when I open them. I ask Beryl for advice but she's snuggled herself into a gap under my desk.

I don't think I'm brave enough to look at the profile yet, especially if she's chosen my profile photo. What if she took a picture of me sleeping last night and uploaded it? Maybe that's why I've got so many messages. Maybe it's people telling me to take my profile down because it's too horrendous. I can't look.

I pick up my 'to do' list to see if there is anything else I can occupy my time with. Number one has been ticked off and so has number three, by Louise, so it just leaves number two, writing my masterpiece, to do. I'll do that later. I then notice there are a few more things to do. I don't remember writing them. Louise. 4) Reply to your MatesDates messages. 5) Go on lots of dates. 6) Meet your Prince

Charming. 7) Fall in love. The word love was surrounded by a cloud of little hearts. 8) Get married and ask Louise to be chief bridesmaid. 9) Have babies. Thanks Louise. Completely ruin the seriousness and sanctity of the 'to do' list with your childish ramblings.

Number two is starting to look a lot more doable compared to the rest. I open my document and read through the page I wrote yesterday. It's not bad. Not brilliant, but not bad. I insert a new page and start writing about my protagonist's first date when she's eighteen. I begin to feel uncomfortable, thinking about the awkwardness of that situation; the strained conversation, the lack of eye contact, the abundance of eye contact, the ... I shudder ... flirting. Who invented flirting anyway? Probably a man. It's normally a man who invents stupid stupid things. Oh ha ha, yes, that story/joke/quip/anecdote was funny, laugh laugh laugh snort laugh spray drink out of my nose. How embarrassing. Watch check; we've only been sitting here for thirty-five minutes. When will this hell be over? Yes, I'll have another drink. No, I'll get them. Yes, I'm sure. Back in a minute. Run to the toilets. Hide for longer than a minute. Breathe breathe. Get drunk. Being drunk makes it so much better.

I push myself away from my desk. I don't think I've ever had a first date that was any better than my first ever first date. Why on Earth would I want to put myself through the trauma of a dating site? I don't know how Louise does it. I need a break.

I scrape the crusty, burnt potato lid away from the sides of the baking dish, and plop the leftover shepherd's pie onto a plate. I contemplate eating it as it is but the smell is quite nauseating. I put it in the microwave and press Auto Reheat and Start. While the plate spins, I finish emptying the dishwasher. I then load it up with all the plates and cups from yesterday. I put the cutlery drawer back in the cabinet. I shove the cutlery in the drawer. It slides about. I really need a cutlery tray. I'll buy one later. The microwave beeps. I pick up my Father Christmas oven glove and carefully take my plate out of the microwave. I take my lunch back to my study. I know, I've been told never to eat where I work, but I'm a busy girl and I've got to write a masterpiece. My screensaver tells me so.

I move my mouse and I'm faced with the MatesDates screen again. The red envelope in the corner is still pulsing, but now there's a number seven in the middle. Seven messages? My heart jumps and my stomach sinks. I put my plate on the floor. I've lost my appetite. Beryl takes her chance and scoffs down the pie.

I click on the envelope and I'm whisked to another page that looks like an e-mail inbox. The seven was right. I have seven messages. I scroll down. The first one is from the MatesDates team, welcoming me, thanking me for joining, giving me tips and hints on how to make my profile better, advice for internet dating safety, a general wish of good luck, and their contact details if I need any help. That's nice of them.

The next message is from JeffingJeffer84. I tentatively open it. A one line message greets me, Hi, thanx for your message. You seem nice but your not my type. Good luck. Jeff. Your not my type! Your not my type!! **Your** not my type!!! Well, Jeff, you're definitely not my type. How could I date someone with such a blatant disregard for grammar? I'm given the option to view his profile, reply to the message or delete the message. I don't dare look at his profile. It might make me want to stab my eyes out with ... I look around for the nearest thing that could be construed as a weapon ... an earbud earphone. I delete the message. Trust Louise to send a message to a guy like this.

I hold my breath as I click open the message from Northern_Ben. I'm glad to see that others struggled with their usernames as much as I did. Naked bungee jumping? Awesome! Have you got any pics? I'm sorry, what? Naked bungee jumping? Now is the time for me to look at my profile.

A giant picture of my face looking vaguely human unravels itself. I don't even remember it being taken, but it's better than the one I would have chosen. The Basics section seems to be the same. Hobbies and Interests: photography, writing, reading, exotic food and culture, music, films, stand-up comedy, socialising, sign-language, archery, pottery, cars, vegetables, 80s cartoons, naked bungee jumping. I delete the last one and pick up my phone ready to call Louise, but her name is already flashing up on the screen. I press the green button.

"What on Earth were you playing at?" I scream.

"Oh you finally answer your phone, and you yell at me for helping you out. Well, that's the last time I'm going to do anything like that for you," says Louise.

"I hope this is the last time you tell the entire world that I like naked bungee jumping," I say.

"You shouldn't be ashamed of your hobbies," she laughs.

I don't say anything.

"Ok, I know I went a bit over the top, but tell me, did you get any messages?" she asks.

"That's not the point," I say. I can feel myself blushing.

"Tell me more, who, who, who? What are they like? Do you fancy any of them? Are you going on any dates? Tell me, tell me, tell me," she rambles.

"Well, I've got seven messages …," I begin.

"eeeeeeeeeeeeeeeeeeee …," I move the phone away from my head. "… eeeeeeeeeeeee. That's really good for a first go. You've only been on there a few hours. I didn't get any messages on my first day, and I sent out hundreds. Hundreds," she says.

"… but I've not had a chance to look at them all," I say.

"Well do it, do it now," she says, aggressively.

I'm too tired to argue, and even if I wasn't tired there's no point arguing with Louise; she'll win anyway.

"Ok," I sigh.

I look at the third message in my inbox.

"Right, this one is from ilovesex69," I say.

Louise lets out a loud guffaw.

"I love those ones," she says in between laughing. "You know, there are sites out there for people just looking for sex, but no, they think it's ok to bug people like us who are seriously looking for relationships."

"You're not seriously looking for a relationship," I say.

"This isn't about me, it's about you. Read on," she demands.

"Well, this is a surprise," I say.

"What?" she asks.

"Well, ilovesex69's message says I love sex lol want to meet up for sex babe ;). Even if I wanted to meet up for sex, babe, how can I when it's clear that you have a blatant disregard for punctuation? I mean, if he can't be bothered with important details, such as punctuation, in his messages, how can I be sure that he'll be bothered with important details during sex?" I say.

Louise snorts down the phone.

"You have so much to learn, little one," she says.

"What do you mean?" I ask.

"Firstly, you will be lucky to find a man on here who knows spelling, punctuation, grammar and syntax as well as you do, so you just have to be tolerant of these small errors," she says.

"But I caaaaaaan't. They're not small errors. They're huge. They're gigantic mistakes and they make my eyes bleed. They make me want to stab kittens and kick up flower beds," I whimper.

"And secondly, you've got to stop being so picky. You've been single for too long for you to be picky. So he doesn't use punctuation, so he's got a receding hairline, so he's from the north, so he's got webbed fingers and eleven toes, so his name is Barry, so what? All men have something wrong with them, but when you've been single for, how long has it been now?" she asks.

"Three years," I mumble.

"When you've been single for three years, you really have to suck it up and put these things on a shelf," she says.

"So you think I should go on a date with ilovesex69?" I ask.

"No, no-one should ever go on a date with ilovesex69 ever but if someone sends you a message and it's not up to your unbelievably high language standards, don't immediately dismiss them. That's all I'm saying," she says.

"I don't have unbelievably high language standards," I lie.

"Do you know how many times I had to write out those Post-it notes before I left this morning?" she asks.

"You didn't need to do rewrites on Post-it notes," I laugh.

"Oh I did. The one on the remote control, I lazily wrote UR instead of your the first time, and then I got into a fluster and wrote you're the second time," she says.

"Well that's just silly, there was no need for that," I say.

"Nuh-uh," she grunts. "You don't know how scary you can get."

I don't say anything. I'm silent in agreement.

"I knew you'd agree," she says.

"So, can I delete our friend who loves sex?" I ask.

"Yes, and for future reference, always be wary of anyone who has the number sixty-nine in their username. You know they're only interested in one thing. Unless it's their age or the year they were born in …," she says.

"The year in which they were born," I correct.

Louise groans. I imagine she's sticking her fingers up at the phone.

"You know I was swearing at you just then," she says.

"I know," I say.

We laugh.

"Shouldn't I even be wary of those guys?" I ask. "I

mean, if their age is sixty-nine, that's a bit old to be sending messages to a thirty year old. And if their birth year is nineteen-sixty-nine, that would make them forty-three, and that's still a bit old, right?"

"Stop being so picky! And you put the maximum age as forty-six, so you're one to talk!" she shouts.

"Ok, ok," I sigh.

"Look, I've got to go now. This was more difficult than I thought. You've only opened one message. Right, I'm going, but you'd better open the rest and reply to the decent sounding ones, even if their grammar isn't perfect, ok? And you can tell me about it tomorrow," she says.

"Tomorrow?" I ask.

"That's it. Go on, just go and forget our lunch date," she moans.

"We didn't have a lunch date," I say.

"Well, we do now. Tomorrow, twelve thirty, Alfredo's. Laters," she says.

"Ok see you tomo ...," I say before she cuts me off.

4

Before I open my other messages, I check the rest of my profile. Considering Louise wrote out the Post-it notes a handful of times, I dread to think how many times she wrote the About Me section.

I read it to Beryl, even though she's not interested. "If my friends could describe me in 3 words they would say that I'm scatty, indecisive and a bit weird sometimes. Well, guess who failed Maths there, Beryl."

She lifts her head, looks at me and tells me that I'm interrupting her sleep.

I continue, "I have an eclectic taste in everything ... Ooh, 'eclectic'; look who swallowed a thesaurus, Beryl. ... from books, to music, to films, to art, to knitwear. She's not wrong there, is she Beryl? I used to be a bit of a snob when it came to art and films and music, and I'd only like things that other people hadn't heard of but after some serious educating I now like pretty much everything. I wouldn't say snob; I just have certain standards. I collect books and cardigans, but don't worry, I'm not a nerd, well not too much of one. Hmm, I pride myself on my nerdiness. I love stand-up comedy, and even though my friends think I should be a stand-up myself I don't find myself particularly funny. I just say and do things and people laugh at me. Harsh, but true. I enjoy writing, and like to experiment with language to create obscure pieces, such as writing poetry with the periodic table of elements (it's a bit difficult to explain, but I enjoy it and it keeps me out of trouble!). Wow, she actually pays attention. I thought she only ever heard her own voice when we're having conversations. I am impressed. I like photography but tend to just point and click and hope for the best. I find interesting things in obscure places, like patterns in walls and rust and peeling paint. That's true. This is pretty accurate so far, isn't it Beryl? I also make arty things with melted wax crayons and masking tape. Well, that makes me sound like a seven year old, or indeed a primary school teacher, but I'll leave it in for now. I have a shih-tzu called Beryl and she's three years old. I collect things, nothing specific, just things. I guess she's right, and saying I collect things is a bit better than saying I never throw things away. Hmm, what do you think Beryl? I have an unhealthy obsession, according to my friends, with grammar, but please don't let that put you off. Also, my mobile phone is always on silent, so if you call and I don't answer, it's not that I'm ignoring you, it's just that I don't know you're calling. Thanks Louise."

That spurs me to turn my phone off silent.

"Ideally, I am just looking to date at the moment, but I would like to meet someone who shares my interests and maybe could introduce me to something new. Well, I am impressed Beryl. I thought she'd try to embarrass me or jeopardise my chances. And as for grammar and punctuation, I'd give her a ninety-eight per cent. I'll tidy it up a bit, but generally it's pretty good."

I notice that she's left the Ideal First Date section blank. I know going for a drink is the typical first date, but that's not my idea of an ideal first date. I'll have to think about that. I have to get through the rest of my messages. I don't like letting things pile up. An awful noise makes me jump. My phone vibrates itself off my desk. That is why I have it on silent. It's Louise again.

"Hel …," I say.

"Who's that?" she asks.

"Lexa," I sigh.

"It can't be," she says. "Lexa never answers her phone."

I let out a half-hearted laugh.

"Seriously," she says. "If you don't tell me who you are and what you've done with my friend, I'm going to call the police."

"Just for you, I turned my phone off silent," I say.

"I'm speechless. It's so unlike you. What's happened? Have you started chatting to someone on MatesDates? Are you waiting for him to call? What's he like? What's his username? Maybe I've been out with him," she says.

"Yes, you are indeed speechless," I say.

"Funny," she says.

"No, I've not started chatting to anyone. I just felt bad for always having my phone on silent," I say.

"Good, finally. So what are the other guys like who sent you messages?" she asks.

"Erm," I mumble.

"You haven't even read them, have you?" she screeches.

"Well, no, not exactly," I say.

"You're useless. I'm coming over and we're going to do them together," she says.

"Aren't you at work?" I ask.

"Yeah, but it's really boring. Why do you think I'm calling you? I'll just say I've got an emergency hospital appointment or something," she says.

"You work in a hospital!" I say.

"I'll get Safa to cover for me. See you in thirty. And please at least open one more message before I get there, ok?" she says.

I sigh.

"Oooooo-kaaaaaay?" she says again.

"Ok," I say.

I'll read the other messages in a minute. I go into the kitchen to get a drink. I open a cupboard and boxes and packets and bags of things fall out. I tidy it up, even though it's not later.

The doorbell rings. I let Louise in. She's carrying a couple of carrier bags.

"Dinner," she says.

I walk into the kitchen. She follows me and dumps the bags on the table. Bottles clank. I look in the bags. Vodka, gin, whiskey, lemonade, beer, and a giant bag of pretzels.

"I see you've got all the food groups there," I say.

She grins, pulls open the bag of pretzels and stuffs a handful into her mouth.

"So?" she says, splattering crumbs.

"So?" I say.

"Did you open anymore messages?" she asks, knowing full well that I haven't.

"Not exactly," I say.

"I knew it! So what have you exactly been doing?" she asks.

I open my kitchen cupboards and show her the neatly, alphabetised system I have for finding my food.

"That's brilliant," she says, slamming a door closed. "The man of your dreams could be waiting for a reply, and you're busy learning your alphabet with the help of your groceries. Seriously, how many jars of peanut butter does one girl need?" she shouts.

"It was on offer," I say, looking at the ground.

"And since when did minestrone soup come before marmalade? And since when did you start liking marmalade?" she shouts again.

"I …," I say.

"Yes, you're useless. Get me a beer, and let's get you the

man of your dreams," she says and snaps her fingers.

Louise walks into my study and sits in the armchair by the window, to the disgust of Beryl. Beryl jumps on her lap and makes herself comfortable. Louise looks at me, holds out her hand and I give her a bottle of beer.

She keeps her eyes on me and says, "You. Sit."

I do as I'm told, trying to stifle a giggle.

"No laughing on my watch," says Louise.

"Sir, yes Sir," I say, and salute.

"What are you waiting for, read away," she says, and takes a sip of her drink.

I open the next message and read, "Hi, I was just browsing and came across your profile. You look very pretty in your profile picture. Is it a recent one? I only ask because a lot of women on here upload pictures from 10 years ago just to attract more men. Blah blah blah."

Louise cuts me off. "What does 'blah blah blah' mean?"

"He's just rambling on about his experiences on here, and how he's not met a decent woman yet," I say.

"Maybe you could be the decent woman he's been looking for," she says.

"Maybe," I say.

"Carry on," says Louise and waves her arm.

"Sir, yes Sir," I say. "Your profile stood out to me as you seem like a normal person, if I can say that without offending you. Most women try so hard to impress, and by doing that they come across as fake. Gah, get on with it."

I take a deep breath and chug a mouthful of beer.

"Cheers for these," I say to Louise, raising my arm. "Blah blah blah eclectic taste blah blah what specific things do you like? Blah blah blah you look like a rock music kind of girl …"

I stop reading and look at Louise. Our eyes widen.

"That's not StuporMan286 is it?" she asks.

I nod.

"That's Mike!" she squeals.

Beryl jumps off her lap and runs to sit by my feet.

I laugh.

"I can't go out with him. I wouldn't be able to keep a straight face," I say.

"I wouldn't let you go out with him. I love you too much to let you go through something like that," she says.

I smile at her.

"And what does he mean that he's not met any decent women on there? We only went out last night. Delete it. Delete him. How rude!" she says.

"Well you did get another guy's number when you were supposed to be on a date with him. That's not really the kind of thing a decent woman would do," I say.

"He touches his crotch when he laughs!" she screams.

"I can't just delete it without replying. He's put in quite a bit of effort. I don't want to be rude and ignore him," I say.

"You have so much to learn, little one," she says.

"I thought you already taught me; to be tolerant of idiots who can't use their mother language properly, and to stop being so picky," I say.

"Aaaaaand, you can't reply to every message you get, no matter how long or impressive it looks," she says.

"That's what she said," I say.

"Look, if you're not going to take this seriously I might as well take my drinks and go home," she says and walks towards the door.

I hold on to her arm and pull her back.

"Men will ignore you. You'll send out a ton of messages and you won't get a reply from all of them, no matter how perfectly your messages are written," she says.

"How rude," I say.

"That's the world of internet dating," she says, shrugging.

I turn back to look at the screen.

"I'm hungry," she says.

"There's a new curry place around the corner. I got a

menu through the door the other day. It's on the fridge," I say.

Louise saunters into the kitchen. Beryl follows her.

"Can you let Beryl out," I yell.

I hear the back door open. I look at my message from Mike. I don't want to ignore him. I can't be that rude. I type Hi Mike, thanks for your message. You seem like a really nice guy but I don't think it would be a good idea if we e-mailed each other, as you went on a date with my best friend, Louise. I think it would be pretty awkward if we took this any further. I wish you luck in finding a decent woman though. Take care. I click the SEND button. Louise sticks her head around the door.

"What were you typing?" she asks.

"Nothing, just had an idea for my book," I lie.

She raises an eyebrow.

"I'm going to walk to the curry place. I need to stretch my legs. What do you want?" she asks.

"Anything, I don't mind …," I say.

"As long as it's not too spicy," we say in unison.

I laugh. She rolls her eyes.

"Yeah, yeah, I know. Korma it is," she says.

I poke my tongue out at her.

"See you in a bit," she says, and walks away.

5

I sit on the back step with a pint glass of vodka and lemonade and watch Beryl fight with a stone. She picks it up in her mouth and throws it around, but it's never well and truly dead. She paws at it, it moves and she throws it in the air again. The whole world exists but to her the whole world is a stone. How lovely for life to be so simple. The front door opens and then closes. I hear Louise huffing and puffing, and struggling with the carrier bags. I don't move from the back step. I just watch Beryl play. The smell of Louise bringing food into the house doesn't even distract her from the stone. I drink back the last mouthful of liquid in the glass and go inside.

I'm not hungry. I pour myself another drink. Louise pulls open all the cupboards in the hunt for plates. In my organisation, I can't even remember where I put them. I don't help her look. I drink. She pours a tub of rice into a bowl; the yellow petals scatter over the worktop. Beryl walks in with her stone between her teeth. She sits by Louise's feet, waiting for whatever will fall on the floor. Her head bobs up and down at every movement Louise makes. Nothing falls. Beryl walks around in a panic, sniffing everywhere for food. You'd think she was starving. Louise knocks some crumbs of naan onto Beryl's head. She shakes, drops her stone and licks the lino.

"Drink?" I ask Louise.

"Gnn n nununade," she says with a mouthful of popadom.

"Gin and lemonade it is," I say as I open the bottle.

She walks into the living room, Beryl at her heels. I guess I'm the drinks waitress tonight. I take the drinks through and then wander back into the kitchen. I'm not drunk. I just feel a bit lightheaded, a bit empty, a bit floaty. My eyes glaze over. I don't cry but I feel like I want to. I'm fine. It must be the drink. I wipe my eyes and take my plate into the living room.

Louise sits on the floor with the tubs of food on the coffee table. Her plate is full. I take some rice and a spoonful of korma, I don't even think I pick up any pieces of chicken, and sit on the floor with my back resting against the sofa. The television is on.

A woman bumps into a man in the street. It's raining. She drops her bags. He bends down to pick them up for her. She bends down too. They both take hold of the same bag. The camera breaks to a prolonged image of her hand delicately resting on his hand, then to their eyes meeting. The rain stops. They stand, still looking at each other, still both holding the same bag. She blinks and turns her face away, half smiling. She clumsily says sorry and pulls her hand away. He holds the bag out for her to take. The sun comes out. He picks up the other bag and passes it to her. She blushes and thanks him. He moves her out of the way as a car drives past, splashing up a puddle near the kerb. They laugh. He asks her if she fancies a coffee, and lo and behold, there is a café just around the corner.

"What is this tripe?" I ask Louise.

"Shhh," she says angrily.

She doesn't even look at me, but she does hold her hand up, palm facing me. Louise doesn't like people talking when she's watching, well, anything.

The couple sit in a booth with a plastic red and white checked tablecloth. The walls are covered with old baseball memorabilia. The waitress is a large set woman, with untidy hair and badly applied make-up. She stands by the table with a grubby looking pad but doesn't say anything. The man says, "Two coffees." The waitress rolls her eyes, nods and walks away. I guess the producer didn't want to pay her. She comes back, pushes two empty cups across the table and fills them from a coffee jug. Both the man and woman reach for the sugar at the same time. They laugh. He lets her take the container. She pours the white powder into her cup and stirs. He does the same. They make small talk; it's not awkward. He's an architect, and is in the middle of a project to rejuvenate the town. She works in a small boutique that sells vintage clothes, but ideally she would like to be a fashion designer. Her mother is sick so she can't move away to go to college. She's actually got some of her designs in her sketchbook. Would we like to see? No we wouldn't. She shows us anyway. The camera leans over her shoulder to show dog-eared pages of scribbles and doodles and fabric swatches and colour charts. He tells her that she's talented. He asks her if she made the outfit she's wearing. She laughs. Do we like it? No, not really. I can't take any more of this gushing.

"I can't watch this," I say. "Things like that don't happen in real life. It's stupid."

Louise waves me away. I go into the kitchen and open the back door. It's not too cold. I walk out onto the grass. I turn around and walk back into the kitchen remembering that I don't have any shoes on, and that I've not cleaned up Beryl's business for a few days now. I finish my drink and put the glass on the sideboard.

"Shut the door, it's cold!" shouts Louise from the other room.

"Shut your mouth, it's loud!" I shout back.

I lean up against the outside wall and pull the door to. The stars are out tonight. I look for Cassiopeia. I can't see it. I try for the plough. I can't see that one either. So much for my Astronomy GCSE. A red light flashes. I pretend it's a shooting star and make a wish. I follow it until I can't see it anymore. I wonder where it's going. I fall to my knees and I cry. Why can't I meet anyone? Why have I been single for so long? What's wrong with me? Why isn't real life like the films? I feel as though I'm looking at someone crying, almost absent from the situation, as though I'd abandoned myself at the time when I needed company the most. Bright colours pulse under my closed eye-lids. My head throbs. I punch out but at nothing; my fists pounding the air in front of my face. My head is telling me to stop but my body won't listen. I can't remember the last time I felt this lonely.

I force out the last tear and it feels cold as it runs down my cheek. I feel stupid for crying. And then I feel stupid for feeling stupid. It must be the drink. I go back inside, lock the door and pull the curtain across to keep what has just happened permanently outside. I pour another vodka and lemonade and go back into the living room. Louise is sprawled out on the sofa asleep and Beryl is standing on her hind legs, leaning up against the coffee table, licking korma sauce from my plate.

I pick up the remote control and turn the television off, just as a soldier shoots some sort of alien creature. I don't think it's the same film from earlier. I look at the food on the coffee table. I'll tidy that up later. I get the duvet out of the airing cupboard and lay it over Louise. She groans and rolls over. I turn the light off and shut the door.

I'm not tired. I'm not anything really. Beryl walks into my study and I follow her. I turn my desk lamp on and sit at my computer. I'm still signed in to MatesDates. I open the next message. It's from PhillyBoyBuilder. The face in the small picture next to his username looks familiar. The message is very short. U hated me wen we was at school. Y u messegin me now?

I take a look at his profile. I recognise the man in the photos. Phillip Jackson! Thanks a lot Louise. A rush of anger darts erratically through me. I grab my phone and write Louise a text. Thanks a lot Louise for sending a message to the boy who made my life a living hell when I was at school. Thanks a lot. I send it. A second later I hear a beep-da-da-beep coming from the other room. I'd completely forgotten that Louise was in the living room. I hold my breath for a moment, waiting for her to burst through the door.

Nothing.

I breathe out. I can't bear to look at his face. I close his profile and delete his message. I notice that a new message has arrived from StuporMan286. It's Mike. Curiosity drives me to open it. I wish I hadn't. **** you, you *****. If you're anything like that **** Louise then I wouldn't touch you with a barge pole. ******* ***** the pair of you. My jaw drops and my heart sinks. There's no need for language like that. I'm glad the site has a swear filter because I'm not in the mood to read what he actually wrote. I delete the message straight away. I could rip him a new one, but I'm classier than that.

I walk into the kitchen and sit with my back up against the washing machine. It's extremely uncomfortable. I drop my head to cry again but nothing comes out. I push myself up against the washing machine in the hope the discomfort will lead to pain and I can start crying. It doesn't work. I can't even cry through frustration. I give up. I pick up the vodka and lemonade and stumble back into my study. The clock tells me it's nearly ten past eleven. I'm tired. My body feels heavy. I pour some vodka into my glass. It spills on my desk. I wipe it up with my sleeve. I do a quiz on the internet. I can only name seventeen of the fifty states in five minutes. I drink some vodka. I shudder. I'm not brave enough to drink spirits straight. I smother it in lemonade. I take another quiz. I can only name six of the eighty-three English counties. I really should have paid more attention in Geography lessons. I laugh out loud. I didn't even take Geography. I giggle. I can't stop. It's not funny. My mouth doesn't stop laughing. Now the tears come. Typical. I do the states quiz again. I correctly guess fifteen states. Stupid quiz.

I have a look at facebase. More status updates about nothing in particular. Fay cooked tuna pasta bake and no-one died ... yet. Safa hates her job - if I have to clear up one more pile of vomit, I'm going to kill someone. Good job I've got access to an unlimited supply of toe tags. Jo why don't any of the pens in my house work? I don't know Jo, I really don't. Emily hates it when ppl post crap bout u n then don't even bother to say it to ur face stop being a coward n just say what u got to say. My head hurts.

I take a deep breath and have another look at MatesDates. I move my mouse to close my computer but the next message stops me. It's from Greg-arious; the user name piques my interest, and the guy in the picture looks quite cute. Short, dark hair, a few freckles, brown eyes and a slightly wonky smile. I quietly read to Beryl, who is back in the armchair by the window, so as not to wake Louise.

"Good morning, Your face was the first face I saw this morning, so had to say hello (and it's certainly not a bad face to see first thing in the morning). Gah, I hope I haven't insulted you with that last sentence in the parentheses. Beryl, he knows the difference between brackets and parentheses. A cheesy comment, but a smart man nonetheless. I think I'm in love! Anyway, I really enjoyed reading your profile; you come across as a bit strange, but I like that. Oh my goodness, I'm full of compliments this morning aren't I? What I mean to say is that you seem interesting, like there are various different layers to you, rather than the one dimensional women I usually come across on here. Most, if not all, are only concerned with their looks, not that you aren't good-looking, because you are. Excuse me while I take my foot out of my mouth. It's just that a lot of the women on here are looking for a sugar daddy to take care of them and their brood of rugrats, and that's just not for me. He seems nice, doesn't he Beryl? He uses punctuation correctly and has a nice range of vocabulary. I am impressed, aren't you? Anyway, sorry, I am prone to rambling every now and then. Beryl is an interesting name for a dog. No word of a lie, that was my grandmother's name, but we always called her Nana Bertie. I have no idea why we did that though. I'll have to ask my parents about that. Well there's another thing to add to my 'to do' list. Beryl, he has a 'to do' list! A 'to do' list! I am impressed that you know how to knit. I don't dare try; I know I'd end up blinding myself with the needles or something. I can be a bit clumsy. Are you knitting anything amazing at the moment?"

I look at the pile of wool on the bookcase shelf. I'm sure knitted rectangles might be amazing to someone. I think they're amazing and Beryl must think they're amazing as she wraps herself up in my knitted rectangles all the time.

I continue reading, "I'm not too sure about the naked bungee jumping. You'll have to tell me more about that, although it really doesn't seem like it would be my kind of thing. So, you're a writer, eh? Would I happen to have read anything you've written? What kind of things do you write? I'm not even sure I can string a sentence together, let alone write professionally. Anyway, I'm sorry about the essay here. I hope I haven't bored you to sleep! I really should get myself off to work. I hope to hear from you soon. Take care, Gregory. P.S. I'm not really a gregarious person. I'm rubbish at thinking of usernames and my friend came up with it. I like your username though!"

I spin my chair around and look at Beryl. She's asleep.

My heart is racing. Gregory seems, well, normal. A bit silly maybe, but I'm a bit silly, sometimes, I guess. I click on his username and I'm taken to his profile. He has three pictures; one of his face that he has clearly taken himself, one of him and some friends posing at what appears to be a house party, and one of him standing underneath the Eiffel Tower. He looks pretty good in all of them. He's handsome but not the type I usually find attractive. I browse his profile. He's six foot one inch tall. Nice. He thinks he's carrying a few extra pounds, but I can't tell that from the photos. He's thirty-two, and he lives nearby. I hold my breath for a second. He owns and manages a gym. He likes films and music, but I think everyone does. He confesses to be a bit of a sci-fi geek, but he reads anything that takes his fancy. He likes cooking, especially Asian food and would like to travel there in the future. He plays in a darts team and has completed five marathons for a cancer charity. He's looking for a woman who can help him kill zombies when they attack. Ha! I like the sound of this one.

I feel sober now. Gregory has sobered me up. I go back to my inbox. I have one new message from Gregory. Hey, I know this is a bit out of the blue, and we haven't chatted properly yet, or indeed at all, but I was wondering if you wanted to go for a drink tomorrow evening. I mean, this is a dating site after all, so we really should go on a date. I fully understand if you think it's too soon, but you seem nice and look nice from your profile and I think talking face to face is a better way to get to know someone, than from hiding behind a computer screen. Let me know what you think. Gregory. My stomach jumps. I click to reply.

6

I wake up to an ear shattering beep-ba-da-beep-beep. I'm on the floor in my study, curled up in the foetal position, wrapped up in my hand-knitted armchair throw. I don't remember how I got here. Beryl is nestled in the crook of my knees. My mobile phone is next to my head. I sit up and pick up my phone. An envelope flashes up on the screen. I have one new message from Louise. What? That wasn't Fat Phil, was it? I didn't recognise him. I'm so sorry. Anyway, get your lazy bum up. We've got a lunch date remember.

The door flies open. Louise stands in the doorway with her hands on her hips, wearing my clothes. I groan and lay back down, covering my head with the blanket. Louise grabs the end and pulls it off me. She grabs my arm and pulls me up. I stumble and fall into her.

"Get in the shower, you reek," she says, pushing me away.

"Good morning to you too," I croak.

I stumble into the bathroom and do my business. My mouth feels like the bottom of a birdcage. I brush my teeth but it doesn't help. I wrap a towel around myself and go into my bedroom. I sit on the edge of my bed. My head throbs and I feel a bit sick. I can't have a hangover. I wasn't drunk enough. My bedroom door flies open. Louise walks in and jumps on my bed.

"Come in Louise, don't bother knocking. It's not like I could have been naked or anything," I say.

She ignores me and makes herself comfortable, followed by Beryl who lies on my pillow.

"You've got a date! Why didn't you tell me?" she squeals.

"I've got a what?" I croak. What is wrong with my voice today?

"A date. With Gregory. Ooh Gregory," she grins.

"With who?" I croak again.

"With whom?" she corrects.

I throw her a glare. She laughs.

"You got a message from Gregory last night asking you out. You left it up on your computer. You know me, I have to have a nose," she says.

Nothing is private with Louise around.

"I don't remember much about last night, only that I'm rubbish at geography quizzes," I say.

My head doesn't hurt but I can't remember getting a message from Gregory.

"Well, you're meeting him this evening for a drink, so pull yourself together because we haven't got much time to get you sorted," she says.

My stomach drops. It's not like me to be so spontaneous. I sit on the edge of the bed. I feel faint. I lie back.

"Hey, don't worry, the first one is always scary, but you can do it. You're a big, brave girl. Now get up, I'm hungry. Alfredo's. Move," she says.

Louise picks up Beryl and walks out of my room. I get dressed. My stomach gurgles. I really don't feel well. My head is fuzzy. I stumble into the hall. Louise is standing by the door with Beryl, holding her lead. I reach my hand into the kitchen and grab a tin of dog food. I put it in my bag and we walk outside. Everything is so loud. The birds, the cars, the children. The children. Why are children so loud all of the time? I let Beryl drag Louise to my parents' house. We walk up their path and the front door is open. My parents don't notice us standing in the hall way. They are too busy dancing to a crackling record spinning on the turntable. I feel better. I let Beryl off her lead and she rushes to Mum's ankles. She jumps up. My parents stop dancing.

"You know you shouldn't do things like that with the front door wide open," I say.

"Hello, love," Mum says.

"Why is the front door open?" I ask.

"Your mother was trying to make bread but managed to burn it. She nearly burnt the house down," Dad says.

I laugh.

"Can you look after Beryl, please?" I ask.

"Of course, we love having her," Mum says.

"Welcome to Hôtel Beryl," Dad says.

"Shush Tom," Mum says. "Ignore him, we love having her, don't we?"

"She eats us out of house and home," Dad says. "It's like having you living here again."

I pull a tin of dog food out of my bag.

"Don't worry Dad, I bought you some dinner," I say.

Louise walks past and heads for the fridge.

"Hello Louise, love," Mum says.

"Karen, Tomothy," Louise says, doffing her invisible cap.

I laugh.

"You do know his name is Thomas?" I ask.

"Yep," Louise says. "But I've called him Tomothy for the past twenty-five years so why change a habit of a lifetime?"

"Are you hungry Louise, love?" Mum asks.

"We're now going out for lunch," I say.

"You don't need to do that," Mum says. "Tom, make the

girls something for lunch."

Dad is looking through a box of dusty records. He lifts his head.

"No, honestly, you don't have to do that," says Louise, pulling a stick of celery out of the fridge. "We've got a private matter that we need to discuss anyway."

I glare at her. She pokes her tongue out at me.

"Ooh, private matter, that sounds exciting," Mum says.

"It's really not," I say. "Come on Louise, I thought you were hungry."

I gesture towards the door.

"Karen, Tomothy, are you busy tonight by any chance?" Louise says.

My parents look at each other, worriedly.

"No, why, love?" Mum asks suspiciously.

"Would you be able to keep Beryl until tomorrow morning?" Louise asks.

"I don't see why not," Dad says.

"What's going on?" Mum asks.

"Nothing," I say. "I'm just busy later."

Louise laughs.

"Yes, she's busy," says Louise, winking.

My parents throw glances around the room. I walk towards the door. Louise doesn't take the hint. She crunches the celery to break the silence.

"Goodbye Beryl, you be a good girl," I say and walk out of the door with a wave. Louise runs after me.

"She's got a date tonight," Louise squeals at my parents.

"With who?" Mum asks.

"With whom," Louise corrects with a wink.

"With whom then," Mum says, rolling her eyes.

I walk back up the path and pull Louise's arm.

"Thank you for taking care of Beryl," says Louise. "She'll be back to pick her up in the morning."

"Thank you, see you tomorrow," I say, blowing them a kiss.

"Have fun tonight," Mum shouts.

I walk off down the road. I'm really hungry now. Louise runs to keep up. I weave my way through the traffic.

"Wait for me," Louise shouts from behind.

I don't wait for her. I walk up to Alfredo's and pull the door open. The waitress shows me to a table by the window. I hate siting by the window. People always stare in and watch you eat. On the other hand, I guess you get bigger portions and nicer looking food. I'd still prefer to sit away from prying eyes though. But I'm not in the mood to argue. Well, not with the waitress anyway. Louise hurries in. Her face is flushed. She glares at me. I glare back. She sits down opposite me and the waitress brings two menus over. I snatch the menu from her and hold it in front of my face so that I can't see Louise.

"Can I get you guys any drinks?" the waitress asks.

"I'll just have a glass of water, thanks," I say.

My mouth still feels like the sole of my shoe.

"I'll have a Bloody Mary, please," says Louise.

The waitress walks away.

"I've got a weird craving for celery today," says Louise.

I hold the menu firm.

"Still not talking to me?" Louise asks.

I close the menu.

"I can't believe you told my parents I've got a date," I hiss, leaning towards her.

"Stop making such a big deal out of everything. It's just a date. You're not going to marry him or anything," she says.

The waitress walks over with our drinks.

"Are you ready to order?" she asks.

I nod, so does Louise.

"I'll have the fusilli porcini," I say, with a stupid Italian accent.

"Has that got any garlic in?" Louise asks the waitress.

"Everything has got a bit of garlic in," she replies.

"See, she's got a date tonight so she can't be too garlicky," says Louise.

I kick her under the table. She laughs through the pain.

"I guess a little bit of garlic is ok. Can you please ask the chef to only put in as much garlic as is absolutely necessary?" she asks.

I kick my foot out again. Louise moves her legs and I end up kicking the table leg instead. The waitress writes something down on her pad.

"And I'll have linguine alla carne," says Louise. "And a side order of garlic bread."

She pokes her tongue out at me.

"Is that everything?" the waitress asks.

"Yes thank you," Louise says.

The waitress takes our menus and walks away. I sip my water and look out of the window.

"I don't know why you're in such a grump," says Louise.

"I'm not in a grump," I say, grumpily.

"Look, it's just a date. You've been on dates before," she says.

"Yeah, but only with people I've known beforehand. I've never been on a date with someone I don't know," I say.

"Well, there's a first time for everything," she says.

I take a sip of my water. We eat, we chat, I worry, Louise relays her first internet dating experience from years ago. It was awkward and uncomfortable, and it doesn't make me feel much better. I feel sick. I walk to the toilet.

I close the cubicle door and pull the lock across. I drop the toilet lid and sit down. Jooley woz 'ere '12. I feel so privileged to be sharing this cubicle with the essence of Jooley. My stomach gurgles. I feel like I'm about to sit an exam. My palms are sweating and my heart is pumping in my throat. The walls close in on me. I gasp for breath. My mind darts from one thing to another and back again. I have no idea what's coming over me. It's like nerves but a more extreme version. It's like exam nerves and job interview nerves and first date nerves all rolled into one, multiplied by a million. I run outside.

Louise follows me. She finds me sitting on the kerb.

"Hey," she says, putting her arm around my shoulders.

"Come with me?" I ask.

"Home? Yeah of course I'll take you home," she says.

"No, tonight I mean," I say.

She sits beside me.

"You want me to come on your date with you?" she asks.

"Yes," I say.

I start shivering and crying. Louise pulls my face up so my eyes meet hers. She takes a compact mirror from her bag and holds it in front of me. My eyes are all puffy, and my cheeks and nose are blotchy and red.

"No-one's going to want to go on a date with you if you look like this," she says.

She snaps the mirror closed and shoves a tissue in my hand. I blow my nose and start laughing.

"What is wrong with me?" I say.

"Too much to list right now," says Louise. "And we don't have the time to go through it at the moment."

I shove her in the ribs with my elbow. We stand up and walk. I still feel queasy. I clearly can't hold my drink as well as I used to. That's a lie. I've always been a lightweight. I am nervous though. It's been too long to even remember when I last went out on a date. I'm not good with people, especially people I don't know.

"Why am I so worried about it?" I ask.

"It's understandable," Louise says. "The first internet date is always going to be scary because you don't know if you're sitting opposite a guy who collects animal bones or has a peculiar fetish. But once you've got this one out of the way, you'll be ready for whatever comes after. Do you remember the one who wanted to take photos of me standing on biscuits in high heels?"

"How can I forget?" I laugh.

I stop laughing.

"It doesn't mean you'll get one of those," Louise quickly says.

"You don't know that," I say.

"You just need to be aware that internet men can be, hmm, strange," she says.

"And what about internet women?" I ask.

Louise ignores me.

"Don't worry," she says. "I'll be there, and Safa will be there."

"You're not bringing Safa, are you?" I moan.

"Well I can't sit in the pub on my own watching you," she says.

"I guess," I say. "But Safa?"

"You've got more important things to worry about other than Safa," she says.

"Like what?" I ask.

I take my front door key out of my bag. Louise snatches it out of my hand and marches up my path. She pushes the door open and walks inside. I follow her into my bedroom.

"Like what you're going to wear tonight," she says.

Louise pulls open my wardrobe doors and stands in front of my clothes with a cocked hip. She *uhms* and *aahs* and shifts her weight to the other hip. Holding onto the doors, she turns her head around to me.

"I was just planning on wearing this," I say, pointing to myself.

She snorts a laugh.

"You can't wear that," she sneers.

"What's wrong with it?" I ask, almost offended.

"It's, well, it's not really "datey", is it?" she says, putting inverted commas around 'datey'.

"It's not like it's a proper date. We're just meeting for a drink," I say.

"Every date is a proper date," scowls Louise. "You have to take these things seriously. He could be the man of your dreams and you'd be sitting there looking like a tramp."

I didn't think I looked like a tramp.

"I just don't want to go over the top and get my hopes up," I say.

"Ok, you choose something to wear, but not what you're wearing at the moment," she says and sits on the edge of the bed.

I rummage through the hangers of various coloured material, hovering on certain things and then moving on quickly.

"I don't know," I wail. "It's been so long since I've had a date."

"You can do it. I won't be here to help you before every date you have," says Louise.

I pull out a pair of jeans.

"Not jeans," Louise says.

"Why not jeans?" I ask.

"They're too casual," she says.

"These are nice ones, look, no holes, no stains, no muddy paw prints," I say, holding them up in front of myself.

"Hmm, ok, what shoes?" she asks.

I kneel down and rummage through the avalanching mountain of footwear and pull out a trainer. I hold it up and she shakes her head. I hold up two more trainers in the same style but in different colours.

"No, no trainers," she says.

"But they're so comfortable," I say.

"Going on dates isn't about comfort. It's about looking good," she says.

"They do look good," I mumble.

She ignores me.

"What about those ones?" she says, pointing at the pile.

"What ones?" I ask, looking at the pile.

"Those purple ones, with the wedge heel," she says.

I hold one up by the strap and twist my mouth in disapproval.

"Have you ever seen me walk in heels?" I ask.

She thinks for a moment.

"No I don't think I have. Put them on," she says.

I buckle my feet into the dangerous contraptions that I bought on a whim because they were in a sale and I liked the colour, and shuffle across the floor on my bottom.

"Stand up," she says.

I hold on to the bed frame and pull myself to my feet. I let go and wobble to the wall.

"Let go of the wall," she says.

I inch forward and stand up straight. My knee gives way and I stumble.

"Ok, you're not the most graceful of creatures, but you'll be sitting down on the date so it won't matter. Keep them on and practise, practise, practise," she says. "Walk and walk and walk and turn and don't fall over."

I march up and down my bedroom. It's almost like walking on a tightrope wire, not that I've ever done that. The floor looks miles away from up here, and my feet have taken on a life of their own.

"Right, that's shoes sorted. They'll at least make the jeans look less casual, and they'll definitely make you look a lot less like a teenage boy!" she says. "Tops."

I whimper again.

"I've never been any good at dressing myself. If it's clean and it doesn't smell too musty, it'll do," I say.

"I have known you for your entire life; I know what your dressing habits are like. Now it's time to change," she says, punching the air.

"Yes, Madam Prime Minister," I say.

"Ok, let's make it easy, pull out all your purple tops or anything that has purple in it," she says.

I yank out most of my wardrobe and dump the clothes on my bed.

"No, no, definitely no, burn it, throw it away, cut this one up and use it as dusters, no, no, no, hmm maybe, maybe this one too, not this one, no, no, this one," she says, pulling out my tops and throwing them across the room.

She hands me the three tops she's chosen.

"Ok, go and put your jeans and shoes on, and each one of these in turn," she says.

"Or you could get out of my room and I could get changed here," I say.

"Or I could leave you on your own and let you make a mess of this yourself," she says.

I walk into the bathroom without breaking my leg. I get changed and open the bathroom door. Louise is standing in the hallway with her hands on her hips.

"So when's the baby due?" she asks.

I look down at myself and flatten down the front of my top.

"That doesn't help. You look fat," she says.

"You look fat," I mumble, and close the door.

I stand in front of the mirror. It doesn't look that bad.

"It does look that bad," Louise shouts through the door.

How did she know? She must be a mind-reader. I change my top. I open the door.

"Bleurgh!" Louise says and pokes two fingers in her mouth.

I shut the door and put on the last top. When I open the door, Louise doesn't say anything. She spins her finger which I take to mean she wants me to turn around. I do it. She claps her hands.

"Yes, that's the one," she says and jumps forward to hug me. "Accessories."

I roll my eyes and follow her back into my bedroom. She pushes me onto my chair and holds up earrings by the side of my face.

"These ones, put them on," she says.

I do it.

"Stand up, give me a twirl," she says.

I do it. I stay upright. I'm impressed with myself.

"Lovely," she says.
I pull a cardigan from a pile on the floor.
"No cardigans," she glares.
"But I'll get cold," I say.
"Tough. Suck it up," she says. "No cardigans on first dates, ever."
I throw it down in a sulk.
"What time are you meeting him?" she asks.
"Half seven," I say.
She looks at her watch.
"It's only three fifteen now!" she laughs.
I pull my shoes off my feet and stomp into the bathroom. I come out wearing my pyjamas.
"I need to eat before I go. Knowing me, I'll spill food all down myself when I'm wearing my "date clothes". It's safest this way," I say.
"Good thinking, little one," Louise says.

***

The doorbell rings. Louise answers it. It's Safa.
"Are you ready for your big date?" she says.
I nod. I start to feel sick.
"We're not making a big deal out of this. It's just a date, a non-sized date," Louise tells Safa. "Isn't that right?"
I nod.
"Well, we're ready to go when you are," Louise says.
I put on my jacket and pick up my bag.
"You're going on a date, not being led to death row," laughs Safa.
Louise links my arm and walks me to the door.
"Got everything?" she asks.
I nod. I mentally run through the contents of my bag. What do I need to take with me that I don't normally carry anyway? Safa squeezes my hand. When she takes it away, I look at my palm. I let the metallic packet fall on to the

ground.

"She doesn't need one of those," Louise says angrily. "She's not like us!"

I pull the door shut behind us and walk out into the evening. It's not too cold but it's not too hot either. I start to feel calmer. We walk. I feel like I'm floating. I don't know if this has anything to do with my shoes or the fact that I'm so excited and so terrified at the same time. We turn the corner. I see him standing outside the pub. I pull back around the corner. Louise and Safa follow me.

"What's wrong?" Louise asks.

"Is that him?" Safa asks, poking her head around the corner.

"Yes, that's him," I say.

I find it difficult to breathe. My stomach dances the bolero. I wrap my arms around my midriff.

"He looks nice," says Safa.

"Stop looking at him," I say, pulling her back. "He might see us."

"Don't you want him to see?" asks Safa.

"I want him to see me, not me and my entourage," I say.

"You'll be fine, don't worry. Just be yourself, but yourself on a good day," says Louise.

I glare at her.

"Smile, and off you go," she says. "We'll hold back and wait until you've gone inside, and then we'll come in and sit on the other side of the bar."

"Don't embarrass me," I say.

"We won't," says Safa. "You'll manage to do that that all on your own. You don't need our help."

"Louise!" I say.

"Safa!" she says.

"Sorry. You'll be ok. Now don't leave the poor man waiting," says Safa.

I walk around the corner and look at the ground. I turn my head but I don't see Louise and Safa. I feel like I'm crossing uncharted waters or something. All exposed and ready to be shot at. The distance between the corner and the bar didn't seem this long when I started out. I approach the man and smile.

"Gregory?" I ask.

"Yes?" he says.

7

We walk inside and up to the bar. The barman comes straight over to us.

"What'll it be?" he asks.

Gregory looks at me.

"I'll get these," he says.

"Oh, er, thanks, I'll, er, have, uhm, a pint of larger please," I say.

"I'll have the same," Gregory says.

The barman pours the drinks. Gregory pulls his wallet from his back pocket. I don't want to stare but I can't help noticing the huge wad of notes. I hope he doesn't think I'm a prostitute or something. I take my drink and walk to an empty table by the window. The front door opens, and Louise and Safa walk in. They blank me and make their way to the bar. I breathe out. We both sit down. I look out of the window and take a sip of my drink. I don't dare look at him. I don't know why. We don't say anything for what seems like hours. We then both blurt something out at the same time.

"After you," he laughs.

"No, you go first," I say.

"No, you, please," he says.

"I was just going to say that this is my first, I mean you are my first, I mean I haven't been on a date before, I mean I have been on a date before but not with someone from a dating site," I babble and offer a half smile.

I gulp down more beer in embarrassment. I'm supposed to be a wordsmith and I can't even get out a simple sentence. This doesn't bode well.

"Don't worry, the first time is always a bit daunting, but I promise it does get better," he says.

"Have you been on a lot of dates then? From the dating site, I mean," I ask.

"A couple, but nothing ever came from them," he says.

"Oh," I say.

"But it doesn't put me off. You fall off one bike, you get on another," he says.

I look at him.

"I mean, horse, don't I? Fall off a horse and get back on another," he says.

I continue looking at him.

"Not that you're a horse. Or indeed a bike," he nervously giggles.

I laugh. He laughs. He has a lovely smile. From over his shoulder at the other end of the bar I see Safa standing up with her thumbs up in the air. I quickly look away. He turns to look behind him. I hope she's sitting back down.

"So," I say.

I feel like I've got the verbal version of writer's block. All words seem to have escaped me. I drink.

"Are you a bit nervous?" he asks.

"Uh-huh," I mumble, dribbling a bit of beer down my chin.

Brilliant. I wipe it with my arm. I don't think he notices.

"Ok, how about I start off, and you join in when you're ready," he says.

I nod.

"Ok," he says, taking a sip of his drink. "My name's Gregory and I'm thirty-two years old."

I laugh.

"Sorry," he smiles. "Well, hmm, ok I'll start with my job."

I nod.

"I currently own and manage a gym. Well it's more of a fitness club. For private members. It's not open to the public or anything. It's just for serious sports people," he says.

I nod.

"You know you see those adverts for gyms and it shows really fit, young, nubile people, running on treadmills or lifting hefty weights, so you think you'll join ..."

I've never thought about joining a gym.

"... and when you turn up, the whole place is full of really fat, really old or really unfit people who are only interested in having a gossip instead of working out?"

I nod, even though I've never stepped foot inside a gym. Not even to ask for directions.

"Well the people you see on the adverts, that's the type of people who use my gym," he says.

"My friend Louise would love that," I say, glancing to the bar.

"Is she a bit of a fitness freak?" he asks.

"No," I say. "She just likes perving on fit men."

He laughs. I drink.

"Well there are a lot of those at the gym, myself excluded," he says, patting his beer belly.

I laugh.

"I've never really been that interested in fitness to be honest, apart from the marathons, but the opportunity came up to buy the building and I had to take it. And I'm glad I did. I love it. There's nothing better than being your own boss. I mean, owning your own business is hard work but it's really satisfying at the end of the day when you can sit back and look at what you've done. And you don't have to answer to anyone else. I hold all the power," he laughs.

"Bit of a megalomaniac then?" I ask.

"Not at all," he says, winking. "Well, maybe a bit."

I laugh.

"I just think that you have to be happy, and I'm lucky that I get to do something I enjoy every day," he says.

I smile. My voice doesn't seem to want to form any sort of question.

"But I don't work all the time," he says. "That's one of the many good things about being your own boss; I can take time off whenever I want. I love camping. I love getting away from the noise and the people and the stress of everything here, and just relaxing with nature."

I nod.

"Have you ever been camping?" he asks.

"Only at music festivals," I say.

"That's not proper camping," he says.

It's uncomfortable and cold and smelly. That's proper camping.

"There's nothing better than falling asleep under the stars," he says.

Not even central heating, a power shower or dry clothes.

"Don't get me wrong, I couldn't live like that. I like my creature comforts, but it's nice to get away every now and then," he says.

I nod and smile. Why can't I speak?

"Do you want me to keep going?" he asks.

I laugh.

"Yes, sorry. Perhaps I need a bit more of this," I say, lifting my glass.

I drink.

"It's ok," he smiles. "So, I'm a bit of a sci-fi geek. I love anything to do with science fiction. I collect comic books …"

I laugh.

"... and character figurines from those 'they're so bad, they're good' nineteen-sixties and seventies sci-fi shows," he says.

And I bet they're in pristine condition, still in their boxes. I giggle.

"Don't laugh," he says. "You collect cardigans!"

I stop laughing and just smile at him.

"I know this will probably make you run for the hills but I'm going to tell you anyway," he says.

I get nervous.

"I don't really like to keep secrets but I've been to a few of those sci-fi conventions," he says. "You know, the ones where hundreds and thousands of geeks get together and dress up as aliens and space commanders and the like, and meet the aged stars of those 'they're so bad, they're good' sci-fi shoes, and buy extortionately priced bits of sci-fi paraphernalia. I know most people think it's weird but I like them and I've made some really good friends from all over the world ..."

His voice is so smooth and delicate. I could drift away on a cloud of his words. I'm not even sure what he's talking about anymore. I finish my drink and realise that I haven't really spoken since starting the pint. He smiles and takes a sip from his glass.

"I'm so sorry," I say. "I haven't said much."

He laughs.

"It's ok," he says. "I know I can ramble a bit."

I smile.

"I've er, I've just got to ...," I say and gesture towards the toilets.

"Oh, right, no worries," he says. "Do you want another drink?"

"I'll get the next round in when I get back," I say.

I stand up. I feel like my head is about to hit the ceiling. I'm sure I wasn't this tall when I came in here. I steady myself and walk towards the toilets. I lean up against the wall next to the hand dryer and count to five. The door opens and Louise walks in.

"How's it going?" she asks.

"Terrible," I wail.

"Why?" she says.

"I think spending all my time with Beryl, I've forgotten how to have a conversation with an actual person," I say.

She gurns her face in the mirror and wipes a glob of mascara from the corner of her eye.

"I can't think of anything to say. He must think I'm really dull. I've just let him do pretty much all the talking," I say.

"Men like talking about themselves, so don't worry," she says straightening her bra.

"But, but," I sigh.

"But nothing. Get back out there, have another drink, and try, just try to say something," she says.

"Hmm, ok," I say.

"Hurry up, before he thinks you've tried to escape by climbing out of the window," she says.

I laugh, grab a quick look at myself in the mirror and leave the bathroom. As I'm walking back to the table I realise that I didn't actually use the bathroom for what it was designed for. I can't go back in now. I'll just have to cross my legs.

"Everything ok?" he asks.

"Yeah, sorry," I say. "A friend called, was difficult to get rid of her."

"No worries," he says. "Drink?"

"Yeah, I'll get them. Same again?" I ask.

He lifts up his empty glass and smiles. I shuffle to the bar and get the drinks. Safa stands next to me.

"How's it going?" she asks.

"Go away," I whisper. "I don't want him to see me talking to you."

I throw a glance to my table. He's looking at his phone.

"Fine," she says, and looks at the barman. "I'll have a double whisky. She's paying," she says to the barman and gestures towards me.

"Ok, ok, just go away," I say.

She takes her drink and sits down. I walk back to my table and put the glasses down, managing to spill a wave of liquid over the table.

"I'm so so so so sorry," I say.

"It's ok, at least it wasn't all over my head," he says.

"Speaking from experience?" I ask.

"She was a nutter," he says.

I decide not to ask any more, just to be on the safe side.

"Ok, I'm going to do some talking now," I say.

He laughs.

"Only if you're up to it," he says and winks.

"I think I can manage it," I say, and take a deep breath.

I open my mouth but nothing comes out.

"Ok, how about a question to get you started?" he says.

I nod. I feel so useless.

"On your profile you said that you're a writer, so what do you write?" he asks.

"At the moment I'm writing a novel, my first one. Well my first serious one," I say. "I've tried to write novels before but I've never been able to finish them. So for a while I spent most of my time writing short stories but it's difficult to get short stories published unless you're an established writer. Not that I've seriously tried to get them published. I guess I'm a bit lazy and I procrastinate far too much," I say.

"And that's where your username comes from," he says.

"Yep," I say, looking down.

"That's cool," he says. "The women that come into my gym are always on the go. It's quite refreshing to speak to someone who admits that they're lazy."

I don't know whether or not that was an insult.

"So what's this novel about?" he asks.

"Not a lot at the moment," I say. "I know what I want to write, but things keep happening and getting in the way of my writing process."

"Like random men asking you out on dates?" he asks.

"I didn't mean that," I say. "I'm just making excuses for my procrastination."

He laughs. It feels so good to be able to talk to a human. His phone rings. He pulls it out of his pocket and looks at the screen.

"I'm sorry, but I do have to take this," he says.

I smile.

"Hello," he says. "What's he done now? Ok. Ok. No, don't do that. I will. I will. I promise. Ok. Ok. See you soon. Yes. I promise. Ok. Ok. Bye. Ok. Bye."

He hangs up.

"I'm really sorry, but I've got to go," he says.

"Oh, ok," I say and look down at my drink.

"No, no, it's nothing like that. It wasn't a get out call or anything, I promise. It's just, well, my sister. She's got an idiot of a boyfriend who gets drunk and violent, and she won't get rid of him because she's scared, and she won't call the police because she's scared. So she calls big brother," he says.

"No, it's fine, honestly," I lie.

"No, it's not fine, but I can't leave her," he says. "I don't want to go, believe me, but …," he shrugs.

I pass him a very weak smile.

"I am so sorry. I have really enjoyed this evening. Listen, let me make it up to you," he says.

I look at him.

"What are you doing Saturday, at about eight-thirty in the morning?" he asks.

"Well, I would usually be asleep, but I'm sure I have an alarm clock somewhere," I say.

"Excellent. Meet me in the park, by the museum shop. Bring Beryl. I'd love to meet her," he says.

I look at him.

"Please," he says and stands up.

"Yeah, ok, why not?" I say.

"You won't regret it, I promise," he says.

He leans towards me and kisses me on the cheek. I giggle like a school girl.

"Again, a thousand apologies, and I'll see you on Saturday," he says and turns to leave.

I slump down in my chair. He quickly turns back to face me. I pull myself up.

"Are you going to be alright getting home?" he asks.

"Yeah, I don't live too far, I'll be ok," I say.

"Good," he says. "Saturday?"

"Saturday," I say, raising my glass to him.

He leaves. I take another sip. I look up to see Louise and Safa standing over me.

"What happened?" Louise asks.

They both sit down opposite me. I feel like I'm at a job interview.

"He got a phone call …," I say.

"Ah one of those," Safa cuts me off.

"No, not one of those," I say.

"What was it? Emergency at home; sister, brother, mum? No, no, his best friend has fallen down a well. Or his gran got run over by an ice-cream van. Or his aunt's husband's brother's dog has contracted rabies and is running rampant throughout the town," she says.

I glare at her.

"His sister …," I say.

"Ha, I knew it," she says.

"Shut up and let her talk," Louise says.

"His sister is having problems with her boyfriend. He beats her or something," I say.

"Classic story," laughs Safa.

Louise and I both glare at her.

"I'm sorry," Louise says and pats my hand.

"He wants to see me again though," I say.

"Classic line," says Safa. "Did he also enjoy the evening and he's really sorry, blah blah blah?"

"Yes," I say.

"Did he make any definite plans with you?" Louise asks.

"He wants me and Beryl to meet him in the park on Saturday morning," I say.

"Well that sounds promising," Louise says. "Doesn't it Safa?"

Safa grunts.

"So what's he like?" Louise asks.

"Nice," I say. "A bit of a geek though. Well actually, a lot of a geek. He goes to those sci-fi conventions where people dress up as aliens."

Louise laughs.

"Get rid of him," Safa says.

"Louise!" I say.

"Safa!" Louise says.

"What?" Safa says.

"Apart from being a complete and utter geek, what's he like?" Louise asks.

"He seems alright," I say. "He owns a fitness club."

"Keep him," Louise says. "If we join we could meet some fit guys."

I look at Louise. She smiles at me.

"Come on, drink up, let's get you home," Louise says.

I leave half a pint on the table. I take my shoes off and walk home barefoot. Louise opens my front door.

"Are you going to be ok?" she asks.

"Yep," I say, stepping inside.

"Speak to you soon," she says.

I wave and push the door closed. I'm tired. I'm a bit drunk. I walk into my bedroom and drop my shoes and bag by the door. I drop onto my bed. I groan. I need a wee. I don't want to get up. I drag myself up and sulk into the bathroom. I do my business and sulk back into my bedroom.

I drop onto my bed.

***

My leg spasms. I jump up. My jeans are twisted. My leg hurts. I limp towards the bathroom. I trip over my bag and shoes in the doorway. I fall. My leg hurts more now. I stand up and hobble onto the cold bathroom floor. I stretch my leg out behind me. The cramp goes. My mouth is dry. I feel dirty. I pull my clothes off. They're clammy. I throw them into the corner of the room and get into the shower.

I step from the steamy bathroom into the cool hallway. I feel better. I walk into my bedroom and get dressed. I pick up my bag, slide my feet into some flip flops, and walk into the kitchen. I'm hungry. I can't be bothered to make anything. I get a slice of bread and hold it in my mouth. I check my bag for my keys, open the front door and step outside. The sun blinds me. I pull the front door closed, eat my bread and walk to my parents' house.

8

I walk up the path and stand on the doorstep. I take a deep breath to prepare myself for the interrogation and knock on the door. I hear Beryl barking. Dad opens the door and Beryl runs out to greet me. I stroke her head. She runs back into the hall and picks up her ball. I follow her inside. Dad is wearing overalls and has a large brown mark on the back of his head.

"What are you doing?" I ask him.

"Just varnishing the window frames in the bathroom," he says.

I don't say anything. I've learnt not to ask too many questions.

"I've got to get back to it. Your mum's in the kitchen," he says as he's walking up the stairs.

Mum sits at the kitchen table surrounded by loaves of bread.

"I just can't get used to this bread making machine you got me," she says.

"What's wrong with it?" I ask.

I take an apple from the bowl on the side. She picks up one loaf and drops it. It bounces. Beryl runs in and fights with it.

"Well, that for starters," she says.

I take a bite from the apple. She throws another loaf at me.

"Catch!" she says.

I drop the apple. Beryl chases it. It rolls in between the washing machine and the dishwasher. I catch the loaf. It feels like it's the weight of a large baby.

"That, for another," Mum says.

I put the loaf on the worktop and bend down to find the apple. It slips out of my hand and Beryl runs outside with it in her mouth.

"Hungry?" Mum asks.

"Not really," I say.

My stomach gurgles.

"Go on, try some of this," she says.

She hands me a plate covered in slices of bread.

"Do I really want to?" I ask.

"I just need an honest opinion. Your dad is useless. You know he eats anything," she says.

"True," I say.

I pull off a corner and put it in my mouth. I leave it there for a moment before I start chewing.

"Yeah, tastes ok," I say. "Wait, eurgh, no it doesn't. What is that?"

"I thought it tasted of washing up liquid, but your father couldn't taste it," she says.

"How on Earth did you get washing up liquid in the bread?" I ask, grabbing a glass and pouring some juice.

"I don't know. I followed the instructions. I followed the instructions on all of them, and they all turned out wrong," she says, pointing to the table. "I don't dare give it to the birds."

"Oh, but you'll give it to your daughter and use her as a guinea pig?" I say.

"Beryl! Beryl! Leave the birds alone," Mum yells into the garden.

I walk into the hall and pick up Beryl's collar and lead.

"You're not going straight away, are you love?" Mum asks.

"Yeah, I've got to get back. Busy busy busy, writing writing writing," I say.

"How's the book coming along?" Mum asks.

"Slowly," I sigh.

"Oh, and how was last night, your daaaaaate?" Mum asks, grinning at me.

"You don't have to say it like that," I say.

"Well, how was it?" she asks again.

"Meh, ok," I say.

"Only ok?" she asks.

"Yes, only ok," I say.

"Isn't he interested in you?" she asks.

"I don't know," I say. "Maybe. I don't know."

"He's probably gay," she says.

"You can't say that every guy who isn't interested in me is probably gay," I say.

"Well, he probably is," she says.

"Well, he's probably not," I say. "We're going out again on Saturday for your information."

"Ooh, where are you going?" she asks.

"I don't know yet," I say.

"Why don't you tell me anything anymore?" she asks.

"I can't tell you what I don't know," I say.

"You're not a teenager you know," she says.

"I know. I've got to go now. Busy busy busy, writing writing writing," I say.

"You said that already," Mum says.

"I know," I say. "So it must be true."

I go out into the garden to get Beryl. She's chewing on the bouncy loaf of bread. She doesn't notice me coming up behind her. I buckle her collar around her neck.

"Who's a beautiful girl?" I say.

She wags her tail and runs inside.

"Thanks for having her," I say to Mum.

"She's no problem, you know we love having her," she says.

I give Mum a hug and she kisses me on the head.

"See you soon," I say.

"Take care," she says.

"Bye Dad," I shout up the stairs.

No reply.

"He's probably got varnish in his ears," Mum says.

I clip Beryl's lead to her collar and open the front door.

"See you soon," I say again.

"Bye, love," Mum says.

She shuts the door.

"Bye, love," I hear Dad shout.

I turn around and he's hanging out of their bedroom window, holding onto the curtain rail, varnishing the outside window frames.

"Bye, Dad," I say.

Beryl and I take a detour on the way home. I want to walk through the park. I'm curious as to what Gregory has planned for Saturday. It's fairly empty. A couple of teenagers rock back and forth on the swings in the children's play area. A man throws a ball to a large, black dog in the distance. A man jogs past me wearing a pair of extremely tight, extremely fluorescent shorts that should never be worn in public. In fact, they should never be worn, ever. A woman cycles towards me with a young boy sitting in a child's seat behind her, his head bobbing to one side under the weight of his large bike helmet. The woman isn't wearing a helmet though. I sit down on a bench in the middle of the park. I choose the one with the least amount of white splatters on it. I look around at the average park, with its average attractions. There's no boating lake, no ice rink, no crazy golf. Nothing of any real interest. I notice the toilet block. I guess that could be of interest to some people. I look over my shoulder to see if there's anything I've missed. I hear someone scream. My head swings back around. I see a man on the ground with a long, pink extender lead tangled around his ankles. Beryl sits by the man's feet, rubbing her head against his leg.

"Oh my goodness, I'm so sorry," I say, rushing over to the man.

I try to untangle his legs from the lead but it seems to make things worse.

"I'm so sorry," I say again.

The man laughs.

"Let me help you," I say, still trying to pull his legs free.

The man carries on laughing.

"Are you ok?" I ask.

He props himself up on to his elbows. I notice that he has ripped a hole in his right trouser leg and his knee is bleeding.

"You're bleeding," I say.

He looks at his leg and drops his head.

"Typical, just typical," he mumbles.

"I really am sorry," I say again. I don't know how it's going to make the situation any better but there's nothing else I can really say.

"Always in threes, isn't it?" he says.

"What is?" I ask.

"Bad things always come in threes," he says.

"Oh," I say.

"As soon as I stepped out of my house this morning, a bird decided to use my jacket as a toilet," he says, pointing to a faded white smudge on his left shoulder.

"That's supposed to be good luck," I say, trying to lighten the mood.

He raises his eyebrow.

"Then a rude woman barged into me when I was at the coffee shop counter making me drop all my change, and a child picked it up and refused to give it back. And when I tried to talk to the child's mother, she said, 'Finders keepers, losers weepers,' and laughed. And now this," he says, throwing his hands up in the air.

"I really am sorry," I say again.

"I know you are, you've said it enough times," he says.

"I'm sorry," I say. "I mean, er ..."

"I know," he says and smiles at me.

He has a really lovely smile, soft and inviting, like I've known him forever. He manoeuvres himself free from Beryl's lead and takes a closer look at his knee. He stands up and hobbles over to the bench I had been sitting on. I follow him and sit down next to him. Beryl jumps onto my lap. He runs his hands through his dirty blonde hair and sighs.

"Can I get you anything?" I ask. "Do you need an ambulance or a lawyer to write up a restraining order?"

He laughs.

"No, I don't think I need an ambulance, but I'll take the lawyer's number if you have it," he says, laughing.

"Let me at least buy you a badly made coffee," I say, gesturing towards the takeaway van. "Please?"

"Yeah, sure, why not? What's the worst that can happen? I've had the three bad things happen to me today so nothing can touch me now. I am invincible!" he says, laughing.

I walk across the path, towards the red and white awning, and buy a tea and a coffee. I put a handful of mini milk tubs and sugar sachets into my pocket and carry the cardboard cups back to the bench. The man takes his cup.

"Thanks," he says.

I pile the sugar and milk between us. He takes a sachet of sugar and pours it into his drink. I pour two tubs of milk and three sachets of sugar into my tea and swirl it around. I forgot to pick up stirrers. My phone rings. I open the side pocket of my bag and look at the screen. It's Louise. I smile at the man and gesture the phone. He nods.

"Hello," I say.

"Where are you?" she asks abruptly.

"In the park," I say.

"What're you doing?" she asks, in a bouncy, sing-song voice.

"Taking Beryl for a walk," I say, looking at the man, smiling.

"You're with Gregory," she gasps.

"No," I say, trying not to let the man guess what Louise was saying.

"You are. You sound weird like you're trying to get rid of me," she says.

"I'll call you when I get home. I've only got one bar of battery," I lie.

"Don't you lie to me. You'd better tell me all the details later," she says.

"Ok, goodbye," I say, and press the red receiver button on my phone.

"Beryl, that's an interesting name for a dog," he says. "Any reason for choosing that name?"

"It's a bit of a long story, but I do like people names for animals, especially grandma and granddad names," I say.

"Well that's a co-incidence. I had a grandmother called Beryl, but for some reason we all called her Nana Bertie," he says.

I choke on my tea. I turn my head away, and splutter and cough over my shoulder.

"Everything ok?" he asks.

"Yeah, I'm fine," I lie. "It just went down the wrong hole, that's all."

I don't like lying but I can't say what I'm thinking. I compose myself and turn back around. I look at him, but I can't see a family resemblance.

"I'm William, by the way," he says, extending his right hand.

I shake it.

"Pleased to meet you William," I say. "Although, I'm not sure you're particularly pleased to meet me."

He looks at me.

"I wouldn't say that," he says.

I giggle like a school girl. Beryl paws at his ankle.

"Pleased to meet you too, Beryl," he says, stroking her on the head.

"And you are?" he says, looking at me.

"Oh, right, sorry, I'm Alexana," I say. "But people call me Lexa."

"Very pleased to meet you Lexa," he says.

"That's a lie, actually," I say. "People generally tend to call me Lexi, which I hate the most, or Alexa or Alana or Alexandra or Anna or Amanda or Andrea.

"Well I will remember that for future reference, Lexi," he says.

I glare at him.

"I'm sorry," he says. "Lexa."

I smile and I'm sure I blush. My cheeks get hot and my skin prickles.

"I'm sorry, have I made you late for work or something?" I ask.

"Firstly, stop saying sorry," he says.

"Sorry," I say.

He glares then laughs.

"And secondly, I'm unemployed," he says.

"All the cool kids are," I say.

He laughs.

"You too?" he asks.

"Hm-mm, something like that," I nod.

"So apart from tripping up innocent passers-by in the park, what do you do with all your time off?" he asks.

"I write," I say. "I'm a writer."

"Really? That's so cool," he says.
"Yeah, it's ok," I say. "Well, I enjoy it."
"That's all that matters," he says.
"I guess," I say.
"What kind of things do you write?" he asks.
I sigh. I don't mean to.
"Sorry, you probably get asked that all the time," he says.
"Firstly, stop saying sorry," I say.
He looks down at his cup and shakes his head.
"And secondly, no, people don't ask me all the time. In fact, people aren't interested in what I write, so I've never had to prepare an answer," I say.
"Well I'm interested," he says.
He seems interested.
"I do a bit of everything; poetry, plays, stories. I'm currently writing my first novel but it's going a bit too slow for my liking," I say.
"What's it about? Your novel," he asks.
"If I told you, I'd have to kill you," I laugh.
"Ah, it's like that, is it?" he laughs.
"To be honest, I've only written a couple of pages. Novel writing is a lot harder than I thought," I say.
"Well you'll have to tell me about it when you've actually written something," he says.
"Yeah, of course I will. I'll just make sure Beryl doesn't try to garrotte you beforehand," I say.
He's flirting with me. I think I'm flirting back. I finish my tea. I notice a pyramid of undissolved sugar in the bottom of the cup. My teeth must hate me.
"Listen, I, er, I know this is a bit forward, and you can say no if you don't want to, but my friend's band is playing at the Arts Centre tomorrow, in the evening, and if you want to, do you want to come along?" he asks.
My heart jumps up into my throat. I can't speak. My mind darts from William to Gregory. I can't date brothers. But it's not like I'm anyone's girlfriend. Going out with two

different people isn't a bad thing. I've only been out with Gregory once and that didn't turn out particularly well, and I did almost kill William, and it's not as though I can't go out with more than one person, even if they are brothers. They might not even be brothers. It might just be a coincidence. There must be hundreds of people who have or had a grandmother called Beryl. But what if they talk to each other and tell each other about me? But it's not like I'm doing anything with either one of them. At the moment I guess I'm just friends with them, friends at most, so it doesn't matter. I can see Gregory in the morning and William in the evening. There's no crime against it. So yeah, why not? Why not go out with William?

"It's ok. I wouldn't accept an invitation from a strange man that I'd tried to kill either," he says.

I find my voice.

"No, sorry, yes. I mean, yes, I would like to go and see your friend's band," I say.

"Really?" he says.

I nod and smile. This is so unlike me.

"I wasn't expecting you to say yes, but great," he says.

I wasn't expecting me to say yes either.

He fumbles in his pocket and pulls out his phone.

"Can I take your number?" he asks.

He blushes. I get my phone back out of my bag and scroll through until I find my number. I pass it to William and he copies my number into his phone.

"Thanks," he says, passing the phone back to me.

My phone rings.

"Only me," he says.

"Thanks," I say.

"I have to hobble home now, but I'll text you later about Saturday," he says.

"Sounds good," I say.

He gets up.

"Thanks Beryl," he says. "I guess only two bad things have happened to me today."

He walks through the park in one direction and I walk in the other. I feel like I'm floating. Two dates on Saturday. Two really nice men. Two really good looking men. I can't help but smile. I like it. I've not felt like this in a long time.

9

"You're a sly horse," Louise says.

She's sitting on my doorstep eating a pasty and reading an old copy of the local paper.

"Don't you have a job to go to?" I ask.

"I'm sick," she says, feigning a cough.

"You're not wrong there," I say.

"Safa's covering for me," she says.

I push my key into the lock and lean on the door. It yawns open. Louise barges past me and heads for the bathroom. I close the front door behind us and walk into the kitchen. I open the back door and let Beryl out. She lays in the shade by the wall. I make Louise a hot chocolate and try to make up a story to tell her what I was doing this morning, but I'm not very good at making up stories.

"Soooooooo?" she says, poking her head around the door.

I shove the mug under her nose.

"Thanks. So?" she says.

"So nothing," I say and walk into the living room.

"What do you mean 'nothing'?" she says.

"I mean nothing," I say, and turn on the television.

"You can't give me nothing. Not after all the help I gave

you," she says.

A woman is suing a man because she broke her arm and she thinks it's his fault. The judge sits at the front of the court room behind a high desk, wearing her black robes. She asks the woman for her side of the story. The woman says that she was at his house and he dared her to get inside his son's plastic car, which was designed to be used by three year olds. She got in and she got stuck. The man wheeled her out onto the road and pushed her along. She was screaming for him to stop but he was laughing so much and he carried on pushing her. They got to the top of a hill and he said he wouldn't push her down it but the car slipped from his hands and she went rolling down the hill. The car was stopped by a kerb but the woman was half thrown out and her arm got caught and she somehow managed to break it. She also had bruises and cuts and other small injuries.

The judge rolls her eyes and asks to see photos of the woman's injuries and the medical report she received at the hospital. The camera zooms in on the pictures of the woman. They show the woman with bruises all over her back and down her legs, and scratches on her cheeks and hands. The judge rolls her eyes again. She flicks through the medical report. She looks at the man and asks for his side of the story.

He tells the judge that the woman has all the details correct. It happened exactly the way she said it. The judge rolls her eyes again. She asks the man how old he is. He says that he's twenty-six. She looks at the woman and asks her the same questions. She says that she's twenty-five. The judge turns back to the man and asks why he dared her to get inside the car. He stifles a laugh and tells the judge that he thought it would be funny. The judge rolls her eyes. She turns to the woman and asks her why she got in the car and she says that she did it because the man dared her.

The judge rolls her eyes one more time and turns to her bailiff. She tells him that she has grandchildren smarter than these two. In fact her dog is smarter than these two. The man and woman giggle, as does the audience. The judge yells at them to be quiet. She leans forward and looks at the woman. She asks her if she's in a relationship with the man. The woman says that they are just friends. The judge tells her to make sure that she never gets into a relationship with the man because he has been spending far too much time with children that he has turned into a child himself. The woman laughs. The judge tells her to stop laughing because she's no better if she would put herself at risk for a dare. She looks at the man and tells him that he's a moron for daring the woman to get into the child's car. She then looks at the woman and tells her that she's a moron for actually doing it.

The woman tries to explain that she thought he would only push her around the garden. She didn't know he was going to take her out onto the road and then push her down a hill. The judge yells at her and asks if she has any mental problems. The woman says she doesn't. The judge speaks slowly and says that she is going to use simple words so that everyone can understand. She tells the woman that she had a choice to get in the car. She chose to get in the car so she is responsible for everything that happened afterwards.

The woman tries to interrupt but the judge raises her eyebrow and tells the woman to be quiet and listen while she is speaking. The woman stops speaking and bites her lip. The judge points to the man and says that he is not responsible for her getting in the car that day. If she hadn't got in the car, he couldn't have pushed her down the hill. The woman tries to speak again. The judge raises her hands. She tells her that the man owes her nothing. Case dismissed.

The adverts start.

"Idiots," I say.

"Stop trying to distract me with stupid Americans," Louise says.

"I'm not trying to do anything," I say.

"You're trying to avoid telling me about Gregory," she says.

"I'm not. You saw what happened last night. That's it," I say.

"And then you were with him this morning," she says.

"I wasn't," I say.

"You were. You had a weird sounding, awkward voice when I called you. The voice you use when you don't want to talk to me because you're busy doing something, or someone, else," she says.

"Well it wasn't Gregory," I say.

"So it was someone," she squeals, her eyes widening.

"No, it was no-one," I say.

"No-one who might turn out to be someone?" she asks.

I go into the kitchen and call Beryl in. I put some meat and biscuits in her bowl and put it on the floor. She takes out a few biscuits and eats them under the table.

"You can't hide from me," Louise says, opening the dishwasher.

"I'm not hiding from anyone," I say.

"You're hiding from yourself," she says in a deep, dramatic voice.

"Hmm," I say.

"Do you ever empty this thing?" Louise asks.

I shrug.

"When I remember to," I say.

She points at the clean plates. I sigh. I noisily put away the plates.

"There's a good girl," she says, patting me on the head.

She puts her mug in the empty dishwasher and shuts the door.

"Tell meeeeee," she pleads, hanging on to my arm.

I tell her. She hugs me.

"That can't have happened. Things like that don't happen in real life, remember," she says, winking at me.

"Shush you," I say.

"I am so happy for you though," she says.

"But," I say.

"No, no buts. We don't like that word," she says.

"But it's important," I say.

"What? Was he born a woman? Is he really old? Is he really young? Is he …," she puts her hand to her mouth. "… ginger?"

"No," I say, pushing her out of the way.

"Well, what's wrong with him?" she asks.

"Nothing's wrong with him," I say. "It's more about the situation."

"I'm not a mind-reader. Spit it out woman," she says.

"I think William and Gregory are brothers," I say.

"Oh," she says.

"Yeah," I say.

"How did you come to that conclusion?" she asks. "Whatever it is, it could just be a coincidence."

"They both had a grandmother called Beryl, but they called her Nana Bertie," I say.

"Oh," she says again.

"Yeah," I say.

"Have you had a look at their facebase profiles?" she asks.

"I don't know their last names," I say.

"You can still search their first names and location," she says.

"I'm not one of those facebase stalkers," I say.

"Nothing wrong with being a stalker," she says. "You can find out stuff without getting caught."

"Hmm," I say.

I walk back into the living room.

"Well it's not like you're married to either of them, so I guess it's ok," Louise says, following me.

"Of course it's ok," I say. "Isn't it?"

"Yeah, it's not weird at all," she says.

"Louise," I glare.

"No, I'm sorry, you're right. You've not made any commitment to anyone, and your MatesDates profile does say that you're interested in just dating at the moment, so Gregory can't complain," she says. "Even if you are going on a date with his brother."

I throw a cushion at her.

"It's not even a date," I say.

"Of course it is," she says.

"It's not. We're going to be watching a band in a tiny room full of people, so it's not like we're going to be alone together. We're not even going to get the chance to talk or anything," I say.

"Well, whatever it is, or isn't, I hope it becomes something," she says.

"Me too," I say. "Maybe."

"Right, I have to go. Safa gets in a right grump if I leave her covering for me for too long," she says.

"Have fun," I say.

Louise groans. She stands up and walks towards the door.

"Don't worry," she says. "I'll see myself out."

"Ok," I say.

The door slams shut. I get up and walk into my study. I turn on my computer but I don't check MatesDates. Two dates is more than enough this week. I go to facebase but can't be bothered to see what everyone is getting up to. I leave it on the screen and open my book. My heart drops at the pathetic excuse for a novel which appears on the screen. I read through what I've written. It's not bad. The house is quiet without Louise. I open my music player and scroll through the songs. I don't know what to listen to. I start up some hip-hop and bounce in my chair. Four tracks pass. I'm still bouncing. I change to some 90s Britpop. I sing with a terrible Mancunian accent. I haven't listened to this album in about ten years. I can still remember all of the words. I sing.

I'm seventeen. I'm standing in a crowded field wearing shorts and wellies and a giant bin-bag rain mac. It's drizzling but it's not cold. My feet don't touch the ground. I'm being carried by moshers, jumping to the rhythm. My arm is above my head, fist pounding the air. I'm singing and shouting and dancing and the only thing that matters in the world is right here, right now. A hand grabs my hand. I don't know who it belongs to and I don't care. We jump. The hand interlocks its fingers with mine and pulls me close. We stop jumping. The crowd around us bumps and pulses. The hand belongs to a boy, to a man, to a boy slash man. He has blonde hair and dark, brown eyes. He kisses me. My friends scream behind me. He gets picked up and thrown, and he crowd surfs to the stage.

I open my eyes. Beryl sits at my feet and stares at me. I click shuffle on my music player and a random song I've never heard before comes on. My phone beeps. I have one new message from Gregory. I don't dare open it. He knows. He knows about me bumping into William. He knows.

I go into the kitchen and make some toast. I can't find the peanut butter. I spread on a thin layer of normal butter and take a bite. I'm not really hungry. I pick up the half-eaten bag of pretzels that Louise left here the other day. I put one in my mouth. It's a bit stale, but it'll do. I take my toast and the pretzels into my study. The angry Cyclops eye winks. I go back into the kitchen and pour a mug of juice. I notice an envelope on the table with a picture of a dog on the front. I don't remember getting this. On the back of the envelope it says Your Pet Insurance Is Due For Renewal. How long has this been sitting there? I open the envelope and scan the letter. Beryl's insurance is due at the end of the month. I check the calendar. I have six days to get it sorted.

I sit back at my computer and search pet insurance. Thousands of results fill the screen. I look for a comparison site. I hate having to fill in all my information. They don't need to know my name and date of birth, and Beryl's name in order to give me a quote. I turn to Beryl.

"When were you born?" I ask.

She yawns. I try to count backwards from this year. I end up in the 1990s.

"You're no help," I say. "You know I'm not very good at maths."

She ignores me.

I click the FIND ME A QUOTE button. An ERROR box pops up. I haven't read and agreed to the terms and conditions. Does anyone ever read the terms and conditions? I put a tick in the box next to I have read and agree to the terms and conditions and click the FIND ME A QUOTE button again. A giant egg timer appears on the screen. I get bored waiting. I do a quiz where I have to guess the famous landmark from its silhouette. I guess eight correctly out of twenty in two minutes.

I click back to the pet insurance quotes. The winking Cyclops is too distracting. I open my desk drawer and toss my phone in there. I notice my passport. I look at my photo. I look like a serial killer. I wouldn't let me into the country if I was working on border patrol. I flick through the empty pages and stop at my Japan stamp. I really need to get more of those. A piece of pretzel lodges itself between two of my back teeth. My tongue can't dislodge it. I put my passport down and go and clean my teeth. I also pluck my eyebrows. I put the tweezers away in the cupboard. A bottle of shampoo falls on my foot. A bottle of shower gel body wash follows. I sit down, cross-legged, in front of the cupboard. I pull out five bottles of shower gel body wash, all in different neon colours and flavours. I flick the lid of the orange bottle open and take a sniff. Apparently I breathe in peach, jasmine and elderberry flower, but my nostrils tell me I can smell soap. Just soap. I line them up by the bath, in rainbow order. I read the ridiculous names of the Revit-alive collection. In a world of equality that supposedly frowns on sexism, the red bottle is called Pamper and the purple bottle is called Indulge, whereas the blue one is Strong and the green one is Active. The orange bottle is just called Relax so I guess anyone can use that.

My hand reaches back into the cupboard and I find more bottles of shampoo and conditioner; all with barely an inch of goo in the bottom of each bottle. One of the bottles is for curly hair. I run my hand over my straight hair. That shampoo clearly isn't mine. Who do I know with curly hair? Maybe that bottle was already here when I moved in. I throw it towards the bin. It's full of cardboard toilet roll tubes. The shampoo bottle bounces off and falls to the side of the bin, taking a couple of tubes with it. I'll clear that up later.

A mouldy bag of cotton wool balls falls forward along with an unopened, out of date bottle of mouth wash. I push those towards the bin. I lie on my stomach and peer into the cupboard. I reach in and my fingers find a flip-flop and a damp cardboard box. I pull out the flip-flop. The strap is broken. I've been looking for that since last summer. I put that near the bin too. I pull the box forward and one side disintegrates in my hand. Beryl tries to eat the clumps of papier-mâché from between my fingers as I rest my hand on the floor. I shake her away and drop the broken box into the bath. I carefully pull the box apart to expose a stack of what appears to be letters and photos. Everything is stuck together in a gunky lump. I wrap the pile in a towel and put it in the airing cupboard. I'll clean the bath out later.

I walk back into my study. A box in the middle of the screen tells me that my session has timed out. I click the refresh button and all of my quotes disappear into oblivion. I sigh. I can't be bothered to go through that palaver again. I'll do it later. My phone beeps again. I ignore it. I imagine that Cyclops getting angrier and angrier and his eye turning into a laser that he will use to escape the captivity of the drawer. He will then use his eye to hypnotise the television remote control, the toaster, the blender, the microwave and the doorbell in order to make a super race of household technology that will rise up and infiltrate the whole street then the town then the country then the whole world, keeping humans captive in our homes, and we will have to work for them. That's an idea for a book. I scribble it down onto a Post-it note. I pull the drawer open and look at my phone's screen. I have one new message from William. I can't look. They both know. I pull the curtains closed and sit on the floor. The eye winks. It won't stop until I read the messages.

I open Gregory's message. Hey, I am so sorry about last night. I am so gutted that I had to leave early. I just wanted to check in to make sure you got home ok and that you still want to meet me on Saturday. If not, I just want to thank you for meeting me the other day. Take care. Gregory xx

I hold the phone to my chest. I feel bad for ignoring him now. I reply. Hey, no worries about the other night. These things can't be helped. Of course I still want to meet you on Saturday. I'm curious as to what you've got planned for eight-thirty on a Saturday morning. Can I get a clue? Do you want me to bring anything?

I breathe a sigh of relief. I open William's message. Hi, this is William, you know, the guy you tried to kill this morning. I just wanted to let you know that the injuries are only minimal so I won't be suing you! An update about tomorrow, if you're still interested. The band is on stage at about 9, so I was wondering if you wanted to meet for a drink beforehand? At 7:30-8ish? Just leave all dangerous weapons at home this time! Wx

I laugh. I feel like I've gotten away with some sort of petty crime, like eating from the bag of grapes as I walk around the supermarket or parking in a disabled parking space while I quickly use the cashpoint. It doesn't stop me looking over my shoulder though.

My phone beeps again. My heart jumps. They're eager. I have one new message from Louise. I know you've had your phone on recently, but remember to have it on tonight. I've got a date with Marco. Love you. Marco? Ah, the waiter she met when on a date with someone else. I text her back. Can't you use Safa as your get out call tonight? I need an early night. I've got that date with Gregory at stupid o'clock in the morning. I panic. Did I just send that to William? No, it's fine. I breathe out.

I reply to William, carefully. Hey, yes, I'm still up for tomorrow evening. Drinks before sound good. I will leave all dangerous weapons at home, but I have to warn you, my arms and legs could be construed as dangerous once I start dancing. Head to toe body armour is recommended.

My phone beeps almost immediately. I'll take my chances, see you tomorrow Wx

I walk into my bedroom, close the curtains, get undressed and climb into bed. Beryl crawls along the floor and curls up on the mat by the side of my bed. I set my radio alarm to go off at half past seven in the morning. I groan and drop my head onto the pillow. Beryl jumps up and climbs over me. She steals most of the duvet, lays her head on my calves and becomes a dead weight. I pull the duvet but it doesn't move. It doesn't matter. I'm too excited. I can't sleep.

10

An awful voice trying to sing wakes me up. The invasive red lines on my alarm clock tell me it's seven-thirty. I groan. Beryl spins around and makes a den out of the duvet. She pulls at the bed covers and wraps herself up like a hoisin duck wrap. Mmm, hoisin duck. I start to salivate. I should have ordered one of those the other night. I drag myself to a sitting position and switch off the dreadful caterwauling that's attacking my eardrums. I get up and open the curtains about an inch. I am blind. The sun shouts through the crack between the fabric panels; 'Let me in, let me in, let me brighten your day.' I groan. I poke my hand out of the window. It feels warm. I feel my eyelids dropping, but a full bladder stops me from falling asleep leaning against the window.

I wander into the bathroom and do my business. My eyes close and my head drops. I hate mornings. I've got a date. I should be excited. I am excited. I open my eyes and get myself sorted.

I open my wardrobe. I turn around to ask Louise for advice. She's not there and Beryl is still sleeping in her duvet den. Make a bit of an effort. I have to make a bit of an effort. I take out a blue dress with butterflies on. I like it. It'll do. I pull on a pair of dark purple tights trying not to jab a fingernail through the material. I succeed. Now for a cardigan. I've got too many to choose from. Dark blue. Done. Look at me being all colour coordinated. Louise would be so proud. My feet find comfort inside a pair of trainers. It's too early for heels, and I don't think I've ever walked Beryl in heels so trainers are the safest option. Hair up or down? I pull it into a ponytail and let it drop. I pull it back and wrap a band around it. I haven't got time to faff around with hair straighteners. I stand in front of my mirror. I only look like I've been run over by a bike rather than a truck, so I guess that's a good thing. I carry Beryl out to the hall, put her lead and collar on, grab my bag, jacket and a handful of poo bags, and we make our way into town.

The town hall clock tells me that it's five past eight. What on Earth am I doing here this early?! I walk over to the museum shop. He's not there. I wait for a few minutes but feel awkward, so I take Beryl for a walk. I wander through the park and Beryl does her business. At least that's out the way so that I don't have to tangle myself up in poop-a-scoop bags in front of Gregory. I drop it into a bin by the entrance gate. I walk along the high street and window shop but don't really pay attention to what's for sale. I feel like I'm going to be sick. I want to go home but I have to walk past our meeting place to get home. I look up at the town hall. It's eight twenty-seven. It's now or never. I walk back to the park.

I see Gregory standing by the museum shop. He grins. I lift my arm and wave. Beryl pulls forward and runs towards him, barking. It's now that I'm glad I'm wearing trainers.

"So this is the infamous Beryl?" he says.

I nod. I'm too out of breath to say anything. Her tail wags and she barks at him.

"Is it ok if I give her a treat?" he asks.

I nod again. He pulls a rawhide bone from his jacket

pocket. She lets out a low growl.

"Is this ok?" he asks.

"Yep," I manage to blurt out.

He kneels down in front of her.

"Make sure she sits before you give it to her," I say.

"Beryl, sit," he says.

She sits.

"Who's a good girl then?" he says, giving her the bone and ruffling her head hair.

"You've got a friend for life there," I say.

"Hopefully," he says and smiles at me.

He stands up.

"So what have you got planned?" I ask.

"Have you eaten?" he asks.

"Nope," I say.

"Good," he says. "Follow me."

I follow him. Beryl carries her bone, tail wagging. A rug is spread out on the grass with a wicker picnic basket sitting in one corner. I laugh.

"After you, m'lady," he says, bowing.

I sit down on the rug and Beryl makes herself comfortable next to me, chewing on her bone. Gregory kneels down and opens the basket.

"I wasn't sure what you liked so I got a bit of everything," he says, pulling out tub after tub of food.

"I eat pretty much anything," I say.

He passes me another rawhide bone. I laugh and put it in my mouth. He laughs. He opens the tubs. The blanket is covered with pots of strawberries and grapes and blueberries and raspberries and cherries, and ripped open paper bags with croissants and pain au chocolats nestling inside, and plastic plates of smoked salmon and cream cheese bagels, and banana muffins.

"I've got some yogurt too if you fancy that," he says.

I am speechless. I drop my jaw. The rawhide bone falls to the ground.

"This is amazing," I say.

"It's nothing," he says. "I just really wanted to apologise for the other night. I really didn't want to leave."

I smile. I imagine we look like one of those happy couples in the MatesDates pictures.

"Well, this is just ...," I say.

For a wordsmith, I find it difficult to pluck adjectives out of the air.

"Thank you," I say.

"The pleasure is all mine," he says.

I love the way he speaks.

"Tuck in," he says, sweeping an arm over the food.

I pick up a pain au chocolat, pull chunks of pastry off and pop them into my mouth.

"Oh by the way," he says and roots around in the basket.

He pulls out a little bunch of flowers and hands them to me. One bloom droops and drops sideways. I am shocked.

"Thank you," I say.

"They're not from me," he says.

"Oh?" I say.

"They're from my sister," he says. "She wanted to apologise for being the reason our date was cut short."

"That's so sweet," I say. "But she didn't need to do that. Tell her 'thank you' from me, please."

"Will do," he says.

I put the flowers down by my leg and pick up a bagel. I take a bite.

"You look really nice today," he says.

I cough and choke. My eyes start to water. Brilliant.

"Hey, are you ok?" he asks, handing me a bottle of water.

I take a sip. I splutter.

"Thank you," I burble.

I wipe my eyes and take a deep breath.

"Are you alright?" he says.

"Yeah, I'm fine thanks," I say. "I just wasn't expecting you to say that."

"To say what?" he asks. "That you look nice?"

"Yeah," I say. "But I bet I don't look so nice now."

"I wouldn't say that," he says. "Red suits you."

I cover my face with my hands. He laughs and pulls them down.

"Ok, I'll make sure you're not eating or drinking whenever I give you a compliment," he says.

I laugh.

"Thank you. A bit of warning would be useful," I say.

He laughs.

"I didn't know if you liked coffee or not, so I brought juice along too," he says, lifting two flasks out of the picnic basket.

"You thought of everything," I say. "Juice please."

He pours some orange liquid into a plastic cup and passes it to me. We eat. We chit-chat. It's nice. He's so easy to talk to. I don't feel like myself. I feel like a better, more confident version of myself. I don't feel awkward or vulnerable. I feel normal, like one of those couply pictures.

"How's the food?" he asks.

"Delicious," I say.

"Well eat up," he says. "If you don't then I will, and do you want to be responsible for ruining this physique? And that's not a good look for the owner of a gym."

He pats his stomach. I laugh. I pick up a handful of blueberries. He pours some water into one of the pot lids and puts it in front of Beryl. She looks up from her bone, growls and then returns to chewing.

"She's busy," I say.

"It's ok, it's there for when she wants it," he says.

I eat more, either out of hunger or nerves.

"Alright, alright, I didn't mean for you to eat it all," he says.

I put my hand down.

"I'm only joking," he says. "It's nice to see a girl who isn't afraid of food."

I look at him.

"Are you saying I'm fat?" I ask.

"No, I, er, I meant, you know, some girls, you take them out for dinner and they eat a lettuce leaf with a side of fresh air and then complain because they've eaten too much," he fumbles.

I can't keep a straight face. I laugh.

"I'm only messing with you," I say.

He wipes his brow with the back of his hand.

"You nearly had me there," he says. "I was trying to think up another apology date for that one."

I smile.

"But it is nice to see a girl who drinks pints and eats bagels and pastries ...," he says.

I pick up some strawberries.

"... and strawberries and doesn't seem to care," he says.

"Life's too short to care," I say.

I wish I'd taken my own advice sooner.

"That's a good attitude to have," he says.

I take a bite out of another pain au chocolat. He looks at me and leans towards me.

"Come here," he says.

I lean towards him and close my eyes. He's going to kiss me. My heart thuds the inside of my ribcage. He takes my chin in his hand. I feel the rough edge of a napkin on my cheek.

"You had some chocolate on your face," he says.

"Oh, did I? Thanks. I can be a bit of a mucky pup," I say, disappointedly.

I laugh but I can't seem to muster a smile.

"Is everything ok?" he asks.

"Yeah, fine," I lie. "I think I've probably eaten too much now."

"Are you sure?" he asks.

"Yeah, I'm stuffed," I say, feigning bloatedness.

"No, I meant are you sure you're ok?" he asks.

"Of course I am, why wouldn't I be?" I say.

"Because I didn't kiss you just then?" he says.

My cheeks flush. I turn my head away so he can't see. He cups my chin with his hand, turns my face back to him and holds my gaze. I lean and he leans until our lips brush. My stomach flips. He takes the side of my head with his right hand, weaving his fingers into my hair. Maybe I should have worn it down today. I do the same; I creep my fingers along his neck and hold on to the back of his head. His hair is so soft, and the kiss is so soft, and my body feels, well, soft. A curious Beryl jumps in between us, barking. He pulls his face away from mine, but his hand stays put.

"I think someone's jealous," I laugh.

I throw Beryl an angry look. She climbs onto my lap.

"Are you eating or drinking anything, or about to eat or drink anything?" he asks.

"No," I say, suspiciously.

"I'm about to give you a compliment," he says. "And I don't want you to choke to death."

I sit up straight and look at him.

"Ok," I say. "Go."

"I just really like your trainers," he says. "Where did you get them from?"

I stretch my left leg out straight and look at my foot.

"I don't know to be honest. I have a collection of them. So whenever I see an interesting pair, I buy them, no matter where I am," I say.

"I've got a couple of pairs but only in black and blue. They don't make awesome ones like that for clown feet," he says, putting his foot up next to mine.

"Wow, is it true what they say about men with big feet?" I ask.

"That we wear big shoes? Yeah, it's true," he laughs.

I want to kiss him again. I don't.

"Is everything ok?" he asks.

I can't hide the grin.

"Good," he says. Have you had enough?"
"Yes, thank you. It was lovely," I say.
"And how was the food?" he asks.
I redden.
"The food was lovely too," I say.
He smiles. He starts to pack the food back into the basket. I eat a few more blackberries and put the lid on top of the tub. I pick it up to put it in the basket. He takes it out of my hand.
"What do you think you're doing?" he says.
"Helping you tidy up," I say.
"This is your 'I'm-really-really-really-really-sorry-for-abandoning-you-the-other-night' breakfast picnic. You're not allowed to do anything other than enjoy yourself," he says.
"But I can't let you clear everything up considering I made most of the mess," I say, pinging crumbs from my skirt onto the grass.
"Do as you're told," he says, leaning forward and planting a kiss on my lips.
I sink back onto my elbows. He pulls away and rubs his nose against mine.
"Yes sir," I say, saluting.
Beryl sniffs her way across the blanket, vacuuming up all the crumbs.
"I bet your house is spotless with her around," he laughs.
"Yeah, something like that," I say.
Beryl carries on with her bone. Gregory moves to sit next to me. He lies on his side, propping himself up on his right elbow.
"Thank you for this," I say.
"Thank you for agreeing to meet me again, after I messed it up first time around," he says.
"First dates are rarely perfect," I say.
"True, so let's call that a pre-first-date date, and count today as our first date," he says. "As long as you think today

was better than the other night."

"Very much so," I say.

He kisses me.

"Good," he says.

My stomach flips and twists and clenches and explodes.

"So, considering this first date has been to your liking, would you be interested in a second one?" he asks.

"I might be," I smile.

"I know you're probably sick of the sight of me today …," he says.

"Far from it," I interrupt.

He kisses me. I don't want him to stop.

"Well, I've got to go into work for a bit this afternoon, but I was wondering if you were free this evening because my friend's band is playing at the Arts Centre and I was wondering if you wanted to go," he says.

My heart drops and hits my stomach on the way down.

"Oh, er, I …," I say.

"It's ok, two dates with me in the same day can't be the most appealing of things," he says, sitting up.

I sit up and face him. He looks disappointed. My mind scrabbles some words together.

"No, it sounds really good, and I would like to …" I say.

"But," he says.

"But," I say, taking his hand. "I don't know if I'm free."

I don't like lying.

"Got another date lined up from MatesDates," he says, faking a laugh.

"No, nothing like that," I say. "It's just my friend, she's, er, well she's a bit indecisive about things, and she can never make her mind up if she wants to do something or not, but I'm going to be seeing her this afternoon so can I text you about it later?"

I know I sound like I'm lying.

"Yeah, that's fine," he says. "But if you're worried about meeting my friends, don't be."

I smile. I'm worried about a lot more than that. He stands up. I do the same, pick up my flowers and walk Beryl backwards so he can fold the blanket.

"Which way are you going?" he asks.

"Down towards the train tracks," I say, pointing.

"Shame," he says. "I've got to go up through town. I was hoping to spend a bit more time with you before I had to go to work."

I blush.

"Next time, eh?" he says.

"Yes, next time," I say.

Beryl picks up her remaining chunk of bone and we all walk to the gate. Gregory stops me, takes my hand and pulls me close to him. He twines his fingers around mine and he kisses me. It's slow and soft and delicious and I could stand here forever. Beryl has other plans and yanks me backwards while in the pursuit of a cat.

"I'm so sorry," I say to Gregory, trying to keep Beryl close to me.

"Well, it was nice while it lasted," he says. "Very nice."

The cat runs. Beryl pulls. I pull her back.

"Thank you for breakfast," I say,

"You're more than welcome," he says. "Hopefully see you later?"

I nod and smile.

"Take care," he says and blows me a kiss.

He walks away, towards the town, and I walk in the other direction towards Louise's house.

11

"Louise! Louise! Get up!" I shout through her letter box. I bang my palm on her front door.

"Louise!" I shout again.

Her next door neighbour opens his front door and leans his torso towards me.

"Is everything alright?" he asks.

"Fine thanks," I say.

He nods and goes back inside.

"Louise! Get out here now!" I shout.

I see a shape moving behind the glass. Louise blearily opens the door in her bathrobe.

"It's not really a good time," she says.

"Is Marco in there?" I say, trying to crane my head around the door.

"Can't it wait?" she says.

"No it can't wait. You let me in right now," I say.

Beryl scurries in through a gap between Louise's legs. Louise reluctantly holds the door open and lets me in.

"Get in the kitchen," she says angrily.

She shuts the door behind me. I get a plate and run it under the tap. Beryl jumps up, eager for a drink. I put the plate on the floor. I unclip the lead from Beryl's collar and put it on the side. She laps at the water. I fill a beer glass with water and drop my flowers in. Muffled voices argue on the other side of the door.

"I'm sorry," Louise pleads.

"Forget it," the other voice says.

The front door slams shut. I pick up the bread board and hold it in front of my face. The kitchen door opens.

"This had better be good," Louise says.

I don't dare speak.

"Come on, out with it," she says.

"Well you know William," I say.

"Oh here we go," she says.

I pick up Beryl and walk past Louise. I open the front door.

"What, so you're going to come round here and ruin my day and then just walk out?" she shouts.

I turn around.

"Look, you got me into this situation. The least you could do is help me," I say.

"What?" she says, leaning against the door frame, arms folded.

I don't want to tell her in the middle of outside, with neighbours twitching their curtains. I walk towards her.

"What 'situation'?" she says.

"William has asked me out to see his friend's band this evening, and …," I say.

"And that's brilliant. Why are you complaining and ruining my day?" she says.

"And, Gregory has asked me out to see his friend's band this evening," I say.

Louise shrugs her shoulders.

"And how is that my fault?" she says.

I put Beryl down. She barks at a gnome.

"If you hadn't signed me up to that stupid dating site I would have never met Gregory and gone on a date with him.

I would never have needed to leave Beryl with my parents. I would never have needed to pick her up the next morning. I would then not have walked through the park and Beryl would not have tangled her lead around William. William and I wouldn't have started talking and he wouldn't have asked me out," I say.

She pushes a pebble with her toe.

"If you hadn't been so insistent that I meet the man of my dreams, I could have been sitting at home writing my novel. It could have been published already. I could be a millionaire right now," I say.

"Well you pretty much are already," she says.

"That's not the point," I say. "The point is ...,"

"The point is, you overreact to small things that can be easily sorted," she says.

"How can this be sorted?" I ask, leaning my head forward to hit the wall.

Louise pulls me inside. Beryl follows.

"Ok, you think this is all my fault," she says, scrunching up yesterday's clothes from the floor and throwing them behind the sofa.

I throw her a look of disgust. She grins at me.

"Right, so seriously, if you hadn't been out with Gregory this week, would you have honestly sat at your computer and written your masterpiece, oh great one?" she asks.

"I might have done," I say.

"We both know you would have alphabetised your shoes by colour or knitted half of a rug or taught yourself how to make chocolate or cleaned out your bathroom cupboard without actually throwing anything away," she says.

I sit down and pick up a magazine.

"Exactly," she says. "So, I have done you a favour."

I look at her.

"I've given your life a bit of excitement," she says.

"No," I say. "What you've given me is a headache."

I lay my head back.

"When was the last time something happened in your life that made your stomach do somersaults?" she asks.

I think.

"When was the last time you actually felt alive?" she asks.

I didn't have an answer. I wail. To my surprise a tear forms in the corner of my eye and rolls over my nose. Louise passes me a box of tissues.

"So how did this morning go?" she asks.

"It was perfect," I say.

"Perfect, eh?" she says. "Details."

"He made me a breakfast picnic in the park," I say.

"I can't believe it," she says. "I've been using that dating site for months and all I ever seem to meet are idiots who have no idea how to treat a woman, and you get a 'perfect', romantic man straight away."

My stomach drops.

"Did you, you know?" she asks.

"Did we what?" I ask.

"You know," she says, puckering her lips.

I blush. She squeals.

"How was it?" she asks.

"Lovely," I sigh.

"So it's easy then. Keep Gregory and dump William," she says.

"It's not easy," I say.

"How so?" she asks.

"Well," I say.

I sit up.

"You know all I have ever wanted was to meet someone, you know, normally. Not through a dating site, but just through life," I say.

"Go on," she says.

"And Gregory is lovely and sweet and handsome and …," I say.

"A good kisser," Louise says.

"And a good kisser," I say. "But it almost seems a bit forced. I wouldn't have met him normally, in real life. Our paths would never have crossed."

"But yours and William's paths only crossed because you met Gregory," she says. "You wouldn't have been in the park at that time of day if you hadn't had to pick Beryl up from your parents."

"You don't know that," I say.

"I do know that," she says.

"But the point is, is that the universe conspired and William and I were in the same place at the same time. That's got to count for something. It doesn't matter how or why we were there. We were just there. That's it," I say.

"So are you trying to convince yourself that the universe wants you and William to be together?" she asks. "You haven't even been out with him yet. He might be the complete opposite of Gregory."

"I'm not trying to convince myself of anything," I say.

"Sure you're not," she says. "Look, how do you know that the universe didn't instigate the conversation between you and Gregory on MatesDates? Your paths crossed there."

"Because the universe knows that I want to bump into someone in real life, like in the films," I say.

"Films aren't real life," she says.

"You know what I mean," I say.

"Normally I do, but this time I have no idea what you're on about," she says.

"Haven't you been listening to anything I've been saying," I say, throwing my arms up in the air.

"Ok, let me try to get this straight. You were single and you were in a bit of a grump that you hadn't been out with anyone in years, and then two guys want to go out with you and you're in a grump," she says.

"Well," I say.

Maybe she was right.

"I knew I was right," she says.

"I just don't know what to do about tonight," I say, dropping my head forward.

"What did you say to Gregory when he asked you," she says.

"I told him that I wasn't sure if I was doing something with a friend this evening and that I'd text him this afternoon," I say.

"Ok, good, that's a simple, believable lie," she says.

"But I don't like lying," I say.

"I know you don't, but sometimes you just have to," she says. "Do you want to see Gregory again?"

"Yeah, I do," I say.

"Ok, and do you want to go out with William?" she asks.

"Well, yeah, just to see if ...," I say.

"Yeah, yeah, if the universe wants you two to be together," she mocks.

"Something like that," I say.

"I assume you're not desperate to see this band this evening," she says.

I shrug and shake my head.

"So text Gregory, apologising that your friend, me, wants you to do something tonight," she says.

"But you know I don't like lying," I say.

"You won't be lying," she says. "We can do something later."

"Ok," I say. "And what about William?"

"Text him and say that something's come up, that you're really sorry, you really wanted to meet up tonight but it's out of your hands, and ask if he wants to meet up another time," she says.

"I really don't like lying," I say.

"You won't be lying," she says. "Something has come up. You're going out with me."

"We can't go out anywhere near the Arts Centre," I say.

"I'm not stupid," she says. "Now get out your phone and

text them. But make sure you send the right text to the right person."

"But what if William doesn't want to see me again?" I ask.

"Then you'll know for sure that the universe doesn't want you to be together," she says.

I can't argue with that logic. I do it. I text them both. I put my phone on the coffee table and stare at it.

"A watched phone never beeps, you know," says Louise.

I turn my head away.

"That's a girl," she says. "Are you hungry? Or did you get your fill this morning?"

She winks at me.

"I could say the same about you," I say. "So I take it the date went well."

"It did until you turned up with your suitcase full of drama," she says.

"I am sorry about that," I say.

"It's ok," Louise says. "He wasn't very good in bed, but I kind of wanted to be the one who kicked him out."

"You're not going to find a decent man if you just keep sleeping with them on the first date," I say.

"No, I'm not going to find a decent man because you're now getting your hands on them all," she says.

"Why do things have to be so complicated?" I cry.

"It's all part of the fun," she says.

My phone beeps. Louise runs forward and snatches it off the coffee table.

"Don't …," I say.

"It's from William," she says.

"Give it to me," I say.

She holds my phone above her head. I reach for it. She switches hands. I reach again. She puts my phone behind her back. I grab her arms and wrestle her to the floor. She holds her hands up. The phone isn't there. She rolls over, stands up and pulls my phone out of her knickers.

"You can keep it," I say.

She wipes my phone down the front of her robe.

"Go on, read it to me," I say. "I don't think I can cope."

I collapse against the sofa.

She puts on a dramatic film trailer voice and says, "Duhn-duhn-duuuuuun."

"Give it to me if you're just going to be stupid," I say.

"Fine, sorry, just trying to lighten the mood," she says. "Ok, he says No worries, hope it's not another lead related injury that's stopping you from meeting me. Or have you managed to get yourself tangled up? Do you need me to call the fire brigade to cut you free? Have a good evening, whatever it is you're doing. Brunch tomorrow maybe? Wx"

"He wants to have brunch with me tomorrow?" I ask.

"I don't know why, but yes, that's what he says," she says.

"Give me the phone," I say and snatch it out of her hands.

I scan over the message quickly.

"See, I wasn't lying," she says.

"I never said you were," I say.

"Don't reply," she says.

"Why not?" I ask.

"You're busy remember," she says. "And I'm hungry. Go make me some food."

"Make it yourself," I say.

"Being your agony aunt doesn't come for free," she says.

She snaps her fingers.

"Food. Now," she says.

"Sir, yes Sir," I say, standing up, saluting and walking into the kitchen. I open the cupboards and pull out random packets of food. I walk back into the living room and dump them on Louise's lap.

12

Louise digs her hand into a bag of popcorn and flicks through the television channels. Everything is 'boring' even though she doesn't settle on a channel long enough to see what's showing.

"Boring, boring, boring," she says. "With all these hundreds of channels, why isn't there anything on?"

"Give me the remote control," I say.

She throws it at me. I don't catch it.

"Useless," she says.

I pick up the remote control and bring up the channel menu. Starting at the beginning, I scroll through the list.

"None of that chat show rubbish," she says.

"Why not?" I ask.

"They're all freaks and weirdos," she says, curling her lip.

"They're interesting," I say. "Those freaks and weirdos are inspiration for my characters."

"What characters?" she asks.

"The ones in my book," I say.

"Oh so you've done some more writing?" she asks.

"Not exactly," I say. "I'm still researching."

"So watching this tripe is research?" she asks, pointing to an extremely overweight woman on the screen who can't fit her huge backside into the chair on the chat show stage.

"Yep," I nod.

"Should have given her a sofa," she says. "So where's your notepad to write down all your 'research'?"

"I have a photographic memory," I say.

"Close your eyes, what am I wearing?" she says.

I can't remember.

"I have a photographic memory for useful and interesting things," I say.

"So I'm not useful or interesting enough to go into your book," she says.

"Do you want me to write about you?" I ask. "Do you want me to write in detail about you; all your faults, all the annoying things you do? Do you really want to find out what I actually think about you?"

"You love me," she says, unperturbed.

"Like a hole in the head," I say.

She throws a handful of popcorn at me. Beryl rushes to the scene of the food shower and scoffs up all the evidence. I pick up my phone.

"Put it down," Louise says.

I cover my phone with a magazine and slump back in my chair.

"Come on, cheer up, we've got to get ready," she says. "We're going out!"

"I'm not in the mood," I say.

"Stop being a grump," she says.

"I'm not a grump," I say.

"Stop being so defensive," she says.

"I'm not being defensive," I say.

"So what are you in the mood for?" she asks.

I shrug.

"Not a lot," I say. "I might just go home."

"Oh thanks, so not only do you ruin my day but you ruin

my night as well," she says.

"If I'm such a bad friend, why are you even friends with me in the first place?" I ask.

"Don't get like that," she says.

"Like what?" I say.

I stand up.

"Dramatic," she says.

"You haven't seen the half of it," I say.

I flounce out of the room, pulling cushions on to the floor and slamming the door behind me. It bounces back open.

"And if you've quite finished," Louise says.

"I'm going to go home," I say. "I had to get up at stupid o'clock to meet Gregory this morning. I could do with a nap."

"You can stay here if you want," she says.

"Thanks, but I just want my own bed and pyjamas," I say.

"Suit yourself," she says.

"Thanks," I say. "And I'm sorry."

"It's ok," she says. "He was annoying me, so you kind of did me a favour."

I walk into the kitchen, pick up my bunch of flowers and Beryl's lead, which I clip to her collar, and open the front door.

"Keep me updated," Louise says.

"I will," I say.

I walk outside and Louise pushes the door closed behind me. We wander home. I shove my front door open. Beryl runs inside. I kick the door closed and take off Beryl's collar and lead. I walk into the kitchen and put my flowers in a glass of water. I pour some biscuits into Beryl's bowl but most of them fall on the floor. I'll clear that up later. Beryl isn't interested. I walk straight into my bedroom, and sit on the edge of my bed. I open William's last message and reread it. He really does want to meet me tomorrow. I wasn't just imagining it. I reply. Brunch tomorrow sounds lovely, but what would be even better is a late lunch, because, well, I can pretty much guarantee I won't be awake at brunch time. Is two-ish ok? I drop my phone onto my pillow and throw my clothes into a pile by the door. My phone beeps. I rush to it. I have one new message from William. Nothing from Gregory. I'm slightly disappointed. I open the message. I'm kind of glad you said lunch. There's no way I'm going to be awake then. Two-ish is perfect. Do you know Hambriento? Wx. I reply straight away. I'm too tired to remember to do it tomorrow. I've never been there but I know where it is, and I've heard it's really nice. See you tomorrow. I drop my phone onto my pillow again. I climb into my pyjamas and collapse onto my bed. I shuffle around until I'm comfortable. Beryl joins me. I lay my head back onto my pillow. My phone digs into the back of my skull. I untangle the contraption from my hair. I click a button and the screen wakes up. No new messages. I put it on my bedside table.

I close my eyes. My fingers locate the remote control and press the 'on' button. I can't be bothered to find something decent and just leave the channel as it is. I'm not really interested in watching anything. I just don't want to be surrounded by silence.

"She's so excited. Iss bin 'er dream since she was born. She laaaves singin'. She's aww-ays singin'. Can't stop 'er singin'. Bin singin' all 'er life, ain't ya? She's briw-yant. Got the voice of a angew. Evrywun says she's briw-yant whenefer she sings, don't they? Sometimes brings a tear to me eye. Y'know," a woman says.

The voice changes. It's the girl. She sounds exactly like her mother, just a higher pitched version of her.

"I'm only firteen buh iss bin ma dream since I was born. I laaave singin'. I'm aww-ays singin'. Can't stop me singing'. Bin singin' all ma life," the girl says.

I hope she sings better than she speaks. The presenter tells her that the judges are ready for her. The audience starts to clap. One of the judges speaks to her.

"What's your name?" the judge asks.
"Smanfa," the girl says.
"And how old are you?" the judge asks.
"Firteen," the girl says.
The audience clap again.
"And what's your dream?" the judge asks.
"T'be er singar," the girl says.
"And how long have you wanted to be a singer?" the judge asks.
"Aww ma life," the girl says.
"Excellent, good luck," the judge says.

The music comes on and the girl starts singing. The audience sympathetically claps but is, in the main, silent. The girl carries on singing, although it can't really be called singing. More like making some sort of noise. Not that I'm an expert but it's pitchy and extremely out of tune. I reach a hand out for the remote control to change the channel but I can't find it. I don't want to open my eyes or get out of bed so I put my pillow over my head. It doesn't drown out the noise. When will this torture end? I'm sure my ears bleed.

The music stops and the girl stops and the audience claps, but it's far from enthusiastic. I shove the pillow off my face. One of the judges speaks.

"Have you ever had singing lessons?" she asks.
"No," the girl says.
"You're so young and you haven't had much singing experience, so it might be beneficial to have some singing lessons, just to learn about breathing and technical skills that will help with your all round performance," the judge says.
"I agree," another judge says. "It was a bit shaky and pitchy. Maybe you were nervous. This is probably the first time you've performed to an audience of two thousand people. It can be very scary. But with some professional help I think you could really improve with your stage presence and singing ability."

The girl doesn't say anything.

"It's time to vote," the first judge says.

"I'm sorry but it's a no from me," the other male judge says.

"It's also a no from me, but good luck with everything," the first female judge says.

"I'm sorry but it's a no today," the other female judge says.

"I'm afraid it's four nos but thank you for coming along today," the final male judge says.

The audience claps. A few seconds later the girl's mother screeches out onto the stage.

"Who the **** do you lot fink you are?" she yells. "You, you can't even sing. 'ow dare you tell my door-ah that she can't sing. She don't need no ******* professional 'elp. You do. When was the last time you 'ad a ******* song in the charts? Come on. You come up 'ere an' sing. See, ya can't. You ain't got the guts or the voice. My door-ah 'as got more talent in her little finger than you aww have aww togevva."

The audience boos.

"You can shu-up an' aww. Shu-up. You don't know what you're tawkin' abaaah. ******* idiots, the lot of ya. You. You've ruined 'er life, takin' 'er dream away from 'er. I 'ope you can sleep tonight, knowin' my door-ah is cryin' 'ersewf to sleep because of you. 'ow embarrassin' for 'er to come on telly and be embarrassed by you. You know nuffin'," she shouts.

"Madam, it is you who has ruined your daughter's life by telling her that she can sing, when she clearly can't, and allowing her to come on television to perform, if that's what you can call it, in front of the entire nation," the first judge says. "You are the reason she embarrassed herself, and you are embarrassing yourself. Please stop lying to your daughter, and start encouraging her to have an achievable dream. And now please get off my stage. Security."

The audience erupts in applause and cheers and laughter.

The adverts start. My ears begin to fill with made up words. *For a healthy digestive system, eat yogurt that contains Immunitum Regulatorium Yummitum. For beautiful hair, use shampoo that contains Smoothatry Locklicious Strengthaserum. For glowing skin, smother your body in cream that contains Bronzitride Moistrocrème Exfolotion.*

I drift in and out of sleep. I dream I work for a sell-o-vision channel. I am demonstrating a product. The crowd are oohing and aahing and clapping and impressed with my product. Everything's going well until I face the judges. The first judge is Gregory. He doesn't like the product and tells me that I'm useless and should get another job. William is the second judge. He likes my product and wants to see more. The final judge is Beryl and she just tries to eat my product. My phone starts ringing. I search through my pockets and my bag but I can't find it. The phone keeps ringing. The judges look at me and roll their eyes. I crawl around on the floor, looking under the table, in between people's legs, but I can't find it. The judges tell me that I'm wasting their time. I apologise and tell them that I'll just be a minute. Once I've found my phone I can carry on with my demonstration. They tell me that my demonstration is over and that I have to go home. I plead with them to let me stay but my phone gets louder and louder until I can't hear what they're saying.

I wake up. I'm sweating. My heart is thumping. I feel like I've run a marathon. My mouth is dry and I feel as though I've been punched in the stomach. I look around. Beryl is still asleep. The screen on my phone is alight. I have one new message from Gregory.

13

My eyes feel sore, as though I've woken up from a hundred-year long sleep. It's dark outside. The television shows a bewildered chat show host interviewing a pop star that he's clearly never heard of. His perfected fake laugh feels like needles behind my eyelids. I can't find the remote control. I stumble out of bed and push the on/off button on the television. I can't remember the last time I pushed that button. The interview is sucked into oblivion where it belongs. I yawn and stretch and feel strangely awake. The red fluorescence of my alarm clock tells me it's eleven twenty-seven.

"I can't believe I've been asleep this long," I say to Beryl.

She's no longer on my bed. I pull on a pair of long socks and wrap my dressing gown around myself. I'm hungry. I've got a craving for potato wedges. I walk into the kitchen and pull open the freezer door. A box vomits ice lollies onto my feet. I shove them uncomfortably into a drawer. I hunt through the compartments, gritting my teeth every time something scrapes against the ice-lined walls. I find the bag of wedges and tip some onto a baking tray. There are too many in the bag for me to eat, but not really enough to leave some in the bag and put back in the freezer. I leave it as it is and throw the empty bag in to the bin. I put the tray in the oven and set the timer for twenty minutes.

I walk into my bedroom and crawl across my bed. I lie on my stomach and reach over to my bedside table. I grab my phone, turn onto my side and look at my messages. Beryl jumps on to the bed and wriggles her way up to just under my arm.

"Let's see what he's got to say," I say to Beryl.

She stretches and yawns. I open Gregory's message. Well I guess it's now your turn for a make up date, but you know, your one has to be a million times better than the picnic in the park. No pressure or anything. Hope you're having a good night whatever you're doing. I'm free all day Tuesday by the way, hint hint. G xx

I roll on to my back and drop my phone to my chest. A weird sensation floods my body. I guess it must be happiness. I've not felt that feeling in a long while. I have no idea what to do on Tuesday though. I panic. What can I do that will be better than that beautiful picnic in the park? Perhaps I should actually take up naked bungee jumping. I close my eyes. My stomach dances erratically. I get up and walk around my bed. Beryl sits up and looks at me, confused. I walk back. I throw my hands up in the air.

The alarm bell rings. I put my phone into my dressing gown pocket and walk to the kitchen. Beryl follows me. I pick up my novelty Father Christmas oven glove and slide the baking tray out of the oven. I tip the wedges in the bowl but most of them miss. I put the tray back in the oven and pick up the escaped wedges. I take the bottle of mayonnaise out of the fridge and squirt a large caterpillar over the wedges. I put the mayonnaise back and take out a can of lemonade. I kick the door closed and walk out of the room.

I don't know where to go. I don't want to watch television. I don't want to get back into bed. I walk into my study and turn on my computer. I wait for it to start up. I look at my clock on the wall. It's nearly ten past eleven. It seems to take forever. I open the music player and set it to shuffle. It's not very loud but sounds loud in the silence of the night. I put my bowl on the side and pick at the wedges. I don't want to look at MatesDates. I do want to look at it, but I don't want to deal with any more men wanting to go out with me just yet. I can't deal with complicated.

I look at pictures of dancing cats, and dogs in hats, and fat people wearing unflattering clothes, and stupid people with incorrectly spelled tattoos, and cute rainbow coloured cupcakes, and funny exam answers, and cartoon character bento boxes, and inappropriate text messages, and superhero wedding attire, and overly fake tanned orange girls doing duck faces in their bathroom mirrors. I look at facebase. Rachel is getting bum implants. I can't read any more. I glance back up at my clock. It's still nearly ten past eleven. I haven't wasted any time here.

I finish my wedges and drink half the can of lemonade. My stomach gurgles. I burp. I fear the windows will rattle out of their frames. Beryl looks at me. I laugh. I feel fidgety. I'm not tired. I don't know what to do. I wander. I look in the kitchen. I look in the living room. I wander back into my study. I sit down and spin around in my chair. I regret sleeping for so long. I get up and walk back out into the hall. I walk and run my hands along the wall. I count my steps from room to room to the front door and back again. I take longer strides the second time around. I stand with my hands on my hips and look up at the ceiling.

"What to do? What to do?" I say.

I open up the back door and Beryl runs outside. I wander into the living room and sit down in front of my bookcase. I look up at the rows of unread paperbacks. I tug at a spine and a book slips out. I flick through the pages. I look at the back cover and scan my eyes over the blurb. It doesn't spark my interest. I squeeze it back in to the row of books it came from. I don't take out any more. I just look. I want to read but I don't know what I want to read. I don't fancy anything new and I can't be bothered to read something I've read before; I know how they all end. I want to be surprised, but not too surprised in a dark house in the middle of the night.

I'm bored and I feel boring. Nothing inspires me to do anything. I wish I could sleep but my mind is too awake. Whose bright idea was it to fall asleep in the early evening? I hear Beryl run in and head straight to my bedroom. I get up and go into the kitchen. I lock the back door and pull the curtain across. I hear Beryl in my bedroom. She's on my bed creating a tornado with the covers, throwing a muddy stone across the untidy duvet. I grab for the stone but she picks it up and runs out of the room. I can't be bothered to chase her. I straighten out the bed clothes. The majority of the material is covered in brown, splodgy paw prints and more indistinguishable brown patches. I turn the duvet over. It's worse on the other side.

I unbutton the bottom edge of the duvet cover and pull out the duvet. I throw the duvet behind me and the cover by the door. I unwrap the pillows from their cases even though they are reasonably clean. I hear the stone ping across the kitchen floor, banging into the cabinets, like a pinball machine. I drop the pillows behind me and throw the cases on top of the duvet cover. I yank off the undersheet and roll it up into a ball. I pick up all the dirty linen and take it into the kitchen. I stuff it into the washing machine and shut the door. I'll set it to wash tomorrow. Beryl takes her eye off the stone and sniffs at the washing machine door. I pick up the stone and put it in the sink. She looks around, puzzled. She hunts for the stone but after a few seconds gets bored and eats some biscuits.

I open up the airing cupboard and pull out some fresh bedsheets. A couple of towels fall onto the floor. I'll pick those up later. I carry the bedsheets into my bedroom stretch the elasticated edges of the undersheet over my mattress. It pings off one corner. I pull it back. Another corner pings off. It's now that I would love to have six-foot long arms. I make sure the back two corners are secure. I push the mattress into the headboard and stretch the undersheet over the other two corners. I turn the pillow cases inside out and pick up the pillows by the corners, one by one, with my hands inside the cases. I flip the cases over the pillows and plump them before throwing them at the head of the bed.

The duvet always causes difficulty. I contemplate leaving the duvet cover off, but the duvet is slightly scratchy when nude and I know I won't want to dress it in the morning. Beryl jumps up on the bed and makes the task all the more difficult. She saunters inside the duvet cover, gets lost and can't find her way out again. She whimpers and paws at the cloth, hoping she can scratch her way out. I climb inside and pull her out. She jumps out of my arms and makes a bed on a pile of my dirty clothes.

I straighten the duvet cover over the duvet and button it closed. I swoosh it up in the air and lay it over my bed. I shoo Beryl off my clothes and carry them into the kitchen. I shove them into the washing machine. I walk back towards my room and notice the towels on the floor. I pick them up. Sheets of paper float to the ground. I remember the damp box from the back of my bathroom cupboard. I drop to the floor and sit cross-legged. I shake the towel and watch the confetti fall. I spread the papers out in front of me. Some are still stuck together. I carefully peel them apart. My eye dances from black and white photo to yellowing envelope to smudged newspaper cutting. I don't know where to begin.

14

I scoop up the papers and carry them into my bedroom. I shut the curtains and turn on my bedside lamp. I bolster up all four pillows on my side of the bed and get up on the bed, wrapping the duvet around me. It smells so fresh and feels like putting on a new pair of socks on the first day back at school after the summer holidays. A not so mucky Beryl jumps up and makes herself comfortable next to me. I lean back against the pillows and rest the pile of papers on my lap. I sort them out and set the photos aside. I start to scan through the other papers but my eyes feel too tired to read. I can't focus on the script. I'm starting to feel drowsy. Even if I could read them, I doubt I would remember anything I read. I straighten the papers and put them on my bedside table drawer so that they don't float away or fall down between the bed and table of their own accord.

The pictures feel a bit sticky. I lift my knees up and make a table by tightening the duvet. I lay the pictures out. There are five in total. I pick up one of the black and white photographs. The corners are bent and tattered but the main image in the centre is clear. A young woman, maybe in her twenties but I can't be sure; I'm terrible with ages, is sitting on a wall by a lake. She seems extremely graceful; her legs swooped to the side, ankles kissing, her hands gently resting in her lap. She looks happy, but she's not smiling an obvious smile. It's shy and coy, but forthright. Dark curls delicately frame her face, I imagine from hours of tying wet rags into her hair. A small hat perches on top of her head. I can't tell if she's wearing make-up, but her skin looks fresh and her eyes look alive. She's wearing a dress that comes just below her knee. I pull the picture closer to my face. The dress has a floral pattern with a wide belt tied up around the middle. I turn the photograph over. In the top left corner a faint pencil squiggle tells me that it's Mullein Park 1947. It's beautifully written, as though someone has taken care to write it. I wonder if the woman wrote it. Or maybe it was the person who took the photograph. I look back at the woman. She looks familiar but I can't put my finger on it.

The other black and white photograph is a lot darker and someone had folded it in half. The wide, white crease line chops a young man in half at the waist. He is standing in front of a door. There's nothing on the walls to indicate where he is. He looks dapper in a pinstripe three piece suit. A pocket watch peeps just below the fold. His shoes are shiny. His hair is parted on one side and he sports a skinny moustache. He stands at a slight angle with his left hand casually in his pocket. He smiles directly at the camera. I turn the photograph over. There is nothing written on the back.

I slide myself down in bed. I hold the man and woman up. Who are they? They must have meant something to someone for them to have kept the pictures, but why were they stuffed in a box and put at the back of a cupboard? Why didn't they get framed? I glimpse at the other three photos. One is black and white and two are in colour. My eyelids drop. I try to keep them open. I can't focus on anything. My eyes close and I drift back.

***

Beryl paws at my hair. Her nails are sharp. I push her away. She climbs on my head. I don't open my eyes. I step out of bed and my foot lands on something smooth and sticky. I reach down and fumble to find my sole. I peel a photograph away from my skin. I drop it back onto the floor. I switch off my bedside lamp and open the curtains. I walk into the kitchen and unlock the back door. Beryl scratches at my ankle. I pull the door open and she runs out and crouches on the grass just outside. She pads back in and I lock the door. I squint my eyes. The green lines on the microwave wriggle and eventually form themselves into a time. It's twelve thirty. I'm surprised Beryl lasted that long.

I feel dreadful, like I've only had ten minutes sleep after being awake for a week. I close my eyes again and feel my way to the bathroom. I turn on the shower and wait for the room to fill with steam before I climb in. I do what I have to do and stumble into my bedroom. I wrap my dressing gown around myself. Beryl hides under the bed as I turn on the hair dryer. She looks at me suspiciously. I aim the dryer at her. She shuffles backwards. My hair flies all over the place. I leave it to drop where it feels most comfortable. It's not like it does as it's told anyway.

I'm not nervous. Why am I not nervous? I should be nervous. Or at least excited. Why am I not excited? Don't I want to go out today? Of course I do. I'm just tired. I'll feel better in a bit. I open my wardrobe. I've got to dress myself again. Sometimes Louise can be useful. I lean back and look out of the window. It looks nice. I pull out a pale blue and white dress and zip myself into it. I carefully roll nude tights up my legs and slip my feet into a pair of black flats. I push my arms into a pale blue cardigan, pick up the photos and put them in my bag. I walk to the front door and Beryl follows me. I buckle her collar around her neck, clip the lead to the collar, put on my jacket, and walk outside.

It's a bit too cold for my liking but I don't have time to change. Beryl must know I've got to be somewhere because she sniffs every lamppost and every wall corner en route to my parents' house. Once we get to their road, and she recognises where we are, she decides she wants to pull my arm out of its socket. I open the gate and she makes a bee-line for the front door. She starts barking. I unclip the lead and knock on the front door. Mum opens the door.

"Hello, love," she says and kisses me on the head.

Beryl runs in.

"Everything ok?" Mum asks.

"Yep," I say. "Can you watch her for a couple of hours?"

"Of course, we love having her here," Mum says.

"Hello, love," Dad says.

He's covered in snippets of duct tape. I look at him and then to Mum.

"He's putting up some shelves," she says.

"Obviously," I say.

"What do we owe the pleasure?" he says.

"She just needs us to look after Beryl for a bit," Mum says.

"Why?" Dad asks.

"Does there need to be a reason for your granddaughter to want to spend time with her grandparents?" I say.

"There usually is a reason," Dad says.

"Well, ok," I say.

I turn to look out of the window and cover my mouth with my hand.

"I'm meeting someone for lunch," I mumble.

"You've got another date?" Mum asks.

"Maybe," I say.

"Oh, love," Mum says wrapping her arms tightly around my shoulders.

I try to wriggle out of her vice like grip. She doesn't let go.

"Limpet much?" I say with my last remaining breath.

"So things are going well with this one?" she asks, finally taking a step backwards.

"Which one?" I ask.

"The one you went out with the other night, when you came here with Louise?" she says.

"Well," I say. "I'm seeing him on Tuesday. I'm seeing someone else today."

Mum takes another step back and folds her arms.

"Don't look at me like that," I say.

"Like what?" she says.

"Like I'm doing something wrong," I say.

"Well are you?" she asks.

"Am I what?" I ask.

"Doing something wrong," she says.

"No, I'm not," I say, even though I'm not too sure.

"Well as long as you know what you're doing," she says.

"I do," I say.

I don't really. She looks at me.

"You look nice," she says.

"Thank you," I say.

"Didn't you want to brush your hair?" she asks.

I run a hand over my head.

"It looks alright," I say.

"No it doesn't," Mum says.

She walks off. I poke my head around the living room door. Dad is sighing at a plank of wood. I feel something yanking at my scalp. Mum is dragging a brush through my hair. It feels like she's ripping it all out. I try to escape her clutches but she's got me trapped. She pulls the brush through my hair. A tear creeps out of my eye. I grab the brush before she can do any more damage.

"See, that looks better already," she says.

I look in the hall mirror. I ruffle my hair. Mum flattens it down.

"I've got to go now," I say. "Bye Dad, bye Beryl."

"Have a good time," Mum says. "Be safe."

"Mu-um," I say.

"You're still my little girl. I want you to be alright," she says.

"I will be," I say.

"See you later," she says.

"Thanks for taking Beryl," I say.

"We love having her," she says.

I stand on the doorstep.

"Oh, before I forget, I found these stuffed at the back of my bathroom cupboard," I say, taking the photos out of my bag and passing them to Mum.

Mum takes a step back.

"You, you mean you cleaned out your bathroom cupboard?" she says.

"Yes," I say.

"Tom! Tom! Call an ambulance. I think I'm having a heart attack. Alexana has cleaned out her bathroom cupboard," she shouts over her shoulder.

"You're not having a heart attack," Dad shouts back. "Because she couldn't have cleaned out anything."

"Thanks Dad," I shout.

Mum laughs.

"I'm not a complete slob," I say.

"Questionable," she says.

She looks at the photos.

"I don't know who they are, but I wondered if you knew anything about them or could find out something about them," I say.

"Hmm," Mum says. "I'll have to ask your dad."

"Brilliant, thank you," I say.

"Bye, love," she says.

"Bye," I say.

She stands at the door waving. I walk away and turn the corner. I ruffle my hair once I'm out of sight. William is wandering up and down outside the restaurant. I catch his eye. He stops wandering and limps towards me.

"Hey," he says.
"Hi," I say. "How are you?"
He limps closer.
"Well the doctor thought it was touch and go there for a moment," he says. "He was thinking about amputation, but he settled on a knee replacement. It should be back to normal in six to eight years."
"Not long until you're dancing for the Russian ballet then?" I say.
He laughs.
"How are you?" he asks.
"I'm really well thanks. And how are you? Really," I say.
"Yeah fine thanks," he says. "You missed such a good night last night."
"I'm sorry," I say.
"No worries," he says. "Next time maybe?"
"Yeah, next time," I say.
He leans towards me.
"You're not going to self-destruct or strangle me with your handbag if I give you a kiss on the cheek?" he laughs.
"I can't promise anything," I say.
He puts a hand on my shoulder and kisses my cheek. His lips are soft. The back of my neck starts to tingle. He smiles at me.
"Hungry?" he says.
"I'm always hungry," I say.
He laughs. We walk to the front of the restaurant. He holds the door open. I walk through and wait by the Wait Here To Be Seated sign. He stands next to me and puts his hand in the small of my back. My skin tingles. Now I'm feeling nervous. Excited. Nervous. A waiter walks towards us.
"Two?" the waiter says.
I nod.
"This way," the waiter says.

He walks towards a table by the window. William pulls out my seat. I sit down, take off my cardigan and put my bag on the floor.

"Thank you," I say.

He smiles at me and sits opposite me. The waiter hands me a menu.

"Can I get you a drink?" the waiter asks.

I scan my eyes over the wine lists."

"Er," I say.

"What I think she means to say is do you have any beer?" William says.

I laugh and hide my face behind my menu. The waiter nods.

"Two pints of your finest lager," William says.

The waiter nods again and walks away.

"How did you know?" I ask.

"You looked terrified at the sight of all those rotten grapes," he says. "A wine drinker's eyes would have lit up at that list."

"You're very perceptive," I say.

"And you're very beautiful," he says.

I laugh. Where did that come from? I hide my face behind my menu again.

"Thank you," I mumble.

"You can put the menu down," he says.

"I can't. There's too much to choose from," I say.

He pulls the menu down. I know my face is red.

"Have you had tapas before?" he asks.

"Kind of," I say.

"How do you mean, kind of?" he asks.

"Well sometimes my friend Louise puts out bowls of different things on her coffee table," I say.

"Like what?" he asks.

"Tortilla crisps, jelly babies, chocolate buttons, popcorn, pretzels, cornflakes, pickle, cheese, cold spaghetti hoops straight from the tin, drawing pins, toenail clippings.

Whatever she has in the cupboard really," I say.

William laughs.

"Well this one is a little bit different," he says. "You pick three or four dishes and I'll pick three or four. We can't really go wrong."

"You sure about that?" I ask.

He slides his chair backwards and winks at me.

"I promise you, no dangerous weapons today," I say.

The waiter brings our drinks over.

"We're not ready yet," William says.

"No problem," the waiter says. "I'll be back in a bit."

He walks away.

"What to have? What to have?" I say.

"Choose anything. It's all really good here," he says.

I look at the menu. The list of dishes is endless. I can't make up my mind.

"Done?" William asks.

"Far from it," I say.

"No rush, take your time," he says, putting down his menu.

I look up from my menu. William is looking at me. I smile. He smiles back. He doesn't stop looking at me. I feel a bit strange. No-one looks at me. Ever.

"I can't decide with you looking at me," I say.

"Well I can't stop looking at you," he says. "It's like you've got some laser beam thing that's holding my head in this position."

"Well close your eyes then," I say.

"Can't do that either," he says.

I pull the menu in front of my face.

"Meanie," he says.

I drop the menu, poke my tongue out and pull the menu back up.

"It's not my fault that you look good," he says.

"Stoppit," I say.

"Can't do that either," he says.

I sigh but my stomach does somersaults. The waiter comes back over.

"Are you ready to order?" he asks.

"I think so," says William.

I put my menu down and William looks at me. I nod.

"Can we have deep fried potatoes with salsa, tiger prawns wrapped in filo, garlic bread, and sweet red peppers stuffed with cheese," he says, reading from the menu.

"Aaaaand," I say.

The waiter turns to face me.

"Garlic mushrooms, tortilla, Spanish meatballs, aaaaaand," I say, taping my finger on the back of the menu, quickly scanning the list.

The waiter sighs.

"And chicken with chorizo," I say. "Please."

"Will that be all," the waiter says.

"And some salad," William says.

"Very good," the waiter says.

He takes our menus and walks away.

"How's unemployed life treating you?" William asks.

"Well …," I say.

"That good, eh?" he asks.

"No," I say. "I was going to say, well, I'm not really unemployed."

"Oh I thought you said you were," he says.

"I kind of am," I say. "It's a bit complicated."

"Complicated?" he says.

"Yeah, a bit," I say.

"Don't you want to talk about it?" he asks.

I look at him. He looks genuine. Something about him makes me feel comfortable in his company.

"I don't mind talking about it, but I don't want it to change your thoughts about me," I say.

"So you kill people and sell their body parts for scientific experimentation too?" he laughs.

I laugh.

"Now my story is going to sound rubbish," I say.

I sip my drink.

"Basically, I don't work because I don't need to work," I say.

He puts his elbows on the table and rests his hands under his chin.

"Tell me more," he says. "I'm intrigued."

"My nan died a few years ago," I say.

"You killed your own grandmother and sold her body parts for scientific experimentation?" he asks.

"Yes, and if you interrupt me again, you'll be next on my list," I say.

"Sorry," he says and winks at me.

"Leading up to her death I was the only one of her grandchildren who actually spent time with her. I didn't do the yukky things like giving her a bath or changing her incontinence knickers," I say.

He pulls a face.

"Thanks, just the image I need before eating," he says.

"What did I say about interrupting me," I say.

I pick up my knife and run my finger along the blade.

"Sorry," he says.

"Good," I say. "Can I continue?"

He takes a sip of his drink and nods.

"I'd go round there and just listen to her stories or take her to the supermarket or yell at idiots on reality television shows with her. I'd sometimes bake her cakes or cook her dinner or get drunk on sherry cocktails," I say.

I pick up my napkin and wipe my eye. William reaches across the table and strokes my arm.

"I'm sorry, you don't have to go on if you don't want to," he says.

"No it's fine," I say. "I just really miss her sometimes."

The waiter brings over a tray of food. He arranges five small plates in the middle of the table. It looks delicious.

He returns a couple of seconds later with the remaining three plates.

"Enjoy your meal," he says.

"Thank you," I say.

"Help yourself," William says.

"I don't know where to start," I say.

I'm sure my eyes are as wide as a child's on Christmas Day or those of a crackhead the moment they've taken a hit. I take a slice of tortilla, a couple of filo prawns, a meatball which is larger than I expected, a spoonful of garlic mushrooms and some salad.

"Hey, don't eat it all," he says.

"You told me to help myself," I say. "You'd better jump in before I take more."

He laughs and grabs the plate of garlic bread.

"So anyway," I say. "Nan passed away, but she was old and it was of natural causes so we weren't surprised. We had the funeral and then the reading of the will. None of us knew that she was loaded. She had more money than any of us knew about."

I cut the meatball in half and shove it into my mouth. It's spicier than I expected. I grab my glass and swallow a mouthful of beer.

"Are you ok?" William asks.

"Fine," I cough.

"So how did she manage to keep all that money a secret from her family?" he asks.

"I have no idea," I say. "It wasn't as though she lived like a tramp. She lived well so we knew she had some savings, but we weren't prepared for the actual figure."

"Which was?" William asks, winking.

"If I told you that, I would have to kill you," I say.

"That's the second death threat I've had from you today," he says.

I grin and do an evil laugh. I cough and choke. Brilliant.

"Are you trying to kill yourself too?" he asks.

"Looks like it," I say.

"At least I now know how much you're enjoying my company," he says. "You want to kill me, and if you can't do that, you'll choke yourself to death."

He grins. I blush.

"Let's just say it was a lot," I say. "So the whole family is sitting around a large table at the solicitors. Me, my parents, Aunt Janet, Uncle Paul and my cousins, Michael, Joshua and Natalie sit along one side of the table. Uncle Terry, his bimbo of a girlfriend, Mel, Uncle Alan, my cousin Hannah, and Aunt Tina sit on the other side of the table. The solicitor garbles through a load of legal jargon that no-one understands. Uncle Terry bangs his hand on the table and tells the lawyer to get on with it. The lawyer starts to read the will. Nan has left a lot of money to charity, to the company that her carers worked for, her postman and the man who works in the off licence. She liked him. He would always ask her for ID whenever she went in to buy her sherry. It gave her a smile. Terry continues shouting that this is ridiculous, that Nan was a stupid old bat didn't who know what she was doing with her money, that she was insane. Dad pipes up and reminds him that she was of sound mind when she wrote the will. He swears and gets out of his chair. The lawyer politely asks him to sit down. Mel coos at him and tells him to calm down otherwise they might not get anything, stupid woman. She doesn't even realise the will's been written and it can't be changed."

I take a breath and shovel some salad into my mouth.

"The lawyer goes on to say that to her children she bequeaths nothing. Can you believe it? Nothing! Terry stands up, kicks his chair over and storms out of the room. We can all hear him arguing with Mel just outside. She's crying, asking him how they're going to be able to afford the round the world cruise and her boob job now. He's shouting at her to shut up. The lawyer coughs and continues. My cousins look all excited. If their parents aren't getting a penny, then surely the rest will be given to the grandchildren."

"Didn't you think that, considering you were one of the grandchildren?" he asks.

"Not really," I say. "I was just curious, mainly. Still wondering where all this money had come from. And to be honest, if she wasn't going to give it to her own children, what chance did the grandchildren have of inheriting it?"

"Do you want the last cheesy pepper?" he asks.

"You have it," I say.

"Sure?" he asks.

"Very," I say.

I chase a chunk of potato around my plate with my fork.

"So the remainder of her money wasn't left to the grandchildren," I say.

"I bet you were disappointed," he says.

"Not really," I say. "The remainder of the money wasn't left to the grandchildren. It was left to one grandchild."

He looks at me. His eyes widen. He points his fork at me. I nod. His jaw drops.

"That's not the best of it," I say.

"It's not?" he says.

"Nope," I say. "The family all throw me dirty looks and start calling me names and accusing me of knowing she had all that money and that's why I spent so much time with her. I couldn't believe how cruel they were being. I had no idea that she had the money. She always put a fiver in my Christmas and birthday cards, even up until she died. She did the same with all of the grandchildren. She never bought anything extravagant or went on amazing holidays or wore flashy jewellery. None of us knew. But it didn't stop them throwing bucketfuls of abuse at me across the table."

"That must have been awful," he says, reaching across the table and holding my hand.

I squeeze his fingers.

"It was horrible," I say. "The fact that my own family

could treat me so badly over something that hadn't been my idea in the first place. I spent time with her because I loved her. She was a wonderful lady and I know so many people who never got to spend time with their grandparents because they died young or they lived on the other side of the country. I wasn't going to take her for granted and assume that she was going to be around forever."

I put down my fork and pick up my glass. I sip my drink and think of my nan. I wipe my eye with the ball of my hand.

"You don't have to go on," William says.

"It's ok," I say. "The lawyer can't calm them down. They're shouting and swearing, and my parents are fighting a losing battle against them. The lawyer leans over to me and says that he'll be back in a minute. He leaves the room and comes back a few moments later with a huge man in a black suit. The security guard asks everyone to leave. We all stand up, but the lawyer looks at me and asks me to stay. This makes matters worse as the whole family know that I'm getting more. At this point I'm crying, and I'm accused of crying crocodile tears. The lawyer closes the door behind my family and tells me that Nan has also left me her bungalow. It's bought and paid for so I don't have to worry about rent or a mortgage. I couldn't believe it."

"I can't believe it," William says.

"And one final thing, the will insisted that if I have any children and one is a girl, I have to call it Beryl after her best friend. I loved my nan but there was no way I could inflict that name on an actual human. And I think it suits my dog down to the ground," I say.

"It does indeed," he says. "She is a little peril. I mean Beryl."

He winks at me.

"So yeah," I say. "I don't work because I don't really need to work."

"So I'm dating a millionaire," he says.

"Not quite," I say.

"I think I'll order some champagne," he says.

I slump back in my chair. My heart sinks.

"I'm only joking," he says. "You loved spending time with your Nan even before you knew she had money. And I've loved spending time with you before I found out you were loaded."

"Oi," I say.

"I am joking," he says. "I promise."

I smile at him. He seems genuine.

"Well, I didn't expect that story," he says.

"I don't think many people would," I say. "That's why I don't really tell people. You find that friends you never knew you had all crawl out of the woodwork, and once you tell them you're not giving them anything, they crawl away."

He looks down at my plate.

"Finished?" he asks.

"Yeah, I'm stuffed," I say. "Don't think I could eat another bite."

"Not even dessert?" he says.

"Well maybe dessert," I say.

15

The waiter takes away our plates and brings us the dessert menu. It's now that I'm glad I'm wearing a dress and not jeans. I don't really know much about first date etiquette but I don't think it's appropriate to open the top button of your trousers after eating. William looks at me and smiles. I pick up my napkin and wipe around my mouth. He carries on looking at me.

"What?" I say, laughing nervously.

"Nothing," he says.

I wipe my mouth again.

"You haven't got anything on your face," he says.

"Oh, right," I say, tracing my finger around my lips just to make sure.

I look at the menu. More choices to make.

"What do you fancy?" I ask him.

"Hmm, something sweet and intense," he says. "And rich."

I blush and look up. He's looking at me, grinning. I roll my eyes. He laughs. I hope he doesn't go on about my money too much. I almost regret telling him.

"How about you?" he asks.

"I don't know," I say. "Something a bit sweet but also quite simple."

He pulls an aghast face. I laugh.

"Or maybe something fruity," I say.

He laughs.

"Seriously though," I say. "I don't think I can eat too much. Well nothing too sickly."

"Go for the trio of minis," he says.

"Yeah I was thinking about that," I say.

"And if you can't eat it, I'll give it a go," he says.

"Oh aren't you kind," I say.

"Anything to help a lady in distress," he says.

The waiter comes back and looks at me.

"I'll have the trio of mini desserts," I say.

"Make that two," William says.

"Can I get you any more drinks?" the waiter asks.

"Can I just get some water, please," I say.

The waiter turns to look at William. He shakes his head.

"Thank you," I say.

The waiter walks away.

"So," I say. "You pretty much know my life history. What about you?"

"What about me?" William says.

My mind goes blank. The more I try to think of questions the more my brain becomes void of words.

"How's the job hunt going for you?" I ask.

It's not the best question but at least it came out with all the words in the right order.

"Don't ask," he sighs.

"That bad, eh?" I say.

"I guess you've never had the worry of being properly unemployed and having to deal with the job centre," he says.

"You'd be surprised," I say.

"Oh so you have?" he asks.

"Yep," I nod. "When I finished university I couldn't find a job so I had to go through all that rigmarole."

"So you know what I'm talking about?" he says.

I nod my head sympathetically.

"So what have they done this time?" I ask.

"Well, I've been unemployed for thirteen weeks now, and they assume that when you've been out of work that long, you've forgotten how to work and so you have to go on a stupid one hour course to help you get back to work. They don't seem to realise that there are no jobs out there to apply for. I apply for all I can, but if I can't find anything, how do they expect me to get back to work?"

"I know," I say. "Where were you working fourteen weeks ago?"

"I had a job that I absolutely loved. I worked for a company that made templates and designs for various advertising campaigns. I mainly worked on making promotional material for music concerts and festivals. I designed posters and fliers and graphics used in television adverts for these events," he says.

"That sounds amazing," I say. "So what happened?"

"Everything was going really well, until our boss sold the company and a new guy took over," he says. "He knew nothing about the business, what we did or anything. But he just walked in, in his flashy suit and started throwing orders around. It was like he thought he was some sort of mafia don or something. Everyone there knew their role and what needed to be done, but he wouldn't let us run smoothly. He wanted to know what everyone was doing all the time."

"Maybe he just wanted to learn what the company was all about," I say.

"Yeah, that's what it initially seemed like, but it was when he started telling us what to do when he had no idea. He hadn't learnt anything but he thought he knew how to do it all," he says.

The waiter comes over to our table carrying a tray with our desserts and my glass of water.

"Thank you," I say.

I look at my plate that houses three very small, but very perfectly formed bowls; one of cinnamon ice-cream, another of warm rice pudding, and the third with sliced apple and caramel filo tart. It looks too good to eat.

"Tuck in," William says.

I push my spoon into the tart. The pastry cracks and crumbles. I scoop it up and shovel it into my mouth, forgetting for a moment that I'm in a restaurant sitting by a window, and I'm on a first date.

"Oh that's so good," I say.

"And now you've got food on your face," William laughs.

I fumble to find my napkin and sweep it across my mouth. Filo flakes fall on to my lap.

"Well now that I've embarrassed myself, you were saying?" I say.

"Yes, right," he says. "Well, a few of us were working on a large-ish project and we had a looming deadline, and we were pretty much working ten hours a day to get it done. About a week or so before the deadline, the new boss decided he wanted to refurbish the entire office because it was untidy and didn't give a good first impression. We're all artists. We're not the tidiest of people. We had paper and ink and drawing materials and computers all over the place. It wasn't the nicest looking of offices but we all managed to get on well and do our own work in our own space. And it wasn't as though any of the clients actually came up and saw our office or anything. It was only ever us in there, and we all got on fine."

He shrugs.

"So, one day, without warning, he tells everyone to get up and get out so he can get these overpaid, pompous interior designers in. These people knew nothing about how our office worked or what kind of space we needed. The team I was working in was so close to getting our work finished. We only needed a few more days and then it would have been done. So I didn't move. I sat at my computer and carried on with what I had to do. The boss didn't like that. I told him that we had to get this work done and the refurb could be done over the weekend. But he wanted it done right there and then. I don't think I was being unreasonable, considering I was doing artwork for a very big client that could have thrown loads more work our way. It was a big deal, you know?" he says.

I nod along.

"Everyone else grovelled down to him, but I'm not that kind of person. I knew my job and what needed to be done. And new desks weren't at the top of the priority list. I took pride in my job, you know? I wanted things done properly. I was sitting at my desk after everyone had left, and suddenly all the lights went out and my computer screen went black. I thought it was a power cut, but he'd turned off the electric to get me out," he says.

"Really?" I say.

"Yep," he says.

"Did you lose your work?" I ask.

"Thankfully no," he says. "It all gets backed up on about twenty different hard drives as we go along."

"That's good," I say.

"Indeed," he says. "So we all had to take a couple of days off while the office was all sorted."

"Paid days off, I hope," I say.

"Yeah, they were paid, but I kept worrying about the project," he says. "I just wanted to get it done. And when we finally got back to work, the office looked like, well, awful. The desks were far too small and they'd been placed at odd angles so it was really difficult to move around without knocking things over or bumping into the back of people's chairs. There was no logical reason for this change up other than it looked nice."

"Seems stupid," I say.

"It was," he says. "But he didn't care. He was like a

child who stamped his feet until he got his own way, and it didn't matter how many people he upset in the process."

I put my spoon down on my plate and push it away from myself.

"I didn't think you could eat anything else," he says.

I look at my empty plate. I laugh.

"I didn't think I could either," I say.

I sip my water. I can feel myself getting bloated. I want to burp but I hold it in.

"Well, we all managed to get back on with our work, and my team finally finished our project with a day to spare, so we were pleased. We made contact with the client and sent it all off," he says.

"That's good," I say.

"You'd think," he says. "We'd worked our backsides off to get it all done, considering we had to take a few unplanned days off. I remember sitting on my chair at the end of the day. I shut my eyes and put my head down on what little free space I had on my desk. After a few minutes a stern voice behind me told me it wanted to have a word. I was shattered. I just wanted to go home and rest, but no matter how much you dislike your boss, you have to speak to them when they ask for a word. We went into this office and he basically told me that he didn't want me to come back into work tomorrow. To be honest, I thought he was joking. I'd had no warnings or anything, and well, that was because I'd never done anything wrong. I kind of let out a laugh but his face was serious. He told me to take everything that belonged to me out of my desk and go home. I almost zoned out. I walked like a zombie to my desk and packed all of my books and things into a cardboard box. My boss came up behind me and told me to leave my swipe card on the desk before I left. I pulled it out of my pocket and let it fall out of my fingers onto my computer keyboard. I carried my box down the stairs and it didn't even hit me when the door closed behind me and there was no way of me getting back in."

"He's not allowed to do that," I say. "He can't just sack you with no reason."

"I know he can't, but he did," he says.

His face drops.

"I loved that job, loved it," he says.

"How long had you been working there?" I ask.

"Years," he says. "Absolutely years. I even did my work experience there when I was at school."

"Wow," I say.

"Yeah," he says.

"I hope you're taking him to court," I say.

"I am indeed," he says.

"Good," I say.

The waiter comes over and takes our plates.

"Would you like any coffee?" he asks.

"No thanks," I say. "I'm fine.

"Just the bill, please," William says.

The waiter nods and walks away.

"Well it sounds like you've got enough experience to walk right into another company," I say.

"You'd think," he says. "But the oh so wise job centre decided that because my last job was in an office, I am suited for office and administration work."

I choke on my water.

"I know," he says. "So I have to apply for minimum wage office assistant jobs rather than getting my teeth into graphic design applications. And the stupid thing is that I'm over qualified. No-one wants someone with a degree in fine art with art history to do their photocopying for them."

The waiter brings over the bill. He puts the tray down and walks away. I pick up my bag and pull out my purse.

"You can put that away," William says.

"I can't let you pay," I say. "Especially as you're not working."

"You're not working either," he says.

"Yes, but ...," I say.

I pull out a couple of notes and put them on the tray. He picks them up and throws them at me.

"You're not paying," he says. "I don't want you to think I want you just for your money."

"I don't think that," I say, although I'm not sure if I believe myself.

"Look, just let me pay for this one," he says. "You can pay for everything else after today, ok?"

He laughs. I laugh.

"Put it away," he says, pushing the money towards me.

"Ok," I say reluctantly.

I stuff the notes back into my purse. William opens his wallet and puts a bank card onto the tray. The waiter walks over with the chip and pin machine. William punches in his number and takes the receipt.

"Thank you," I say.

"My pleasure," he says.

I stand up. I wobble a bit. I didn't think that pint made me drunk while I was sitting down. I steady myself on the back of my chair. I pick up my bag and cardigan. William stands up.

"I've just got to ...," I say, gesturing to the toilets.

"No worries," William says. "I'll meet you outside."

***

William is leaning up against a wall across the road from the restaurant. I walk over to him.

"Er ...," he says, pointing at me.

"What?" I say.

I look down at my front. A fat, red, tomato sauce caterpillar crawls down my dress. I wrap my cardigan around me.

"Why didn't you tell me?" I say.

"I only noticed now," he says. "I was too busy looking at

your face in there."

"How embarrassing," I say.

"Not as embarrassing as tripping up a kerb," he says.

"Did you do that while I was in the toilet?" I ask.

"Maybe, I can't remember," he says.

"It's not embarrassing if no-one's there to see it," I say. "Do it again."

He does a fake trip but manages to fall over his feet. He grabs on to my arm to steady himself. A couple pushing a pram walk past. They look at us like we're mad. William finds his balance but he still holds on to my arm.

"I had a really good time," he says.

"Me too," I say.

"And now that I know you're rich, well, that makes it a million times better," he says.

He winks at me. I jokingly hit him in the arm. He twists my arm around my back and holds me in a position where I can't move.

"Didn't I tell you that I've got a black belt in kushikatsu," he says.

"Don't talk about food," I say, holding my stomach.

"What do you mean?" he says.

"Kushikatsu," I say. "Deep fried Japanese kebab. Delicious, but I've eaten too much this afternoon to think about more food."

"Since when have you been an expert in Japanese cuisine?" he asks.

"Since I went there a couple of years ago and fell in love with their food," I say.

"You should have said," he says. "We could have gone for sushi."

"Next time," I say.

He loosens his hold and turns me back around. My legs get in a tangle. I stumble. He holds me up. I look at the ground.

"Are you ok?" he asks.

"Yeah, fine," I say. "I just don't think spinning me around like that is a good idea, especially after everything I've packed away today."

He takes a step back.

"Oi," I say. "I'm not going to be sick."

"Are you sure?" he asks.

"Yes," I say.

He walks towards me.

"So it's safe for me to do this?" he asks.

He leans in and kisses me. I'm not surprised. I was expecting it. I can taste our meal on his breath but I don't mind. Our teeth bump. We both pretend it hasn't happened. His lips are soft but the stubble that frames them is itchy. He kisses well but all I can think about is Gregory and how delicious he was. I pull away. I feel guilty.

"What's up?" he asks.

"Sorry," I say. "Just got a bit of food stuck in my back teeth."

I hate lying, but I can't seem to stop. It's starting to come all too naturally to me.

"Do you want me to get it for you?" he asks, slithering his tongue towards my mouth.

"Eurgh, get off," I say, pushing him away.

"I was only joking," he says.

"I know," I say, prodding around with my tongue to find the fake piece of food.

"Got it?" he asks.

"Yep," I lie.

"So where were we?" he asks.

"Just about here," I say, pulling his face towards mine.

We kiss. I try to force Gregory out of my head but I can't. William pulls my body towards his. He wraps his arms around me. I do the same. He feels very comfortable. Apart from the stubble, I don't want him to stop. Someone walks past.

"Get a room!" they shout.

William pulls back. I look over my shoulder.

"Ignore them," William says to me.

The moment has gone. I smile awkwardly.

"Did you say you studied fine art?" I say.

"Yeah," he says. "Do you want to see some of my work?"

"Er, ok," I say.

He takes my hand and we walk along the pavement. We don't really say much but the silence isn't awkward. It's almost as though we don't need to say anything. We walk through town and along some roads that I don't recognise. I start to feel nervous. My hand starts to sweat. He squeezes my hand.

"Don't worry, we're nearly there," he says.

I smile. We walk down an underpass. It smells of wee. I hold my breath. You hear stories of what happens to girls in underpasses. Someone's going to hear a story about me, I just know it.

"Here we are," he says.

We stop in front a section of graffiti on the wall.

"Ooh, you rebel, you," I say.

"Do you like it?" he asks.

I take a step back. I don't know much about art but it's really good. Kind of abstract with lines and shapes and colours.

"I really like it," I say.

"You're not just saying that?" he asks.

"No, I really really like it," I say. "I'd definitely have something like this hanging on my wall."

It's really cold in the underpass. I shiver. William stands behind me and wraps his arms around me. I sink back into him. His painting is amazing.

"I wish I had the skills to do something like this," I say.

"Aren't you arty?" he asks.

"I am a bit," I say. "My dad is a painter and he always wanted me to follow in his footsteps, but I don't have the patience to learn how to do it properly. I tend to make more of a mess than a masterpiece. Saying that, my dad always manages to get more paint on the back of head and in his ears than he does on the canvas, so I guess I have followed in his footsteps after all."

"What kind of thing do you make a mess of?" he asks.

"I glue wax crayons onto canvas and melt them with a hairdryer," I say.

He laughs. I don't.

"Really?" he asks.

"Yep," I say.

"I've never seen anything like that," he says.

"It's pretty cool," I say. "It's all about chance. You can't plan the outcome. You can have an idea of what it will look like, but it always surprises you."

"I might have to give that a go," he says.

"Hey, don't steal my idea," I say.

"Because you didn't steal the idea from anyone, did you?" he asks.

I shove him backwards. He bumps into the wall. I bump into him. He wraps his arms around me tighter. I lean back on him. He drops his face into my neck and kisses me. I keep my eyes fixed on his art. It is electrifying. I just want to touch. William turns me around and kisses me along my collar bone. My knees feel weak. I get angry at myself. I don't like feeling clichés. A child rides his bike past followed by his tutting mother. William looks up and throws her a smile then returns to my neck. He runs his hands softly down my back. I move my hands to his neck and bury my fingers in his hair.

My phone starts ringing loudly. I try to ignore it. It gets louder. I drop my head. William doesn't leave my neck. I fumble in my bag for my phone. The screen is alight with MUM & DAD.

"I have to take this," I say. "It's my mum. If I don't answer this, she'll think something terrible has happened to me."

"Ok," he says, not moving from my neck.

I try to push him away with my free hand but he just holds it down.

"Hello," I say, trying to sound normal.

"Is everything ok?" Mum asks.

"Yep," I say, trying to hold my breath so that she won't hear my heavy breathing.

I try to wriggle free. He moves up to my ear. I let out a groan. I bite my lip.

"Where are you?" Mum says.

"Just out," I say.

"I just wanted to make sure you were ok and not dead," Mum says.

"I'm ok and I'm not dead," I say.

"Do you know when you'll be round to pick up Beryl?" she asks.

"Soon," I say.

"Are you sure you're ok?" she asks.

"Yep," I say.

"You don't sound it," she says.

"I'm fine," I say.

"Has he upset you?" she asks.

"Nope," I say.

William catches my eye. He winks at me. I laugh. I mouth 'stop it' but he doesn't stop.

"Well, we'll see you soon," she says.

"Yep," I say.

"Bye," she says.

"Bye," I say.

I hang up.

"Dude, that was my mum," I say to William.

"I know," he says, kissing my cheek. "But you loved it."

I did but I didn't admit to it. I laugh and poke him in the side. He jumps and moves away from me.

"You've found my weakness," he says, feigning a cry.

I point my finger at him and wave it like a fencing sword.
"Where are your kushikatsu skills now?" I ask.
He laughs.
"Hah!" I shout.
"Keep back," he says.
I put my finger in my cardigan pocket.
"You're safe," I say. "For now."
"How's Mum?" he asks.
"Fine," I say. "She was just checking up on me."
"You sure she wasn't just being nosy?" he asks.
"Well, that too," I say.
"Mums can be a bit like that," he says.
"Well your mum hasn't called," I say.
"That would be quite difficult," he says. "She's dead."
I laugh. He doesn't. My heart sinks.
"I'm so sorry," I say, wishing the ground would open up.
"You should have seen your face," he says, laughing.
I hit him in the arm.
"That was cruel," I say.
"I'm sorry," he says, winking at me.
"No," I say, folding my arms and turning my back to him.
He wraps his arms around me and nuzzles the back of my head.
"I'm sorry," he says.
"What for?" I ask.
"For everything," he says.
"Good," I say.
I turn around. He grins at me. He has a very genuine smile and sweet eyes. I want to fold him up and put him in my pocket. I take his hand and walk out of the underpass. Natural daylight hits my eyes and I cover my brow with my hand.
"Where to now?" he asks.
"I'm sorry but I really should get going," I say sadly.
"Oh," he says. "That's ok."
"I don't want to," I say.

"So why are you?" he asks.

"My parents are looking after Beryl and I said I'd only be a few hours, and I don't want to take them for granted," I say.

"No," he says. "That's understandable. As long as you enjoyed yourself and you're not trying to escape."

"Of course not," I say. "I really enjoyed myself, and I loved seeing your art. You'll have to show me some more."

"Really?" he says.

"Yes," I say. "Why so surprised?"

"Most people think I'm a vandal with no concept of art," he says.

"Well, you are a bit of a vandal," I say. "But a really skilled one."

He blushes.

"You're blushing," I say.

He covers his face with his hands. I pull them away.

"It's cute," I say.

He holds on to my hands.

"You're cute," he says.

I try to cover my face with my hands. He holds them down.

"So if you want to see more of my art, does that also mean you want to see more of me?" he asks.

"Nope, I just want to see your art," I say.

"Tough, we come as a package," he says.

"Well, I suppose I can see you again," I say. "If I have to."

"You have to," he tells me.

I don't get a chance to disagree as he pulls my face to his. I can still taste our meal. It doesn't bother me. The kiss comes to a natural end.

"Let me know when you're free to see more of me," he says. "I mean my art."

"Will do," I say.

"Don't leave it too long," he says.

"I won't," I say.

"Will you be alright getting home?" he asks.

"Erm," I say, looking around.

"Don't you know where you are?" he asks.

"Not really," I say.

"Uh-oh, didn't your parents ever teach you about going into underpasses with men you've only just met?" he asks, smiling.

"They did warn me that there are some right weirdos out there," I say.

"Good job I'm not one of them then," he says, laughing.

"Good job indeed. Can you get me back to the high street, please? I can make my way home from there," I say.

"No problem, my lady," he says, taking my hand in his.

We walk back through the dark tunnel, along the roads I still don't recognise, and end up on the high street, near the park where we first met. He pulls me close and gives me a long, slow kiss. My skin is on fire.

"I have to go," I say.

"I know," he says. "Can you do me a favour?"

"I can try," I say.

"Can you thank Beryl for nearly killing me the other day," he says.

"Will do," I say.

"Take care," he says.

"You too," I say.

"You've got to go, you know," he says.

"I know," I sigh, walking away.

16

Beryl starts barking before I've even opened my parents' gate. I click the latch behind me and the bullet runs from a suddenly open front door. She jumps up, scratching a large hole in my tights. Mum stands on the doorstep.

"How did it go?" she asks.

"Fine," I say.

I walk inside.

"Only fine?" she asks.

"Yep," I say.

"You're not a teenager anymore," she says. "You can say more than one word to me you know."

"I know," I say.

I walk into the kitchen and get a glass of water.

"How has she been?" I ask.

"Perfect, as always," Mum says.

"Did you have a chance to look at those photos?" I ask.

"Yeah," she says. "Where did you find them?"

"Pay attention," I say. "I found them at the back of my bathroom cupboard when I was doing some cleaning."

She feigns stumbling backwards.

"You did that joke before," I say.

"I thought I'd give you a chance to tell me where you actually found them," she says. "But if you want to stick to the cleaning story, that's fine."

I glare at her. We sit at the kitchen table.

"A lot of people wouldn't believe you," she says, patting me on the arm. "But I do."

She grins. I roll my eyes.

"So do you know who they are?" I ask.

"I didn't recognise anyone," she says. "But your dad did."

"Oh?" I say.

"Did you find anything else with the photos?" she asks.

I remember the pile of papers in my bedside table drawer.

"Yes," I say. "There was an envelope and letters and I think there was a newspaper article or something."

"Didn't you read through those? They might have given you some idea of who the people are in the photos," she says.

I look at her.

"But your mind and body was probably so traumatised after all that cleaning that it just shut down," she says.

"You're not funny, you know," I say.

She laughs.

"Well I'm laughing," she says.

I ignore her.

"It was weird how all these things were stored, if I can even use that word," I say.

"What do you mean?" Mum asks.

"Well they were just put in a box and shoved right at the back of the bathroom cupboard," I say. "I'm just surprised that none of us found them after Nan died. I just hope the papers haven't been ruined."

Dad walks in. He has a swoosh of blue paint just above his eyebrow.

"Evening," he says.

"How goes it?" I ask.

"Tough," he says, walking over to the kettle.

He fills the jug with water and puts his mug on the side. He spoons some coffee and some white hot chocolate into the mug.

"Mocha?" he asks me.

"I don't like coffee," I say.

"I know," he laughs.

The kettle clicks and he pours the hot water into his mug. He stirs his drink and puts the spoon on the side. He walks out of the room. I follow him. He has blue paint on the back of his head. He sits down at the stool in front of his easel. He sips his drink. I stand next to him.

"What do you think?" he asks.

I look at the painting. It's pretty good.

"Rubbish," I say.

Beryl plods in and stretches herself out on the floor.

"I can never get a sensible answer out of you," he says.

"Well, ask me a sensible question then," I say.

"Karen," he shouts to Mum. "Your daughter is being stupid again."

"Nothing to do with me," Mum says, standing in the doorway.

"What's it supposed to be?" I ask Dad.

"I don't know yet," he says.

"Well how can I comment on it when you don't even know what it is?" I ask.

He sips his coffee again.

"So who are those people in my photos?" I ask.

He gets off his stool.

"Let me just wash my hands," he says, leaving the room.

I perch on the stool and look at his painting. I think about Williams graffiti. I smile. Dad walks back in and sits at his table. He moves his drawing books and pencils to the side. I sit down opposite him. Beryl jumps on my lap. Dad lays out the photos in front of us. He picks up the black and white picture of the woman sitting by the lake.

"This is my mum," he says.

He passes it to me.

"She was about eighteen or nineteen years old here," he says.

I look at her. I knew I thought she was familiar.

"This was taken in a park near where she used to live when she was younger," he says. "She loved it there. I remember she used to take me there when I was little. And your Uncle Alan. Terry, Janet and Tina hadn't been born then. We used to take bread down to feed the ducks in the lake. We'd sit on the wall and dangle our feet into the water and compete to see who could get the most ducks to come and eat our bread, but Alan would always scream whenever the ducks came too close and they'd get scared away."

He takes the photo out of my hand. He doesn't speak. I pick up the picture of the man in the suit.

"Is this Granddad?" I ask.

"No," he says. "I don't know who this is."

He puts the picture of his mother down and picks up the one of the man.

"It's not any of my uncles," he says.

He brings the photo closer to his eyes.

"I really don't recognise this man at all," he says.

I pick up the other three photographs. They're all of the same building, a theatre, but taken years apart. The oldest one is a black and white picture of the theatre front. The building looks so inviting. The sweeping nineteen-twenties writing on the sign over the front doors reads Talbot's Theatre. It looks like there's a canopy held up by two columns. The windows in the doors are covered with art deco stained glass patterns. There is such a sense of genuine nostalgia in this picture and I've never even been there.

"Where is this?" I ask Dad.

"I don't know," he says.

He taps the picture against his thumb.

"It must have been important if Nan has all these photos

of the same place," I say.

"Yeah," he says, vaguely.

"Did you ever go there when you were little?" I ask.

"Not that I can remember," he says.

The next photo of the theatre is in colour. It shows the theatre looking nearly as stunning as in the black and white picture, but you can see that it's aged. I don't know whether or not it has something to do with being in colour, but the building looks a bit grubby. Not too shabby, but just a little bit uncared for.

The last photo is in colour. It looks quite recent, well ish, maybe from the eighties. It's a bit faded but the theatre is very clear. The windows have been boarded up, and the once coherent sign now reads T lb t' Thea e. The white columns are now grey and dirty, and a tree appears to be growing out of the roof. Weeds queue up on the pavement outside. Gnarled tree branches claw at the chipboard covering the windows. It looks almost invisible, as though it had been disguised to fade into the background.

I lay the photos out, side by side. There are no cars. No people. It doesn't even look like there are any buildings on either side of the theatre. It almost makes me feel a bit uneasy, as though the place didn't really exist. Or like it's some sort of set for a television programme.

"Maybe those letters and things you've got at home could help shine a light on this," Mum says.

I hadn't noticed her come into the room. Dad holds the picture of his mum. He misses her. I miss her. I pick up the three photos of the theatre and the one of the suited man. I leave Nan's photo with Dad. He needs it more than I do.

"I keep meaning to read them but don't seem to have the time at the moment," I say. "I'll get around to it. Eventually."

Mum smiles at me.

"I'm going to go," I say.

"Don't you want to stay for dinner?" Mum asks.

"No thanks," I say. "I ate far too much this afternoon."
"Sure?" Mum says.
"Sure," I say. "But thank you. And thanks for looking after Beryl today."
"We love having her," Mum says.
Mum chases Beryl into the kitchen. Beryl hides under the table. Mum creeps up and scoops Beryl up in her arms. I put her collar around her neck. She runs to sit by the front door.
"I'll see you on Tuesday," I say.
"Tuesday?" Mum says.
"Oh yeah," I say. "Can you look after Beryl on Tuesday?"
"Got another date?" Mum asks.
"Maybe," I say.
"Who with this time?" she asks.
"Oh there's too many now," I say. "I can't remember."
I laugh. Mum just looks at me.
"You haven't been on this many dates in your whole life," Mum says.
"Thank you for that," I say.
"I'm just saying," Mum says.
"Well don't just say," I say irritably.
"Is someone tired?" Mum asks.
"I'm going home now," I say.
I walk towards the door and clip Beryl's lead to her collar.
"Love you," I say to Mum.
"Love you too," Mum says to me.
"Bye Dad," I shout. "Love you."
We walk outside into the cool early evening air. I pull my cardigan around myself and hurry home. I unclip Beryl's lead, push my front door open and let her run through. I dump my stuff on the floor and shut the door with my back. I lean up against the door and slide down to sit. I kick off my shoes. I feel sad. I feel angry. I feel lonely but

I really don't want company. My mind darts from William to Gregory. I can't focus on either one of them. Why do things have to be so complicated? I bang the back of my head into the door. Beryl barks.

"There's no-one there," I say to her. "It's just me."

Beryl walks in a circle at my feet and curls up in the corner. I unbuckle her collar and drop it to the floor. I want to cry but no tears come. So long with no-one and now I've got two. And not just any two but a lovely two. A kind two. A good looking two. A funny two. A sweet two. A really easy to get along with two. A I can't make a choice between the two two. Decisions. I've never been any good at decisions. Even when I don't like one of the options, I still can't decide. But I like both of the options. Why do I have to like both of them? And why do they have to like me? Life was so much easier when no-one liked me. When I was apparently invisible to all men. Stupid Louise. Stupid Louise and her stupid bright ideas. Stupid me for listening to stupid Louise. What's wrong with being single? Nothing. I can wear my pyjamas all day and eat lard if I want to. But no, I now have to start taking care of myself. I have to start brushing up on my social skills and learning to hold my tongue. I'm not socially acceptable. I'm awkward and uncoordinated and clumsy and pedantic and messy and I talk too much about things that no-one else cares about. I talk too much about things that I sometimes don't even care about. No-one ever likes me. Never. Now there are two. Two. At the same time.

"Who would you pick, Beryl?" I ask. "You've met them both. What do you think of them?"

Beryl yawns.

"I know you tried to kill William," I say. "But you could have done that affectionately, maybe. And don't just pick Gregory because he gave you treats. You have to make a rational, logical and well thought out decision. Go."

Beryl doesn't move. I scratch her behind the ears. She

shakes her head.

"Useless," I say.

I rest my head back. My hair tickles my neck. I think of William. I think of how attentive he was. I think of how he was looking at me even though I didn't know he was looking, and how he carried on looking after I caught him looking. I think about the underpass and his artwork and the way he held me and the way I felt comfortable in his arms. I think of Gregory and what we're going to do on Tuesday. What are we going to do on Tuesday? I can't think.

I stand up. I'm tired. I fish my phone out of my bag and switch it off. I don't want anything or anyone to interrupt me tonight. I just want to sleep. I wander into the kitchen, putting Beryl's collar and lead on the worktop, and unlock the back door. Beryl looks outside. She doesn't move.

"Bed time?" I ask.

She turns around and runs out of the room. I lock the back door and pull the curtain across. I walk out of the kitchen and knock Beryl's collar off the side. I go to step over it but manage to stand on the buckle with full force. A horrible sensation shimmies up my leg and bounces back into my foot. I cry out in pain but still no tears fall. It hurts. It hurts like standing on children's building blocks. As though the building blocks are made of scorpion tails and nettles and broken glass. I touch the sole of my foot. It feels like it's bleeding. My tights are still intact. I look at my fingers. No blood. It is excruciating. I want to collapse. I want to be dramatic and flail about, but it doesn't have the same effect when there's no-one here to see it. I hobble to my bedroom and sit on the edge of the bed. I feel like every ounce of life has been drained from me. Maybe there is a hole in the bottom of my foot, and my very life essence has dribbled out between the kitchen and here. I'm too tired to go and look for it.

I get undressed and throw my clothes into the corner. I pull the curtains closed. I remember that my dirty bed clothes are still in the washing machine, unwashed. I'll sort that out later. My body finds my pyjamas and manoeuvres itself into bed. My mind is travelling in a hundred directions at once.

    I close my eyes. I don't want to go to sleep because tomorrow will come quicker and I'll have to deal with things then. I don't want to stay awake because everything hurts. It all hurts. Far too much. My foot throbs. My head pounds. My heart beats. Slowly. I start to cry.

17

I don't sleep. I can't get comfortable. My pillow is too hot. I turn it over. It's too cold. My foot still hurts. My legs are fidgety. My feet start dancing. I get cramp. I don't want to get up. The pain won't go. It sinks its teeth into my calf. It bites and bites and gnaws and digs its jagged fists into the muscle. I get up and run as best as I can into the bathroom. I flatten my foot against the tiles. It's so cold. I stretch my leg, pulling my calf muscle. My toes contort. I don't need this. Why is this all going on? I'm too tired to deal with this. Too tired. I rest my hands on the edge of the sink and stretch my leg out behind me. My leg feels like it's going to snap in half. I stamp my foot.

I turn on the tap and cup my hand under the running water. I sip from my palm. The pain eases. I slump down on the toilet and drop my head. I laugh. I can't believe how stupid I am. I stood on a buckle. I got cramp. Two men are interested in me. That's no reason to cry. I remind myself of all the babies in Africa dying of AIDS. What are my problems?

I walk back into my bedroom. I flop onto the bed.

***

I wake up. I feel awake. I look at my clock. It's eight forty-nine. That can't be right. I sit up and look at it straight on. It's eight fifty. I stand up. My leg twinges. I kick it out in front of me. The twinge goes. Beryl is still asleep. I open the curtains and walk out into the kitchen. I throw a plastic liquid bubble into the washing machine and start it up. It whooshes into action. Beryl saunters into the kitchen. She stretches like a cat. I pull open the curtain to the back door and unlock it. Beryl jumps into the garden. I wash up her bowl and fill it with delicious meaty chunks of unknown beef parts in an appetising congealed gravy jelly mixture. Before I've put the bowl onto the floor, Beryl is back in, licking her lips. I leave the back door open. The fresh morning air is welcome today.

I walk into the hall and pick up my bag. I take out the photos and look through them again.

"Who are you?" I say to the suited man.

He doesn't say anything. He just smiles at me, casually, with one hand in his pocket.

"You've got a secret. I know it," I say to him. "What are you hiding?"

I carry him and the theatre into my study and drop them next to my keyboard. I turn on my computer and I turn on my phone. I expect an angry winking Cyclops eye, and there it is. The screen lights up. I have one new message from William. None from Louise. I'm slightly concerned. I open the message. The time stamp tells me he sent it at three twenty. Hey, I hope I don't wake you with this but I had to do it as soon as I got home and send it to you as soon as I was done. It's not even dry yet. Thank you for today, or is it yesterday now? Please let me know what you think. Wx

It's a picture message. I click to open the picture. My screen fills with blocks of colour. I can't tell what it is. I rotate my phone. It's no clearer upside down. My computer is on. I untangle the serpent menagerie of cables that have slithered under my desk, and pull out my phone connector cable. I find a free USB port and plug it in. It doesn't fit. I turn it around and plug it in. It still doesn't fit. I turn it around and plug it in. It goes in smoothly. I attach my phone to the other end and click to transfer files. I find the picture William sent me and save it on my computer. I clickety-click it open. My face fills up the screen.

I slide my chair back. I can't believe what I'm seeing. It's a graffiti spray painted picture of my face. It's colourful and evocative and tasteful and beautiful and dark. It's me in so many ways. I don't know how he managed to capture everything about me after only having spent a few hours with me. I roll forward and touch the screen. He's got my nose right. My eyes. The scar on my lip. Most people don't even notice that. I'm speechless. No-one has ever done anything like that for me.

I unplug my phone from my computer and reply to his message. Thank you. I don't know what to say other than thank you. It's lovely. I can't believe you did that. Thank you again!

I step up and walk backwards. It's so abstract but so realistic at the same time. I pick up my phone again. I text Louise. Are you dead? Haven't heard from you in a day. Went out with William yesterday and it went really well, thanks for asking. Look what he sent me at half three this morning. I attach the picture to the message and send it.

I'm hungry. I go into the kitchen and pour a bowl of cereal. A few flakes fall on the floor. I crunch them underfoot. Beryl eats them. I slosh over some milk and take the bowl back to my study, with a spoon and a packet of crisps. I know I shouldn't eat where I'm working but I'm too busy to eat anywhere else. The Cyclops is winking. I have a new message from Louise. What on Earth is that? I'm not dead. I've been at work, and I've actually had to do work. Can you believe it? My boss is on my back.

Apparently I've been slacking off. Had meetings and warnings and tellings off. Got to go. She's got eyes everywhere.

I text back straight away. It's supposed to be me. He does graffiti art. He painted a picture of me. Isn't it romantic?! I don't expect a reply but one comes through almost immediately. It's from William. I'm glad you like it. I was worried that I'd overstepped the mark but once I'd sent you the message there was no going back. It's not finished but you can have it once it's done. Wx

I keep looking at the image on my screen. Why are they making it so difficult for me? Why can't one of them be an ignorant pig? Maybe inappropriately politically incorrect? A kitten killer? Something, anything to turn me off them. But no. It's all picnics in the park and bespoke artwork.

I put my bowl down on my desk and pick up the photos. I lay them across my keyboard. I look at the black and white theatre. It's so inviting. I wonder where it is. I wonder what happened to it. I do an internet search for Talbot's Theatre. Not much comes up. I can't refine my search as I don't know where it is. I do an image search but that's equally as futile. I turn the photos over. No-one has been kind enough to write anything on the back. I hold the boarded up picture.

"Where are you?" I say. "Or do you even exist anymore? Maybe you've been knocked down. Maybe you're a housing estate now."

I remember the letters in my bedside table drawer. I walk into my bedroom and climb over my bed. I pull open the drawer and find the papers. They're crisp and almost cardboardy in places.

"That bathroom cupboard did you no good," I say.

I put on a pair of socks and wrap a dressing gown around me. It's not as warm as the sun leads me to think. I take the papers into my study and lay them out on my desk. I take my empty breakfast bowl back into the kitchen. I don't want to spill milk on everything. I close the back door.

I sit back at my desk and pick up the papers. I notice the pet insurance renewal letter poking out from under my peanut butter pen jar. I've only got a couple of days to get it sorted. Why do I always leave things to the last minute? Why do last minutes arrive so quickly? I put down the bathroom cupboard letters.

"I've just got to do something. Don't go anywhere," I tell them.

I scan the letter. Blah blah blah Thank you for insuring Beryl with us blah blah blah vet fees increasing ... 24-hour vet phone helpline ... just call us on the number at the top of this letter to renew your insurance. It's more expensive than I'd thought it would be, but I can't be bothered to hunt around for anything cheaper. I pick up my phone and punch in the numbers. I press two for insurance renewals. I am in a queue. My waiting time is seven minutes. I sway to the panpipe music. I am in a queue. One of their operators will be with me shortly. My waiting time is seven minutes. I drum my fingers on the desk. I imagine I'm in a music video for the song that's seeping into my ears. I'm using it as a backing track for a hip-hop remix. I bounce. The woman interrupts to tell me that I'm in a queue. I know I'm in a queue. I spin myself around in my chair. One of their operators will be with me shor... A human voice speaks to me. I slip off my chair.

"Oh, hi, hello, yes," I say. "I'd like to renew my pet insurance."

***

I wiggle my mouse. The screensaver disappears. I want to find out about Talbot's Theatre. How can it not exist on the internet? Everything exists on the internet. Maybe someone has added something about it over night. I remember the washing machine. I walk into the kitchen. A red Cyclops eye stares at me from the corner of the room. It's not angry or demanding like my phone. It doesn't wink. It just gazes forward, perhaps thinking about something else. I click open the door. I smell lavender. I look around for my basket. I don't think I have one. I open the back door. I wander into the hall for a pair of shoes. I slip my feet into the flats I wore yesterday. I pull a bin bag out of the drawer and parachute it open. I yank the duvet cover, pillow cases, sheet, and clothes out of the washing machine and stuff them into the bin bag. I carry it outside and drop it on the ground. There are already some pegs hanging on the washing line. I reach into the bag and pull out a pillow case. I swoosh it out in front of me to straighten it up, and clip it to the line. I do the same with the other three cases. A couple of birds fly into the tree. They perch on a branch and look at me.

"Don't you even think about it," I say to them. "I've got my eye on you."

They stare at me. I'm not going to win in a staring competition against birds. Do birds even blink? I hang up my clothes and straighten them as much as I can. That'll save having to iron them later. I try to straighten my sheet and duvet cover. I get myself in a tangle. I can't find an edge. I throw the heavy material over the line and shove a couple of pegs on to hold them in place. I kick up the bin bag and catch it. I look at the tree. The birds have gone.

"You've got a whole garden to do your business in," I shout. "Don't you dare think about doing it over here."

I wave my arms near the washing. One day I know I'll be that crazy lady that kids are scared of. They'll dare each other to come and ring my doorbell or jump over my garden gate and spy through my windows. I'll just set up booby traps to make the experience a whole lot more terrifying for them. I'll have to put that on my 'to do' list.

I walk back into the kitchen. I leave Beryl outside. She's happy playing with a stone. She can also keep an eye on those birds. I don't think I'll get dressed today. I sit down at my desk. The angry Cyclops winks. I have one new message from Gregory. Hey, I hope you're ok and that you've had a good weekend. I hope I didn't scare you off talking about going out on Tuesday. If you're busy, no worries, we can sort something else out. Gx

I feel guilty. I don't want him to think I'm ignoring him. I feel awful. I reply straight away. I am so sorry, I haven't been ignoring you. Tuesday is fine for me. I've got a few ideas. Do you want to do something during the day?

I do an internet search for interesting date ideas. I browse the pages of bowling, boring, ice-skating, dangerous, tandem bicycle ride, perilous, aquarium, terrifying. I look at a picture of a couple standing in a narrow tube surrounded almost entirely by water. A shark swims over their head. What if it bangs its nose into the tube and a crack forms and water drips through and the crack gets bigger and the tube floods and they drown to death? Or even worse, they get eaten to death? Not my idea of a fun date, thank you very much.

I go to facebase and type Alexa needs some ideas for an interesting/unusual date. I delete it. I don't really want people asking me questions about it all. It's bad enough Louise knowing the ins and outs of my personal life, let alone the rest of the world. I glance down at the other status updates. Haylee what hav I dun now stop hiding n say it to my face. Rachel can't sit down. Do I really want help from these people?

I go back to the internet search and change interesting to random in the hope that something more to my liking will come up. Indeed lots of random ideas pop up; dressing up as ninjas and doing parkour through town, pretending to be foreign tourists, finger painting, doing everything backwards, crazy golf, hide and seek in a supermarket, treasure hunt, going for a walk and collecting rubbish and seeing who has the most interesting piece of rubbish. I'm sure some people find those things fun, but I'm not sure

Gregory would. Well, maybe the crazy golf. Everyone likes that.

I've not played crazy golf in years. Thinking about it, I've not been to the seaside in years. Well not properly. I've walked Beryl along the beach, but I haven't eaten ice-cream and candy floss and lost hundreds of two pees in the amusement arcades or had a horse and carriage ride along the sea front and danced badly on those stupid dance machines and eaten fish and chips under the pier and built sandcastles in, well, forever. That's what we'll do.

My phone beeps. I have one new message from Gregory. *Glad you're ok and that I haven't scared you off. During the day is good for me, but not too early though. I had to meet a girl the other day and it was far too early in the morning. So what have you got planned? No don't tell me. I like surprises. Gx*

I text back straight away. I don't want him to think I'm ignoring him anymore. What kind of person would want to meet up at stupid o'clock in the morning? They must be mentally unhinged. *How about I pick you up in the car park behind the cinema at about ten-ish? Or is that still too early?*

I put my phone down on the desk and pick up the envelope. Nothing is written on the front. I carefully open it and pull out the papers from inside. They're neatly folded in three. I unfold them and hold them open. There are only two pages in total. It feels thicker. The handwriting is beautiful, all swooshy and scripty. The author has used blue ink but it has faded and smudged in some places. I look at the Post-it notes scattered around my desk. The writing on them looks like a monkey has stuck a pen up its nose and then sneezed. The stunningly written letter puts me to shame. I turn my back to my desk and read the letter. It's dated Monday 9th June 1958. There's no return address, which is strange. *Dear Miss Bell.* Who are you, Miss Bell?

I pick up my phone and dial my parents' number. I scan my eyes over the letter but don't actually take any in. Mum answers.

"Hello," she says.

"Dad there?" I ask.

"Hello to you too," she says.

"You already said that," I say.

I hear her pass the phone to Dad.

"It's your daughter," she says to him.

"Hello," he says.

"Hi, what was Nan's maiden name?" I ask.

"Bell," he says.

"Ok, thanks, bye," I say.

"Bye," he says.

I hang up the phone. So Miss Bell is my nan. But surely in nineteen fifty-eight she would have been Mrs Wright. I pick up my phone again and hit redial. Mum answers the phone again.

"Hello," she says.

"Dad there?" I ask.

She sighs.

"Hello," Dad says.

"When did Nan and Granddad get married?" I ask.

"Er," he says.

I know he's sitting there counting years on his fingers.

"They met just after the war had ended and started courting," he says. "And I was born in nineteen fifty, so they would have been married a year or so before that, so nineteen forty-eight, forty-nine."

"Ok, thanks, bye," I say.

"Bye," he laughs.

I hang up the phone. So it couldn't be Nan. But it couldn't be Janet. She wasn't born then, I don't think. I pick up the phone again and hit the redial button again.

"Hello," Dad says.

"Dad there?" I ask.

"This is your father," he says.

"I knew that," I say. "I was just testing."

He laughs.

"When was Aunty Janet born?" I ask.

"Nineteen fifty-nine," he says.

"Ok, thanks," I say.

"Anything else?" he asks. "I'm about to have a nap."

"Did Nan have any sisters?" I ask.

"No, just two brothers. My Uncle Edward who died in the war and Uncle George," he says.

"That's what I thought," I say.

"Why do you want to know?" he asks.

"I'm just doing some research," I say.

"What for?" he asks.

"Just trying to piece together the letters and pictures and things I found in my bathroom cupboard," I say.

"What? When you were cleaning?" he laughs.

"Yes," I say.

He carries on laughing.

"Laugh more old man," I say. "I might just have a few more questions when you're napping."

He stops laughing.

"Well, yes," he says. "I'll let you get on."

"Yes, thanks, you've been helpful," I say.

"If you need anything else, call me next Tuesday," he says.

"Will do," I say. "Ok, thanks, bye."

"Bye," he says.

I hang up the phone. So Janet wasn't born when this letter was written, and Nan had no sisters. I scribble people and dates down onto a Post-it note. I get up and sit in the armchair by the window. I read the letter. Dear Miss Bell, I am afraid that I have to be the one who writes this letter to you but your behaviour is despicable. I am loathe to speak to you in person for fear of tongues wagging. A woman such as yourself should concern herself with her own husband rather than the husbands of her acquaintances. I beg of you, stop what you are doing. Stop before your children are harmed. If you are intent on working, I have a friend who is in need of a seamstress. I can arrange a meeting if you are interested. Your current choice of employment is unholy and immoral. I would like to draw to your attention to your Holy Bible, Matthew chapter 5, verse 28 when Jesus Christ spoke to his disciples from atop a mountain. "But I say unto you, That whosoever looketh on a woman to lust after her hath committed adultery with her already in his heart." I beg, please do not encourage the Lord's men to commit adultery. Remember, in 1 Corinthians chapter 6, verses 9 and 10, "neither fornicators, nor idolaters, nor adulterers, nor effeminate, nor abusers of themselves with mankind, nor thieves, nor covetous, nor drunkards, nor revilers, nor extortioners shall inherit the kingdom of God."

I come to the end of the first page. It appears that my grandmother was a prostitute. If I was reading about any other person, I would laugh. But it's my own grandmother. My dad's mum. I'm not sure if I want to read the rest of this letter. I do though.

I cannot sit by and let you lead these men into damnation. I pray for you daily that the Lord will cleanse you of your sinful nature and restore you to the wholesome young woman that I know you are. I pray also for Frank and your boys that they do not get caught up in your world of deceit. Think about what you are doing. Think about the effect your actions are having on others. God bless. Reverend John McAdams.

I reread the letter. This can't be about Nan. But the reverend mentions Granddad Frank. The boys must be Dad and Uncle Alan, if Janet wasn't born yet. So does that mean that my dad and my uncles and aunts might be half-siblings? No, it can't be. I fold the letter up and put it back in the envelope. I look at the clock. It's nearly ten past eleven. I look at the time in the corner of my computer screen. It's too early to phone Dad again; I might just speak to Mum, only until I've got all the facts. Although I'm not sure I want all the facts. I pick up all the photos and papers and put them in a plastic wallet. I fold the top over and put them in my desk drawer. I don't want to read anymore today.

I hear a tapping on the window. It's raining. I run to the kitchen and pick up the bin bag. It's not raining heavily but I don't want to leave the washing out there just in case. I pull the clothes off the line. Pegs fly in all directions. I'll pick those up later. Everything feels dry ish, apart from the duvet cover and undersheet. I carry everything inside and shut the door behind me. Beryl shakes herself.

I drop the bin bag on the floor and pull the airing horses out from the side of a cupboard. I carry everything into the living room. I wrestle with the contraptions, trying to hook plastic hooks over plastic lips without anything pinging out of place and poking me in the eye. Eventually, one stands as it's supposed to. I hang some of the clothes on the rails in the middle and cover the whole thing with the duvet cover. The other horse rebels against my authority. One leg slides outwards like a ballerina flexing before a performance. The protruding shelf unclips half of itself from its rail and threatens to go all the way.

"Don't you even think about it," I say.

I bend down to straighten up the leg and the shelf lets itself fly free. The main body of the horse collapses and takes me with it. I am entrapped by an inanimate object with a mind of its own. I escape and stand up. One of the hooks is caught in my hair. I untangle myself and roughly pull the horse into position.

"Stay," I say, pointing menacingly at it.

I hear it slip but only slightly. I hang up the pillow cases and some clothes on the middle rails and hang the undersheet over the top. I hold my breath as the horse drops slightly under the weight. I stand with my arms open to catch it if it falls, even though my reactions have never been very quick. It stays. I walk out of the room.

I'm hungry. I open the fridge. I know there's nothing particularly edible in there. I really need to do some shopping but not today. I'm not going to get dressed today. I open the freezer. My body needs something healthy. My hand goes for a box of microwave burgers. I have to pull myself back. I take out the box of microwave burgers and find a box of fishcakes. I put them on the side and put the box of microwave burgers back. I open the bottom drawer and pull out a bag of frozen peas. I cover a baking tray with foil and put a fishcake in the middle. It looks small and lonely by itself. I tip the box and another cake falls out. I turn the dial to two hundred and put the fishcakes in the oven. I pour the peas into a saucepan, cover them with water and put the pan on the hob. I turn the dial to four. I set the timer for twenty minutes.

I hear the airing horse plummet to the ground. It has defeated me. I don't want to fight. I leave it where it is. I'll sort it out later. I go back into my study and sit at my computer and search for Talbot's Theatre again. Various theatres situated in large towns and cities pop up, but nothing about Talbot. I thought the internet was supposed to know everything.

I notice my phone is winking at me again. I have one new message from Gregory. Ten-ish is fine. Car park behind cinema is fine, but you do know that cinema dates are a bit cliché so I hope we're not staying there. Don't give too much away but do I need to bring anything? Gx

I start to type a reply. Just bring your gorgeous self. I delete that. I can't write that. Or can I? I mean we've kissed so he knows I like him. I retype it. I giggle. I feel like a schoolgirl passing notes in class. Just bring your gorgeous self and maybe a jacket. Well definitely a jacket. Knowing my luck it'll rain. And some sunglasses just in case it goes the other way.

I wander into the kitchen and wrestle the vacuum cleaner from behind the table. It doesn't defeat me. I pull out the cable and plug it into a socket in the hall. I switch it on. It growls. Beryl runs into my bedroom. I push the vacuum cleaner along the hall, sucking up crumbs that Beryl has somehow managed to miss. I try to vacuum up the letters on the mat by the front door but they refuse to disappear up the tube. I kick them into the corner. I'll look at them later.

The timer beeps. I switch off the vacuum cleaner and leave it in the hall. I drain my peas through a sieve and pour them into a bowl. I open the oven, put on my Father Christmas oven glove and take out the baking tray. I turn both dials to zero. I tip the fishcakes on to the peas, put the baking tray back in the oven and shut the oven door. I drop the oven glove onto the side and take a fork out of the cutlery drawer. I walk into the living room, sit down and turn on the television.

A fat child waddles across the screen. A fat woman sits uncomfortably on a chair, with her fat rolls hanging over the sides. The chat show host sits in a chair next to her. The woman is crying.

"How old is your daughter?" the host asks.

"She's four," the mother says.

"And how much does she weigh?" the host asks.

"Five and a half stone," the mother sobs.

The audience gasps.

"That's more than twice the weight of an average four year old," the host says. "Most ten year olds aren't even that heavy."

"I know," the mother sobs.

I dig my fork into my food and eat.

"I don't know what to do," the woman says.

The host stands up and walks into the audience. He sticks his microphone in the face of a woman who has her hand up.

"What do you feed her?" the audience woman asks.

"She'll only eat crisps and chocolate," the mother says.

The audience woman grabs the microphone out of the

host's hand.

"What?" the audience woman says. "Have you heard of fruit and vegetables?"

"She drinks strawberry milkshakes," the mother says.

"This is worse than child abuse," the audience woman says. "How can you sit there and say that you only feed her junk? Haven't you heard of diabetes?"

The audience claps. The host snatches back the microphone.

"You're on the show today to get some help, aren't you?" he says.

"Yes," the mother says.

The audience boos. The mother sobs into her tissue. Another audience member grabs the microphone from the host.

"What is wrong with you?" the audience woman asks. "How can you need help? Is there something wrong with you? When you go shopping you pick up some carrots and some apples rather than crisps and chocolate."

The audience claps. The mother looks angry. She tries to stand up but she's wedged tightly in the chair.

"You don't know anything," the mother shouts. "You don't know anything about me."

"We know you're an unfit mother," someone from the audience shouts.

The audience claps. The mother cries. The child sits on the floor.

"It's not my fault," the mother shouts.

I can't watch any more. I switch the television off and finish eating my food. I take my bowl into the kitchen and put it into the sink. I walk back into the hall and switch the vacuum cleaner on again. I push it towards the living room. The clothes horses are still on the floor. I can't be bothered to try and manoeuvre the vacuum cleaner around them. I drag the contraption to my study and clean the carpet in there. I pull the end off the hose and run it along the bookshelves. Cobwebs glisten in the sunlight. I can't remember the last time I did the vacuuming. I run the hose along the top shelf. A book falls down. I switch off the vacuum cleaner and pick up the book. I've not read it in years. The cover is covered in dust. I wipe it down my leg. It's one of my childhood favourites. I sit in the armchair and open the book. On the inside of the front cover is a child's scrawl. Alexana Wright Age 7. I turn the page and I read.

Beryl jumps on my lap. I put the book down. I've got about ten more pages to read. I'll finish that later. I stand up and walk into the hall. Beryl follows me. I unplug the vacuum cleaner lead and walk back into my study. I push the vacuum cleaner into the corner and throw the cable over it. I turn off my computer and walk into the kitchen. I'm bored. I don't know what to do. I open the back door and Beryl runs out. I put some bread in the toaster and push it down. The toast pops out. I take the peanut butter jar out of the cupboard and a knife from the cutlery drawer, and smother the toast. I leave the jar and knife on the side. I eat my toast and stand at the back door, watching Beryl play. Beryl plods in. I shut and lock the back door, and pull the curtain across.

I don't know what to do. I walk into my study and pick up my book. I take it into my bedroom and put it on the floor next to my bed. I close the curtains, put on my bedside lamp and get undressed. I get into bed. Beryl joins me. I set my radio alarm clock for eight o'clock. I lie on my side, pick up my book and read.

I finish the book and put it back on the floor. I switch off the lamp and close my eyes. I can't sleep. I'm too nervous. I'm too excited. Tomorrow is so close and so far away.

***

The weatherman tells me it's going to be a sunny day with a slight chance of rain. I groan. My stomach jumps. I get out of bed, open the curtains and walk into the kitchen. I unlock the back door and Beryl runs out. I open the fridge. I'm too excited to eat. I have to eat something. I can't. I'm too nervous to eat. Beryl comes in and I lock the back door.

I walk into the bathroom, get undressed and have a quick shower. I wrap a towel around myself and stand in front of my wardrobe. Slight chance of rain. Jeans it is then. I get dressed, put Beryl's collar around her neck, clip her lead to her collar, pick up my bag and walk outside.

18

I unlock my car. Beryl climbs up over the driver's seat and sits on the passenger's seat. I sit down and throw my bag on to the back seat. Beryl stands on her hind legs and leans her front paws against the window. I shut my door and turn the key in the ignition. The car coughs. I can't remember the last time I drove anywhere. Mum's voice claws its way into my head. *Make sure you start it up every day even if you're not going anywhere.* I don't ever tell her when she's right and this is one of those times. I turn the key again. The car splutters like a forty-a-day smoker. One more turn and it purrs. I drive to my parents' house. I pull into the driveway. Mum is sitting in the front garden reading a book. She gets up and walks over to me. I'm glad because I don't really feel like getting out of the car. Beryl claws at the window in excitement. She climbs on my lap and whimpers. Sometimes I think she loves them more than she loves me. But then I guess grandchildren love their grandparents mainly because they aren't their parents. You can get away with so much more with your grandparents.

Mum opens the passenger door. Beryl shoots out.

"Where are you off to?" Mum asks.

"The seaside," I say.
She looks up at the sky.
"It's not going to rain," I say.
"No, of course not," she says. "Have fun."
"I will," I say. "See you at some point later."
Mum pushes the door closed.
"Thanks for taking Beryl today," I say.
"We love having her," Mum says.
"See you later," I say.
"Bye," Mum says.

I reverse out, narrowly missing a lamppost. My heart drops into my shoes and my stomach jumps into my throat. I stop the car in the middle of the road and look around. I take a deep breath, wipe my sweaty palms down my jeans and drive into town. Gregory is standing on the pavement just outside the car park. I pull up next to him and roll down my window.

"How much for a couple of hours?" I ask.
He walks away from me.
"Oi," I shout. "Don't you walk away from me."
He turns around. I poke my head out of the window. He laughs.
"I didn't recognise your voice there," he says.
"Get in," I say.
He does. I lean over my seat and pull my bag on to my lap. I root around.
"What are you looking for?" he asks.
"Gag, handcuffs and blindfold," I say.
He leans back.
"Well you said you didn't want to know where we were going," I say.
"Well that explains the blindfold," he says. "But what about the gag and handcuffs?"
"Once we start driving, I'm going to start singing," I say. "I don't want you complaining about my choice of music, or trying to escape."

He laughs. He leans forward, puts his hand behind my head and pulls me towards him. He kisses me. It's as lovely as I remember. I panic. Can he taste William? No, why would he? I've brushed my teeth since then. And how would he know what William tastes like? He's not going to be kissing his brother. Stop thinking and enjoy the kiss. He pulls back.

"Do I really need a blindfold?" he asks.

"Hmm," I say.

"What if I promise to look at you the whole journey and shut my eyes whenever we pass a place sign?" he asks.

William looked at me. He looked at me so much that he was able to paint a picture of me from memory.

"Ok, I think I can let you get away with that," I say.

"Good," he says.

He kisses me again. He doesn't have stubble. I find what I'm looking for in my bag. I pull out a cassette tape and put it in the tape player.

"You play tapes?" he asks, surprised.

"Yep, love them," I say.

"Me too!" he says.

"There's just something about a mixtape, I don't know, something, hmm …," I say.

"I know exactly what you mean," he says.

"A mix CD doesn't have the same feel to it," I say.

"Totally," he says.

I smile. He laughs.

"I can't believe you like tapes," he says.

"I know," I say. "Kids these days will never know the pleasure of pulling a cassette out of the player and leaving a tangle of tape behind …," I say.

"And having to roll it back in with a pen," he laughs.

He's finishing my sentences.

"Exactly," I say. "That's all part of the fun. And when the tape is really old and stretched, and a once straight forward song has turned into a wiki-wiki-wah remix."

"You're so old school," he says. "I love it."

I'm glad he said 'it' and not 'you'.

"What's on here then?" he asks, pointing to the tape player.

"A little bit of everything I like," I say. "So you'll probably hate it."

"If it's anything like you, I'm sure I'll really like it," he says.

I laugh and look down at my lap.

"Are you ready?" I ask.

"Indeedy," he says.

I start the car and pull away. The tape crackles and the music blares out. Gregory turns the volume dial down to eleven. I click it down to ten.

"Still too loud?" he asks.

"No, I er," I say. "I have a bit of an issue with the volume dial."

"How so?" he asks.

"Don't laugh," I say.

"Well I'm going to now," he says.

I don't say anything.

"I'm only joking," he says, touching my leg.

"I don't like the volume being on any odd numbers unless they're a multiple of five," I say.

He laughs.

"I told you not to laugh," I say, pouting.

"Aww, I'm sorry," he says, rubbing my leg.

I poke my tongue out at him.

"Is there any reason for that?" he asks.

"I'm just a bit odd," I say.

"No arguing there," he says.

I move his hand off my leg.

"But I like odd," he says.

I move his hand back on to my leg. He smiles. I start singing quietly.

"Don't hold back on my account," he says.

"If you insist," I say.

I sing loudly. He looks at me and prods my arm.

"What are you doing?" I say.

"I was just wondering if there is a volume dial on you," he says.

"Ha, no such luck," I say, and carry on singing.

The road is pretty clear, thankfully. I don't really fancy exposing my road-rage self just yet. I pull into a backstreet and park up.

"Where are we?" he asks.

I look up at a dilapidated hotel, The Sunrise Lodge, with peeling, yellow paint on all the window frames and hanging baskets of dying flowers on either side of the front door. There are no vacancies.

"I was going to take you in there and have my wicked way with you," I say. "That's what the handcuffs were really for."

He looks at the hotel.

"Classy," he says.

I reach over my seat and get my handbag. I open the door and get out of the car. He stays seated. I lean down and look at him.

"I'm a bit scared," he says.

"Don't you trust me?" I ask.

I laugh. He whimpers.

"Come on," I say. "Get out."

"Demanding, eh?" he says.

"Well, you're more than welcome to stay in the car all day," I say. "But I'm off to have some fun."

I close the door and slowly walk away. I count to three under my breath. Just as I get to three I feel a hand wrap itself around my hand.

"I knew you couldn't resist me," I say.

"I just saw the net curtains twitching up there," he says, pointing at the hotel. "Didn't really feel safe."

I turn around and press the button on my car keyring.

The car's lights flash.

"Aww," I say. "I'll keep you safe."

I pull our hands up to my lips and kiss his finger.

"Is your car going to be alright there?" he asks.

"Even if my car gets smashed or stolen, the cost to repair it or get a new one will be less than the cost of the pay and display car parks around here," I say.

We walk past more decaying buildings that looked like they could have been beautiful once. Gregory stops walking.

"Is everything ok?" I say.

"I just wanted to do this," he says.

He kisses me.

"What was that for?" I ask.

"Does there need to be a reason?" he says.

"I guess not," I say.

We carry on walking. We stop at the kerb that meets the main road.

"Are we where I think we are?" he asks.

"And where might that be?" I ask.

"Are we at the seaside?" he asks.

"Yep," I say.

He grins.

"I absolutely love the seaside," he says.

I smile at him. He looks genuinely excited.

"I went out with a girl once," he says. "I mean, I'm sorry, I know it's not good dating etiquette to talk about past relationships."

"It's ok," I say. "What were you going to say?"

"Well, we weren't together that long, but whenever we went out we had to act her age. We had to go to wine bars and museums and art galleries and drink espressos and dress smartly and walk with poise. I wasn't allowed to just be silly."

"I like museums and art galleries," I say.

"So do I," he says. "But I wasn't allowed to touch anything."

"I don't think anyone's allowed to touch anything," I say.

"In some places we went, there were tactile exhibits where you could, I don't know, get a piece of paper and lay it on a replica urn and rub a wax crayon over it to make a pattern, or put on a chainmail smock and a Roman helmet and stand next to a scary mannequin from the nineteen eighties dressed as a centurion and have your picture taken. I was never allowed to do that. *Those things are for children, Gregors, and we're not children, are we?* I hate it when people shorten my name, and she knew that."

"Ha," I laugh. "Me too. Well I hate it when people shorten it to something they want to shorten it to. The amount of people who think it's ok to call me Lexi. That's not my name. I've never introduced myself as that. Don't assume I like to be called that just because you like to say it. My name is the name I tell you. Use it as it is. Don't go making up a new one."

He laughs.

"Sorry, it's one of my pet hates," I say. "I'm calm now."

I take a deep breath.

"Well she always got her own way," he says. "A bit of a spoilt brat."

"She sounds fun," I say.

"Very," he says. "That's why we weren't together for that long."

He looks sadly at his feet.

"And I wasn't allowed to show that I was excited or happy," he says. "I couldn't jump or run or throw my hands up or shout or anything."

"Well, all that is going to change today," I say.

I hold on to his hand and look for a break in the traffic. I run forward and pull him along with me. I rush down an alley between a café and an amusement arcade. We reach the promenade. I don't stop running. At the edge of the concrete I let go of his hand.

"Jump!" I shout.

We fling our bodies gracefully off the pavement on to the soft sand. I lose my footing and fall sideways. I lay on my back with my eyes closed, laughing. I hear a thump land next to me.

"Are you ok?" asks Gregory.

"I'm fine," I say. "You?"

"I'm amazing," he says.

"I know you are," I say.

I push him on to his back and lean over him. I kiss him. I let myself fall on to his chest.

"People are looking," he says.

"Only adults worry about people looking at them, Gregory," I say. "And today, we're not adults."

He flings his arms around me.

"You're a little star, you know?" he says.

"I know," I say.

I get up and brush myself down. Gregory puts his hands on my head and pushes his fingers into my hair.

"You've got half the beach up in there," he says.

"I'll keep it," I say. "As a souvenir of the day."

He smiles.

"So what do you want to do first?" I ask.

"Get some food," he says. "I'm really hungry."

We clamber off the beach and walk along the promenade. I sit down on a bench and untie my laces. He sits next to me. I take off my trainer and tip out a little mound of sand on to the ground. Gregory does the same.

"Nice socks," I say.

He wiggles his cartoon charactered toes.

"Don't tell me," I say. "You were only allowed to wear black socks?"

"Sometimes dark blue," he says. "And white ones, but only when we were playing tennis."

I feign death and slide down the bench.

"But we're having fun today," he says. "So no talking about her."

I nod. He stands up.

"Climb on," he says.

"What?" I say.

He turns his back to me and pats himself on the shoulders.

"You'd better be stronger than you look," I say.

"Get on," he says.

I stand on the bench and wrap my arms around his neck. He stretches his arms out to the side and I cling my thighs to his waist. He puts his hands on my bottom and hoists me up. He hooks his hands under my knees and walks.

"Where to?" he asks.

"Food," I say.

"Directions?" he says.

"Straight on," I say. "And then left, there, by that bin."

We make our way back on to the main road.

"There," I say, pointing to a shop.

"Really?" he asks.

"Yep," I say.

He carries me to the shop. Hanging on the canopy above the front of the shop are plastic bags of pink and blue and yellow candyfloss bobbing in the breeze. A large window is wide open and a woman sits on a stool reading a magazine.

"Good morning," Gregory says to her.

The woman stands up and puts her magazine down. She doesn't say anything.

"Two bags of candyfloss, please," he says.

"Pink, blue or yellow," she says, unenthusiastically.

Gregory turns his head as far as he can and looks at me.

"Pink," I say.

"And a blue one," he says.

The woman picks up two bags and passes them to me. I hold them in front of Gregory's face.

"Pound," the woman says.

I lift up my leg and Gregory pulls his wallet out of his pocket. He puts a pound coin down on the window ledge.

"Thanks," he says to the woman.

She slides the money towards her and puts it in the till. She picks up her magazine and sits back on her stool. Gregory carries me away.

"She was a happy bunny," I say.

"Very," he says.

"You can put me down now," I say.

He drops me. I hand him the bag of blue candyfloss.

"Did you know that candyfloss in French is barbe à papa?" I say.

"I did not," he says.

"It means Dad's beard," I say.

"I did not know that either," he says.

"I don't remember much from my French lessons, but I do remember funny sounding words," I say.

I open my bag of candyfloss and pull a chunk out. I put it in my mouth. It melts immediately.

"Like what?" he says, eating some of his candyfloss.

"Er," I say. "Un phoque is a seal, une pompelmousse is a grapefruit. And erm, well I can't think of any more right now."

"Ok, so maybe we won't have our next date in France," he says.

"Oi," I say.

I pull out a strand of candyfloss and stick it to my face just below my nose. I look at Gregory. He bursts out laughing.

"Hold still," he says.

I start laughing. Gregory pulls his phone out of his pocket and takes a photo of me.

"What are you doing?" I ask.

"I'm starting up a folder for blackmailing purposes," he says. "Just in case, you know."

"Hey," I say. "Delete it. Delete it."

"Nope," he says, putting his phone away.

He shoves a handful of blue into his mouth and laughs.

We walk along the seafront.

"How's your sister?" I ask.

"She's fine, thanks," he says. "It's complicated, and it's difficult to tell your sister that she's making the wrong choices, but I guess I'll always be there to pick up the pieces. That's what big brothers do."

"Have you got any other brothers or sisters?" I ask casually.

"Nope, just me and Gemma," he says.

My stomach flips. I feel free.

"How about you?" he asks.

"Just me," I say. "But when you have perfection first time, you know you're going to be disappointed with anything that comes after."

He laughs.

"Wait here," I say.

I shove my half eaten bag of candyfloss at Gregory and walk in to a shop. I pick up a red square bucket shaped like a castle with turrets, a green round bucket, and two blue spades, and take them to the counter. The unimpressed teenager holds out his hand. I lay a five pound note on his palm. He doesn't say anything. He drops some coins on the counter. I fumble to pick them up. The boy looks at me like I'm an inconvenience. I hold the buckets and spades behind my back and walk outside. Gregory is leaning against a lamppost holding his blue candyfloss.

"Er, where's mine?" I ask.

"You'll never believe it. It's kind of a funny story really," he says.

I look at him.

"Yes?" I say.

"Well this giant seagull flew down and snatched it out of my hand," he says. "He was holding a knife and everything."

"Uh-huh," I say. "And it's just a coincidence that you've got pink smudges on your lips."

"That must have happened when you kissed me," he says. "Transferral or something."

"I haven't kissed you in a long time," I say.

"Well, anyway, what have you got there?" he asks.

"I don't know if you deserve to have this now," I say.

"I'm sorry," he says, making puppy dog eyes. "I'll be on the watch for rogue seagulls and will do my utmost to protect your foodstuffs from these beasts from now on."

"Good boy," I say.

"Sooo?" he asks, stretching his head around to look behind my back.

I hold out the buckets and spades in front of me. His eyes widen.

"You're allowed to be excited," I say.

He jumps and punches the sky.

"Now give me your candyfloss," I say, pulling the bag out of his hand.

I give Gregory the buckets and spades and I run off. He chases me to the beach. I put the last piece of candyfloss in my mouth and put the plastic bag in the bin. The beach is empty apart from a couple of dog-walkers and a woman unsuccessfully trying to teach her child how to eat an ice-cream cone. There is more ice-cream down his front and on the ground than in his mouth. He seems to be enjoying himself and that's all that matters.

"The best sand is the wet stuff near the sea," I say, marching ahead.

"You sound like an expert," he says.

I look over my shoulder and turn around so that I'm walking backwards.

"I am indeed," I say.

He jogs to catch up with me. I sit down on the sand, and take my shoes and socks off.

"Good thinking," he says.

He sits down opposite me, and takes his shoes and socks off.

"You've got really hairy toes," I laugh.

"Yeah, well you've got a really hairy …," he says. "… mum."

"It's not her fault, it's a hormone imbalance," I say.

He pokes his tongue out at me.

"You've also got a blue tongue," I say.

"Hab I?" he asks, poking his tongue out as far as it'll go, going cross-eyed in the process.

"Give me a bucket," I say.

He passes me the green one.

"Oh, so you get to have the fancy one," I say.

"I'm still traumatised after that seagull attack," he says. "I need something to comfort me, and this bucket reminds me of a bucket I had as a child."

He holds the bucket against his cheek and strokes the side.

"Ok, you win," I say. "This time."

I dig up some of the sand and shovel it in to my bucket. I pat down the top once it's full and tip the bucket upside down. I bang the handle of the spade on the bottom of the bucket and gently pull the bucket up. My tower stands perfectly. Not a crumble, not a crack.

"What's that?" Gregory asks, pointing over my shoulder.

I turn my head around.

"What?" I say, turning back.

I notice a demolished tower in front of me. I look at Gregory. He shrugs his shoulders.

"Seagull," he says.

"Yeah, yeah, of course it was," I say.

He scoops sand in to his bucket and pats it down. He turns it over and pulls the bucket off. I stab the castle in the side with my spade. The castle collapses. He looks at me. I shrug my shoulders.

"Seagull," I say.

"I don't think you're taking this seriously," he says.

"I don't think you are," I say.

"It's not my fault," he says. "It's the seagulls."

I look in the sky. No birds of any description. A few grey clouds though. I stick my spade into the ground and flick some sand at Gregory. He tries to grab my spade. I wave it around and hit him in the side of the head. I drop the spade and lean forward.

"I am so so sorry," I say.

I laugh. I can't help it. Gregory holds his hand on his head.

"Are you ok?" I ask.

"Am I bleeding?" he asks.

"I can't see," I say. "Take your hand down."

I hold his head in my hands and move his hair. He winces.

"No, you're not bleeding," I say.

He grabs me around the waist and pulls me on top of him.

"Stupid seagulls," I say.

He kisses me.

"I think the last time I was hit in the head with a plastic spade at the seaside, I must have been about six or seven, by Gemma who wasn't too impressed at me drowning her doll in the sea," he says.

"Weren't you a delightful brother," I say.

"I've matured a lot since then," he says. "I now kill dolls with a lethal mixture of nicotine, vodka and crack cocaine."

I laugh. He kisses me again.

"You're an idiot," I say.

"Well I probably am now that I've been hit in the head," he says. "That must have killed a few million brain cells."

"You had that many to start with?" I ask, surprised.

He pushes me off him. I feel something plop on my arm. I look down. That had better not be a bird. It's not. Something plops again. It starts raining. We pick up our shoes and the buckets and spades, and run towards the pier. We stand under the wooden planks and protect ourselves from the weather. We drop everything on to the sand. I laugh.

"Typical," I say.

"It's ok," he says.

He holds my hands and pulls me towards him. He wraps his arms around me. He's so warm. I nuzzle in to his chest and wrap my arms around his back. He smells good. I breathe him in. I think about William and his arms around me, and how safe I felt in that dingy underpass with him. Gregory leans back.

"Are you crying?" he asks.

I touch my face. My cheek is wet. That's because of the rain. I sniff. My nose is running. I get a tissue out of my bag.

"No," I say. "I'm just a bit cold."

"Aw," he says, pulling me back towards him. "Let's warm you up."

He rubs his hands up and down my arms. I feel safe with him under this dingy pier. We kiss. The rain stops.

"You want to make a move?" I say.

"Sure," he says.

We pick up our shoes and the buckets and spades. We walk to the steps and sit down. I rub as much sand off my feet as I can, and redress them. Gregory does the same.

"What do you want to do with these?" he asks, holding up a bucket.

"We'll give them to the first kid we see," I say.

He grabs my hand and kisses it. I smile. We get up and walk to the top of the steps. A woman is standing nearby leaning against the railings. She's looking at her phone. A child sits on the floor driving a small car around her feet. I smile at her to try to catch her attention but she's focussed on her phone.

"Hi," I say to her.

She doesn't look up.

"Excuse me?" I say.

She sneers at me. I smile.

"What?" she barks.

"I was just wondering if your child would like these," I say, holding up my bucket and spade.

"Nah," she says, and looks back down at her phone.

My stomach sinks. I turn and walk away.

"Maybe we'll give them to the second child we see," I say to Gregory.

We wander around the pier. I stop in front of a shabby fun-house mirror. My legs look two inches long and my body stretches on for miles until it reaches my tiny head. I bob up and down. My proportions change with each movement. I hear a 'click' behind me.

"What are you doing?" I ask.

"More blackmail material," he laughs.

I drag him away. A man and a woman sit on a bench. Two children sit between them sharing a tray of chips. I pull Gregory towards them.

"Hi," I say to them.

The couple look up at me. The children carry on eating.

"I know this is going to sound strange," I say. "But would your children like these?"

We hold out the buckets and spades. The man stands up.

"Are you sure?" he asks.

He has a very gentle sounding voice.

"Of course," I say.

He takes them.

"Thank you so much," he says.

He sounds sad.

"Michael, Andrew, look what the nice man and lady have given you," he says.

The boys look up and grin at us. They give their chips to the woman and reach out their arms.

"What do you say to the nice man and lady?" he says.

"Thank you," the boys say.

"You are more than welcome," I say.

The woman wipes her eyes.

"Thank you so much," she says.

"No problem," I say. "I hope you enjoy them as much as we did."

We turn to walk away. The man touches my arm.

"Thank you," the man says.

"You're welcome," I say.

"It's just …," the man says. "Well, the boys really wanted to come to the beach and me and my wife weren't sure if we could afford it, but we didn't want to disappoint them. They were so hungry but we could only afford one tray of chips. The prices here have really shot through the roof. I guess they're getting ready for the tourist season. I'd hoped we could buy them a bucket and spade to share but we didn't have the money and then you came along."

He sighs.

"Just thank you," he says. "You've really helped us, and they're so happy."

He turns around and looks at the boys. They're using the spades as swords. I smile and hold back a tear. The man walks back to his family. Gregory and I walk away.

"Now I'm crying," I say.

Gregory puts his arm around my shoulders and pulls me into him. We walk along the pier. I put my arm around his waist. At this moment the world is perfect. There's no war, no famine, no disease. Only two happy little boys and a very happy thirty year old woman.

"Get in there," Gregory says, pointing to a wooden cut-out, showing a muscly man lifting a barbell over his head.

"Blackmail?" I ask.

"Yep," he says.

I stick my head through the cut-out face hole and grin. He takes a photo.

"Your turn," I say.

He stands behind a very fat woman wearing an unflattering swimming costume, and pokes his head through the face hole. I get my phone out of my pocket and take his picture.

"Blackmail?" he asks.

"I'd never be so cruel," I say. "It's just for my own personal amusement."

He laughs.

"Excuse me," he says to a middle aged woman. "Can you take our photo please?"

"Of course," she says.

"One more," he says to me, nodding towards one with two face holes cut out.

The woman stands in front of us. Gregory is a very attractive mermaid and I am the sailor who has caught the mermaid in his net. The woman takes the picture.

"Thank you," Gregory laughs.

"Yeah, thank you," I say to Gregory.

I take his hand.

"Popty ping," he says.

"Excuse me?" I say.

"It's a microwave," he says. "In Welsh."

I look at him.

"It's the only funny foreign word I know," he says.

"A bit of a delayed reaction there," I say.

"I only just remembered it," he says.

"Where did you learn that?" I ask.

"I can't remember," he says. "I think I heard it on the radio."

I laugh.

"I'm hungry," I say.

"Ditto," he says.

"I think we'd better go somewhere inside, you know, just in case we bump into any more of those thieving seagulls," I say.

"I'm afraid I can't do that," he says.

"Why not?" I ask.

"It's the law, when you come to the seaside, that you have to eat your chips at the beach," he says. "The law."

"Well if it's the law," I say.

"It is," he says.

We walk towards the entrance of the pier. The smell of chips gets stronger.

"Just chips?" he asks.

"Yep, just chips," I say.

"Two large chips," he says to the man in the van.

The man scoops the chips into polystyrene trays and wraps them up in paper.

"Salt and vinegar's just on the side," he says, pointing to the side of the van.

"Thanks," I say.

Gregory passes some money to the man.

"Salt and vinegar?" I ask him.

"Are bears Catholic?" he asks.

"Not that I'm aware," I say, confused.

"Oh, well, yes, loads of salt and vinegar," he says. "It's the law."

"Wow, so many laws that I haven't heard of," I say. "I've actually broken this law a few times, but don't tell anyone."

I put my finger up to my lips.

"Don't worry," he says. "I won't."

He smiles at me. I give him his chips. I balance mine on the ledge and sprinkle over the salt and vinegar. Gregory does the same. He passes me a wooden fork. We walk along the sea front and sit on a bench. I put my parcel on my lap and open up the paper. It's so warm on my thighs. They smell so good. I stab my fork into the biggest chip and direct it towards my mouth. Gregory pulls the chip off my fork and eats it himself.

"Seagulls," he says.

I slide to one end of the bench and wrap my arm around my chips. I stuff a few in to my mouth. They're so hot and salty and delicious. I eat and eat and don't look up.

"Did you ever eat chips out of newspaper?" he asks.

"No," I say sadly.

"Me neither," he says. "I would have loved to though."

"I know," I say. "There's something very seasidey about chips in newspaper."

I eat a few more chips. My pile seems never ending. I sit back and groan.

"Ok?" he asks.

"I'm full," I say.

He looks over at my lap.

"You've hardly even touched these," he says.

"I know, but I'm stuffed," I say.

I wrap the paper around my uneaten chips and pass it to Gregory.

"I need a drink," I say. "Don't let any seagulls eat my lunch."

"I'll try," he says. "But I can't promise anything. They're sneaky, they are."

"Uh-huh," I say. "Do you want anything?"

"Yeah, whatever you're having," he says.

I walk along the promenade to a café. A machine in the window swirls blue and red liquid around a plastic box.

"One red and one blue ice slush, please," I say to the woman.

She takes a plastic cup, puts it under the nozzle and pulls down the handle. The red liquid drops slinkily into the cup. It levels out at the top. She drops a straw into the drink and passes it to me. She does the same with the blue one.

"Thank you," I say.

I pay her and walk back to the bench.

"A seagull came along, but I told it to go away," he says.

"Well done," I say and kiss him on the head.

He grins like a child.

"Red or blue?" I ask.

"Er, red," he says.

I pass him the cup.

"Correct answer," I say. "Blue is my favourite."

I put the straw in my mouth and suck. A shot of ice shoots into my mouth. My tongue numbs. My eye twitches.

"Ow ow ow," I say, rubbing my eye.

"Ice headache?" he asks.

"Mm-hmm," I say, winking.

"Have a chip," he says. "The heat will counter balance the cold."

"Ooh, that sounds scientific," I say.

"Yes, I'm a qualified seaside foodologist," he says.

I eat a chip. The pain eases. I sip a bit more gently.

"Look who's got a blue tongue now," he laughs.

I poke my tongue out at him. He laughs.

"I really can't eat any more," I say.

"Lightweight," he says.

"I'm just not a big fat fatty," I say, poking a finger in to his stomach.

"Oi," he says, poking a finger into my waist.

I scream, wiggle and fall off the bench. A group of teenagers walk past. They laugh. I blush.

"Ticklish, eh?" he asks.

"No," I say, pulling myself back on to the bench. "It was a seagull."

"A seagull?" he asks.

"Yeah," I say. "It flew pretty close. Didn't you see it? I had to dive on to the ground to avoid being snatched away in its claws."

"Riiiight," he says.

I compose myself.

"Do you want the rest of my chips?" I ask.

"No, I think I'll pass," he says. "I'm going on a diet."

"Ok, I'll just give them to the seagulls then," I say, standing up.

"Don't you even think about it," he says, pulling my arm.

I sit down and he takes the chips. I slowly sip my blue ice slush. We don't speak. It's nice, not awkward. I look out at the sea. It's calm. The grey clouds have gone. The sky is bright. It's not too cold. My phone shatters the silence with an angry beep.

"I'm so sorry," I say. "I thought I had it on silent."

"It's ok," he says. "You answer it."

I pull my phone out of my bag. I have one new message from William. I look at Gregory and then back to my phone. I don't open the message. I turn my phone on silent.

"It's nothing important," I say.

It might be, I don't know. I try to push it out of my mind.

"Finished?" I ask Gregory.

He screws the empty chip papers into a ball and slurps the last bit of red liquid from the bottom of the cup.

"Yep," he says.

I stand up.

"I could do with a nap though," he says, closing his eyes.

"Only old people have naps after lunch," I say. "And today we are children."

He grumbles.

"I s'pose so," he says, ambling up and walking over to the bin.

He throws the papers at the bin like a basketball. They go in.

"If I'd done that, they probably would have ended up on my head," I say.

He laughs. I stand up on the bench.

"Carry me," I say, holding my arms out.

"I can't even carry myself," he says.

"But I eated too much," I whimper.

"So did I," he says.

I don't move.

"Caaaaaawwy meeeee," I whinge, stamping my feet.

He walks over, stands in front of the bench and turns his back to me. I climb on. He drops down on to the bench.

"I can't," he says.

"Useless," I say. "Fine, I'll walk myself."

I stand up and jump off the bench.

"Where to now?" he asks.

"This way," I say, and walk away from the beach towards the main road.

"Slow down," he says. "I ate too much."

"That's not my fault," I say. "Now quick march."

"It was your fault," he says.

"How so?" I ask, stopping next to a flower bed in the shape of an anchor.

"If you'd eaten all your chips, I wouldn't have had to eat them, and I wouldn't be feeling so full," he says.

"I didn't hold a gun to your head and force you to eat them," I say.

"I'm surprised you didn't, considering you hit me in the head with a plastic spade earlier," he says.

I change my direction.

"What's that smell?" he asks, putting his hand over his mouth.

"I was thinking, considering you can't really move, we'd get carried for a bit," I say.

I walk towards a line of horses and carriages. A large bag hangs under the horses' hind quarters, one end attached to their waist and the other end attached to the front of the carriage.

"That," I say, pointing to the bag. "That is what that smell is."

I walk up to the man standing by the horse at the front of the line.

"How much for one way?" I ask.

The man points to the sign indicating prices. I pay him.

"Come on," I say to Gregory.

"Is it safe?" he asks.

"Of course it's safe," I say.

"I, er," he says, waving his hand towards himself, beckoning me over.

"What's up?" I ask.

"I've got a bit of a phobia of horses," he whispers.

"Oh," I say.

"I know it's stupid, but they scare me," he says. "It's those teeth. They're so …"

He takes a step back.

"… big," he finishes.

I hold his hand.

"I promise you it's safe," I say. "And I'll be here the whole time, so you've got nothing to worry about."

The man opens the door to the carriage. We walk towards the horse. The horse whinnies. Gregory grips my hand.

"It's going to be ok," I say.

I climb in to the carriage and sit down on the soft red and blue blanket. Gregory sits next to me. He's holding his breath.

"Breathe," I say.

"Uh-huh," he says, his eyes darting from side to side.

The man sits on a seat at the front of the carriage and holds on to the horse's reins. The horse turns on to the road and pulls us along.

"You can pretend to be the Queen up here," I say.

I start waving my hand royally. Old people on the pavement wave back at me. I laugh. Gregory stares straight ahead at the horse.

"How do you know it's not going to just run off?" he asks.

"Well, I don't," I say. "But that guy knows what he's doing. Just relax."

I push his shoulders down into the back of the seat.

"There," I say.

I lift his arm up and put it around my shoulder. He looks at me and smiles.

"Thank you," he says.

"No worries," I say. "It was only a couple of quid."

"I didn't mean that, but thank you for that," he says, kissing me on the head. "I meant for not laughing at me."

"Why am I going to laugh at you?" I ask.

"Because of my stupid fear of stupid horses," he says.

"I bet you a million quid that if you spoke to every person along this road and asked them what they were scared of, it would be something stupid," I say.

"You think?" he says.

"I know," I say. "We're all irrational creatures. Come on, I can only listen to things if the volume is an even number or a multiple of five."

He smiles.

"See," I say.

"You're amazing," he says, kissing me on the lips.

"I know," I say.

"So what are you scared of?" he asks me.

"Ha," I say.

"Come on, you've got to tell me," he says. "I told you mine."

"But only because we were in a situation where your fear presented itself," I say.

"Stop being all philosophical and tell me," he says.

"Ok, but you've got to promise not to laugh," I say.

"I promise," he says, crossing his heart.

"Ok," I say.

I take a deep breath.

"Rabbits," I say.

"Rabbits?" he says.

"You're not allowed to laugh," I say.

"I'm not laughing," he says, covering his mouth.

"You are," I say, pushing his arm away.

He laughs.

"I'm sorry," he says. "But rabbits?"

"I had a traumatic experience with an Easter bunny when I was little," I say. "I've never gotten over it."

"Aww," he says, pulling me in to his chest and kissing me on the top of the head.

The horse slows from a trot to a walk. The carriage

stops.

"That wasn't so bad, was it?" I say.

Gregory smiles at me. The man opens the carriage door. I put my right foot on the small step and reach my left foot towards the pavement. I fall forwards. The pavement is a lot further away than I anticipated. Everything moves in slow motion. My hands let go of the side of the carriage and my arms fly out in front of me. I've got nothing to hold on to. I pull at the air in the hope I can find my balance again. I fall in to the man, knocking him in to the side of the carriage. He reaches for me. I fall in a crumpled heap on the pavement. I laugh.

"I'm so sorry," I say to the man.

"No mind," he says. "Not the first time a lovely lass 'as thrown 'erself at me."

He leans forward and puts out his hand. I take it and he pulls me to my feet.

"Owt broken?" he asks.

I wiggle my feet, legs, hips and arms.

"I think everything is still where it's supposed to be," I say.

I look up at Gregory. He's still sitting down with his hand over his mouth.

"Don't rush to help me or anything," I say.

"I'm sorry," he says. "But the horse ..."

He stands up and jumps from the carriage, nearly as gracefully as I had jumped. He steps backwards towards the back of the carriage.

"It was looking at me," he says.

I look to the man.

"Thank you," I say.

"No mind," he says, and shuts the carriage door.

I hobble over to the wall and lean against it.

"I am really sorry," Gregory says, walking towards me.

I rub my ankle.

"You're going to have to piggy-back me everywhere

now," I say.

He turns around.

"Your carriage awaits," he says.

I jump on his back. He walks a short way along the path. The miniature road train pulls up to the kerb just in front of us.

"I'll save your back," I say. "We can get the train."

I jump off Gregory's back and walk towards the train.

"I'll get this one," Gregory says to me.

The driver unhooks the chains from the carriages and a few people get out. I climb in to the train and sit on a seat clearly designed for children or people with no legs. I angle my legs diagonally across the carriage. Gregory climbs in and sits with his legs going diagonally in the other direction.

"Luxury travel," I say.

He holds my hand and kisses it.

"I am really sorry about that," he says.

"It's ok," I say.

"It's not. You were falling and I was scared rigid just because that horse turned its head around and looked at me," he says.

"He couldn't even look at you," I say. "They wear blinkers."

"See," he says. "So even more reason to show that I'm an idiot."

"Being scared of horses doesn't make you an idiot," I say. "You're just an idiot, regardless."

He looks at me. I laugh.

"I know," he says. "But still."

"If it makes you feel any better, if that carriage had been pulled by a rabbit, I would have shoved you out of the way so that I could escape. I might not even have got on. So you were a lot braver than I would have been," I say.

"You're just being nice," he says.

"One thing you will learn about me is that I don't say things just to be nice," I say. "I don't like lying to make someone feel better."

I turn my head away. I remember the text from William. I feel like a fraud. A hypocrite. Gregory squeezes my hand.

"Are you ok?" he asks.

"Yeah, I'm fine," I say. "My ankle just twinges a bit."

I'm not lying. My ankle is throbbing.

"Let me have a look," he says.

I slide around on the wooden seat and lift my foot up. A family gets on the train a few seats behind us. The children keep shouting *choo choo*. The first few times are cute. It starts to grate after the twentieth time. I untie my shoelace and pull off my trainer. Some sand pings out. The train driver walks along the side of the train making sure everything is secure. His voice comes over the tannoy.

"Here we go," he says.

He rings a bell. The train does a U-turn and holds up the traffic. I hold on to my seat. I don't want to fall out of another vehicle. The train runs smoothly down the designated train path. Gregory puts pressure on my foot.

"Be careful," I say. "I'm ticklish."

"I know," he says.

"You don't," I say. "My foot could fly out at any time and kick you in the nose."

He holds my foot at arm's length.

"Does this hurt?" he asks, pushing my toes backwards, then forwards.

"A little bit," I say.

"Well I don't think anything's broken," he says.

"You're not a doctor though," I say. "So I think you should carry me everywhere just to be on the safe side."

He tickles me in the side. I nearly slide off the seat.

"Those seagulls," he laughs.

The train pulls to a stop just by the row of horses and carriages.

"Are you going to be ok?" I ask.

"Yep, I'm big and brave," he says.

The train driver unhooks the chain. I pull on my trainer and do up the lace. Gregory stands on the pavement and holds out his hand. I take it.

"M'lady," he says, doffing his invisible cap.

"Thankee kind sir," I say, stepping carefully off the train. I limp out of the way of the horses.

"I've just got to …," I say, pointing to a toilet block.

"Good thinking," he says.

***

I sit down on a bench and wait for Gregory. I take my phone out of my bag. I have three missed calls from Louise. I'll call her back later. The small envelope at the top of the screen reminds me of William's message. My finger hovers over the buttons; to open or not to open? Gregory makes my decision for me. He walks towards me. I put my phone back in my bag.

"Are you ok?" he asks me.

"Yeah, I'm fine," I say.

"If your foot hurts too much we can go," he says.

"No, we've got so much more to do," I say. "I can't let a stupid broken foot get in the way."

I stand up and put my arm around his waist. He puts his arm around my shoulder. I start to walk. He doesn't move. I turn around. He kisses me. He's so tender. I could collapse here if he wasn't holding on to me.

"Thank you for today," he says, looking me in the eye.

"No mind," I say, mimicking the horse man's voice.

"I mean it," he says. "I haven't felt like this in a long time. It's refreshing."

He kisses me again. I forget the pain in my ankle.

"Are you ready?" I ask him.

"Lead on," he says.

I walk towards the main road, avoiding the horses.

"Hungry?" I ask.

"Not yet," he says.
I walk down some steps towards a cabin.
"Crazy golf?" he asks.
"Yep," I say.
"I'm rubbish at crazy golf," he says.
"Good," I say. "Because I'm a bad loser."
He laughs. The unimpressed girl looks up at us. I smile. She continues writing a text. It takes a few moments. She slides her phone in to her pocket.
"Two," I say.
She pulls two golf clubs out from under the counter and passes them to Gregory. She digs her hand into a bucket and pulls out a red and a blue golf ball. She hands them to me. I put them in my pocket. She slides a score card across the counter with a short pencil. I root around in my bag for my purse. Gregory beats me to it and pays the lady. He passes me a golf club. I hold it like a sword and aim it for his chest. The girl coughs and points to a sign behind her. All golf clubs are to be used as golf clubs and not weapons. I laugh. Gregory pushes me through the door. We enter Treasure Trove Island.

I put my golf ball down on the Astroturf. I am faced with a giant skull missing a couple of teeth. I hit the ball, swinging the golf club like a professional player. I miss the ball. Gregory laughs. I tap the ball gently. It rolls forward about four inches and then rolls behind me. I stand, defeated.

"Start as you mean to go on," Gregory says to me.

"For all you know I could be luring you in to a false sense of security," I say. "I might be pretending that I'm rubbish and then I turn out to be a professional crazy golf player."

"And are you doing that?" he asks.

"No," I say. "But I might be."

I take a step back.

"Show me how it's done then," I say.

Gregory crouches down and puts his ball on the ground.

He stands to the side, licks his finger and holds it up in the air. He points.

"A north-westerly wind today," he says.

"That's south," I say.

"Don't interrupt an expert while he's at work," he says.

"I won't," I say. "But I will interrupt you."

I laugh. He goes to hit the ball. I tap him behind the knee with my golf club. His knee buckles and he stumbles forward. He turns around and looks at me.

"Don't tell me," he says. "Seagulls?"

I nod, looking innocent, holding my golf club behind my back.

"Sort it out," I say. "We're going to be here forever."

He hits the ball. It rolls through a gap in the skull's mouth. He jumps excitedly around the other side.

"It went in," he shouts.

"No it didn't," I say. "You're lying."

"Have a look if you don't believe me," he shouts.

"I believe it's in the hole," I say. "But I also believe that you kicked it in there."

He leans around the skull and forces his bottom lip into a pout.

"Go on then," he says. "Show me how it's done."

I do.

19

We stand at the last hole. I look at the score card.

"You really are rubbish at this," I say.

"And not only are you a bad loser, you're also a bad winner," he says.

"Shut up and take your shot," I say.

He puts his ball down. He crouches down and winks. He aims his golf club in front of him.

"All you've got to do is hit the ball up the slope, in to the pirates' chest of booty and down through the giant bracelet. It's huge, you can't miss," I say.

"That's what she said," he says, winking.

"Just do it," I say. "I want my victory ice-cream."

"That's what she said," he says, winking.

I growl. He hits the ball. It rolls up the slope and then rolls back down.

"Don't hit it too hard," I say. "It'll go in the lake."

"I know," he snaps.

"Alright," I say, stepping back.

"I'm sorry," he says. "I'm just concentrating."

He hits the ball; it rolls all the way up the slope and plops down the hole. It rattles down a tube and disappears. I look at the score card and add up the scores.

"There's no need for that," he says, snatching the score card and screwing it up.

I kiss him.

"Ok, I think I can handle getting kissed every time I lose at something," he says.

I kiss him again. A woman behind us coughs.

"Have you finished here?" she asks, abruptly.

"Sorry, yes," I say, smiling.

Gregory and I walk away. We give our golf clubs back to the unimpressed girl and walk towards the main road.

"Go on," he says. "I know you want to."

"Want to what?" I ask.

"Do a victory dance," he says.

"How did you know?" I ask.

"Your hips have been shaking since about half way around the course," he says.

"Well ....," I say.

"Go on," he says. "Just get it out of the way."

I shake my arms and hips and bend my knees and bounce. I stop.

"Done?" he asks.

I do one more hip shake.

"Done," I say.

"Good," he says. "Now, do I remember right that you said something about ice-cream?"

"You are indeed correct," I say. "And I know just the place."

We cross the road and walk towards a van.

"What do you want?" I ask Gregory.

"Er," he says.

"It's all the same, ice-cream in a cone, but dipped in whatever you want," the man in the van says.

Gregory's eyes widen when he sees tubs of nuts and sprinkles and sweets and chocolate.

"Any time today," I say.

"Space rocks popping candy," he says.

The man in the van holds a cone under the ice-cream nozzle. The vanilla cream curls to a peak. He then rolls it in the tub of orange crystals and passes it to Gregory. He grins like a child.

"And I'll have chocolate hundreds and thousands," I say.

I pull a note out of my purse and pass it to the man. He hands me my ice-cream and my change. I drop the coins in my bag.

"Thank you," I say to the ice-cream man.

We walk back across the road.

"Hey, weren't you supposed to treat me to the ice-cream because I won at golf?" I ask.

"Yes, I think I was," he says, embarrassed.

"Don't worry about it. You can just owe me two next time," I tell him.

"How is it?" I ask.

Gregory opens his mouth. The air is filled with fizzing and popping and crackling.

"Guh-lisus," he says.

I smile at him.

"Want to try some?" he asks.

I look at him suspiciously.

"I'm not going to put it on your face," he says. "I'm not going to waste my delicious ice-cream doing that."

I look at him suspiciously.

"I won't," he says.

I hold on to his wrist and guide the ice-cream to my mouth. He jerks his arm and the ice-cream splodges into my cheek.

"Thank you," I say, rolling my eyes.

He pulls me close and licks the ice-cream off my cheek.

"Mmm, tastes even better if you eat it this way," he laughs.

I wipe my face with my sleeve.

"Go on," he says, holding his ice-cream out to me.

I lean in, he moves his arm. I look like a pigeon pecking at the ground.

"Hold still," I say.

"I am," he says. "You're the one who's moving."

I walk away.

"I didn't want any anyway," I say.

I start eating mine. He catches me up.

"Ok, I really won't do anything this time," he says. "I promise."

I look at him. He crosses his heart. I take a bite. My mouth fills with fizzing and popping and crackling. I hold my mouth open.

"S'gug," I say.

I eat some of my chocolate sprinkles. I wish I'd gone with the space rocks popping candy. It's starting to get dark. We sit on a bench. Strings of coloured bulbs above us light up. Amusement arcades run up and down the length of the main road. Their lights flash and shimmer and pulse. I slide up close to Gregory and put my head on his shoulder. Everything feels so magical, like it's something more than an ice-cream on a bench at the seaside.

"Do you need to get home any time soon?" I ask.

"No," he says. "Unless you're trying to get rid of me."

"Far from it," I say. "I've just got one more thing I want to do."

"Sounds interesting," he says.

"It was my absolutely most favouritest thing to do in the whole wide world when I was little," I say.

He laughs.

"I couldn't wait for the summer holidays when my parents would bring me up here," I say. "It was the highlight of our days out."

I pop the last bit of cone in to my mouth.

"Well I don't know what could be better than that ice-cream," he says.

"You'll see," I say.

We walk down the road towards a red and yellow glow. We walk under the giant Lucky Star Amusements sign and head to the money change machine. I slide in a five pound note and press the 2p button. A loud rattle of coins falls into the tray. I scoop them up and put them in a plastic tub. I hand it to Gregory. He grins.

"I love the two pee machines," he says. "Thank you."

He kisses me. I put in another five pound note and collect my two pees in a plastic tub.

"There's an art to the two pee machine, you know?" I say.

"Oh I know," he says. "You have to walk around and look at each machine individually before choosing one."

"Yep," I say. "You have to look for the one with the most prizes in, but also the one that has a lot of two pees balancing precariously on the ledge."

"And keep an eye out for sneaky kids and grannies who are ready to jump in and steal the loot," he says.

"Yes!" I say.

We walk around the arcade, watching teenagers shooting zombies with plastic guns and racing motorbikes along Spanish streets and spending a fortune trying to grab an oddly shaped toy with a claw that doesn't want to grip.

"Never do those," I say.

"I know," he says. "They're a fix. You can probably buy those toys in town cheaper."

I notice a machine with a balancing pile of coins. I drop a two pee in to the slot. It bounces down and lays flat on the moving shelf. It moves backwards and forwards and backwards. Nothing happens. Gregory walks around to the other side.

"Got my one," he says.

I drop another two pee in. The shelf slides fluidly. My two pee pushes a couple of two pees off the shelf. They land on the pile. Nothing happens. I can feel my palms sweating. I hear coins drop on the other side of the machine.

"How much?" I say.

"Twelve pence," Gregory says.

I drop another two pee in. It rolls to the edge and drops down the side. I hear money fall. I look in my tray. Nothing.

"Yes!" Gregory shouts from the other side. "Got some strawberry hair clips."

"They'll suit you," I say.

I drop another two pee in. The shelf slides and pulls it to lay down flat. It pushes one coin off the shelf. The shelf pushes into the fallen coin. Nothing happens. I start to get angry. I hear more money fall on the other side. Gregory bends down and looks at me through the glass.

"This is great," he says, grinning.

"Yeah," I say.

I drop two two pees in at the same time. They bounce in different directions. They land flat. The shelf moves backwards. A row of coins drop off the shelf. The shelf slides forwards. The machine rattles as the huge pile of coins drop and fall in to my tray.

"Yes!" I shout.

"What did you get?" he asks.

"Loads of money," I say, scooping it into my tub. "And a plastic diamond ring."

"Ooh, look at you, princess," he says.

I try to squish it on to one of my fingers.

"It doesn't fit," I say.

I drop in a couple more two pees, but nothing happens. I think I've had the jackpot from this machine. A child loitering behind me rushes to my machine when I walk away. I walk around and stand behind Gregory.

"Given up on that one?" he asks.

"Yep," I say. "I got all I could out of that one."

I waggle my little finger at him. The plastic glitters under the neon lights of the arcade machines.

"Beautiful," he says.

I laugh. He turns his head around and leans forward. A strawberry hairclip clings to his short hair with all its might.

"Suits you," I say.

"Thanks," he says.

"Are you staying on this one?" I ask him.

"Yep," he says.

I drop a couple of two pees into his machine, kiss him on the cheek, and walk away. I hear a few coins drop. I don't know if it's Gregory's machine. The pings and clangs and repeated tinny tunes all merge into one sound. I wander around and drop coins into various machines. I don't really get anything back. I don't mind. I find a machine that looks like it's about to overbalance soon. I robotically drop my coins into the slot. This one has two moving shelves sliding at different speeds. My coins bounce in different directions. A few drop in to the tray. I pick them out. A hand covers my eyes. I take a breath in.

"Hold out your hand," he says.

It's Gregory. I pass my plastic pot into my left hand and hold my right hand out, open. A small, cold object drops in to my palm.

"Ok," he says. "Open your eyes."

The hand moves away. I look down. I'm holding a small, brown dog keyring.

"It's Beryl," he says.

"It looks nothing like Beryl," I laugh.

"Doesn't it?" he says.

"No," I say. "She's got a brown and white head, and a brown body."

"Oh," he says. "Guess I was paying more attention to someone else that day."

I smile and look down. I hug him.

"Thank you," I say.

I loop the ring over my finger and let the dog dangle.

"This can be Meryl," I say.

"Meryl it is," he says.

I root around in my bag for my car keys and attach Meryl to them. Gregory puts his empty plastic pot on top of my machine.

"Well that's me out," he says.

I drop in my last few two pees. A few more drop out with a plastic bracelet.

"Matches the ring," he says.

I put those two pees back in to the machine. Nothing happens. I wait a few moments just to make sure nothing happens. Nothing happens. I yawn.

"Is someone sleepy?" he asks.

"Yeah," I say. "I think I am."

"So you want to go home?" he asks.

"Yeah," I say. "I think I do."

He hugs me and kisses me on the top of my head. We walk out of the arcade. The roads are full of cars driving up and down at stupid speeds. They have flashing lights that pulse under the cars' bodies. Their windows are rolled down and *vwoomp vwoomp vwoomp* music beats out.

"You can tell you're getting old when all music starts to sound the same," I say.

"Oh, was that music?" Gregory says.

"That's another sign you're getting old," I laugh.

We slowly wander along the pavement, avoiding teenagers throwing chips at each other and scantily-clad women throwing abuse at each other. Gregory puts his arm around my shoulder and pulls me close to him. He's so warm. I close my eyes and rest my head on his shoulder. We stop walking.

"I know you want to get home," he says. "But can you hang on just one more minute?"

"Yeah," I say.

Gregory walks over to a booth with giant stuffed toys hanging from the roof beams. I pull his arm. He walks back to me.

"They're a fix," I say. "Just like those claw machines."

"Trust me," he says.

He walks towards the booth. I look at the sign. Score three aces to win a prize. A wall is covered with hundreds of different playing cards. I can't even see three aces. Gregory gives the man a pound coin. The man gives Gregory three darts. Gregory throws one dart. Ten of clubs. He throws the second dart. It bounces off the wall. He throws the final dart. Four of hearts.

"Never mind," I say.

The man pulls the darts out of the wall. Gregory gives him another pound. The man gives Gregory the darts. Gregory throws one dart. Ace of spades. He throws the second dart. Ace of diamonds. He scans the wall looking for the third ace. He looks at me and winks. He throws the final dart and hits the ace of hearts right in the middle of the heart. I clap. The man rolls his eyes.

"What d'you want?" he asks, pointing to the stuffed toys.

Gregory looks at me.

"The pink dog," I say.

"I knew you were going to say that," Gregory says.

The man unhooks the dog and hands it to Gregory. We walk away. He passes me the dog. Its head is huge, but its body is really small. I can't carry it and see where I'm going at the same time. I wrap my arms around the dog's neck and stumble forward.

"Thanks," I say, turning around and hitting Gregory with the dog.

"No mind," he says.

I laugh.

"When were you going to tell me that you're an expert dartist?" I ask.

He laughs.

"Do you play a lot?" I ask.

He laughs again.

"What's so funny?" I ask.

"When I was younger, I used to spend a week in the

summer holidays with my grandparents ...," he says.

"Nana Bertie?" I ask.

"Glad to see you were paying attention," he says. "But no. My other grandparents. My mum's parents. Anyway, I went the same week every year and that was the same week that the town had a summer fayre, with all the trimmings. Food and stalls and shows and bands and fireworks. And there was always a travelling fair ground, with dodgems and a fun house and a ghost train and the waltzers and some sort of terrifying contraption that spun around and went upside down and inside out."

"Not your thing?" I say.

"No," he says. "But I did love the waltzers. And the one thing that I loved more than the waltzers was the daughter of the guy who ran the waltzers."

"Aww, a little crush," I say.

"It was more than a crush," he says, hurt. "It was love."

"And how old were you?" I ask.

"Eleven," he mumbles.

"Eleven?" I laugh.

"I was in love," he says.

"Ok," I say.

"And how old was she?" I ask.

"Fifteen or sixteen," he says.

I don't say anything.

"She was beautiful and all the boys followed her everywhere. She didn't really seem that interested. I wanted to do something that would make me stand out from the rest of them," he says.

"Well, being eleven was a big thing that made you stand out from the other boys," I say.

"Funny," he says. "I wanted to win her a prize and then I could win her heart."

"Ah clever," I say.

"So I walked up to a booth pretty similar to that one," he says, pointing behind us. "And handed over my money and got my darts. I think that was the first time I'd ever held darts. They were a lot heavier than I thought they would be. I lunged them towards the cards and hit absolutely nothing. So I paid for another three darts and threw again. I think I hit one card but the other two darts bounced off the board. I didn't give up. I think I must have spent all my pocket money trying to get a teddy bear holding a heart for her."

"Did you do it?" I ask.

"Not that summer," he says. "But the next summer they came back and I tried all over again. I threw those darts like it was no-one's business. I'd matured into a strong twelve year old. My hand-eye coordination had improved. And the girl was even more beautiful than I remembered."

"What was her name?" I ask.

"I don't know," he laughs.

"Ah, true love," I say.

"Shuttup," he says. "So I tried again and again and again with those darts, and eventually I got it. I hit one card. I hit two cards. I hit three cards. All dead in the centre."

He throws his hands up in the air and smiles.

"I couldn't believe it," he says. "The man shoved a toy at me, but I'd got the bug. I wanted to throw more darts. I dropped the toy on the ground and bought more darts. I won another toy and then another."

"Wow," I say. "The nameless girl must have been impressed with you."

"I forgot about her," he says. "I just wanted to throw darts at cards."

I laugh.

"I stopped staying with my grandparents when I was seventeen," he says. "And I've not thrown darts at cards since then, so I just wanted to see if I could still do it."

I struggle to hold up the giant, pink dog.

"Well you can," I say. "But what was with having two goes?"

"The darts they use aren't the same as the ones they have

in pubs," he says. "These guys on the stalls weight them so it's more difficult to win prizes. You think you're throwing it in a straight line but it will veer off to the left or the right. So you have to give them one go and throw them randomly just to see what they'll do."

"Aah," I say. "Sneaky."

We walk down a dark road. The dilapidated hotels look a lot scarier in the dark especially as the glowing lights of the seaside are now behind us. I speed up my pace as best as I can with a stuffed dog in tow. I fumble in my purse for my car keys. My finger finds Meryl. I pull them out and press the button. My car's lights flash. I pull open the driver's door and pull my seat forward. I stuff my handbag and the pink dog through the gap and it flollops on the back seat. I click the seat down and get in the car. Gregory looks at me. I shut the door and pull my seatbelt across me.

"I don't think you realise just how much fun I've had today," he says.

"I've had a really good time too," I say.

"Thank you," he says.

He leans towards me. I lean towards him. The seatbelt doesn't let me move. I nearly garrotte myself. Gregory releases the seatbelt. It slides across my body. He pulls me further towards him. He kisses me. A deliciously passionate kiss. I want to climb across the car and sit on his lap. I don't. But I want to. A couple of men walk past and scream obscenities at us. That spoils the mood. I pull away and laugh. I clip my seatbelt back in and start the car. I eject the cassette tape and turn it over.

"It's time for side two," I say.

20

"Do you want me to drop you off at home?" I ask Gregory.

"If it's not out of your way," he says.

I follow his directions and pull up outside his house. I turn off the engine. The air feels awkward. I laugh nervously. He looks at me.

"I, er," he says.

I turn my body to look at him.

"Do you, er," he says. "Do you want to come in?"

I look down at my lap.

"No, sorry," he says. "I shouldn't have asked. It's only our second date and I know girls have rules about things like that. Anyway, sorry, ignore me."

I look at him and smile.

"Girls might have confusing rules but I don't," I say. "However, I've got to pick Beryl up from my parents."

He smiles.

"It's ok," he says. "I understand."

"And I'm shattered," I say. "I would probably fall asleep as soon as I sat down."

I laugh. He doesn't believe me.

"Honestly, it's fine," he says. "Well thank you for today. You are well and truly forgiven for not coming out on Saturday night."

I laugh. He leans across and kisses me. I'm too tired to enjoy it.

"Drive safely," he says.

"I'll try," I say.

"I'll give you a call or a text soon," he says. "If you're free later this week and fancy doing something."

"Yeah sounds good," I say.

"Good," he says, kissing me again.

He gets out of the car. I pull the giant, pink dog into the front seat. I don't like driving alone at night. The dog might look like a passenger to unsuspecting murderers and they'll leave me alone. Gregory leans down.

"What's this one called?" he asks, patting the dog on the nose.

"You choose," I say.

"Cheryl," he says.

"Original," I say.

"Good night," he says, blowing me a kiss.

"Good night," I say, catching his kiss.

He shuts the door. I text Mum. I'll be round in five minutes. Can you please bring Beryl out. I'm too tired to get out of the car. X I drive to my parents' house. Mum stands by the door with Beryl on her lead. I pull up by the gate. Beryl pulls Mum towards my car. I open the passenger door. Beryl cowers between Mum's legs.

"This is your new friend," I say to her. "Say hello to Cheryl."

Mum picks up Beryl and puts her in the passenger footwell.

"Have a good time?" Mum says.

"Uh-huh," I say. "Tired."

"Ok, good night," she says. "Drive safely."

"Night," I say.

I pull away and turn my music up loud. I sing along loudly to keep myself awake. I stop the car opposite my house. It's eerily quiet. I pull my bag from the back seat, unclip Cheryl's seatbelt, drag her out of the car, put her on the roof and pull Beryl across so she can jump out of the driver's door. I lock the car and walk across the road, dragging both Beryl and Cheryl. I unlock my front door, barge my way in and let Beryl off her lead. I throw Cheryl into the hall. Beryl barks at her. I shut the front door and wander into the kitchen. I take a mug from the side and fill it with water. I drink it down in one go. The barking stops. I look out to see Beryl humping Cheryl's face.

"I knew you'd like her," I say.

I leave Beryl to enjoy herself and walk into my bedroom. My eyes sting. I can't keep them both open at the same time. I keep alternating my winking eye after a few seconds. I feel like a flamingo sleeping on one leg. I put the mug down on the windowsill and shut the curtains. I wriggle out of my clothes and leave them where I stand. I pull on my pyjamas and get into bed. With one eye open I text Mum. Home. Tired. Sleep.x

The envelope at the top of the screen reminds me I have a message from William. I text Louise. Phone back on silent. Busy today. Are you free tomorrow? Need your help. Sleep now. Text me back. I won't hear it.

I'm too tired to be overly coherent. She'll understand. I open William's message. I worked on it solidly for a day and it's finished! Are you free Friday so I can pass my work of art to my muse? Wx

A picture fills my screen. I can't really see it with the one eye I have open, mainly because it wants to close.

***

I wake up not remembering having fallen asleep. My phone is still in my hand. I accidentally push a button when

I put it on my bedside table. I have one new message from Louise. Have to work in the morning - boo. But can skive the afternoon - yay. Got some news. See you at two-ish. I don't reply.

I look for Beryl. She's not on my bed. I get up, pull the curtains open and walk out into the hallway. She's asleep on Cheryl's stomach. I tip-toe past into the kitchen. I open the back door and Beryl comes charging out. She runs around the garden like she's on speed. I have no idea where she gets her energy from. She spins around, chasing her tail and then collapses on her stomach. Her tongue lolls out the side of her mouth. She springs up and runs towards the tree and does her business in the shade.

I look around the garden at piles of her business and the yellow patches of grass that surround them. I really should clean those up. I carefully make my way to the shed and pull open the door. It smells musty in there, like a DIY store. I pick up a coal scuttle from just behind the door and the spade part from a broken shovel. I turn the scuttle upside down on the grass, and hit the base with the spade, to wake up any spiders that might be in there. It lets out a muted clang. I tentatively pick up the scuttle, hoping that all spiders and bugs and creepy crawlies have run away. I give it a shake just to be on the safe side.

A ninja spider scurries along the outside of the scuttle and across my hand. I throw the scuttle across the lawn and scream. I flap my arms around; rubbing my arms and legs to make sure the spider isn't on me. I run back inside, still flapping. I feel sick. It's in my nose. It's in my ear. It's laying babies. I poke my finger into my ear. I can feel it, walking around, making a home for itself. I shudder. I find a pair of trainers. I tip them upside down and bang the soles with the ball of my hand. No spiders fall out. It's still in my ear. I put my feet in my trainers and raise my right shoulder up to my right ear. If I can cut off the oxygen supply, the spider will die. I squash my head down on to my shoulder.

If it dies, I'll have a dead spider in my ear. Is that worse than a live spider? I go into the bathroom and take a cotton bud out of the cupboard. I run it under the hot tap and then poke it into my ear. I wiggle it around and pull it out. I don't dare look at it.

I hold it in front of my face. There's no spider on the end of it. I've pushed the spider further into my head. It's in there. I can feel it. I take a hair band off the shelf and pull my hair into a ponytail. The spider runs out of my ear and darts across my cheek. I flail my hands around my face. I swish my head from side to side. A couple of stray hairs float into the sink. They're mine.

I walk back into the kitchen. I open the cupboard under the sink and take out a pair of yellow rubber gloves. I twist them and bundle them into a ball in my hands to make sure there's nothing alive in there. I put them on and walk outside, poking a large, yellow finger into my ear every now and then. I pick up the spade and the scuttle and make an abstract dot-to-dot route around the garden, scooping up the dots as I go. There are a lot of dots.

The grass is getting long. I'll sort that out later. I open the dustbin and tip out the contents of the coat scuttle. A shower of *bump-bump-bump* hits the bottom of the bin. The smell makes me feel sick. I close the lid. I leave the scuttle and spade just by the back door. I don't want to go back into the shed. I walk inside and kick my trainers off. They skid under the kitchen table. I pull the gloves off and throw them at the sink. One lands on the draining board, the other flops on the floor. I'll sort that out later. Beryl walks in and sits by her bowl. I open a tin of some meat product disguised as beef in gravy. I spoon it into her bowl and mix in some biscuits. She picks up a few biscuits in her mouth and walks into the hall. She drops them on the carpet and slowly crunches her way through them. She then comes back in and does the same thing again. I pick up her bowl and put it down in the hall. She looks at me and walks away. I leave the bowl where it is.

I walk into the bathroom and turn the shower on and climb out of my pyjamas. I pick up my clothes. A spider runs out of my trouser leg and scurries towards a crack between the bath and the wall. I shiver and sweat. I close the toilet seat and crouch on top of the toilet, keeping my eyes on the crack. I jump from the toilet seat to the door. I put my pyjamas down and run into my room and pull on a dressing gown. I pick up my pyjamas and go outside. I shake them until my arms feel like they're going to fly out of their sockets. I peg them onto the washing line. Anything in there will definitely have to drop out eventually.

I hurry back inside, pick up the rubber gloves and pull them on. I go back into the bathroom and unravel a roll of toilet paper. I poke it into the crack between the bath and the wall. The room is steaming up from the shower. The toilet paper disintegrates in my hand. The crack is blocked. I take off my dressing gown and rubber gloves and climb into the shower. I quickly wash. I don't want to spend more time than I need to with that beast.

I wrap my dressing gown around myself and walk into the hall. I pull the bathroom door closed behind me. I walk into my bedroom and take a towel off the radiator rail. I wrap it around my hair and pile it up on my head. My ear gurgles. I shake my head. I walk into the kitchen and get a glass of water. I take it into my study. It's nearly ten past eleven. I've got loads of time before Louise gets here.

I put my glass on my desk and slide open the drawer to my right. I take out the plastic wallet containing the photos and papers. I pull a large piece of paper out. It's folded in half and then in half again. I carefully open it up. It creaks. The paper is very thick. There's a big, yellow stain on the back, where the folds meet in the middle. A small sliver of paper pings on to the floor. I lean down to pick it up. A few more pieces of paper fall off my lap. I slide off my chair and sit on the floor. I lay the large piece of paper in front of me.

It's covered in smaller pieces of paper that appear to have been cut from various letters. The handwriting on each piece of paper is different. I flatten everything out and pick up the escaped pieces from the carpet. I lay them on top of the larger piece of paper. Some of the ink has faded from the dampness of the bathroom cupboard but many are still legible. Evelyn, I am pleading; stop, stop immediately. I run my finger over the words. Harry is my husband, not yours. You can't have him. My eye scans the page. Your exploits are appalling and I'm losing everything because of you and Your sinful behaviour will be punished, mark my words and My family will never be the same and You have turned the once stunning Talbot's Theatre into a sordid den of disrepute.

What was she doing? What made these people so angry? I slide out the other papers. The doorbell rings. Beryl barks.

"Hang on," I shout.

I fold up the paper and put it back inside the plastic wallet, and put it in the drawer. I pick myself up off the floor and walk out of the study. I close the door behind me and walk to the front door. I pull it open and Louise rushes in.

"Is everything ok?" I ask.

"No it isn't," she says.

I close the door and walk into the living room. The dishevelled airing horses have both collapsed. I move them to the side of the room with my feet. I'll tidy up the clothes later. Louise lies down on the sofa.

"Drink?" I say.

"Water," she says.

"You know where the tap is," I say.

"I can't," she says, lolling her head to the side.

I walk into the kitchen and get Louise a glass of water. I walk out. Beryl drags Cheryl in to the living room by her leg. She stops in the doorway and starts humping her face again. I climb over both of them and pass the glass to

Louise.

"What's up?" I ask.

Louise sips her water. She looks like she's been crying.

"Have you been crying?" I ask.

"I don't know," she says, bursting into tears.

She sits up. I sit down next to her.

"I'm pregnant," she says.

"You're what?" I ask.

"I know," she says.

She cups her hands in her lap.

"How?" I ask.

"I know it's been a long while for you, but I think you remember how," she says.

I get up.

"There's no need to be like that," I say.

"I'm sorry," she says. "I'm just so confused."

I sit back down and put my arm around her shoulder.

"Is it Pablo's?" I ask.

"Marco," she says. "And yes."

"Have you told him?" I ask.

She shakes her head.

"You're the first person I've told," she says.

"Is that why you were calling me yesterday?" I ask.

"Yes," she says. "Where were you?"

"We can talk about that later," I say. "We just need to get you sorted out first."

She smiles and hugs me.

"Why didn't you call Safa?" I ask.

"You know as well as I do that she's an evil witch with a heart of stone," she says.

I laugh.

"It's not her fault she's Scottish," I say.

Louise laughs.

"How late are you?" I ask.

"A day," she says.

"A day?" I ask. "Is that all?"

"What do you mean 'is that all?'?" she asks.

"Well a day doesn't mean that you're pregnant," I say.

"So how many days do I have to be late to mean that I'm pregnant?" she asks.

"I don't know," I say, flustered.

"Come on," she says. "When you were pregnant, how many days late were you?"

"I've never been pregnant," I say.

"Exactly," she says. "So you don't know. A mother knows. A mother knows."

She starts crying again.

"It could just be stress," I say. "I mean, you've been having a few problems at work."

She shakes her head.

"A mother knows," she says again.

"Have you taken a test?" I ask. "Or been to the doctor?"

She shakes her head.

"Right, that's what we need to do," I say.

"We?" she asks.

"Well you came to me for help so I'm going to help you," I say. "Stay here."

I hurry into my bedroom and pull my towel off my head. My hair still isn't dry. I half-heartedly rub it with the towel. I kick the door closed and pull on some clothes. I lift up my arm and sniff my armpit. It'll do. I walk back into the living room, slide my feet into some flip flops and pick up my bag.

"I'm going to town and I'm going to get you a pregnancy test," I say. "Anything else you want?"

She shakes her head.

"Thank you," she says. "I owe you one."

"What, a pregnancy test?" I ask.

"You know what I mean," Louise says.

"Well we've got to sort my life out when I get back," I say.

She drops her head back on to the sofa. I hurry out the front door.

***

"Louise," I call out as I walk inside the house.

She doesn't answer. I look in the living room. Nothing. I look in the kitchen. The back door is open. I look outside. Louise is standing in the middle of the garden holding Beryl in her arms like she's a baby. She's bobbing up and down, pointing around the garden.

"And that's a tree and a birdy. And do you know what noise birdies make?" she says to Beryl.

"You're an idiot," I chirp.

Louise turns around.

"I was just testing it out," she says. "You know?"

"No, I don't know," I say. "Now put my dog down."

Louise leans down and Beryl jumps out of her arms. She runs indoors to get away from the crazy woman. I pull the pregnancy test box out of my bag and wave it at Louise.

"I don't need to go to the toilet yet," she says.

"Tough," I say. "You're going in there and you're going to wee on the stick, even if it takes you all day."

She snatches the box out of my hand.

"And shut the door this time," I shout.

She stomps to the bathroom like a teenager having been told to tidy their room and slams the door. I sit in the hall by my bedroom door. Beryl drags Cheryl into the hall and humps the living daylights out of her.

"How many sticks in that box?" I shout.

"Two," Louise says. "Why?"

"I think you might need to save one for Beryl," I laugh.

"It's not funny," Louise shouts.

"If I make you laugh, you might wee quicker," I say.

"I'm holding it in on purpose," she says.

"Come on," I say. "I've got things to do."

"Like what?" she asks. "What's more important than me?"

"Well, I thought for once that I could be the most important one," I say.

"Never," she laughs.

I hear the sound of water hitting water. A start stop tinkle.

"Eew," Louise shouts.

"What's wrong?" I say.

"I got some on my hand," she says.

"Well you're in the right place to wash it off," I say.

The toilet flushes and the door opens. Louise is standing by the sink, scrubbing her hands with more than enough soap. The blue, plastic stick is balanced on the edge of the sink.

"How long have we got to wait?" I ask.

Louise picks the box up from the floor and passes it to me. I scan the instructions on the back.

"Did you wee on the right end?" I ask.

"I weed all over the stick and all over myself," she says.

"Well I guess that'll do," I say.

I read the box.

"Ok," I say. "Three minutes."

Louise walks past me and makes her way to the kitchen. She pulls open the cupboards and fridge.

"Haven't you got anything to eat in this place?" she asks.

"What do you want?" I ask, leaving the stick in the bathroom.

"I don't know," she snaps.

"It's going to be alright," I say.

"They all say that," she snaps again.

"Who do?" I ask.

"People," she says. "You find out you're pregnant and single and the first thing people say is that it's going to be alright. Women have been having babies for millions of years and I'm sure there are more success stories than there are things that go wrong so statistically yes things are going to be alright. But you don't know. You don't know for a fact that it's going to be alright. You can't see into the future. You don't even know what's going to happen in the next five seconds."

She punches me in the arm.

"Ow," I say. "What was that for?"

"You probably thought that standing here, in your kitchen, that everything was going to be alright, but it wasn't. You got punched in the arm," she says.

"You punched me in the arm," I say, rubbing my arm.

"But you couldn't have predicted that," she says. "You didn't know what was going to happen. I've seen pictures. I'm going to get fat. I'm going to get stretch marks. I'm going to get saggy boobs. And then the baby might come out all deformed. It might not have all its fingers or toes or it might grow up to be a serial killer or …"

She drops her head and brings her hand up to her eyes.

"Or," she says. "It might be ginger."

She gasps and feigns sobbing. I roll my eyes, walk towards her and give her a hug. This is the longest three minutes of my life. I keep an eye on the microwave clock. I'm sure time is moving backwards. Louise wipes her nose on my top.

"Thanks," I say, wiping myself with kitchen towel.

She leaves the fridge open and walks towards the door.

"Time's not up yet," I say.

She sighs and leans against the door frame. I pick Beryl's bowl up and wash it out.

"Do you have to be so loud?" she snaps.

"Do you have to be so snappy?" I ask.

"I'm stressed," she says.

"And you think I'm not?" I say.

"Are you pregnant?" she asks.

"Are you?" I say.

She doesn't say anything. I dry the bowl and take some dog biscuits out of the cupboard. I put the bowl on the floor and sprinkle the biscuits in, in the hope that Beryl will leave

Cheryl alone. She doesn't. I look at the microwave clock.

"Do you want to look?" I ask. "Or do you want me to?"

"I'll do it," she says, walking towards the bathroom.

She stands in the doorway, holding the door frame.

"I can't do it," she says.

"Do you want me to?" I ask.

She nods.

"Mm-hmm," she says.

I bend down and walk under her arm. I kick the box towards her.

"So what should happen if you're pregnant?" I ask.

I pull off some toilet paper and pick up the driest end of the stick. She picks up the box and looks at the back.

"Two pink lines equals pregnant," she says.

"So what does three lines mean?" I ask.

She reads the box again.

"Two lines means pregnant. One line means not pregnant," she says. "But there's nothing about three lines."

"Must mean you're having an alien," I say.

She snatches the stick out of my hand.

"There's only one pink line," she shouts, throwing the stick at me.

I duck out of the way. The stick hits the window and drops into the bath.

"So you're not pregnant," I say.

"Those tests aren't a hundred per cent accurate anyway," she says.

"I know," I say. "A mother knows."

"Get out of the way," she says, walking towards me. "All this stress is playing havoc with my bladder."

I walk out of the bathroom and pull the door closed behind me. I sit on the floor and have a tug of war with Beryl, using Cheryl as the rope.

"False alarm. I'm not pregnant," Louise shouts. "Have you got any ...?"

"In the bag behind the bin," I shout back.

"Thanks," she says.

"Any time," I say.

The toilet flushes and Louise emerges with a smile on her face.

"So my problem has been solved," she says. "What's going on with you?"

"You're right," I say. "I haven't got any food in this place. Go and get some and then we can talk."

Louise sighs and pulls the front door towards her.

"Thank you," I say.

She pulls the door closed.

21

Louise bursts through the door with a couple of carrier bags.

"I didn't expect you to do my weekly shop," I say.

"This is lunch," she says.

I look at the clock. It's three fifty-six.

"Went to the bakery," she says.

She gives me one carrier bag. I take it and walk into my study. I sit at my desk. Louise sits on the armchair by the window. Beryl drags in Cheryl. I open my carrier bag and pull out a can of lemonade. I put that on my desk. There are four small paper bags in the carrier bag. I open one. It's a giant sausage roll. The next is a huge chicken salad sandwich. Most of the salad has fallen out and is sitting in the bottom of the paper bag. There is a glazed doughnut in the next bag, covered with pink icing and muli-coloured sprinkles. The final paper bag houses a large, almost the size of my face, cream filled Belgian bun.

"Which cake do you want?" I ask.

"They're both for you," she says. "I've got the same."

I take a bite out of the sausage roll. Pastry crumbles down my front. Beryl is enjoying herself too much with

Cheryl to notice.

"So?" Louise asks.

"Well," I say.

"Don't you mean 'Will'?" she laughs.

"Funny," I say, not laughing.

"Sorry," she says, opening up her sandwich and pulling out the tomato slices.

She holds them between her forefinger and thumb and wiggles her arm at me.

"Nu-huh," she whinges.

"They're not going to kill you," I say.

I reach out and take them. I squish them inside my sandwich.

I eat more of my sausage roll. I don't say anything.

"Am I going to have to beat it out of you?" she asks.

"I don't know where to start," I say.

"At the beginning is normally a good place," she says.

"Funny," I say, not laughing.

I open my can and drink.

"I went out with Gregory yesterday," I say.

Louise squeals.

"Tell me everything," she says. "Details."

I tell her everything.

"So where's the problem?" she asks, biting into her cake and squirting cream out of the sides.

"The problem is that I went out for dinner with William on Sunday afternoon and he's lovely too," I say.

"Oh no," she says. "Life must be so tough for you."

"It is," I say. "And William painted a picture of me."

"What?" she says. "That thing you sent me the other day?"

"It wasn't finished then," I say. "He sent me a finished picture."

"Let me see," she says.

I turn on my computer and plug my phone in. I transfer the file and open it up so it fills the screen.

"That's a pretty good likeness," Louise says. "I never wanted to say anything about that green growth under your chin, but I guess I don't need to now."

"That's a shadow," I say.

"I don't think so," she says, turning her head on its side.

"Be nice," I say. "It's sweet. He didn't have to do anything like this. But he did."

"Are you sure it's sweet?" she asks. "It might be a bit creepy."

"How so?" I ask.

"Well he spent the whole date looking at you and then he goes home and immediately paints you," she says.

"And?" I say.

"Well anyone who wants to look at you for that long and then paint you so he can see your face at home must have something wrong with them," she says.

"If you're not going to be helpful, don't bother saying anything," I say.

"Sorry," she says. "Seriously though, that is a pretty decent picture, considering he's only met you twice."

"I know," I say.

I transfer it to facebase as my profile picture.

"Has Gregory done anything like that?" she asks.

"Well he made that picnic in the park," I say.

"Not really the same thing," she says. "But that is romantic."

"I don't know which one to pick," I whine.

"Do you have to pick?" she asks. "Why can't you go out with both of them?"

"Because I wouldn't want that done to me," I say. "I'm really starting to like both of them and it isn't fair on either one."

"Especially as they're brothers," she says.

"Here's the thing," I say. "They're not brothers. Gregory said he only had a younger sister. No brothers."

"Well that's good," she says. "But it's odd that two

people had a grandmother called Beryl who they called Nana Bertie."

I slap my palm to my forehead.

"They must be cousins," I say.

"Oh yeah, I didn't think about that," Louise says.

"But neither of them mentioned having cousins living nearby," I say.

"You've only spent a handful of hours with each of them," she says. "You're not going to know their entire family history in that time."

I open the paper bag containing the doughnut. I eat it in three bites. I feel sick. Louise pulls me off my chair.

"Sit over there," she says, pointing to the arm chair by the window.

I move, taking my chicken salad sandwich with me. Louise sits at my desk. She opens up a spreadsheet. I can't see what she's typing.

"What's that for?" I ask.

"It's a pro/con list for both of them," she says.

"I can't write a pro/con list," I say.

"You're not writing one," she says. "I am."

I pull a piece of chicken out of my sandwich and put it in my mouth.

"So we'll start with Gregory," she says.

"Ok," I say.

"So the most important thing," she says. "Is he a good kisser?"

"That's the most important thing?" I ask.

"Yes," she says. "So?"

"Yes, he's a very good kisser," I say.

"Pro," she says. "What kind of job does he have?"

"What does that matter?" I ask.

"I need to know that you'll be taken care of, with treats and meals out and day trips and weekends away to European capital cities," she says.

"He owns and manages a gym," I say. "It's kind of a

private members club."

"Ooh, posh," she says. "So he has money?"

"I have money," I say.

"I know," she says. "But a woman deserves to be treated like a princess no matter how much money she has that she didn't earn herself."

"Hey," I say. "I'd give all the money away just to have Nan back again."

"I know," she says. "I'm sorry."

I eat more of my sandwich even though I'm not hungry anymore.

"So pro for money," she says. "But con for owning his own business. Long working hours. But pro as he can take time off whenever he wants. But con as it can be stressful."

"So is that pro or con?" I ask.

"Both," she says.

"Ok," I say.

"And if he's passionate enough about health and fitness to actually buy his own gym, he must be pretty fit himself," she says.

"Kind of," I say.

"And that brings us nicely on to looks," she says.

"I can't judge him on his looks," I say.

"Yes you can," she says. "You need an attractive man so that there's a fifty fifty chance that you'll have good looking kids."

"Oi," I say, taking a slice of tomato out of my roll. "Do you want this in your hair?"

"Is he taller than you?" she asks, ignoring my threat.

"You've seen him," I say.

"I wasn't really paying attention," she says. "I had to keep Safa out of trouble."

"Yep," I say. "He's about six foot two."

"So that's definitely a pro, for you and your abnormally long legs," she says.

"Do you want to keep insulting me?" I ask.

"Only if I have to," she says. "And is he good looking?"

"You saw him," I say.

"But do you think he's good looking?" she asks.

I think about it.

"Well," I say. "Yeah he is."

"You had to think about that," she says.

"Well he's not typical of guys that I find good looking," I say. "He's not ugly, but …,"

"Buuuut?" Louise says.

"But I can see why people would think he's good looking," I say.

"What's wrong with him?" she asks.

"He's a bit too clean cut for my liking," I say. "There's nothing wrong with that, but you know what a slob I am."

Louise nods.

"Oi," I say.

"You said it," she says.

"But you're not supposed to agree," I say.

"So looks goes in the con column," she says, typing.

"That's not fair," I say. "He's not bad looking."

"But he's not your type," she says. "Lookswise."

"Hmm," I say.

"Romantic?" she asks.

"Well he did give me that picnic in the park," I say. "And he invited Beryl and gave her biscuits. Not many men would want to go on a date with someone and her dog."

"True," Louise says. "So that's an automatic pro."

"Well …," I say.

"What?" she asks.

"Yesterday," I say. "We went out, and I know it was my date to say sorry for not going to see that band with him the other Saturday, but I paid for a lot of things."

"You've got the money," she says.

"I know that and you know that," I say. "But he didn't know that."

"Hmm," she says.

"I don't mind paying, you know that, and he did pay for some things but he didn't really offer for the things he didn't pay for, and I know he did the picnic and I didn't pay for anything, but we were out for the whole day yesterday and I did drive, but I know it was my decision to go there," I ramble.

"The world isn't like it used to be," Louise laments. "Women's Lib means that we now have to pay for ourselves. Men aren't allowed to be chivalrous anymore. He might have wanted to pay but didn't say anything because he didn't want to offend you. You know how crazy women can be."

"Yeah, some think they're pregnant when they're clearly not," I say.

"Men have to walk on eggshells around us," she says, ignoring me. "He may have had a pyscho ex-girlfriend who insisted on paying her own way. Give him the benefit of the doubt."

"Stupid Women's Libbers," I say.

"How old is he?" she asks.

"Thirty-two," I say.

"Finally someone who's older than you," she says.

I grin.

"And finally," she says. "Is he good in bed?"

"I don't know," I say. "We've only had two and a half dates."

"Well," she says. "Does he look like he'll be good in bed?"

"I don't know," I say. "You can't tell just by looking at someone."

"You can," she says, looking me up and down. "I bet you're useless."

"Thanks," I say. "Way to fill me with confidence."

"We'll just leave that blank," she says. "We can fill that in later."

I look at her.

"So that gives Gregory five pros and two cons," she says.

"So far, he's in the lead."

"I've got another con," I say.

"Oh?" Louise says.

"Well," I say.

"Come on," she says. "Spit it out."

I open my mouth and show her my chewed up sandwich.

"And you wonder why you've been single for so long?" she says.

"And now I've got two men who want me," I say, laughing.

Louise rolls her eyes.

"Well," I say. "You know I've always wanted to meet someone like they do in films?"

Louise nods.

"I met Gregory on a dating site," I say. "That's not how I imagined I'd ever meet someone."

"You can't be picky," she says.

"I know," I say. "Just put it in the con column. Just for now."

Louise reluctantly types.

"Well he's still five-three up," she says.

I nod.

"Now William," she says. "Same categories. Is he a good kisser?"

"Yes," I say.

"Sounds like there's a 'but' there," she says.

"But, he's got stubble and it's itchy," I say.

"So con for kissing," she says, typing.

"No," I say. "Apart from the stubble, the kisses are really nice. Put it in both."

"Ok," she says. "Job?"

"He's unemployed," I say.

"Con," she says.

"It wasn't his fault," I say. "He was unfairly dismissed."

"So he was sacked?" she asks.

"Yes, but it wasn't his fault," I say.

"You said that already," she says. "So what did he do?"

"He designed advertising for events, like posters and television adverts and fliers and things," I say.

"So he's a bit arty?" she asks.

"Yeah," I say.

"Well, he doesn't have a job" she says. "So that's a con, but he's arty and you like artiness so that's a pro."

"Ok," I say. "I can go with that."

"How tall is he?"

"About my height," I say. "Maybe a bit taller."

"Con," she says.

"Why's that a con?" I ask.

"Well, you can't wear your trainers when you walk down the aisle, and if you wear heels you'll be taller than him and that'll make the wedding photos look strange," she says.

"We've only been on one date!" I say.

"All marriages start with one date," she says.

Sometimes her logic is too flawless to argue with.

"Height, con," she says, typing. "Now, do you find this one attractive?"

I blush.

"That's a yes then," she says.

"He is more my type," I say. "I guess that goes along with being arty."

"Romantic?" she asks.

"Well we've only been on one date, and that was to a restaurant which is a bit obvious, but he did pull out my seat and he told me to order whatever I wanted and he paid for it even though he's unemployed," I say.

"That is pretty generous," she says.

"And I told him about Nan," I say.

"What did you do that for?" she asks, spinning around in her chair.

"Well he asked me if I'd had any luck finding a job and I said I didn't really need to find one and it kind of led on from there," I say.

"You could have always lied," she says.

"I don't like lying," I say.

"But you didn't have to tell him," she says. "Now you'll be wondering if he's actually interested in you or your money."

"Well firstly, I don't have that much money," I say. "And secondly, he paid for everything even after I'd told him about Nan. And I offered to pay half. And he still insisted on paying. And don't forget that he painted that picture of me. And he wants me to have it. That's pretty romantic."

"Ok," Louise says. "We'll put that in the pro column for now, but we'll have to keep an eye on that."

I tear off some chunks of bread and drop them on the floor.

"Beryl," I say.

She ignores me.

"Beryl," I say again.

She chews at Cheryl's ear.

"Well there's some food on the floor if you want it," I say.

"And how old is he?" Louise asks.

"Twenty-nine," I say.

"Con," she says.

"How is that a con?" I say.

"You always go for men that are younger than you," she says. "That is when you do actually go for men. And you always end up breaking up."

"I've broken up from guys who were older than me too," I say.

"But there have been more younger than older," she says. "Which makes it a risk zone."

"Ok," I say. "And one final pro. We met how people meet in films."

Louise laughs.

"Come on," I say. "Beryl tangled his legs up in her lead.

That's how many a romcom romance has started."

"And as in all romcoms, something goes horribly wrong," she says.

"And then it all works out and they live happily ever after," I say.

"Films and real life aren't the same thing," she says.

"You don't know that," I say. "You've just not met anyone who's happened upon love in such a way."

Louise looks at me.

"Put it down," I say.

She types.

"And again, I bet you don't know if he's good in bed," she says.

"Of course not," I say. "We've only had one proper date."

"So William has five pros and four cons," she says. "Which makes Gregory the clear winner."

"How?" I ask. "They both have five pros."

"But Gregory only has three cons. William has four," she says.

Beryl plods over and scoops the bread pieces into her mouth. She walks back to the other side of the room and shares them with Cheryl.

"Oh if only life was that easy," I say.

"You'd rather spend your time humping a giant, pink dog than going out with two lovely men who want to be with you?" she asks.

"Sometimes, yeah," I say.

"You're a strange one," she says.

"I know," I say.

"Well, I can't help you," she says. "But you're going to have to make your mind up pretty quickly if you're sure you don't want to carry on dating both of them."

"You know I don't do decisions," I whine. "You choose for me."

"I can't," she says. "But I know someone who can."

"Who?" I ask.

She looks at Beryl.

"She's met both of them, right?" she asks.

"Yep," I say.

"What did she think?" she asks.

"Well Gregory gave her bones, so she's going to like him," I say. "And she tried to kill William."

"Well there's your answer," she says.

22

"I've got an early start in the morning," Louise says, shuffling towards the front door.

"You mean you're actually going to work tomorrow?" I say.

"Eventually," she says. "I've got a pedicure first thing. Now that I'm not pregnant anymore, I've got to get myself back out dating."

I laugh. She does a twirl.

"Sorry for earlier," she says. "It was hormones or something."

"Right," I say.

I open the door and she steps out. Beryl is too busy with Cheryl to notice.

"Let me know your decision," Louise says. "When you finally make one."

"When have you ever known me to make a decision?" I say.

"True," she says, and walks down the path.

I shut the door. I walk into the kitchen and open the back door. Beryl looks at me and then at Cheryl. She plods outside and does her business. I pick up Cheryl. One of her legs is hanging by a thread. I get a pair of kitchen scissors and perform an amputation. I put both parts on the worktop. I'll sew them up later. Beryl comes in. She sniffs the ground looking for Cheryl.

"She's just had to go to the hospital," I tell Beryl. "It's only a small operation. She'll be fine."

Beryl paws at her ball but is unimpressed. I lock the back door and pull the curtain across. I walk to my bedroom, turn the light on and walk out. I go into my study and pick my phone up from my desk. Louise's pro/con list sits in the printer tray. I pick it up. I can't make my mind up based on how tall they are or how old they are. I take the page with me and drop it on my bed. I sit down, partially crushing the paper. Beryl jumps on the bed and snuggles into my thigh. I wake up my phone and look at William's last message. No-one apart from my dad has ever painted a picture of me. I think it's romantic, no matter what Louise thinks. I smile.

I reply to his message. That's amazing. I am impressed. I can't wait to see the real thing. Friday is good for me. What time? Where?

I lean over my bed and reach for the charger cable. I push the metal end into my phone. It won't go in. I turn it over and push it in. It won't go in. I turn it over again and push it in. It won't go in. I get frustrated. I turn it over one more time and push it in. It won't go in. I hold the phone and the end of the cable close to my eye and slowly try to put it in. I realise that it's my camera charger cable. I throw it on the floor and pick up the right cable. That slots in to my phone with ease. I let my phone fall from my hand on to the pile of books by my bed. I turn the light off, close the curtains, get undressed and put on my pyjamas. I lie down and close my eyes.

I'm on the judging panel. I look to my left and right but I'm the only person sitting behind the desk. I have two giant red buttons in front of me. I don't dare press either one. Gregory walks on to the stage. He's wearing a skin tight, black leotard. The audience cheer. I look behind me. There's no-one there. He does a dance across the stage, jumping and spinning and pirouetting and doing the splits mid-air. He stops where he started, frantically waving his jazz hands. The audience applaud. I look behind me. There's no-one there. I look at the stage. William is there. I look for Gregory. He's gone. William does the same dance as Gregory. He stops where he started, frantically waving his jazz hands. The audience applaud. I look behind me. There's no-one there. I look at the stage. I'm at home watching myself on the television. The presenters face the camera and explain that I have to make a decision about which act I want to send through to the live final. They tell me that the atmosphere is tense in the studio. The camera returns to me. I can see myself. I move close to the television screen. I see my hand hovering over the buttons. One is William. One is Gregory. The camera shows the stage. Both men stand in huge Perspex boxes with seaside grabber game claws hanging above them. The presenters look down the camera and explain that once I've made my decision, I have to press the button of the one I want to send through to the live final. The claw will drop and pick up my choice. He will be lifted up and removed from the box. The one I don't choose will have to stay in the box forever. The camera returns to me. My eyes move from left to right to left to right. I look around for some help. The lights are off. The presenters have gone. I close my eyes and slam my hand down on one of the buttons. It makes a horrible noise like a police car siren. It's so loud. It doesn't stop. Someone turns the lights on. I can't see who I've chosen. There's a white glow that fills every piece of everywhere. I can't see anything. I put my hand over my eyes. The siren keeps going. I can't hear anything. I run. I trip.

I fall out of bed. My knees hit the carpet but they could have been hitting concrete. I cry out but I don't make any noise. My torso slides slowly, dragging the duvet with it. I curl myself up under the mound of material. Beryl digs her way in. My mouth is dry. I poke my head out. There's no cup there. I cough and unwrap myself from my burrito casing. I stand up. My knees buckle. I pull up one pyjama trouser leg. A bruise has started to form. I hobble to the kitchen. The floor is cold. I stand on the mat by the sink and turn the tap on. Red and blue lights flash from behind the roller blind. I pull it up. An ambulance is parked in the middle of the road causing a traffic jam. I turn the tap off. I put my hands on the edge of the sink, lean forward and push my face up to the window, avoiding impaling my eye on my cactus farm.

A paramedic, in a green onesie, wheels a stretcher out of one of the houses opposite. It looks like there is someone on it but I can't make out who it is. Not that I know anyone who lives along my road. I really should make more of an effort. Whoever it is, they're not in an industrial bin bag so I guess that's a good thing. People are coming out of their houses. There are already a few people loitering on the pavement. They should mind their own business. The paramedic puts the stretcher in the back of the ambulance and slams the doors shut. He gets in and the yellow van zooms off down the road. The people stay outside, looking at each other. Hands contain gasps of sympathy.

I open the fridge. No milk. I pull a box of cereal out of the cupboard and dig my hand inside. I eat the raisins, banana chips and dried apple fragments, and drop the brown flakes back in to the box. I wander into my study and sit down on my desk chair. Beryl follows me in, sniffing the ground. I crumble a few flakes in my hand and sprinkle them on the floor. She eats a couple then jumps on to the armchair by the window. She rests her chin on the arm. She looks forlorn.

"What should I do today, Beryl?" I ask.

She lets out a puff of air. I remember the dismembered Cheryl sitting on the work top. I take my box of cereal back out to the kitchen and put it away. I pick up all of Cheryl's parts and carry her into the living room. The collapsed clothes horses are still on the floor. I'll sort them out later. I put Cheryl on the coffee table. I open the cupboards at the base of the Welsh dresser for Nan's sewing kit. I pull out road maps to places I've never heard of, folders full of my bank statements, a couple of out of date calendars; one from two thousand and two and the other from nineteen ninety-six, a Christmas biscuit tin containing batteries of various shapes and sizes, a navy blue fluffy slipper, a packet of unopened sheer nude tights, a jam jar full of old coins, a stack of photo frames housing the generic smiley family pictures that are in there when you buy them, and in the last cupboard, an ornate sewing box.

I sit on the floor and put the box on the coffee table. I carefully open the lid. Spools of different coloured thread nestle in their own little compartments. Three metal thimbles roll around in a larger compartment, with a needle threader and a slightly unravelled tape measure. A crumpled paper bag of odd buttons is squished into one of the compartments with thread. I pull out the cotton looking for something that resembles the fluorescent fuchsia of Cheryl's fur. The closest match is a red so that will have to do. I'm sure Beryl won't notice. I put it on the coffee table.

I pull out the top layer and put that on the coffee table. The bottom of the box is a mess. A darning mushroom sways its stem from side to side. I pick up a small circle of needles. They're not needles. They're pins. I find needles in a small plastic container. I put the box of needles next to the thread. I curiously look at the other things in the bottom of the sewing box. A small pair of scissors, a folded up doll's dress pattern, some safety pins attached to a piece of white material and a folded up photograph. I unfold the photograph. It's extremely old and feels like it will split in four parts, where the folds have been forced. I lay it on the table. It's a black and white image of a woman. There's something familiar about her face. She's standing side on, but her face is towards the camera. She's wearing a rather revealing dress. Even though it's long and reaches the ground, there is a very long slit up the side and she's poking her leg out so that her whole leg, from ankle to thigh, is exposed. She's also wearing stockings, a suspender belt and high heeled shoes. She's holding a large feather fan in her right hand. It covers her torso. Her other arm is up in the air. I look closely at the face. Why does she look so familiar?

I leave the photo where it is, and put everything that I don't need back in the sewing box. I unroll a length of cotton and rip it from the spool. I tie a knot in one end and put the other end in my mouth. I lick it to a point and aim it at the eye of the needle. I wink, hold the needle steady and move the thread towards the hole. It goes through first time. I pull the thread through and start to sew the leg closed on itself. I push the stuffing in and close the gaping hole. I tie the cotton off and throw the leg behind me. Beryl picks it up and carries it on to the sofa. She grips it in her teeth and flings it around her head. She makes sure it's well and truly dead before using it as a pillow.

The photo catches my eye. I hate not knowing who it is. She looks so familiar but there's something not quite right about the image. I carefully slide the photo onto my hand and flip it over. There's nothing on the back. I turn it over.

"Who are you?" I say.

The photo doesn't say anything. I put it back on the table. I rethread the needle with a longer length of cotton. I put Cheryl under my arm and hold her leg gash closed. Stuffing keeps popping out. Sewing this bit is more difficult than her actual leg. I sew it shut but I know Beryl will chew it open in no time. I put the needle and thread back in the box and leave it on the coffee table. I pick up the photo and take it into my study. I put it in a plastic wallet and lay it on my keyboard.

"Who are you?" I say.

The photo doesn't say anything.

"Useless," I say.

I go back into the living room. Beryl has chewed Cheryl's leg gash open and is pulling out the stuffing. I pick Cheryl up and put her on top of the bookcase. I pull my duvet cover, undersheet and pillow cases off the airing horses. I carry them to the airing cupboard and stuff them onto a shelf. I go back into the living room and bundle up my clothes. I lean the folded airing horses against the wall. One falls over. I'll pick that up later. I drop my clothes on to my bed.

I wander into my study. I look at the clock. It's nearly ten past eleven. I touch the photo of the scantily clad woman. I tilt it to see if I can get a better look at her face. I put it to the side. I open my desk drawer and take out the papers from the back of the bathroom cupboard. I look for the picture of my nan. Dad's still got it. I know this woman isn't my nan. They're not the same person. Everything is different; face shape, hair colour, smile, the way they carry themselves. It's obviously not her.

I look at the man in the suit. He's standing in a similar position to the sewing box woman. I look at her. I look at him. Although the woman's face has been distorted slightly because of the condition of the photograph, there is a similarity between the two. Something in the eyes. I cover her mouth and nose with my left hand. I cover his mouth and nose with my right hand. Their eyes are eerily similar. Twins, or at least siblings.

I put them all in the drawer and turn on my computer. I open the imaginatively titled file, book, and look at my novel. Barely even five thousand words. My great idea clearly doesn't have legs. I spin around in my chair and look at my books.

"How did you get all your ideas?" I ask.

My house is very quiet today.

"And once you got your ideas, where did you find the time to write them down?" I ask.

Maybe I should stick to writing short stories. I close my novel and open a blank page. I write a story about a man who buys a car, but at the same time his friend gives him a car. Both cars are nice and comfortable to drive and look shiny and new. He only has a one door garage so he knows he can't keep both cars. He really likes the car he bought himself, but the one his friend gave him is a classic. He would love to keep them both but he knows he has to sell one. He can't make a decision.

I laugh and push myself away from my computer. I'm hungry. I have a quick shower and pull some clothes on. I put Beryl's collar on her, clip the lead to it, pull Cheryl from the top of the bookcase and bundle them all in the car. I drive to my parents' house. Mum is in the front garden pulling out weeds from her flowerbeds. Dad is sitting on a chair drinking a cup of coffee.

"Why did you pull that flower out?" Dad says to Mum.

"What flower?" she asks.

"That one," he says. "The pink one that you just pulled out."

Mum runs her hand through the pile of weeds lying beside her on a bin bag. She holds up a scrawny plant.

"Yes that one," Dad says.

"That's not a flower," Mum says. "It's a weed."

"Well I don't know," Dad says.

"No you don't know," Mum says. "That's why you're over there and I'm over here. If I left this to you, I don't know what I'd end up with in my flower beds."

Beryl jumps over me as I open the driver's door. She runs straight towards Mum and rolls around in the mud. I clamber out of the car, dragging Cheryl behind me.

"Got another date?" Mum shouts.

"No," I say.

"So to what do we owe this pleasure?" Dad asks.

"Can't a daughter come and see her parents for no reason?" I say.

"They can," Mum says. "But what do you want?"

"I'm hungry and I haven't got any food," I say.

"So you thought you'd come and eat us out of house and home," Dad says.

"So I thought I would drop Beryl off here for a bit so she wouldn't be left alone and I could go and do some shopping," I say. "But if you're offering to feed me, I'm not going to say no."

"No-one was offering to feed you," Dad says.

Beryl jumps on his lap and leaves muddy paw prints all over his trousers.

"What's that?" Mum asks.

"Cheryl," I say. "Don't you remember? She was sitting in the front seat the other night when I came to pick Beryl up."

"That's right," she says.

"She had a bit of an accident," I say. "I was wondering if you could sew her up."

"Couldn't you do it?" she asks.

"I tried," I say. "But Beryl undid all of my hard work."

Mum stands up, drops her gardening gloves on the ground and reaches her arm out to grab Cheryl.

"Be careful," I say. "You might want to wear gloves. This is Beryl's new love interest."

Mum takes Cheryl by the ears and carries her indoors. Beryl sits by Dad's feet. He takes a dog treat out of his pocket and pops it in her mouth. He doesn't think I notice. I do. I get back in the car. I start the engine and push the tape into the player. I sing. Dad waves at me. I smile and wave back. I drive to the supermarket and park uncomfortably close to a car that has been selfishly parked over two parking spaces. I open my door. My car is a couple of inches inside the line. I get out, satisfied. I root around in my purse for a pound coin and unlock a trolley. I push it across the car park and walk through the giant automatic doors.

The supermarket is cold. It's not too busy. I walk through the fruit and veg. I lean on the push-bar and stop by the lettuce. I pick up an iceberg. I put it in my trolley. I pick up a cos. I look at it. I lean over my trolley and pick up the iceberg. I look at them both. Both lettuces, both nice, both extremely similar but with minor differences which don't really matter in the greater scheme of things. I like them both. There's nothing wrong with having them both. I won't eat them both at the same time with a meal. I prefer cos with tuna mayo salad. But I like iceberg in cheese and piccalilli sandwiches. I put them both in my trolley. There's nothing wrong with buying two types of lettuce.

I push the trolley along the aisles, only stopping at brightly coloured boxes and tins that are in buy one get one free offers. I lay two boxes of apple and cinnamon instant porridge, two tins of tuna, two fajita making kits, two vegetarian pizzas, two packets of mini chocolate bars, two tubs of coleslaw, two blocks of mild cheese, two bottles of ketchup, two trays of dog food, two jars of tomato and basil pasta sauce, two bags of fusilli pasta, two tubes of toothpaste, two rolls of clingfilm, two tubs of ice-cream and two different but also similar lettuces on to the conveyor belt. The cashier beeps the barcodes across the scanner. She doesn't say anything. She doesn't look up. I stuff my food haphazardly into carrier bags. She scans quicker than I can pack. I dump the carrier bags in the trolley and look at the cashier. She still doesn't say anything. I put my card in the chip and pin machine.

"Cashback?" the cashier asks.

"No thanks," I say.

She presses a button on her till. She turns her head away and fiddles with some carrier bags to make it obvious that she's not looking at me or my pin number. I press the number keys and then the green button. She puts her hand on a cocked hip and waits for the receipt machine to spew out the paper. She pulls it off and passes it to me.

"Thanks," I say.

She doesn't say anything. I push my trolley towards the front doors, holding my breath as I pass through the security gates. It doesn't beep. I'm free. I get back to my car. A woman is clumsily climbing into the car next to mine through the passenger door. I open my boot and load in my carrier bags. The woman reverses out of her space and stops just behind me.

"I couldn't get into my car," she shouts.

"Ok," I say.

"You parked too close," she shouts.

"You parked over the white line," I say.

"You could have parked anywhere else in the car park," she shouts.

"And you could have parked within the designated parking space white lines," I say.

"I had to climb through the passenger side. I ripped a hole in my tights," she shouts.

"Because you parked over the white line," I say.

"If you'd had a passenger, they wouldn't have been able to get out," she shouts.

"I didn't have a passenger though," I say.

She drives off shouting obscenities. I close my boot and take my trolley back to the trolley-park. I push the chain into my trolley and my pound coin pops out. I walk back to my car, get in and drive back to my parents'.

They're all inside. I leave the dog food in the car. I struggle to the front door with the shopping. I knock on the door with my foot. No-one answers. I put down the shopping and knock. No-one answers. I open the letterbox and look in.

"Hello," I shout.

Beryl starts barking.

"Where's Nanny and Granddad?" I ask.

She jumps up at the door. I see some legs walking down

the stairs. The door opens. Mum stands there wearing yellow rubber gloves and sweating. I cringe.

"Toilet's blocked," she says.

Beryl jumps over the shopping and claws the bags.

"Why are you bringing that in here?" she asks.

"I bought all the buy one get one free offers," I say. "I don't want it all."

I walk inside. Dad walks down the stairs holding a broken plunger.

"Nice to see you've bought some food to replace the stuff you and Louise eat whenever you're here," he says.

I struggle with the bags into the kitchen.

"Thanks for the help," I say.

I dump the bags in the middle of the floor. I put one box of porridge in the cupboard along with one of the fajita kits. I take out a tube of toothpaste and a roll of clingfilm, and put them on the side. I put one block of cheese and one tub of coleslaw in the fridge. I look at the rest of the food. I'll keep that. Dad walks in from outside carrying a mallet and a crowbar.

"Ooh, toothpaste and clingfilm," he says. "You've outdone yourself here."

"There's some cheese in the fridge and some porridge and a fajita kit in here," I say, opening the cupboard door.

"Hmm," he says, walking past me.

"I'm going to go," I say. "Before the ice-cream melts."

"Where's our ice-cream?" Dad asks.

I shrug. Mum puts Beryl's collar on her and clips on the lead. She opens the door and I walk out.

"Thanks for taking care of Beryl," I say.

"It's no problem," Mum says. "We love having her."

I open the boot and put the carrier bags back into the car. I close the boot and open the driver's door. Beryl jumps in and makes herself comfortable on the passenger seat.

"Take care," Mum says.

I wave and reverse out of the driveway.

23

I think about William and Gregory. I force myself to believe that I'm not doing anything wrong and that I don't need to make a decision right now. I pull up outside of my house and park on the other side of the road. I really should build a driveway. I'll put that on my 'to do' list. I pull my handbag over my head. It hangs across my body. I check over my shoulder for traffic and get out of the car. I lock Beryl in the car and quickly take the carrier bags from the boot and run them across the road. I put them on my doorstep and run back to the car. I get Beryl out and lock the car. I hurry her across the road and unlock my front door. I unclip Beryl's lead, open the door and she runs inside. I pick up the carrier bags and struggle in after her. I shove the door closed and drop the bags. I put my handbag on the floor and kick off my shoes. Beryl jumps up at me. I unbuckle her collar. She sniffs at the door.

"What's up?" I ask her.

She looks at me.

"Oh, Cheryl!" I say. "We'll have to get her next time we're at Nanny and Granddad's."

Beryl lies down by the door. I pick up the carrier bags

and take them into the kitchen. I shove the pizzas and the ice-cream into the freezer and leave the rest on the side. I'll sort that out later. Something's missing. The dog food. It's still in the car. I'll get that out later. I'm hungry. I open the cupboard and pull out an oven proof dish. I pour some pasta into the dish and cover it in pasta sauce. I give it a stir. A few bits of pasta jump out and hit me in the stomach. I kick them under the oven and wipe the red sauce off my front. I grate some cheese over the top and put the remainder in the fridge, along with the coleslaw. I take out a beef tomato from the fridge and give it a bit of a squeeze. It's very ripe. I shut the fridge door and put the tomato on the chopping board. I slice the tomato with a bread knife and put the slices on top of the pasta. I shake the cheese grater over the floor and watch the yellow confetti fall. Beryl eats it up. I stir the pasta, mixing in the tomato slices and the grated cheese, and put it in the oven. I turn the oven to two hundred degrees and set the timer for forty minutes. I put the rest of the shopping away and walk into the living room. Beryl follows me.

I pick up the remote control and turn on the television. An enthusiastic American woman is talking about "'erbs" and "scallions" and "skillets". She chops something and throws it into a pan. It hisses and bubbles. The camera moves in and shows a close up image of the food. I think about William. I think about Gregory. William. Gregory. William. Gregory. Wigory. Grelliam. I drop my head back. I pick up the remote control and flick through the channels. I don't pay attention to anything. I can't make a choice. I can't. My mind can't focus on anything. I walk into the kitchen. There's still twenty minutes until my food's ready.

I wander. I walk around the kitchen, out into the hall, up and down the hall, into my bedroom, around my bed and back again, back into the hall, into my study and I stop. I look out of the window. Nothing's happening outside. I turn around. Nothing's happening inside. I walk back into the hall and pick up my handbag. I reach in and pull out my phone. I drop my bag on the floor. The Cyclops eye is winking. I press a button to wake up the screen. I have one new message from William. *I've got to go to the job centre on Friday morning – oh joy. Should be finished at about half 11. If you don't mind being seen in that part of town, do you fancy meeting me there? You can pick up your painting and we could get some lunch if you want. Wx*

I walk into the living room and sit down. I smile. I'm excited. Maybe I should choose William. We didn't meet on the internet and he's romantic and sweet and he paints. And we didn't meet on the internet. I can't make my mind up now. I'll see how it goes on Friday. I don't want to rush the decision and make the wrong one. I reply to William's message. *I might have to wear a disguise but I will meet you at the job centre. But you will owe me big time for forcing me to be seen in public there. See you tomorrow.*

The timer beeps. I put my phone on the coffee table and walk into the kitchen. I put on my Father Christmas oven glove, open the oven and take out the dish. I close the oven door, put the dish down on the hob and find a clean plate. I grab a serving spoon from the hook on the wall, scoop out a couple of spoonfuls of pasta and dollop them on the plate. I open the fridge and take out a can of lemonade. I close the fridge door with my foot, find a clean fork and pick up my plate of food. I walk into my study and put my plate down on my desk. I switch my computer on and look at the clock. It's nearly ten past eleven.

I sit down and stick my fork into the pasta. I bring the fork up to my mouth, stretching out a globule of cheese, and blow on the food. I eat it. It's hot. I open the can of lemonade and drink. Beryl plods in and sits in the armchair by the window. She rests her head on the arm of the chair and closes her eyes. I eat some more pasta. My computer screen flickers to life. I go on the internet and watch videos of dancing cats, and dogs rescuing children from the sea, and talking birds, and sneezing pandas, and a cappella choirs singing cartoon theme tunes, and breakdancing toddlers, and men miming to Euro-pop songs, and people doing flash mobs in supermarkets, and teenagers falling off skateboards, and men who take a photo of themselves every day for a year just to see if they change. They don't.

I check facebase. I don't know why though. Rachel has posted new photos to the album My New Bum. I won't look at that. Max i h8 telly y's their nuffin on. I sigh. Safa - another day, another dollar, another dirty old man's bed to clean. That's more than enough information.

I look at the clock. It's nearly ten past eleven. It feels like I've been sitting here longer. I take my plate out to the kitchen and put it on the side by the sink. I really should do some writing. I walk back into my study and sit at my desk. I open the document entitled book. I scroll to the end of the text and start a new paragraph. The main character is an old woman now. She's outlived her husband, and although she misses him, she doesn't want to miss out on life. She refuses to be one of those miserable old women who sits in front of the television all day and shouts at you if you call them when one of their programmes is on. She's carefree, a go getter, an adventurer, a forward thinker. She takes chances and risks and doesn't think about the consequences. She's confident and brave and blasé. She doesn't sit around and mope and whinge and complain. She doesn't procrastinate, that's for sure. She's cheery and feisty and sometimes a little bit rude, but people let her get away with it because she does it with a wink and a smile. She never says 'back in my day' because every day is her day. She wears bright pink and orange and blue and dances to the muzak in supermarkets and sneaks five pound notes into her grandchildren's hands when their parents aren't looking.

She books herself on an old people's Mediterranean cruise. She goes on her own. She meets men and dances with them in the on-ship ballroom. She lets them buy her a drink and walk her back to her cabin but she never lets them kiss her, not even on the cheek. She promised her husband 'til death do us part, but in her heart she would feel like a cheat if she did anything with any other man. She still wears her wedding ring but on her right hand. She tells inquirers that she's far too young to think about settling down. They laugh.

She doesn't share a room. She likes being able to spread herself out in a double bed. Sometimes she likes to walk around naked but she doesn't tell anyone that. She sits alone at meal times and doesn't invite anyone to share her company, but she doesn't decline if someone asks if they can sit with her. She likes to watch people. They fascinate her. She keeps a notebook and a mechanical pencil in her handbag and sometimes makes sketches of the most interesting looking people.

Her children worry about her. Or to be more precise, they worry that she's spending their inheritance. She knows what they think of her but she doesn't care. She's worked hard for her money and she's going to enjoy it while she's got the chance. She's happy.

I lean back in my chair and push my keyboard away from me. I wish I could be like her. Maybe I will be when I'm older. Maybe when my husband dies, it will be a wakeup call telling me that life is far too short and that I should grab every opportunity with both hands. Maybe I'll be sitting by his death bed in a sterile, unfriendly hospital with machines beeping either side of him, and tubes running in and out of him, and he says something but I can't hear him, so I move my head closer to his face and with a croaky voice he tells me to never forget him. I promise that I will think of him every day and that I'll love him forever. He'll cough and I'll hold his hand, and he'll tell me not to cry which will make me cry even more, and he'll tell me not to mourn. He'll tell me to enjoy my life and I'll tell him that I won't be able to enjoy it without him. He'll struggle to breathe and I'll hold my breath and he'll close his eyes and nurses will rush in and everything will move in slow motion and I'll cry out and someone will hold me and everything I've ever known will disappear in a split second and doctors will shout and machines will beep and curtains will close and I'll fall to my knees and my mind will go blank.

Maybe I'll be sitting in my bedroom on the morning of the funeral and I'll look at his side of the bed and the unruffled bed clothes and I'll think of him in the hospital and I'll think of him before he got ill and I'll cry a little but I'll stand up and walk over to my dressing table and I'll take a red scarf out of the drawer and tie it around my neck. And I'll open my wardrobe and take out a red handbag and put on a red pair of shoes and I'll walk downstairs and my whole family will gasp and I'll watch his coffin disappear into the ground and I won't say 'goodbye'. I'll say 'see you soon'.

I start to cry. I take a deep breath. I'm getting upset about a life that I don't even have. I don't have it because I don't have a boyfriend let alone a husband. I save what I've written and close the document. I don't want to write any more.

My phone beeps. I have one new message from William. You're getting an awesome painting. Isn't that enough? Wx. I laugh. I reply. Throw in some ice-cream and I might forgive you for forcing me to wait outside the job centre. I feel better. I open my document and look back at my story. I read through what I've just written. It's not bad. I like it. My phone beeps. I have one new message from William. Just be thankful that I'm not forcing you to wait for me inside the job centre. Have you seen those questionable stains on the sofas? Wx. I laugh. I have seen those questionable stains. I reply. Good point. I'll definitely meet you outside.

I'm not tired but I don't want to do anything. I shut down

my computer and walk into the bathroom. Something in the bath catches my eye. It's Louise's pregnancy test. I unravel some toilet paper and hold it in my hand. I lean over the side of the bath and drop the toilet paper onto the stick. I scoop it all up and quickly put it in the bin. I scoop out the bits of dried cardboard box and drop them in the bin. I put the plug in the bath and turn on the hot tap. I close the toilet seat and sit down. The room fills with steam. I relax. I open the bathroom cupboard. I'm the mood for indulgence and take out the purple bottle of shower gel body wash. I put the bottle on the side of the bath and turn on the cold tap.

I walk into my bedroom, get undressed and pick up my dressing gown. I walk back into the bathroom, shut the door, drop my dressing gown and climb into the bath. I turn off the taps, lie back and rest my head. I close my eyes and sink my body down as far as it will go.

The water goes cold. I don't want to get out. My fingers are wrinkled and my toes are numb. I pull the plug out with my toes and place it on the side of the bath. I watch the water level go down. I get out and wrap myself in my dressing gown. I open the door and walk into the kitchen. I'm hungry. I scoop out one spoonful of pasta into a bowl and put it in the microwave. I press the Auto Reheat Meal button then the Start button. The microwave whirs into action. I open the back door. Beryl rushes out, runs around the garden and does her business under the tree. She runs back in. I lock the door and pull the curtain across.

The microwave beeps. I put on my Father Christmas oven glove, open the microwave and take out the bowl. I pick up the fork I used earlier and walk into the living room. I turn on the television. A man is screaming at another man. He wants to know where his daughter is. The second guy doesn't say anything. The first guy grabs the second guy around the throat and pushes him into a wall. The first guy punches the second guy in the jaw. Blood seeps from between his lips. The first guy yells in his face. He wants to know where his daughter is. The second guy laughs. He parts his lips and shows blood smeared teeth. Red drops dribble from his chin. The second guy speaks in an extremely wooden Russian accent. He tells the first man that he's going to kill the first guy's daughter and then he's going to kill him. The first guy punches the second guy again.

The door of the warehouse explodes open and a group of men wearing masks and carrying machine guns run in. More men jump out from behind crates and boxes. They shoot at each other. Bullets fly and men fall until only one man is left standing. Or indeed crouching behind a collapsed shelving unit. He points his gun out and follows with his face. He looks left and then right and jumps out from his hiding place. He creeps through the maze of dead bodies. He hears a noise behind him. A man covered in blood slowly lifts up his arm. His hand shakes under the weight of the gun he's holding. He aims it at the first man. The first man shoots his gun. He's out of bullets. The dying man pulls the trigger on his gun. The first man dives out of the way of the bullet, reaches into his sock, pulls out a knife and throws it. It moves in slow motion through the air and lands directly between the dying man's eyes.

Someone slowly claps. The only alive guy after the shoot-out turns around. A fat man stands at the top of a metal staircase. He takes a cigar from the inside pocket of his coat. He puts it in his mouth and lights it with a match that he takes from his trouser pocket. He flicks the still lit match down the stairs. It somersaults in the air and eventually burns out. It drops at the feet of the first man. He looks at the match and then at the man at the top of the stairs. The man at the top of the stairs laughs. The man at the bottom of the stairs asks him where his daughter is. The man at the top of the stairs tells him that he'll never see his daughter unless he gives him a hundred million dollars. He has twenty-four hours to get the money. The fat man's phone rings. He puts his hand inside his coat and takes out his mobile phone. He presses a button and puts the phone to the side of his head. He speaks in Russian. There are no subtitles. He puts the phone back in his pocket and looks at the man at the bottom of the stairs. He tells him that he has twenty-three hours. The fat man laughs and turns to walk away. A gun is fired. The fat man falls backwards. He tumbles down the stairs. Blood trickles out of the hole in his forehead.

A wonderfully coiffured woman stands at the top of the stairs wearing ripped, dirty and bloody clothes. She has a smear of grease on her left cheek. She calls down to the man at the bottom of the stairs. He has to hurry up. They haven't got much time. She knows where his daughter is.

The adverts start. I don't care where his daughter is. I turn the television off and take my empty bowl into the kitchen. I walk into my study and pick up my phone. I walk into my bedroom and throw my phone onto my bed. I put on my pyjamas and climb into bed. Beryl jumps up beside me. I reach out for my phone and open a new text message. *I'm sorry for the short notice but could you look after Beryl tomorrow? I'll bring her round at about eleven-ish. Thanks.x* I send the message to Mum. I turn my phone on silent and put it on the floor. I set my radio alarm clock to go off at nine o'clock. I lie on my back and close my eyes.

***

A man abruptly shouts a weather report into my ear. It's going to be sunny with the chance of showers. I reach my arm out from under the duvet and fumble to switch the radio off. Silence. I reach my arm down to the floor and pick up my phone. I have one new message from Mum. *Of course. We love having her. See you tomorrow.* I pull myself up and out of bed, and open the curtains. I walk to the kitchen, open the back door and Beryl runs outside. I pour a sachet of microwave porridge and some milk into a bowl and put it in the microwave. I set the timer to two minutes and press the Start button and then stand by the back door.

Beryl barks at the birds sitting on the washing line. I call her in. She ignores me. I leave her to it. I look at the mess in the kitchen. I'll sort it out later. The microwave beeps. I put on my Father Christmas oven glove and take out the bowl. I take a spoon out of the cutlery drawer, sit down at the kitchen table and eat. I lean to look outside. It's cloudy but the sky is blue. It doesn't feel too cold. I stand up and lean against the door frame. Beryl rolls around in the grass. I scrape my spoon around the bowl to get at the last bits of porridge which are stuck to the side. I turn around and put my bowl in the sink. I call to Beryl to come in. She does. I shut and lock the back door.

I walk into the bathroom, get undressed and climb into the shower. I do what I have to do in the bathroom and then I go into my bedroom. I quickly dry myself off and find some clothes. I put on a pair of jeans and a white t-shirt. My feet find their way into a pair of trainers. I buckle Beryl's collar around her neck, pick up a cardigan, put it into my handbag along with my phone, clip the lead to Beryl's collar and walk out of the house. I pull the door closed behind me and I walk to my parents' house.

Dad is standing in the front garden holding a digital camera to his face.

"Hello," I say.

"Hello," he says, not moving the camera.

"What are you doing?" I ask.

"I'm trying out some new paints," he says.

"Looks like a camera to me," I say.

"Funny," he says. "I'm taking some pictures of clouds for reference, but the camera isn't working or something because when I look at the screen, the pictures are all dark and blurry."

I walk up to him and take the camera out of his hand.

"It sometimes helps if you have the camera the other way

around," I say, handing the camera back to him.

He looks up to the sky and presses the button on the top of the camera. He pulls it away from his face and looks at the screen.

"Oh," he says. "Aren't you clever?!"

"I must have been adopted," I say.

"So what was I doing?" he asks.

"Taking close up pictures of your nose," I say.

Mum comes out of the front door. Beryl runs up to her. I pass Mum the lead.

"Thanks for this," I say.

"It's no problem," she says. "We love having her, don't we Tom?"

"Nyuh-huh," Dad says, leaning his head back with the camera pushed up against his face.

"What are you up to today?" Mum asks.

"Another kind of date," I say.

"Ooh," Mum says.

"I'll pick Beryl up this afternoon," I say.

"Aren't you going to tell me anything else," she says.

"I love you," I say.

"I meant about your date," she says.

"I can't tell you anything," I say. "It hasn't happened yet."

"That's not what I meant," Mum says.

"I know," I say. "See you later."

I turn around, walk through the gate and make my way into town.

24

I sit on the wall outside the job centre. A couple walk up and loiter on the pavement drinking from lager cans. I avoid eye contact and pull out my phone. It's only eleven twenty-three. I put my phone away just in case I get mugged. The couple each squash their cans in their hands and throw them on the ground. I try not to look but I can't help it. The man catches my eye. He burps at me and laughs. The woman laughs. She doesn't have any front teeth. They walk past me and through the job centre doors. I choke on the smell that they leave outside.

The door opens.

"Ready?" William asks.

"Yeah," I say. "Are you ok?"

"I just want to get out of here," he says.

"You're not the only one," I say.

We walk off. We don't say anything to each other. He slips his hand into mine. I like it. We walk out of town.

"I'm sorry," he says. "But that place just gets me, you know."

I nod and smile.

"Thanks for meeting me," he says.

"Well I can't wait to see this painting," I say.

He stops walking. He turns to me and kisses me. His stubble isn't as scratchy as I remember it. We walk.

"I just can't believe the people in there have managed to get jobs," he says. "They're so stupid. Surely you have to take some sort of literacy test before being allowed to use a pen and write things in front of other people. I mean, how can they not know the difference between AC-cept and EX-cept? I wanted to rip the pen out of her hand, stab her in the face with it and then rewrite everything. I had to sign my name to that statement."

"Don't even get me started on things like that," I say.

"I'm sorry," he says.

"There's no need to apologise," I say.

"But they look at me like I'm some sort of uneducated inbred bumpkin just because I haven't got a job," he says. "As I came out, this couple walked in and they looked like they didn't know how to say ten words between them, let alone know how to spell them. The guy couldn't even tie his own shoelaces."

He looks at his shoes. I look. No laces.

"Are you sure you know how to tie laces?" I ask.

He laughs.

"It just takes me a while to unwind after I've been in there," he says.

"It's ok," I say. "Honestly."

"You're sweet," he says.

"Rant away," I say. "I'll be your ear to bash."

He squeezes my hand.

"I'd just like to know the screening process for applicants there," he says. "Do you just turn up and grunt at them and they give you a job."

"Do you want to know a secret?" I say.

"Go on," he says.

"Promise not to tell anyone," I say. "I'm not proud of this."

"Ok," he says.

"I used to work at the job centre," I say.

He lets go of my hand. He stares at me.

"I'm afraid we can't see each other anymore," he says.

I turn to walk away. He grabs my arm. I turn around. He smiles.

"I've thought about it long and hard and I think I can get past this," he says. "But it's going to take some time."

"I understand," I say. "Thank you."

He laughs and kisses me.

"How did you end up there?" he asks.

"I was unemployed for such a long time and a job came up to work in a call centre. It didn't say where, but I applied anyway. Ages later I got called for an interview at a hotel. There were loads of other people there and we were like on a conveyor belt; one in, one out. I had my interview in one of the hotel's bedrooms," I say.

"Ah, one of *those* interviews," he says, winking.

"No," I say, shoving him into the road.

He laughs.

"I then found out it was for the job centre, and not actually for a call centre," I say.

"Strange," he says.

"I know," I say. "I got offered the job, and as you know, if you're offered a job, no matter how much you don't want it, you have to take it. So I went to the induction and I was sat in a room with a bunch of morons. We were actually taught how to be rude and ignorant."

"Were you taught how to be stupid?" he asks.

"No, most of them brought their own bag of stupid along, and kept dipping in there throughout the training courses," I say. One girl didn't know where she lived or what a lighthouse was."

I laugh.

"I wish I could say that I was surprised," he says. "But I'm not."

"It was painful," I say.

"How long did you work there for?" he asks.

"Two whole months," I say.

He laughs.

"How did you manage to escape?" he asks.

"I don't know how it happened, but I got offered a job in an office that I'd applied for ages ago," I say. "Apparently, the person they hired didn't turn up. And I am eternally grateful for that."

"Well I'm glad that you managed to get out safely," he says. "And have lived to tell the tale."

"It was traumatic," I say. "But I think I'm over the worst of it."

He puts a sympathetic arm around my shoulder.

"Nearly there," he says.

We cross the road.

"It's getting to the point now where I'd take any job, no matter how awful it is, just to get out of going to the job centre every week," he says.

"Well you're not there now," I say.

"I know," he says.

He puts his hand into his pocket and pulls out a bunch of keys. He stands outside a red door.

"Ok, just to warn you, excuse the mess," he says. "I just don't want to shatter the illusion of me being a lazy, good for nothing, unemployed bum."

"As long as nothing starts moving of its own accord," I say.

"I can't guarantee that," he says.

I laugh. He unlocks the door and pushes it open.

"After you," he says.

I walk in and fall over a tandem bike leaning against the hallway wall.

"Mind the bike," he says.

I look up at him from the floor. He leans down and pulls me up.

"Fancy a ride?" he asks.

"I can't ride a bike," I say.

"You don't seem like you're too good at walking either," he says.

He laughs.

"Perhaps you'd better go first," I say.

He squeezes past me. I hold on to his shoulder. I climb over piles of magazines and slalom around washing machine innards.

"Unfinished collage projects," he says. "And unfinished sculpture projects."

"Ah," I say.

We walk through the hall and turn into the kitchen.

"Can I get you a drink?" he asks.

The kitchen looks like mine. Piles of things everywhere.

"No thanks," I say.

He walks over to the freezer and pulls the door open. He slides one of the freezer drawers towards him.

"Ice-cream?" he asks.

I look in. The draw is full of boxes of rocket lollies and cones and choc ices and fruit splits and ice-cream sandwiches, and tubs of different flavours.

"Wow," I say.

"Well I wasn't sure what you liked," he says.

"You bought all of these for me?" I ask.

"Not just for you," he says. "I like rocket lollies."

I look down at my feet and smile. I'm going to choose William.

"Maybe in a bit," I say. "I just want to see the painting first."

"Ok, ok," he says.

We walk through a door at the end of the kitchen. I step down into a conservatory. It's very cool. The windows are covered in sheets of newspaper. Stacks of canvasses lean up against the walls. The floor is soft with decorators' sheets. There are bags of spray paint cans overflowing in all corners of the room.

"So where is it?" I say, excitedly.

He walks over to a large sheet covering what I assume to be a canvas. He stands next to it. It must be about five foot square. I point at it.

"Is this it?" I ask, excitedly.

He pulls the cloth from the back and lets it drop to the floor at the front.

"What do you think?" he asks.

I am speechless. It's amazing. The photos he sent didn't do it justice.

"Say something," he says. "Please."

"I'm sorry," I say. "I just can't put it into words how amazing it is."

"I thought you were supposed to be the one who's good with words," he says.

"So did I," I say.

My hands find a home on my cheeks. I walk backwards and take in the whole picture. It looks like me in every way.

"You are so talented," I say.

He smiles at me.

"So you like it?" he asks.

He walks towards me and I throw my arms around his neck.

"No, I don't like it," I say. "I love it."

I kiss him.

"This is so special," I say. "Is it a bit narcissistic if I hang it in my bedroom?"

"Not at all," he says. "I'm so glad you like it."

He stands behind me and wraps his arms around me. He puts his face into my neck. I can feel his breath on my skin. I nuzzle back in to his body.

"I love it," I say, leaning in and looking at the painting closely.

"How are you with travelling on the bus?" he asks.

"Fine," I say. "Why?"

"Well unless you fancy trying to get this bad boy to your house on the back of a tandem, I think we're going to need to lug it on the bus," he says.

"Good point," I say.

"I've got some bubble wrap upstairs," he says, running out of the room.

I take another step back. I can't wait to get it home. There's a knock at the door.

"Can you get that," William shouts from the top of the stairs.

I walk to the front door, carefully avoiding the tandem and turn the door knob. I pull the door towards me. William runs down the stairs, long jumps over a pile of papers and stands next to me with his arm around my waist.

"Hey," William says. "What do you want?"

The man says nothing.

"Where are my manners?" William says.

I look at the ground. I squeeze my eyes shut. I don't think I cry. I hope I don't.

"This is my cousin, Gregory," he says, looking at me. "And this is …"

"I know who this is," Gregory says, turning around and walking away.

"What?" William says.

I move in slow motion. I want to stay with William but I want to run after Gregory.

"I'm sorry," I say to William. "Please, let me explain."

"Well I wish someone would," he says.

"Just give me a minute," I say, running out of the door and along the pavement.

"Gregory," I shout.

He doesn't turn around. He keeps walking. I catch up with him and pull his arm. He stops walking. He doesn't turn around.

"What were you doing there?" he asks.

I open my mouth to speak but nothing comes out.

"And why did he have his arm around your waist?" he asks.

"I'm sorry," I say.

He turns around.

"Why are you sorry?" he asks. "What have you done that you need to be sorry for?"

He knows. I look down. I open my mouth to speak.

"Don't bother," he says.

"Please let me explain," I say.

"What is there to explain?" he asks.

All words escape me.

"I'm waiting," he says.

"I didn't mean for this to happen," I say.

"You mean that you didn't mean to get caught," he says.

I don't say anything. He has the right to be angry with me.

"I met you first," I say.

"And is that supposed to make me feel better?" he asks.

"No," I say. "I just meant that I met you on purpose and, well, meeting William was more of an accident."

"What does that even mean?" he asks. "At least get your story straight in your head before you spout incoherent lies at me."

"I'm not lying," I say.

"But you're not being truthful either," he says.

"I am," I say. "But it's complicated."

"Ah yes," he says, "Complicated. Women love that word. They normally use it when they can't make their mind up about what they want."

I don't say anything. Nothing I say is going to make things any better.

"Just tell me," he says.

"What?" I ask.

"Have you slept with him?" he asks.

"No," I say, looking him in the eye.

"So why were you there today?" he asks.

I take a deep breath. I don't want to lie to him.

"He painted a picture of me," I say. "I was just there to pick it up."

I look back at the ground.

"I didn't mean to …," I say.

"What?" he says. "You didn't mean to keep dating both of us at the same time, especially when you found out we knew each other?"

"No," I say.

"Just don't bother," he says. "Go on, run back to William and your painting."

"Gregory," I say.

He walks away. I cry. I didn't mean for any of this. I walk back to William's house. My painting leans against the wall next to the closed front door, wrapped in bubble wrap. I knock on the door. It opens. William is holding his mobile to his ear.

"Hi," I say.

"You've got your painting," he says. "What more do you want?"

I don't say anything.

"Look, don't bother trying to explain," he says. "I'm talking to Gregory now."

He waves his phone at me.

"I didn't mean for this," I say.

"Yeah yeah, tell someone who cares," he says.

He pushes the door. I put my hand up to stop it closing.

"What?" he says.

"Can I just explain?" I ask.

"No," he says, and pushes the door closed.

25

I stand on the pavement, awkwardly holding the painting. An old man with a walking stick hobbles up to me.

"Everything alright?" he asks.

"Yes, I'm fine, thanks," I say.

"You don't look too fine," he says, passing me his handkerchief from his top pocket.

"No, honestly," I say. "I'm fine, but thank you."

I wipe my eyes with the back of my hand. I've been crying.

"Well do you at least want a hand with that?" he asks, pointing to the painting.

"No, thank you," I say. "I can sort it."

"It's no bother," he says. "I can ask my neighbour. He's a strong young man. He can help you carry it to your car."

He walks towards William's front door. I panic.

"Thank you," I say. "But I don't have a car. I'm just going to call a taxi. But thank you."

"Suit yourself," the man says, opening his front door.

I pull my phone out of my bag and call a taxi. I ask for a large car that can carry a five foot square canvas. It'll be about fifteen to twenty minutes. I wait.

***

The taxi driver helps me get the canvas out of the back of the car. He leans it up against my wall. I pay him. I struggle to the front door and let myself in. I lean the canvas up against the hall wall. I text Mum. Can you please keep Beryl til tomorrow. I just need some time on my own. I switch my phone off and put it in my bag.

I drag myself into the kitchen and open the freezer. I hate being a cliché but I want ice-cream. I touch the tub of triple chocolate fudge. I look at the tub of strawberry and vanilla cheesecake. I pick up the cheesecake ice-cream, take off the lid and sit it on the side to melt. I take a spoon out of the cutlery drawer. I really need a cutlery tray. I should write that on my 'to do' list. I'll do it later. I pick up the ice-cream and take it into the living room. I put the tub and spoon on the coffee table.

I walk into my bedroom and pull my duvet off the bed. I drag it behind me into the living room. I sit on the sofa and wrap the duvet around me. I pick up the ice-cream and spoon. It hasn't melted enough. The spoon won't go in. I turn on the television. A lion is eating a zebra. It rips the flesh from the body like it's tissue paper. The lioness climbs in and wraps her paws around the zebra's neck. It looks like she's hugging him. She rips a chunk out of its neck. I flick through the channels. I don't even see what's on. My thumb keeps pressing the remote control button but all I can see is Gregory's face when I open William's door. I feel like the me from my dream the other night where I'm watching myself. I'm not actually there. It isn't actually me. It's just a television show. Everything in the television isn't real. The lion doesn't really eat the zebra. It's only television.

I pick up the tub of ice-cream. I can't see the spoon. I'm crying. The tears blur my vision. I reach out and grab at the coffee table. I knock some things on the floor. I don't care.

My hand finds the spoon. I scoop it through the softened ice-cream and direct it to my mouth. I sob.

How can I have been so stupid? This is why I don't do things. This is why I sit at home with my computer and my dog and I don't get involved in life. This is why I ignore the door unless I'm expecting someone. This is why I order my shopping online. Things are simple. But once you start talking to people and going out and doing things, that's when it all gets complicated. I don't deal well with complicated. I'm not used to it.

I look at the television. A soft spoken woman tells me that if I have constipation I should take her magic tablets. A walking tablet, carrying an axe, cuts poos that won't shift. I'm glad I didn't pick the chocolate ice-cream. I change the channel. An over enthusiastic man wants me to buy his super blender that converts into a mega abs workout machine. I don't want that. I want things to go back to the way they were. I want to be jealous of Louise going out on date after date. Maybe even a bit bitter. Maybe even cry myself to sleep night after night because I'm so lonely and alone and no-one will ever want me. I want to feel scared of dying alone once Beryl leaves me. I want to listen to sad songs that remind me of people I love that don't love me. I want to pretend that I'm too busy with work or my writing and that's why I'm still single. I want to write about love and romance and project myself onto the main character. I want to feel frumpy and unattractive. I want to feel absolutely anything other than what I'm feeling now.

I can't believe I hurt two wonderful people. I can't believe I couldn't be honest with them from the start. If only I hadn't joined that stupid dating site. I never wanted to do it in the first place. I did, but I didn't want it to turn out like this. If only I'd busied myself with something other than the internet. Stupid internet. It ruins so much.

I sob and eat and sob and eat and eat and eat and sob. I feel sick. My spoon hits the cardboard bottom of the tub. I scrape out the last of the ice-cream and drop the tub and spoon on the floor. I lay my head back on the arm of the sofa. Every part of me hurts. I want to sleep. I want to sleep the past couple of weeks away. Couple of weeks. Ha! Why am I upset about a couple of weeks? I only knew them for a couple of weeks. It's not like I was actually in a relationship with either of them. So I couldn't have cheated on either of them. So why are they so angry with me? It's not like either of them wanted to make it official. It's not like we talked about anything like that. So where's the problem? If they wanted to date other girls, I wouldn't mind. I would mind. I'd hate it. I'd hate it even more if it was with someone I was related to. What have I done?

I don't know what's on the television. It's just noise. Noise and pictures that don't mean anything to me. I close my eyes and cry until I can't cry anymore, until I end up sounding like a child throwing a tantrum.

***

I wake up. It's dark. The television is still on. I don't know what's on. I get up and find my bag. I pull out my phone and turn it on. I wait for it to start up and hold my breath. I have one new message. My heart drops. It's from Mum. What's happened? Are you ok? I reply. I'm fine. Tell you about it when I pick Beryl up. I open a blank message. I don't type anything. I want to talk to them. I want to explain. I want to know how they're feeling. I just want to explain. I type. I'm sorry. I delete it. Please can we talk? I delete it. Can all three of us meet? I delete it. Bad idea. Very bad idea. I'm sorry. I know I don't deserve it but please give me the chance to explain. I select Gregory's and William's numbers from my list of contacts and click send.

A lump forms in my throat. I feel drunk. I open the fridge. There's a beer at the back. I get the bottle opener out of the cutlery drawer and open the bottle. The cap pings off. I can't see it. I take a sip. It doesn't taste very nice. I take my phone and the beer into the living room. I flop down on the bundled up duvet. It's so soft. If I don't move, I will be in a pure state of comfort forever. I burp. The comfort disappears. I press buttons on my phone to wake up the screen. No new messages. I text Louise. It's all over. The phone falls out of my hand. I laugh.

I turn the volume down on the television to ten. Everything sounds loud at night. A group of naked men and women ride bikes through the streets of a town somewhere to join a naked bike riding rally. I feel sick. I change the channel. A fast-speaking man is frantically painting someone's bathroom walls with a roller coated in vomit coloured paint. People behind him are trying to fix a cabinet on to the wall. It falls and the mirror smashes. The frantic man makes a joke about bad luck. He's not funny.

I run to the bathroom. I pull up the toilet seat and sit on the floor. I drop my face into the bowl. I gag. I smell beer and ice-cream. I don't want to smell that. I cry. I'm not sick. I let myself drop to my back. The tiles are cold on my arms. I pull a towel off the rail and scrunch it under my head. I pull another one down and cover myself with it. My stomach gurgles. I don't want to leave the room. Just in case.

My leg spasms. I bite the inside of my cheek. I jump up. The pain is too much. I fall against the sink. I don't open my eyes. I stretch out my leg. I'm so cold. I shiver. I sneeze. My foot clenches. My toes twist. I lift my foot and reach down. I rub the sole of my foot. I dig my knuckles into the arch. I put my foot down on the tiles and stand on tip toes. It hurts. It hurts so much. I walk to my bedroom. I push my hands up against the door frame and stretch my leg out behind me. My calf muscle tightens. I fall to my knees and crawl along the carpet. My leg feels hot. I climb on to my bed. There's no duvet. I cry. I wrap my dressing gown around myself.

***

I wake up. I'm lying diagonally across my bed. My neck aches. My pillows are on the floor. I'm tired. I don't want to lie down anymore. I get up. I walk to the living room. I get my phone out of my bag. I've got one new message from Mum. You're not fine. Tell me what's wrong. I reply. Everything's gone wrong. Can you keep Beryl for a while. I just need some time to sort things out. Not in the mood to talk. I text Louise. Come round. I need to talk. I sit down on the sofa and lay my head back. I shut my eyes.

***

"Hey, hey, wake up!" a voice shouts.
Something pounds against the living room window.
"I can see you!" the voice shouts.
I drop my head to the side.
"Open the door, I need to wee!" the voice shouts.
It's Louise. I get up and open the front door.
"You look terrible," she says.
She barges past me and walks to the bathroom. She shuts the door. I shut the front door. The sun is too bright. The toilet flushes. Louise walks out of the bathroom doing up her trousers.
"What's happened now?" Louise asks. "Found another perfect man?"
I cry. She walks towards me and wraps her arms around me. I blubber into her neck.
"It can't be that bad," she says.
"It's not," I say. "But it feels like it."
"You get yourself in the shower and I'll try and get some food together," she says.

"I'm not hungry and I don't feel like having a shower," I say.

"Well you need to eat and you smell disgusting," she says. "So get in there."

I look down at myself. I'm still wearing my clothes from yesterday. I lift up my arm and have a sniff. I don't care. She pushes me towards the bathroom. I peel my clothes off and dump them on the floor. The shower feels wonderful. I don't want to get out. Tiny fingers dance over my skin. It's so relaxing. Louise bangs on the door.

"Come on," she says. "You can't stay in there all day."

I get out and wrap a towel around myself.

"What's this?" Louise shouts.

I poke my head around the bathroom door.

"What's what?" I ask.

She points to the canvas.

"It's me," I say.

Louise is pulling the bubble wrap off the painting.

"So this is the painting?" she says.

"So it seems," I say.

I walk into my bedroom and shut the door. I find some clean clothes and put them on.

"It's actually pretty good," she shouts. "Considering it's you."

I open the door. The painting is staring at me from the other end of the hall.

"Cover it up," I say. "Or turn it around. I don't want to look at it."

I walk into the kitchen.

"Where's Beryl?" she asks.

"At my parents'," I say. "Where's my food?"

"I didn't think you were hungry," she says.

"I changed my mind," I say.

Louise takes a bowl out of the cupboard, finds the box of cereal and pours out a flurry of flakes.

"Where's all the fruit?" she asks, looking in to the bowl.

"I ate it," I say.

She pours on some milk and passes me the bowl.

"Voila!" she says.

"Thanks," I say.

I take a spoon out of the cutlery drawer and walk into the living room. Louise follows me.

"So why are you in such a grump?" she asks.

"I'm not in a grump," I say.

I sit on the sofa and pull the duvet around me.

"I know you're lazy," she says. "But this isn't like you."

She pulls the duvet off me and drags it out of the room.

"Hey," I shout.

"Do you need me to buy you a pregnancy test?" she asks, walking back into the living room.

"I wish," I say.

I spoon a mound of flakes into my mouth. Milk dribbles down my chin. I wipe it with my sleeve.

"You wanted me here," Louise says. "If you're going to be all cryptic, I'm going to go. You know I can only do the celebrity crosswords."

I put my bowl on the coffee table.

"They found out," I say.

"What?" she says.

"Yep," I say.

"Who?" she asks.

"William and Gregory," I say.

"When?" she asks.

"Yesterday," I say.

"How?" she asks.

"It's a long story," I say.

"As long as your book?" she asks.

I look at her.

"Tell me," she says.

I tell her. She looks at me.

"But they're men," she says. "They're not supposed to get attached that quickly."

"I wouldn't know," I say.

"Take it from me," she says. "Men hate it when women are clingy or they want something serious too soon. They always want to keep it casual."

I pick up my bowl. The cereal flakes have turned to mush.

"There has to be something more to this," she says.

"Like what?" I say.

"I don't know," she says. "Some sort of sibling rivalry, maybe."

"But they're not siblings," I say. "They're cousins."

"Cousling rivalry then," she says.

"That's not even a word," I say.

"If you can say it and can understand what it means, it's a word," she says.

Flawless logic. I put the bowl back on the coffee table.

"All I'm saying is that it sounds a bit off," she says. "You've only known them a couple of weeks, if that, and they both dump you because you went out with each of them twice. Most men wouldn't care. And it's not as though you'd made anything official. No-one was your boyfriend and you were no-one's girlfriend."

"I know," I say. "But it doesn't stop me feeling bad."

"You just need to forget about them," she says.

"I can't," I say. "I really liked them."

"You liked the attention," she says.

"When have I ever liked attention?" I say.

"You don't like to admit you like it," she says. "But you do."

"Do I?" I say.

"Yes," she says.

"And since when did you qualify to become a practising psychoanalyst?" I ask.

"It's just obvious," she says.

"Why?" I ask.

"How long has it been since you last had a date?" she

asks.

I don't say anything.

"And how long has it been since you flirted with someone, like a shop assistant or a bus driver?" she asks. "Just a smile or a laugh or an eyelash flutter or a hair twirl."

I laugh.

"I can't remember you ever doing anything like that," she says. "But I know you've wanted to. I know you've wanted to have those stomach flipping feelings that make you feel alive for a few seconds."

"It's never bothered me," I say.

"Stop lying to me," she says. "You're not very good at it."

I look at her.

"So to have two men, two really nice men, giving you those stomach flipping feelings all the time, after so long without them …," she says.

"You don't have to go on about it," I say.

"I just mean, you must have liked it," she says. "Anyone would have liked it."

"Ok, I liked it!" I shout. "So what?"

"I just mean that you didn't do anything wrong," she says.

"So why do I feel like I do?" I ask.

I feel like I'm going to cry.

"Things happen, and things don't always go how we would have wanted them to go," she says. "But it's how we deal with them that matters. You can sit around all day eating ice-cream and feeling sorry for yourself, or you can forget about them and move on."

I don't want to forget about them and move on.

"It's like this," she says. "If they liked you, really liked you, then they would have let you explain. At least."

"Hmm," I say. "Maybe."

"But they didn't even want to listen to you," she says. "So move on. Find someone better."

I smile.

"Preferably only one at a time this time," she says.

"I think I want to give men up," I say.

"No you don't," she says. "What you want to do is get back on the horse or the bike or whatever it is and find another man. Remember, you have to kiss a lot of frogs before you find your prince."

"Swallow a book of clichés?" I ask.

"Look, you asked me here to help," she says. "So I'm helping. I could be at work, but no, I'm here, for you, like you were here for me the other day."

"I know," I say. "I'm sorry."

She smiles.

"It's not as bad as you think," she says. "But the sooner you move on, the better you'll feel."

"Are you skiving another day off work?" I ask.

"It's only a day," she says. "It doesn't matter. Safa's covering for me again."

"But you've already had a warning," I say.

"It wasn't really a warning," she says. "More like a suggestion."

"A suggestion?" I say.

"They suggested that I stop having so many days off," she says.

I stand up and take my bowl into the kitchen.

"Fancy a pizza?" I ask.

"Yeah," she says. "Got a menu?"

"I went shopping the other day," I say.

Louise stands in the doorway and feigns a faint.

"Funny," I say.

"Do you even know how to use your oven?" she asks.

"Be nice to me," I say. "I'm suffering."

"You're annoying is what you are," she says. "Now cook."

"Sir, yes Sir," I say, saluting.

I open the freezer and pull out a vegetarian pizza.

"That's not a pizza," Louise says. "Where's the meat?"

I pull out the box of microwave burgers and wave it at Louise.

"Definitely not," she says. "I know I eat a lot of rubbish, but I have no idea how you manage to eat those."

"So pizza it is," I say.

Louise shrugs. I turn the oven to two hundred and put the pizza in. I set the timer for fifteen minutes. I look up. Louise has gone.

"Louise!" I call out.

She doesn't say anything. I look in the living room. She's not there. I look in my study. She's sitting at my desk and my computer is on.

"What are you doing?" I ask.

"Finding you a date," she says.

"What?" I ask.

"Nothing serious," she says. "Just someone who looks like they'll be fun, someone who can take your mind of this mess, someone you can go out with once and never see again."

"But what if I like them?" I ask.

"You won't," she says.

"So what's the point?" I ask.

"Things don't always need a point," she says. "But you need to get used to just going out with men. Just. Going. Out."

I sit in the armchair by the window.

"Wow, you've got twelve new messages," she says.

"From who?" I ask.

"From whooooom," she says.

I don't say anything.

"It doesn't matter from whom," she says. "We're starting afresh. We're going to find the guys. They're not going to find us. It's our choice who we go out with."

"Us?" I say. "We?"

"You," she says. "You."

I nod.

"I thought you weren't interested," she says.

"I changed my mind," I say.

She laughs.

"Ok, let's get started," she says. "First thing is to delete all of these old messages."

"You can't do that," I say.

"I've already done it," she says.

I slump down in the armchair.

"Now who do we have here?" she says.

26

"How about this one?" Louise asks. "markyboy216."

"What's he like?" I ask.

I can't really see the screen from where I'm sitting. I can't be bothered to move.

"He's quite good looking," she says.

"My good looking or your good looking?" I ask.

"Probably more mine than yours," she says.

"Next," I say.

"Maybe you should go for someone different," she says. "Someone not your type."

"Maybe," I say.

"It's not like you want a relationship with any of these," she says. "You just want to date, nothing serious."

I get up and walk over to the book case. I take down a ball of wool and two knitting needles. I sit on the armchair and cast on a row of stitches. I knit.

"And what does he want?" I ask.

"He wants to date but nothing serious," she says.

"Ok, so he's your good looking," I say. "What else?"

"He's thirty-one, six foot, hairdresser, no pets, occasional smoker, occasional drinker," she says.

"Hmm," I say. "Ok. Interests?"

"Sports, pub, films, havin a laff," she reads from the screen.

"He's having a laugh if he thinks anyone is going to be interested in that profile," I say.

Louise throws me a glare.

"Stop being a snob," she says. "How many times do I have to say this? You're not looking to be in a relationship with any of these guys. You're just going to go out with them. Date but nothing serious."

"I know, I know," I say.

"I'll send out the messages," she says. "You don't need to do anything other than turn up on the date and have fun."

"I guess," I say.

The timer beeps. I put my knitting on the window sill. I walk into the kitchen and take the pizza out of the oven. I get a pair of scissors and cut the pizza into eight pieces. I open the fridge and take out two cans of lemonade. I carry it all into the study.

"I've sent out three messages," Louise says.

"To who?" I ask.

"To whoooooom," she says.

I shove the plate of pizza towards her. She takes two slices and puts them down on my desk. I put a can of lemonade next to them.

"To that first guy, markysomethingorother," she says.

"Uh-huh," I say, taking a bite from a slice of pizza.

"And this one," she says, pointing to the screen.

"What's he like?" I ask.

"He's probably a bit more your good looking," she says, opening her can.

"That's more like it," I say.

"He's twenty-six," she says.

I choke on my pizza.

"I know," she says. "He's younger than I'd normally let you go for. But it's dating. Nothing serious."

"I know," I say. "I keep forgetting that. So apart from being young enough to be my son, what's he like?"

"He's an electrician, likes the normal things, seems relatively harmless," she says.

"What's his name?" I ask.

"His username is KMB44," she says.

"And his real name?" I ask.

"No idea," she says.

"And who's the other guy?" I ask.

"Pretty much the same, inoffensive, middle of the road," she says.

"Hmm," I say. "Ok."

Louise drops her crust on the floor. She looks at me.

"Oh yeah, Beryl's not here," she says.

She leaves the crust on the carpet.

"She can eat it when she gets home," I say.

Louise rolls her chair towards me and takes another slice of pizza.

"So what did you say to them?" I ask.

"The same kind of thing I send out," she says. "Hi, your profile looks interesting, fancy meeting up for a drink, it's easier to get to know someone face to face rather than through countless e-mails, blah blah blah, let me know if you're free this weekend or next week."

"Isn't that a bit forward?" I ask.

"Apparently men like that," she says. "Men like confident women."

"Well they're not going to be impressed when I turn up and am all shy and dull," I say.

"No, they're not," Louise says. "So just make sure that you're not your normal self."

I look at her. She laughs. I pass her the plate.

"Do you want anymore?" I ask.

She takes the plate. I walk out of the room. I wander into the living room. My phone is on the floor by the sofa. I pick it up and wander back into my study. I press a button to wake up the screen. I've got no new messages.

"Are you expecting something?" Louise asks.

"No," I say and put my phone on the bookcase.

"You didn't text them, did you?" she asks.

"Why do you ask like that?" I ask.

"Because it's a stupid stupid thing to do," she says.

"Why's it stupid stupid?" I ask.

"They both said they didn't want to see you again," she says.

"They didn't actually say that," I say.

"But they implied it," she says. "Walking away from you and shutting a door in your face doesn't say that they want to be friends."

"Hmm," I say.

"And if they don't want to see you again, I can bet that they don't want to hear from you again," she says.

"But I just want to explain," I say.

"I know you do, but they're angry," she says. "Even if they let you explain, there's a chance they won't hear what you say. So you'd just be wasting your breath and even make the situation worse."

"Seriously, what books have you swallowed?" I ask.

"Books?" she says. "Since when have I read books?"

"Well you're going to read mine," I say.

"Yes, I'll read it once it's written," she says. "How's that going by the way?"

I look at her.

"So back to your psychobabble," I say.

She laughs.

"A lot of the patients at the hospital watch American talk shows," she says. "I can't help watching them too."

"You could try and do your job," I say.

"I'm boosting morale with the patients," she says.

"That would be good if that was your job," I say.

"If I hadn't watched those shows, I wouldn't be able to help you," she says. "Stop complaining."

"I'm not complaining," I say. "It's just unlike you to have decent advice."

"I won't bother then," she says.

"I'm sorry," I say. "And thank you."

"You're welcome," she says.

"So what should I do now?" I ask.

"Right now?" she asks.

"No," I say. "About William and Gregory."

"Nothing," she says.

"Nothing?" I ask.

"Nothing," she says.

"Why not?" I ask.

"Do you want to go out with them again?" she asks.

"I don't know," I say. "Maybe."

"Which one?" she asks.

"I don't know," I say.

"Well you have to make a choice," she says. "Did you text both of them?"

I nod.

"The same message?" she asks.

I nod again.

"So you don't really care which one you end up with?" she asks.

"I don't know," I say. "I was emotional."

"And that's why you should never text when you're emotional," she says.

"I just want to explain," I say.

"I know, but you can't," she says. "Just leave it. If they want you, they can get hold of you."

"I just want to say sorry," I say.

I sink back into the chair and close my eyes.

"Do you want me to go?" Louise asks.

"I don't want you to go," I say. "But I don't think I'm going to be much company."

"You're never much company," she says. "But I still stick around."

I look at her.

"Has anyone replied?" I ask.

"You're eager," she says.

"No point moping around," I say.

"Exactly," she says.

She turns around and refreshes the screen.

"Nope," she says. "No new messages."

"Fancy a walk?" I say.

"Where to?" she asks.

"Parents'," I say. "To get Beryl."

"Yeah," she says. "Why not? I'm still a bit hungry."

I stand up and lean over Louise's shoulder. I refresh the screen one more time. No new messages. I shut everything down. Louise gets up and walks to the front door. I pick up my phone and press a button to wake up the screen. No new messages. I call my parents. The phone rings. I wait.

"Hello," Mum says.

"I'm on my way to pick up Beryl," I say.

"Is everything ok?" Mum asks.

"Yeah," I say.

"It's not, is it?" Mum asks.

"So why did you ask?" I ask.

She doesn't say anything.

"Sorry," I say. "I'll see you in a bit."

"See you in a bit," she says.

"Oh, make sure you've got some food," I say. "Louise is with me."

27

I walk into the hallway and open the airing cupboard. I pull out a sheet and carry it with me to the front door. I lean the painting up against the wall and cover it with the sheet.

"Why did you do that?" Louise asks.

I look at her.

"You didn't like it when I showed you the pictures," I say.

"A girl can change her mind," she says. "Or not even make it up."

I look at her.

"Joke!" she says.

I don't laugh. I open the front door. I walk out. Louise follows me. I walk back in. I pick up my bag. I sigh.

"Even more useless than usual, eh?" Louise says.

"Yep," I say.

I walk outside again and pull the door closed.

"Are you sure you've got your keys?" she asks.

"Nope," I say, shrugging.

I walk away from my house. It's warm. I'm not sure what the time is. I look at my arm. I'm not wearing a watch.

"It's nearly four," Louise says.
"Really?" I ask.
"Yep," she says.
"I must have slept for hours last night," I say.
"And today," she says.
"I don't feel any better for it," I say.

I sigh. We don't speak for the rest of the walk. I don't mind that. We walk up the path to my parents' house. I knock on the door. Beryl barks. Mum answers the door. She's holding a guitar stand and the metal frame to a dolls' pram. Beryl jumps up at me. I bend down and pick her up.

"Hello," Mum says.

I walk in.

"Hello Louise, love," Mum says to Louise.

"Karen," Louise says to Mum.

"I made you a sandwich, Louise, love," Mum says to Louise. "It's in the fridge."

"Cheese and pickle?" Louise asks.

"Of course," Mum says.

"Thank you," Louise says, skipping into the kitchen.

Mum looks at me.

"You look terrible," she says.

"Nice to see you too," I say to Mum.

"Is everything ok?" she asks.

Louise walks into the hall, holding a plate in one hand and half a sandwich in the other hand. She takes a bite.

"She got dumped," she says with her mouth full.

I glare at her.

"Who by?" Mum asks.

"By whooooom," Louise says.

I glare at her.

"By whom," Mum says.

Louise laughs. I carry Beryl into the kitchen and put her down in her bed. She runs out and sits by Louise's feet waiting for a crumb to drop. I sit down.

"By both of them," Louise says.

"I knew it was a bad idea," Mum says.

"What was a bad idea?" Dad asks, walking through the kitchen holding a large cassette player from the eighties.

"Tomothy," Louise says, doffing an invisible cap.

"Eating us out of house and home again Louise," Dad says.

"Of course," Louise says.

"Didn't I say to you, Tom, that she shouldn't go out with two men at the same time?" Mum says. "Didn't I say to you that it was a bad idea?"

"Indeed you did," he says. "What's happened?"

"She got dumped," Louise says.

"Who by?" Dad asks.

"By whooooom," Louise says.

Dad rolls his eyes.

"By both of them," Louise says.

"Well it was a bad idea," Dad says.

I stand up and walk to the sink. I take a mug off the draining board and pour myself some water. I sip from the mug. My eyes well up. Mum leans the guitar stand and pram parts against the freezer. Dad walks into the back garden with the cassette player.

"What happened?" Mum asks.

"I don't want to talk about it," I say.

I sit back down. Dad comes back in and takes the guitar stand and pram parts into the garden.

"Basically," Louise says. "She was at William's picking up a painting he'd painted of her and Gregory knocked on the door. She answered the door and it all kicked off. Apparently Gregory and William are cousins."

I glare at Louise. Mum gasps.

"Did you know?" Mum asks me.

"She thought they were brothers to start with," Louise says. "But then she found out that Gregory has a sister but no brothers. But they had to be related because of the Nana Bertie thing, so the only other solution was that they were cousins."

Mum looks at me.

"Doesn't that make you some sort of inbred?" Louise asks me.

I glare at her.

"Well you knew something like this was going to happen," Mum says.

"She knows," Louise says.

"Why didn't you choose one and let the other down gently?" Mum asks.

"If she had a choice of one, she couldn't make a decision," Louise says.

Mum nods.

"Well now you won't have any distractions and you can focus on your writing," she says.

Dad walks back in.

"Yes, get that masterpiece written," he says. "I want to retire."

"You're already retired," I say.

He walks past me and out of the kitchen. His feet pad up the stairs carpet.

"How's your writing going?" Mum asks me.

"Yes," Louise says. "How is it going?"

"I've got ideas," I say.

"Ideas don't get published," Mum says. "Words get published."

"I think I'm going to change direction with it," I say.

"It has to have a direction in the first place for you to change it," Louise says.

"Don't choke on your sandwich," I say.

"I won't," Louise says. "It's delicious. Is this new bread?"

"Homemade bread," Mum says.

"So you've finally mastered it?" I say.

Dad walks through the kitchen carrying a standard lamp without a lampshade or a plug. He takes it into the garden.

"So what's this new direction?" Mum asks.

"I don't want to say anything yet," I say.

"Which means you have absolutely no idea what you're doing," Louise says.

I glare at her.

"It's going to be a bit more complicated than my initial idea," I say. "I just need to get writing to see if it has legs."

"Sounds interesting," Mum says.

Louise puts her plate into the dishwasher. She takes a mug off the draining board and puts it down in front of the kettle. She fills the kettle with water and pushes the switch. The kettle glows blue.

"Hot chocolate, Karen?" she asks Mum.

"No thanks Louise, love," she says.

Dad walks back in.

"Hot chocolate, Tomothy?" she asks Dad.

"Drinking us out of house and home?" he says.

"Of course," Louise says.

"I'll have a coffee," he says.

Louise gets another mug. She opens the cupboard above the kettle and takes out a jar of coffee and a jar of hot chocolate powder. She gets two spoons out of the cutlery drawer and walks back to the mugs. She spoons coffee into one mug and hot chocolate powder into the other. The kettle clicks done and she pours the boiling water into the mugs. She stirs with both hands. Dad walks into the kitchen carrying a stack of rewritable CDs. He puts them down on the table and takes the mug that Louise is holding out for him.

"Thanks," he says.

"Anything else I can get for you?" Louise asks.

He sips his coffee.

"This'll do for now," he says.

He puts the mug on the table and picks up the CDs. He takes them into the garden. Louise follows him to the door.

"What's all that for?" she shouts.

"We've been clearing out the loft," Mum says.

I stand up and squeeze past Louise. A pile of useless junk sits in the middle of the garden. Beryl fights with a vacuum cleaner tube.

"You know you're not allowed to start a bonfire with this stuff," I say. "You'll kill the neighbours with the toxic fumes."

"You spoil all our fun," Mum says.

Louise walks over to the pile and kicks a three-legged plastic patio chair.

"I'm building a sculpture," Dad says.

"It's not very good," Louise starts.

"I haven't started yet," Dad says. "I'm just sorting out all of our junk to see what I can use."

"I might have some junk for you," Louise says. "If you want it."

"Yeah, the more the merrier," Dad says.

Louise puts her mug on the patio table and walks towards me. She puts her arms around my waist and picks me up. My feet drag on the floor. For such a short woman, she's surprisingly strong. She carries me towards the pile. She drops me on the grass next to a tyreless bicycle wheel. Beryl jumps on me.

"I'll see what else I've got and I'll bring it round later in the week," Louise says.

"Much appreciated," Dad says. "But this bit of old tat will drag down the overall image of the installation."

He taps me in the side with the toe of his boot. I feign death. Beryl climbs over my stomach.

"Where's Cheryl?" I ask Mum.

"I had to perform a lot of surgery on her," Mum says. "Beryl managed to pull off all her limbs, so she's a bit of a stumpy thing."

I stand up.

"So what kind of sculpture are you going to make with all this junk?" Louise asks.

Dad takes a step back and puts his hands on his hips.

"I don't know yet," he says. "But it doesn't always have to be something. It can just be a thing. The unknown destination after a journey along unchartered roads is a lot more interesting than a walk to the shops."

"That's a bit too phisolophical for my brain," Louise says.

I laugh.

"Philosophical," I say.

"That's what I said," Louise says, turning around and walking inside.

I walk into the kitchen. Louise and Mum are sitting at the table.

"Are you girls doing anything tonight?" Mum asks.

I shake my head.

"Well it's not like she's got any dates lined up," Louise says.

I glare at her.

"Do you want to stay for dinner?" Mum asks.

I don't really want to.

"You don't have to ask me twice," Louise says.

Dad walks in.

"Get the barbecue started Tom," Mum says. "The girls are staying for dinner."

"Eating us out of house and home," Dad says. "When you moved out I thought that would be the last we saw of you."

He turns and looks at Louise.

"And you," Dad says to Louise.

Louise smiles.

"Don't listen to him Louise, love," Mum says. "You're always welcome here."

Dad shakes his head and walks towards the stairs.

"Tom," Mum says to Dad. "Barbecue."

He turns on his heels and walks outside. Mum walks to the freezer and pulls the door open. A breath of icy air hits me.

"What do you girls fancy?" she asks.

"Meat," Louise says.

"Meat it is," Mum says.

Louise points to me.

"She made me eat a vegetable pizza earlier," she says.

"What?" Mum says. "No meat."

"No meat," Louise says.

"That's not a real pizza," Mum says.

"That's what I said," Louise says.

Mum slides a freezer drawer towards her and rummages through the food. She pulls out a bag of homemade burgers, a bag of homemade barbecue sauce marinated chicken wings and a bag of shop-bought Lincolnshire sausages because my dad prefers those ones and do I know how difficult it is to make homemade sausages? I can imagine.

I walk over to a cupboard, open the door and take out a large bowl. I put it on the side next to the chopping board. I open the fridge and take out some lettuce, a handful of baby tomatoes, a cucumber and a carrot. I close the door and put the salad on the side. I take a red onion from the vegetable rack. I rip and slice and chop and mix it all in the bowl.

"Your dad made some really nice mustard salad dressing," Mum says. "It's in the strawberry jam jar in the fridge."

I open the fridge door.

"And he made some ketchup too," she says. "Although that's not as nice as the shop bought one, so get them both. Your dad's one is in the cream cheese tub. Be careful, the lid's not very secure."

I look in the fridge for any food that looks like it's in the wrong container. I find the jam jar and the shop bought ketchup. The kitchen fills with smoke. I cough.

"A little help here," Dad shouts.

"What have you done wrong?" Mum says.

"Why's it always my fault?" Dad says.

"Because you're the only one out there," Mum says.

She throws her hands up in the air and sighs.

"Men!" she says, walking outside.

Louise shuts the door. The smoke disappears. I put the jars on the side.

"Do you think we'll ever be like your parents?" she asks.

"I hope not," I say.

"I'm being serious," she says.

"Well you can be the man," I say.

"I didn't mean that," she says.

"I know what you meant," I say.

"I mean, married for all those years and still happy," she says

"You think they're happy?" I ask.

"Don't you?" she says.

"They're always bickering," I say.

"But isn't that part of the charm?" she asks.

She picks some lettuce leaves out of the salad bowl and puts them in her mouth.

"I mean," she says. "They've been together for a hundred years, and they may bicker, but they're still together."

"I guess," I say. "I've never really thought about it. They're just my parents. Maybe it's because they're both a bit odd; they know no-one else would put up with them so they have to stay together."

Louise laughs.

"Well it would be nice to have someone," Louise says. "Even if it is only someone who puts up with me because no-one else will."

"I put up with you because no-one else will," I say.

"Well maybe me and you will end up like your parents," she says.

"You're still being the man," I say.

She laughs. I pick up the salad bowl and walk to the back door. Louise picks up the ketchup and salad dressing. I open the door and we go outside. The air smells burnt.

"How do you want your burgers?" Mum asks. "Burnt or really burnt?"

"I'll just go for burnt to start with," Louise says.

"I don't see you doing any better," Dad says to Mum.

"Well it's difficult to be a backside driver at a barbecue," Mum says.

I laugh.

"Backseat," I say.

Mum glares at me.

"Your father won't let go of the tongs," she says. "How am I supposed to cook without tongs? I don't have asbestos hands you know."

"Get in the kitchen woman," Dad says. "And bring out the plates and the rolls."

"Get in the kitchen, bring out the plates and rolls," Mum mimics.

Mum kisses Dad on the lips. I put the salad bowl on the table.

"Get a room," I say.

"Ok then," Mum says. "Come on Tom."

Mum walks towards the back door. Dad puts down the tongs and follows her.

"Hey," I say.

My parents laugh.

"Well you told us to," Mum says.

I drop my head and cover my eyes with my hand.

"We don't need any more burnt or very burnt bits of meat," I say.

Mum walks over to me and gives me a hug. She leans behind me and picks up the tongs.

"Ah-ha!" she says. "Now you get in the kitchen and get the rolls."

Dad salutes and walks inside. He brings the plates out and puts them on the table, with some knives and forks and a serving spoon for the salad.

"Where are the rolls?" he asks.

"In the tall cupboard," Mum says. "You can't miss them."

"I looked in there," he says. "Where else would they be?"

"They'd be in the cupboard where they always are," Mum says.

"Well they're not there now," he says.

Mum sighs and puts the tongs down. She walks towards the door.

"Men!" she says, walking inside.

Dad winks and scurries towards the barbecue. He picks up the tongs and turns a burger.

"Thomas Winston Wright!" Mum shouts.

"You're in trouble," Louise says.

"Are you still here?" Dad asks.

Mum stands at the back door with one hand on her hip and the other hand holding out a bag of rolls.

"Where did you find them?" Dad says.

"Where do you think?" Mum snaps. "In the tall cupboard. Where I said they'd be."

She puts them down on the table.

"I knew they were there," Dad whispers to me. "But I couldn't let her have control of the tongs for too long."

"I heard that," Mum says.

She goes back inside and brings out a jug of water with pink plastic ice cubes floating at the top. She puts it in the middle of the table. She reaches her hand through the back door and picks up four beakers. She puts them on the table. Dad loads the meat on to a large plate and brings it over to the table.

"Grub up," he says.

28

I sit down, take a roll and put a burger inside.

"Haven't we got any plastic cheese?" I ask.

"I knew you forgot something," Mum says to Dad.

He ignores her and piles a mound of salad onto his plate. Louise takes the serving spoon out of his hand and serves herself some salad, carefully making sure she doesn't pick up any tomato. Dad opens the jam jar and spoons some dressing over his lettuce. Louise takes the jar out of his hand and pours the dressing on to her plate. I take a bite out of my burger.

"You know I found those pictures and things in the back of the bathroom cupboard?" I say.

"What? When you were cleaning?" Dad asks, laughing.

I glare at him.

"Are you sure you can't remember that theatre?" I ask.

"I know my memory is bad, but it doesn't ring any bells at all," Dad says.

"Hmm," I say.

"What's this?" Louise asks.

"Apparently our dear daughter was doing some cleaning the other day," Dad says.

Louise laughs.

"I don't believe it," she says.

I pour myself some water. A pink plastic ice cube plops into the beaker. I scoop it out and drop it back into the jug.

"And on this apparent cleaning escapade she found an old photograph of Mum, a photograph of a man, and three photographs of a theatre, the same theatre but years apart," Dad says.

"Oh I forgot to tell you," I say. "I found another photograph in Nan's sewing box."

"What? While you were doing some more cleaning?" Dad laughs.

I turn to face Mum.

"It was another black and white photo, of a woman, not Nan, wearing not very many clothes," I say. "She looks almost burlesque or something. There was also something really familiar about her face. I just happened to look at the picture of the unknown man and that's why the woman looked familiar. They've got the same facial features. They must have been brother and sister. But I still don't know who they are."

"I can't help you, I'm afraid," Dad says.

I pull apart a chicken wing with my knife and fork.

"You eat it like this," Louise says, picking up her own piece of chicken.

She rips the meat off with her teeth like a Neanderthal, covering her chin in barbecue sauce.

"I just don't like the bone in my mouth," I say.

"And that's why you're still single," says Mum.

Louise chokes. I blush.

"Mother!" I say.

"Karen!" Dad says.

"What?" Mum says.

"Anyway," I say. "Moving on. There was another thing."

"What was that?" Dad asks.

"Well it's a bit delicate," I say.
"How so?" Mum asks.
"Well," I say. "There was a letter from a vicar addressed to Nan, but he used her maiden name."
"There's nothing wrong with that," Dad says.
"But it was dated after she got married," I say.
"Oh," Dad says.
I eat some salad. I don't know how to put it politely so I just say it.
"It implies that she was a prostitute," I say.
Mum drops her fork.
"I'm sure it didn't," Mum says.
I look at Dad.
"I don't want to believe it," I say. "But I can't think of any other explanation."
"What did it say?" Dad asks. "The letter from the vicar."
"I can't remember exactly," I say. "But it was something about begging her to stop what she was doing as it could badly affect her husband and sons, and that she should be concerned with her own husband and not the husbands of other women."
"There has to be some other reason," Mum says.
"I hope so," I say. "But there was also a large piece of paper with smaller bits stuck on. These smaller bits look like they're excerpts from letters from an array of people asking her to stop doing what she's doing and saying that she's sinful. I don't know what to make of it all."
Dad pushes his plate away.
"Dad," I say. "I'm sorry."
He stands up and walks inside.
"Have you still got this letter and other bits of paper?" Mum asks.
"Yeah, at home," I say. "There are some other papers and things with it. They might be able to shed some light on it all."
"Haven't you read them?" Mum asks.

"Not yet," I say.

"Well wouldn't it have been a better idea to get all the information before telling your father that his mother was a prostitute?" Mum shouts.

"I didn't think …," I say.

"No," she says. "You never do."

"I'm sorry," I say.

"Perhaps if you didn't just sit around at home all day, and actually interacted with human beings and not just your dog, you might learn how to behave around people," she says.

Mum gets up and walks inside. Louise doesn't say anything. I feel horrible. I cry. Louise stands up and walks behind me. She wraps her arms around my shoulders.

"I didn't mean to …," I say.

"I know," she says. "Maybe it would be best if you just went home and slept off these past few days."

I nod. Louise lets go. I stand up.

"Can you get Beryl?" I ask her.

"Sure," she says.

I walk inside. No-one's downstairs. I walk towards the stairs and put my foot on the first step. I hear my parents' muffled voices. I take my foot off the step and walk back into the kitchen. I rip a page out of Mum's shopping list pad and scribble a note. I am really sorry. I didn't mean to upset Dad. I don't write anything else just in case I put my foot in it again. Louise walks past me with Beryl under her arm. She takes her into the hall. I look in the living room for Cheryl and her appendages. She's not there. I won't go upstairs. Louise has buckled up Beryl's collar. I take the lead and open the front door. Beryl runs out. I follow with Louise. I pull the door closed as quietly as I can.

Louise gives me a hug. I sink my head into her shoulder.

"I have to have to have to go to work tomorrow," she says, sighing. "But if you need me, text me and I'll call you on my break. If the witch allows me a break."

"Thank you," I say.

Beryl jumps up at Louise. Louise crouches down and scratches the back of Beryl's head.

"Come on," I say to Beryl.

"It'll be ok," Louise says.

"I know," I sigh. "Thanks."

"Any time," she says.

I walk away. Beryl walks alongside me. A cat wanders across the pavement. Beryl darts forward. I trip off the kerb and twist my ankle. I think about the beach and the horse and carriage ride and Gregory and the kiss in the rain under the pier. My ankle really hurts. I pull Beryl back. I click the extending lead into place and hold her tight next to me. I hobble. Home seems a lot further away than normal.

I'm tired. I'm tired and I'm lonely and I'm fed up. I open my gate and walk up the path. Beryl pulls to the door. I put the key in and turn it. I push the door open and walk inside. I unclip Beryl's lead and unbuckle her from her collar. I throw them on the floor along with my bag and shoes. I push the door closed behind me.

I pull the sheet off the painting. I lean the canvas up against the door and walk back. I sit down at the other end of the hall and cross my legs. I stare at the painting. It's breath taking. I feel bad for thinking that about something that is essentially a picture of my face, but it's not that I find myself breath taking. I just can't believe that someone who only spent a few hours with me could create such an accurate portrait. And I can't believe that he would want to.

I've been such an idiot. I crawl along the carpet towards the door. I sit down directly in front of the canvas. I put my hand out to touch it. I don't. I look to my side and pull my bag towards me. I find my phone and hold it in my hand. I know there'll be nothing there but I press a button to wake up the screen anyway. I have one new message from William. My stomach drops. My heart thumps. My palms heat up. I put my phone on the floor and wipe my hands on my knees. I pick up the phone and look at the screen. I don't want to open it. My thumb moves towards the button to open the message. I click it.

__29__

I close my eyes. I feel like I'm opening my exam results. I know I've failed but I've still got to look at that piece of paper confirming it. I half open one eye. The screen is too blurry to read. I open both eyes. You're right, you probably don't deserve it, but my ex-boss sacked me without giving me the chance to fight my corner. I'd be a hypocrite if I didn't let you explain whatever it is that you feel the need to explain. William.

I let go of the phone and start crying. I drop backwards and lay down. The tears roll in all directions over my face. I feel relieved. I run through hundreds of potential conversations in my head simultaneously. I sit up. I can't predict what he's going to say. I wipe my face with my sleeve. I pick up my phone and reply to William's message. Thank you and I'm sorry. When are you free to meet? I send it just as it is. I don't want to say too much to make things any worse.

I stand up and walk into the kitchen. I open the back door and Beryl runs out. She jumps through the long grass. I really have to get that sorted. It's too late to drag the lawnmower out now. I'll do it tomorrow. Beryl hurries back inside. I shut the door, lock it and pull the curtain across. I walk into my bedroom. Beryl follows me. She jumps up on the bed and makes herself comfortable. I put my phone on my bedside table. I close the curtains, get undressed and look at my bedroom floor. I can't actually see the floor. I pick up a couple of pairs of jeans, some underwear, seven socks, a few tops and a cardigan. I carry them into the kitchen and stuff them into the washing machine. I put a plastic liquid bubble in too, shut the door and start the machine. It whooshes into action.

I walk back into my bedroom and get into bed. I find the eighth sock hiding under my duvet. I pull it out and throw it across the room. I lie on my back and let my head sink into my pillow. I pick up my phone and hold it in both hands on my chest. The washing machine bubbles and gurgles. It's relaxing. I turn on to my side and press a button to wake up the screen. I text Mum. Hey, I'm really sorry about earlier. Please give Dad a hug from me. I know it can't be true, about Nan, but I had to tell him. I'll bring everything round for you to have a read. Maybe you can make things a bit clearer. Xxx

My phone beeps. I didn't think Mum could text that quickly. I have one new message from William. I feel excited. I know I shouldn't but I can't help it. I know there's nothing to be excited about. I guess I'm just a wishful thinker sometimes. I open the message. I've gone away for a few days visiting friends. Just need to clear my head. I don't know when I'll be back but I'll let you know. We can arrange something then. I suppose that's all I can hope for right now.

I feel empty. I don't like the thought of him being away for a few days. Or even longer. I miss him. I miss the way he wrapped his arms around me when we looked at his painting in the underpass, and the painting of me in his conservatory. It doesn't matter that he's not taller than me or that he's not older than me. I can't believe Louise made me do that list. He's creative and sweet and generous and he liked me enough to immortalise my face in spray paint. And he wants to give me a chance to explain. That's got to mean something. But with him being away and Louise having to work, I can focus on my book. I can at least try to get something solid written without too many distractions.

I turn my phone on silent and put it on the floor. I pull the duvet up to my chin and close my eyes.

***

I wake up. Beryl is pawing at my hair. She lies across the top of my head. I can't sit up. I push her off. She does a backwards roll off the pillow. I get up, open the curtains and walk to the kitchen. I open the back door. Beryl runs out and barely manages to make it off the step before doing her business. I leave her to it and do my own business in the bathroom, keeping my eye on the toilet paper filling the crack between the bath and the wall. I walk back into the kitchen. Beryl crawls through the grass on her stomach. I sigh. If I cut the grass now, I can get it out of the way and not have to worry about it later.

I walk back in the house and find some trainers. I put on my dressing gown and walk into the bathroom. I pick up the yellow rubber gloves off the floor and squeeze my hands inside them. I look out into the garden and stare at the shed. I bravely march up to the door and pull it open. The lawnmower is towards the back on the left side. I put one foot inside and lean forward. I can't reach it. I step a bit closer but still can't reach it. I move both feet inside the shed. It's so small, like a doll's house. A doll's house full of people-eating spiders. My eyes dart from side to side. There's a spider web hanging from the bottom of a shelf. There's no spider on it. I pull up the hood of my dressing gown and take a few steps further inside. I pick up a gardening fork and move it out of the way. I knock down a paint can with the handle of the fork. It doesn't explode open. I leave it. My foot gets tangled in the hose. I kick it. It tangles itself around my leg. I trip forward and steady myself on a patio umbrella. I reach down and pull the hose. It slides out. I throw it towards the back of the shed. I lift the umbrella out of the way and use it to clear a path. I shuffle forwards, pushing some crates to the side, and reach out for the lawnmower handle. I pull it towards me. It stutters along the floor, pulling the crates with it. I manoeuvre the contraption to the door. It gets stuck. I yank the lawnmower and it frees itself. One of the crates falls forward and lands on its side on the floor. The lid cracks. I'll sort that out later.

I drag the lawnmower into the middle of the garden and unravel the orange cable from around the handle. I walk inside, unplug the kettle and plug in the lawnmower. I push the switch down. I walk outside and pick Beryl up. I carry her into the hall, put her on the carpet, walk back into the kitchen and close the door. I walk outside and switch the lawnmower on. It hums and splutters as I push it through the grass. The lawnmower glides erratically over the ground. I push the machine forwards and pull it backwards. The plastic box on the back fills up with grass. I switch off the lawnmower, unclip the box and empty the contents into the bin. I start again. My arms ache. The lawnmower stops moving. I shove it forward. It stutters. I turn around and drag the lawnmower. The box fills up. I empty it. I look at the garden. It looks messier now than it did before I started. I push the mower back over the areas I've already mowed. The box fills up again. I don't empty it. I'm too tired. I pull the lawnmower towards me and push it up by the wall. I go into the kitchen and turn off the plug.

I open the kitchen door. Beryl runs out and rolls on the cut areas of grass. I walk over to the shed and push the crates back. I pick up the crate that has fallen on the floor. It's not as heavy as it looks. The lid falls off. I drop the crate trying to catch the lid. It smashes on the ground and a wave of material falls out. It's a creamy cotton piece of fabric. I pull out the crate fragments and put them on the grass behind me. I'll give them to Dad for his sculpture. I stand up and hold an edge of the material between my yellow thumb and forefinger. I flick it out in front of me. It's dusty. I cough. I run the edge through my hands and find two corners. I flick it again. I turn around and spread it out on the grass. Beryl lays out on it. It is covered in large stain patches of pale yellow. I look back into the shed. There's a small, metal tin on the ground where the crate smashed. I pick it up.

It's rusty and dented. I try to open it. It's locked. I put it on the ground and walk into the kitchen. I look on the kitchen table at the junk I cleared out of the cutlery drawer. I pick up the four sets of keys and take them outside. I sit down on the material and put the tin on my lap. I lay they keys out in front of me. One set clearly won't fit. They look like the front door keys to a mansion or a castle. I pick up the second keyring. One key looks promising. I poke it into the hole in the front of the tin. It's just slightly too big. I put those keys back on the ground. The next lot appear to be general front door keys with maybe a padlock key on there too. They all look too big. There are a couple of small keys on the last keyring. The first one is too small but the second one fits. It's always the last one you try. I turn the key but it doesn't move. I jiggle it around. I take it out and put it back in. It doesn't turn. It makes a horrible, scratchy noise, like fingernails down a blackboard. It sets my teeth on edge.

I stand up and walk into the shed. I don't go in too far. I look around and pick up a claw hammer from a shelf. I sit back down and pick up the tin. I slide the claw under the lip of the lid. I put the tin on the ground and hold it down with my left hand. I hold the handle of the hammer in my right hand and pull it up. The lid doesn't budge. I move the hammer to a corner and try to pull it off again. Nothing happens. I pull the claw out and hit the tin with the flat end of the hammer. The tin dents but doesn't open. I stand up and throw the tin at the tree. It lands about three feet in front of me. I kick it. Beryl looks up at me. I smile at her.

I turn around and pick up the hammer. I throw it into the shed. It clangs against a paint tin. I shut the shed door and attempt to fold up the material. I put it under my arm and pick up the box. I take them into the kitchen and put them on the kitchen table. The red light on the washing machine reminds me that my washing is done. I don't want to hang it out now. I want to do it later. But it will smell if I leave it in the machine.

I open the washing machine door. I get a bin bag out of the drawer and parachute it open. I pull the still damp clothes out of the washing machine, stuff them in the plastic bag and drag it outside. The bag bumps over the varying lengths of grass. I pull the clothes out and hang them on the line. I look up. There are no birds today.

I pick up the bin bag, take it inside and put it back in the drawer. I take off my rubber gloves and put them on the draining board. I push the back door. It doesn't shut. I look down and see the orange lawnmower cable. I unplug it from the wall and throw it outside. I'll put it away later.

I kick off my trainers in the hall and walk into the bathroom. I turn on the shower and dump my dressing gown and pyjamas in the corner of the room. I climb in the shower and wash the smell of the shed off my skin.

My house phone rings. Only one person ever calls me on that. I step out of the shower and wrap a towel around myself. I walk into my study and pick up the phone.

"'allo muvvah," I say.

"Actually it's your farver," Dad says.

"Oh hello," I say.

"How are you?" he asks.

"I'm fine thanks," I say. "How are you?"

"I think I'm ok," he says.

"I'm sorry about yesterday," I say.

"I know you are," he says. "I'm sorry too. I didn't mean to react like that. I just didn't expect you, or indeed anyone, to say what you said."

"I didn't like saying it," I say.

"I know," he says. "You're sorry, I'm sorry. Let's leave it there."

"Deal," I say. "So what do you want?"

"Charming," Dad says. "Can't a dad call his daughter for a chat every once in a while?"

"This is the first once in a while that you've ever called me," I say.

"Are you busy today?" he asks. "Have you got anymore tidying and cleaning planned?"

He laughs.

"I'll have you know that I've already mowed the lawn, put out the washing and tidied some of the garden shed this morning," I say, only partially embellishing the truth.

"I'm impressed," he says. "You could do with a break. Fancy having your old dad over for lunch?"

"Of course," I say.

"See you in half an hour then," he says.

"Ok," I say. "See you in a bit."

I hang up the phone and walk into my bedroom. I look on the floor for some clothes. I pick up a pair of pyjama trousers, a lone sock and my giant, purple jumper. Where have all my clothes gone? I drop everything, open my wardrobe and find some clean clothes there. Some I haven't worn in ages. I get dressed. I sit at the kitchen table and try to get the lid off the tin. It won't budge. The doorbell rings. Beryl barks.

"Just a second," I shout.

I pick up the painting and struggle into the living room. I cover it with the sheet. I walk back into the hall and open the front door. Dad is standing on the doorstep holding a large fruit box from the supermarket. A slightly smaller glass oven dish sits in the middle of the box. It contains a steaming hot shepherd's pie. I take the box out of Dad's hands and carry it into the kitchen. He follows me, making a fuss of Beryl. I put the shepherd's pie on the hob.

"Your mother's worried that you're not eating properly," he says.

"I am," I say. "But thank you."

He holds an odd shaped pink think out to me. It's Cheryl.

"What happened to her?" I ask.

"Your mother!" Dad says.

Beryl jumps up.

"Give it to her," I say.

Dad throws Cheryl into the hall. Beryl bounds after her. He drops Cheryl's arms and legs by the door.

"Tea?" I say.

"That would be lovely," Dad says.

"You know where the kettle is," I say.

"Charming," he says.

"I'm not your slave," I say.

"So it's ok for me to be your slave for twenty odd years but you can't even make your poor, old, decrepit father a drink," he says, dropping on to a chair.

"Fine," I say.

I flick the switch on the kettle. Nothing happens. I pick it up and put it back down on its base. I flick the switch again. Nothing happens.

"Sometimes helps if you plug it in," Dad says.

I glare at him. I pick up the plug and put it in the socket. I switch it on at the wall and flick the switch on the kettle. It glows blue. I find a clean mug and put a teabag in it.

"What happened to the teapot?" Dad asks.

I look around the kitchen.

"I have no idea," I say.

Dad laughs. The kettle steams and clicks off. I pour the water over the teabag and watch it float to the top of the mug. I pass the mug to Dad.

"Thank you," he says. "I do have a bit of an ulterior

motive for being here."

"I knew it," I say. "What do you want?"

Dad opens the cutlery drawer and takes out a teaspoon.

"You could really do with a cutlery tray," he says.

"Yeah I know," I say. "I'll sort that out later."

He stirs the teabag around in the mug, dunking it under the water. He squashes it against the inside of the mug with the spoon and scoops it out. He drops it in the bin and puts the spoon in the sink. He takes a sip.

"I was wondering if I could have a look at those letters," he says.

"Yeah, they're in my study," I say.

"Ah, the land where time stands still," he says. "Is it still nearly ten past eleven?"

"Of course," I say. "You wait here. I'll just go and get them."

I walk past Beryl fighting with Cheryl in the hall and go into my study. I open my desk drawer and take out the letters and photos. I notice my 'to do' list on my desk. I pick up a pen and after Louise's list of stupidities I write 10) Buy a cutlery tray. I close my desk drawer and walk back into the kitchen. Dad's not in there. I walk to the living room.

"Dad?" I say.

"In here," he says.

"Thanks for being so specific," I say.

I walk into the living room. Dad is standing in front of my giant face. I pick up the sheet and cover the canvas.

"I was looking at that," Dad says.

"This isn't an art gallery," I say.

"Who did it?" he asks. "They really captured your likeness."

"It was just someone," I say. "Don't you want to look at these?"

"In a minute," he says.

He pulls the sheet off the painting and takes a step back.

I walk past him and sit on the sofa. He leans in towards the painting.

"What sort of paint is this?" he asks.

"Spray paint," I say. "Are you hungry yet?"

"In a minute," he says.

I slide the magazines, newspapers, letters, papers, folders and remote controls to one end of the coffee table and lay out the pictures and papers from the plastic wallet.

"See how similar these two look?" I say, holding up the photo of the suited man and the photo of the burlesque woman.

"Who painted it?" he asks.

"No-one important," I say.

"Was it one of your young men?" he asks.

I look at him.

"Well I don't know what you call it nowadays," he says. "Back in my day you just went out with someone, one person, and then you were boyfriend and girlfriend."

"I know," I say. "And the chaperone would walk between you and the women weren't allowed to show their ankles."

He laughs.

"But yes," I say. "It was one of the men I went out with."

"He's very good," Dad says. "Why didn't you keep hold of him?"

"Do we really need to talk about this?" I ask.

"Not if you don't want to," Dad says.

"I don't," I say. "So come and sit over here."

He walks over to the sofa and sits down next to me. He puts his mug of tea on the end table.

"So what have we got here?" he asks.

"Well these are the photos of the theatre and this is the unknown man," I say, pointing to the photos. "And this is the woman I found in Nan's sewing box. Be careful. The photo looks like it could fall apart at any time."

He holds the photo in his palm and brings it close to his

face.

"Do you know who it is?" I ask.

"She doesn't look like anyone I remember," he says. "Mum didn't really have friends. Especially none who would dress like this."

"But don't you think she looks like him?" I ask, pointing to the unknown suited man.

"There is some sort of resemblance," he says. "But I still don't know who they are."

He puts the photos down.

"Is this the letter from the reverend?" he asks, picking up the letter.

"It is," I say. "Are you sure you want to read it?"

"I have to," he says. "I need to know what it says."

He picks up his mug and takes a few sips of tea. He puts the mug down and holds the envelope in both hands. He carefully opens it, takes out the papers and unfolds them. I don't say anything. His eyes scan the pages.

"Are you ok?" I ask.

He doesn't look at me. He keeps his eyes fixed on the letter.

"I can see how you would have thought that this reverend was saying that Mum was a prostitute," he says. "But you know her. You know she couldn't have done anything like that. You know she loved your granddad. She didn't even want to think about getting remarried after he died. She believed in one man for one woman forever. There is no way she would have done anything like that. No way."

"I know," I say. "But what else could it be?"

He puts the letter back in the envelope and puts it on the table.

"What's this?" he asks, picking up the folded sheet of paper.

"Careful with that," I say. "It's cut out and stuck on bits of other letters from other people. But some of them have come unstuck. And others, you can't really read very well."

He unfolds the paper and presses it out flat on the table. A few pieces of paper slide off. He puts them back in place. He leans forward and reads over the snippets.

"You know when something happens and you read about it or hear about it and you think that it can't possibly be true or that it's partially true but the story's been embellished," he says.

"Yep," I say.

"This is one of those times," he says. "None of this seems real, but it must be."

He picks up his mug but he doesn't drink.

"But I know it's not what we think it is," he says. "I just know."

I think of Louise. A mother knows. I laugh.

"What's funny?" Dad says.

"Nothing," I say.

"There has to be another explanation," he says. "There just has to be."

"There are some more bits in there," I say, pointing to the plastic wallet.

"Fancy taking a break?" Dad says. "I'm hungry and I just want to stop thinking about this for a bit.

"Ok," I say, and walk into the kitchen.

Dad follows me and closes the living room door. He sits down and hovers his mug over the kitchen table.

"How can I believe you tided the bathroom when you've got all this mess here?" he asks.

I open the back door and wave my arm outside.

"Washing done, lawn mowed," I say. "Busy me can't keep everywhere clean all at the same time."

Dad stands up and looks out the door.

"You mowed the lawn, eh?" he says. "Some of it grew back really quickly and some of it not at all."

I push him back and shut the door.

"I would have sorted it out if you hadn't turned up. It's all your fault I didn't finish," I say. "So shush."

He laughs.

"Look, all you have to do is pile things up and you can make some room," I say, walking over to the kitchen table.

I put my pile of unopened letters onto a chair and slide the rest of the junk to the other end of the table. Something falls on the floor. I bend down and pick up the jelly mould in the shape of a teddy bear. I put it back on the pile. Dad looks at me.

"I'll sort that out later," I say.

Dad puts his mug down on the table.

"Haven't you got any placemats?" he asks. "Or coasters?"

"Of course I have," I say.

"Where?" he asks.

"Well I don't know," I say.

I get two plates and put them on the bread board. I scoop some shepherd's pie onto each plate and put one plate into the microwave. I press the Auto Reheat button, and then Start. The microwave buzzes into action.

"What's this?" Dad asks, picking up the tin.

"Well," I say. "When I was cleaning out the garden shed this morning …,"

Dad lets out a belly laugh. I glare at him.

"Sorry," he says. "I just find it so hard to believe."

"When I was cleaning out the garden shed this morning I managed to drop one of those old crates that have been in there ever since I moved in, and that tin and that sheet thing were in there," I say.

"What's in it?" Dad asks.

"I don't know," I say. "I can't get it open. I found a key that fits though. It just won't turn."

He picks up the tin and the key. He puts the key in the hole in the front of the tin and wiggles it around.

"Hmm," he says, holding the tin up close to his face.

The microwave beeps. I open the door and take out the plate. It's hot. I should have put on my Father Christmas oven glove. I put it down in front of Dad.

"Thanks," he says.

I give him a knife and fork. He takes them with one hand and with the other he shakes the tin.

"Hmm," he says.

I put my plate in the microwave and start it up. Dad doesn't touch his food.

"Have you got anything to get rid of rust?" he asks.

I look at him and shrug my shoulders.

"You don't think I do any sort of normal cleaning," I say. "So why on Earth would I have rust getter-ridder?"

"I didn't know if Mum left any here," he says.

I walk to the cupboard under the sink and open the doors. I crouch down and peer in. It smells. I close the door.

"Nope," I say.

"None in the shed?" he asks.

I shrug again.

"I thought you cleaned out the shed," he says.

The microwave beeps.

"I did," I say. "But there was this spider and then I dropped the crate and found the tin and then you called, so I didn't have time to look properly."

I open the microwave door, put on my Father Christmas oven glove this time and take the plate out. I put it on the table opposite Dad. He doesn't look up. He fiddles with the key in the lock of the tin. The key gets stuck. He puts the tin on the chair next to him. I get a glass of water and a knife and fork. I sit down. Dad digs his fork into the potato.

"How's the writing going?" he asks.

I laugh. I eat. The food is hot. I take a sip of water.

"Slowly," I say.

"Why's that?" he asks.

"I don't know," I say. "Just haven't really had any inspiration."

"What have you got so far?" he asks.

"Hmm," I say. "Well, I want it to be a semi-fictional

account of my life, but with the main character being a million times more interesting than me."

Dad nods.

"I've written about her first day at school and her first date," I say. "But that's about it. I don't really know where to go with it."

"What do you mean?" he asks.

"Well I don't know if I want it to be in the style of an autobiography, kind of chronicling all major events of her life in order. Or maybe a diary, but I think that's been done before. Or maybe her as an old woman looking back on her life, perhaps telling her grandchildren stories from her youth," I say.

"They all sound good," Dad says.

"Hmm," I say. "But I can't seem to focus on one thing or put it into any sort of order."

"Isn't it a bit egotistical, writing about yourself?" he asks.

"Isn't it a bit egotistical, painting all those self-portraits?" I ask.

"Don't talk back to your father," he says, winking.

I ignore him.

"When you study creative writing, you are constantly told to write about things you know," I say. "And what do I know better than myself? And I'm not writing completely about myself. Some things are based on me and some things are made up."

I eat. The food's not so hot anymore.

"But I've had a few ideas for something completely different," I say.

"Oh?" Dad says.

"I don't really want to say too much just yet because I'm still not sure what direction I want it to go in," I say. "But it's something completely different from my original idea."

"Sounds intriguing," Dad says.

"I hope so," I say.

I chase a pea around my plate with my fork. It escapes

on a wave of gravy. I pick it up with my fingers. I pick up the plate and lick up the gravy. I put the plate down and lean back in my chair.

"That was good," I say.

I drink some water. I pick up my plate and Dad's plate and carry them to the sink.

"Dishwasher broken?" Dad asks.

I open the dishwasher. It's empty apart from a mug. I put in the plates from lunch, and the bowls and glasses and cutlery that are sitting in and around the sink. Dad drinks down the last of his tea and passes me his mug. He picks up the tin.

"Let's get you open," he says.

He walks outside. I pick up Beryl's bowl and scoop out some shepherd's pie for her. I put it on the side until the food has completely cooled. I walk outside. Beryl follows me, carrying one of Cheryl's limbs. Dad is making noise in the shed. I look in. He's standing with his hands on his hips looking around.

"Did you find a chisel in here?" he asks.

I shrug.

"Or a crowbar?" he asks.

I shrug again.

"Where's the hammer you were using earlier?" he asks.

"I threw it over there," I say, vaguely pointing at the back of the shed.

Dad sighs. He climbs over the crates and the patio umbrella and the garden hose and picks up the hammer. He leans down. I can't see what he's doing.

"Ah-ha," he says.

"What?" I ask.

He doesn't say anything. Something clatters. Dad stands up and turns around. He walks towards me holding the claw hammer I used earlier and a chisel.

"Where did you find that?" I ask.

"In the tool box," he says.

"What tool box?" I ask.

"The one at the back in the corner," he says. "Which you clearly would have seen when you tidied up in here."

"The spiders," I say, pushing my finger into my ear.

"Hmm," Dad says.

He walks over to the door and sits down on the step. He puts the tin between his feet with the lid pointing away from him. I pick up Beryl. He puts the chisel under the lip of the lid where the lock is, and hits the end of the chisel with the hammer. The lid pops open and swings on its hinge. I put Beryl down and clap. Beryl walks over to the tin and sniffs at the contents. Dad puts his hand inside the tin.

"What is it?" I ask.

30

"It's a book," he says.

He turns it over.

"A diary," he says.

He opens the front cover.

"Property of Evelyn Rose Wright (née Bell) 1949," he reads, putting the tin down.

He shuts the front cover.

"I can't read this," he says. "It's my mum's personal thoughts and feelings. And there are things in here that I probably don't want to know about."

"But it could tell us something about all those letters and things," I say. "The one from the reverend is dated nineteen-forty-eight."

"Fifty-eight," he says.

"Oh," I say. "But aren't you still curious?"

"It's from the year before I was born," he says. "So there's definitely going to be something in here that I don't want to know about. I think we should just get rid of it."

"We can't do that," I say. "It's a part of history."

He runs his finger along the spine.

"I just don't think it should be read," he says. "Diaries

are private things.

"But she's not here anymore," I say. "She's not going to know. It's not like we've snuck into her bedroom and rooted around under her bed and stolen her diary."

"I just wouldn't feel comfortable," he says.

"Well can I read it?" I ask.

He holds the diary in both hands and looks at the front cover. He sniffs back a tear.

"I miss her so much," he says.

He drops the diary on his lap and brings his hands up to his eyes. I never know what to do when Dad cries. It happens so rarely. He stands up and walks inside, holding the book. I follow him and wrap my arms around him. He kisses me on the head. He passes me the diary.

"If you do read it, please don't tell me what it says," he says.

"So you don't mind me reading it?" I ask.

"I don't know," he says. "If it was written by anyone else I wouldn't have a problem, but it's my mum and it doesn't feel right if I look at it. But I guess it's ok if you do."

"Do you want to look over the rest of those papers?" I ask.

"I think I'm going to go home now," he says. "I'm not really in the mood. I hope you don't mind."

"Of course I don't mind," I say.

He gives me a hug.

"Any time you fancy coming round for lunch again, you're more than welcome," I say. "Just make sure Mum makes something nice for us to eat again."

"Will do," he says.

He walks to the front door. Beryl brings him one of Cheryl's limbs to play with.

"No doubt your mother will dump you on us at some point soon, so I'll see you then," he says to Beryl, stroking her head.

He pulls the pink limb out of her teeth and throws it along

the hall. She chases after it. Dad opens the door, kisses me on the head and leaves. I push the door closed and look at the cover of the diary in my hand. It's a deep blue with the word Diary printed across the centre in gold coloured script. I run my finger over the word and feel the indentations of the lettering. I open the front cover and read the beautifully hand penned lines; Property of Evelyn Rose Wright (née Bell) 1949. I trace my fingers over the swirls of the letters, theatrically spiralling over the double l. The background for these words is equally as dramatic. The paper lining the inside cover is smooth to the touch. The base is the brightest sapphire colour, flecked with twists of whites and reds, like the waves of patriotic gymnasts' ribbons.

The book smells musty, as though it has been sitting in the shed for years, but it also has that delicious aged aroma of a second hand bookshop found in the basement of a Victorian house. The pages are yellow around the edges. I sit down on the floor by the front door and lean up against the wall. I lift my knees up and rest the book against my thighs. I carefully turn the first page. It creaks as it moves. The first few pages are blank. I close the diary and then open it in the middle, and I see the most amazing page of writing. I scan my eyes over the page. I don't take in the words. I just look at the lines and how everything joins up so perfectly. It looks like one of those handwriting fonts on the computer. There are no mistakes or scribbles. It's beautiful.

I close the diary. I feel awkward. I don't think I should be reading it. I stand up and walk into my study. I put the diary in my desk drawer. Maybe I'll read it. Maybe I won't. Just right now I don't feel like I should. I walk to the living room and open the door. I tidy up the papers and photos from the coffee table and put them back in the plastic wallet. I take them into my study and put them in the drawer with the diary.

I go back into the living room and turn on the television.

I sit down on the sofa and lift my feet onto the coffee table. A woman is suing her daughter for all the money she spent on her when she was a child. The woman explains to the judge that throughout her life she has spent thousands of dollars on her child. The judge asks her what she spent the thousands of dollars on. The mother lists food, clothes, diapers, hospital and doctors' bills, school supplies, holidays, birthday and Christmas presents, parties and toys amongst the things she bought for her daughter. The judge looks at the mother. She leans forward and shouts at the woman. She tells her that those are all normal things that parents buy for their children. A child needs diapers and food and shouldn't be expected to pay for those things. The daughter stands there, not saying anything. The mother puts her hands on the table and leans forward. She starts to speak. The judge tells her not to speak while she's speaking. The mother takes her hands off the table and stands up straight. The judge shouts at the mother. She tells her that she chose to have a baby and by choosing to have a baby, she is choosing to pay for all the expenses that come with having a baby. The mother opens her mouth to speak. The judge shouts at her and tells her not to interrupt her while she's speaking. The mother apologises. The judge asks the woman if she owns a car. The mother says she does own a car. The judge asks her if she's ever had to take the car to the mechanic or to the car wash, or if she's ever bought gas and oil, or reupholstered the seats, or bought new tyres. The mother nods. The judge shouts that the mother needs to speak up. The woman says that she has done those things. The judge asks her if she expects her car to pay for those things. The audience in the court room laughs. The judge shouts at the mother. She tells her that she chose to have a car; therefore she chose to have those expenses. She chose to have a child; therefore she chose to have those expenses.

The mother opens her mouth to speak. The judge gives the mother permission to speak. The mother says that she didn't choose to have a child. She says that the pregnancy was a mistake and she hadn't wanted the baby. The judge holds her hand up. The mother stops speaking. The judge tells the mother that her daughter did not choose to be born. She needed to be fed and clothed. She might not have needed toys and holidays, but they are things that you buy for children to make their lives more bearable and enjoyable. They're not things that can be sued for.

The mother opens her mouth to speak. The judge tells her that she doesn't want to hear what she has to say. The mother says that she didn't want to have a child. The judge stands up and looks directly at the mother. The judge tells the mother that the child didn't want to have a mother like her, but unfortunately that's the way things have ended up. The judge looks at the daughter and asks her if she has a job. The daughter says that she's in college at the moment and has a part time job. The judge asks the daughter if she has any children. The daughter says that she doesn't. The judge tells the daughter that if she does ever to decide to have children, she can't sue them once they reach eighteen years of age for eighteen years' worth of expenses. The daughter smiles. The mother raises her hand. The judge tells her to put her hand down and that she should be ashamed of herself. Her case is dismissed. The bailiff tells everyone that they may be excused.

I turn the television off. One dose of stupidity is enough for one day. I walk into my study and turn on my computer. I look at some pictures of dogs wearing shoes. They bore me. I think about MatesDates. I don't look at it. I do some online window shopping. I find some books, CDs and DVDs to add to my wishlist. I put them in order of priority so that Father Christmas knows what I want. I want far too much.

I do a quiz about the most popular boys' names beginning with A through the decades, from the eighteen-eighties to the two thousands. I have eight minutes. I type Albert, Alfred,

Andrew, Adam, Arthur, Anthony, Alex, Alexander. I have seven minutes. I can't think of any more. I click the Give Up button. The timer stops and the rest of the answers are filled in. Who on Earth would name their child Alvin? I look through the quizzes. I can't be bothered to find out how much I don't know about things I don't really care about. I spin around in my chair.

I open MatesDates. I have one new message. I feel a bit disappointed. I don't open it. I browse men in my area. I scroll down the page. No-one catches my eye. I click Next at the bottom of the page. I scroll down the page. I click on one guy's face. He looks ok. He's a primary school teacher. He probably loves kids. He probably has hundreds of stories about the funny things that the kids in his class say. The stories are probably cute to start with but they'll probably get boring after a while. I click back. I scroll through the next page. No-one looks particularly interesting.

I give in and click the envelope which is pulsing at the top of the screen. I have one new message from KMB44. I open the message. Hi, thanks for your message. Most women on here aren't particularly interested in actually meeting up. They chat and send e-mails but as soon as you ask them out for a drink they're either busy or they just ignore you. So thank you for changing my view of women on here. As by chance I am free next week. Well, I'm free on Monday. I work all day Saturday and Sunday in my dad's shop, and then babysit my nephew most weekend evenings. My sister is an exotic dancer and she makes most of her money those nights. But I'm free Monday afternoon, maybe for a cheeky beer garden beverage. Let me know how you feel about that. Take care, Seth.

He seems nice. I reply. Hey, thanks for your reply. I'm sorry for the delay but I've had a busy couple of days. I hope you manage to see this message before you have to go off on your babysitting duties. A cheeky beverage sounds good. I don't know if you have a favourite pub but The Salmon Tree has a pretty decent beer garden and they sell the best cheesy wedges I've ever tasted. How does two-ish sound? Have a good evening and hopefully see you tomorrow.

I send it. I wish I hadn't. I feel sad and angry. I don't want to lead him on. I know it's not going to go anywhere. I open his profile. He is quite good looking and he did reply to Louise's message from me. He's an electrician and I don't know anything about electricity so that might be an interesting conversation. And he's just looking to date, nothing serious, so I guess he's probably going out with other people too and not looking for a relationship just yet. There's nothing I can do about it now. The message has been sent.

I go into my bedroom and pick up my phone. I open a new text message. What are you doing tomorrow afternoon? Are you free to look after Beryl for a couple of hours? I'm going on a date with one of those randoms you messaged the other day and I don't fancy having to explain it to my parents. You can come round and eat all my food and fall asleep on the sofa to your heart's content. I send the message to Louise.

I take my phone with me and walk back into my study. I sit down and look at Seth's pictures. He is actually more than quite good looking. He's quite a bit good looking. An envelope pops up in the top corner of my computer screen. I click on the envelope. I have one new message from KMB44. That was quick. I open the message. Hey, 2-ish at The Salmon Tree sounds great. Sorry for the brief reply. My nephew wants to look at videos of dancing cats. He's pushing my arm away as I type. See you tomorrow. Seth. Well I have to go now. I look at my phone. The Cyclops eye winks. I have one new message from Louise. Yep, what time? Remember you're just dating, nothing serious. I remember. I reply. I know, I know. I'm meeting him at two-ish, so half one? I send it.

I put my phone on my desk and turn to my computer. I refresh the screen. No new messages. I refresh the screen again. No new messages. I refresh the screen again. No new messages. I push my mouse away. I look up at the clock. It's nearly ten past eleven. It's late. I'm not tired. I don't want to do anything. I spin around in my chair. I slow to a stop. I open my desk drawer and look inside. I take out the diary. I run my hand over the cover. I put it on my desk and close the drawer. I shut down my computer and walk out of the room. Beryl follows me. I walk into the kitchen and open the back door. Beryl runs outside. I want to open the diary but I don't want to open it at the same time. It has to contain something interesting, why else would she have written a diary and then hidden it if it wasn't interesting. But at the same time I wouldn't want anyone reading my diary, even if I was dead. Not that I'd ever write down anything too embarrassing. I can't imagine my nan ever doing anything embarrassing. So I'm sure there's nothing too incriminating in her diary. It'll probably just be about things like baking and housework and my granddad. And back then it was all lie back and think of England, so there's no way she would have written about anything like that.

Beryl comes back in, walks over to her bowl of water and laps at the liquid. I take her food bowl from the side. The piece of shepherd's pie is cold now. I put it on the floor and she eats. I put the diary down on the side and shut the back door. I lock it and pull the curtain across. I put the leftover shepherd's pie in the fridge and take out a handful of chocolate bars. I pick up the diary and walk into my bedroom. Beryl follows me. I put the chocolate and diary on my bedside table. I open one bar of chocolate and eat it in two bites. They must be getting smaller.

I close the curtains and get undressed. I put on my pyjamas and sit down on my bed. Seth doesn't have my phone number. I don't have his. How am I supposed to let him know if I'm running late? I never run late so I won't need to call him. But what if he needs to call me? What if something happens outside of his control and he doesn't want it to look like he's standing me up? I can't be bothered to turn my computer back on. I stand up and slide my feet into some trainers. I hurry into the kitchen, unlock the back door and pull a bin bag out of the drawer. I walk to the clothes line and pull my clothes off the washing line. Pegs ping off in all directions. I'll pick those up later. I stuff my clothes into the bin bag and carry them into the kitchen. I lock the back door and dump the bin bag on a chair. I kick my trainers into the hall and walk back to my bedroom.

I lean all four pillows up against the headboard and I get into bed. I pull the pillows about until I'm comfortably sitting up. I open another bar of chocolate and eat it in two bites. They definitely are getting smaller. I drop the wrapper on the floor. I pick up the diary and slide my knees up towards me. I rest the book on my knees and slowly open the front cover.

31

The pages feel so delicate. I turn each one as if it was made of puff pastry. I look at Beryl. She's asleep. Nothing happens for most of January. Or perhaps she didn't get the diary until the twenty-sixth of January.   Great news. Frank returned from the meeting with the biggest smile on his face that I had ever seen, he could not contain it. He walked into the kitchen, picked me up and spun me around like I was a rag doll. I told him to put me down, which he did, but he held me close to his chest. 'This is where it starts,' he said. 'Everything changes from here on in.' My dear diary, it is true, everything is going to change and I am so excited.

I turn the page over. Thursday 27th January ~ We went to have another look at the building and it is just so beautiful.   From the outside it is so warm and welcoming. I could have stood and looked at it for hours. Frank became irritated with me when I wouldn't go inside. From under the canopy he shouted that I would catch my death if I stood out in the rain for too long but I honestly had not noticed that it had started raining. I ran across the road, avoiding the puddles at the kerbside, and stepped inside. Frank locked the door behind me. He took my coat, and once I had brushed myself off, I looked up. I was speechless. It was more amazing than I had remembered it. The ceiling was so high in the lobby and the carpet was so soft underfoot. Frank took my hand and we walked up the stairs. The brass banisters shone. At the top of the stairs Frank told me to close my eyes and he guided me forward. I heard him pull the door open and he walked me forward a bit further. The temperature dropped and I shivered but that feeling did last for long, as Frank told me to open my eyes and the butterflies danced around in my stomach. I opened my eyes and saw the most incredible, magical sight. I had never imagined it could ever look like that. I felt like I was a child again. I wanted to run and touch and explore everything. Frank had to return to work so we had to leave. He said we could have a better look around on Saturday. I wanted to stay there. I wanted to dance.

Friday 28th January ~ Frank has been spreading the word and interest is high. He has spoken to a number of men at the pub and even some from the factory, and they want to come along. Ronald already wants to get involved and he will be joining us tomorrow so that he can get a feel for the place. I will be glad for the additional assistance as I know Frank will be too busy behind the scenes, as it were, to help elsewhere. Frank is the thinker and I am the doer. Goodnight my dear diary. I will convey my news tomorrow.

I turn the page over. I yawn. I slouch further down into bed. Saturday 29th January ~ The sun shone on us today. It was frightfully cold but I was too excited for it to bother me. Ronald was already there, waiting for us outside. He stood under the canopy and waved us across the road. I could see from the glint in his eye that he was as excited as I was. Frank took the key from his pocket and unlocked the door. I walked in and gazed in awe at the ceiling as though

***

Beryl paws at my chest. I push her away. I open an eye and look at the clock. It's eight forty. I move. It hurts. I'm still sitting up. My knees are still pulled up. I straighten my legs. It hurts. Beryl jumps off the bed and sits by the door. I roll myself out of bed. Something falls on the floor. I reach down and find the diary. I pick it up. It doesn't look damaged. I put it on my bedside table. I stand up. It hurts. I feel like I've been in a fight. I stretch my arms up. It hurts. I shuffle towards the kitchen. I unlock the back door. Beryl runs outside. I pick up her bowl. It hurts. I wash out the bowl and dry it. I put it on the side and lean down to open the fridge door. It hurts. I take out a tin of dog food and scoop what's left in the tin into the bowl. I kick the fridge door closed and leave the tin on the side. I'll sort that out later. I get a handful of biscuits and mix those in with the meat. I put the bowl down on the floor. It hurts.

Beryl comes in and heads straight for the bowl. I close and lock the back door. I walk into the bathroom and sit on the edge of the bath. I slide the plug into the plughole and turn on the hot tap. I stand up and reach my arms above my head. I fight through the pain and stretch. My neck clicks. My back realigns. My legs refuse to properly straighten. I slump on the toilet. The bath fills up. I turn off the hot tap and turn on the cold. I drop my pyjamas into a pile by the door and get into the bath. My muscles cry out in relief. I sink under the water. I don't want to get out.

I dry myself off with a flannel. I really need to bring some towels into the bathroom. I'll put that on my 'to do' list. I take my pyjamas into my bedroom. I pick up my dressing gown and wrap it around myself. I open the curtains. I walk into the kitchen and open the fridge. It doesn't hurt. I scoop some shepherd's pie out onto a plate and put it in the microwave. I press the Auto Reheat Meal button and then the Start button. The microwave whirs into action. I put the rest of the shepherd's pie back into the fridge and shut the door. I pour myself a mug of water and take it into the living room. I put it down on the coffee table and pick up the remote control. I turn on the television. I walk back into the kitchen and take a fork out of the cutlery drawer. The microwave beeps. I put on my Father Christmas oven glove, open the microwave and take out the plate. I walk into the living room and sit down on the sofa. I put the plate on the coffee table.

A super skinny woman on the telly tells me that she's lost so much weight on the 'pay-a-pound, lose-a-pound' diet. She stands in an immaculately clean and tidy living room, wearing the skimpiest outfit imaginable. I'm sure this is not appropriate for morning television. She walks around her living room, caressing furniture as she goes. She stops by the fireplace and takes a framed photo from the mantelpiece.

"This was me, only three months ago," she says, excitedly.

The camera zooms in on the photo. The same woman stands there in a badly fitting tracksuit. She's slouching forward, pushing her stomach out. Her hair is dirty and she's not smiling. The woman throws the photo behind her, lifts her arms up in the air, cocks a hip and does a twirl.

"And this is me now, after the pay-a-pound, lose-a-pound diet," she says. "It's so simple. The more money you pay, the more weight you lose."

I lean forward and stick my fork into my food. I pick up the plate and lean back on the sofa. I eat.

"Every morning, as soon as you wake up, you text the word 'help' to your very own, special diet hotline number," she says, holding up her mobile phone and pretending to press the buttons. "It only costs you one pound per text and you will immediately receive a text back, giving you a health and fitness tip for the day. If you are serious about losing weight, you will follow those tips to the letter. I did and look at me now."

She does another twirl. I choke on my food. I take a sip of water from the mug. She provocatively bends over the sofa and picks up what looks like a parachute.

"Just three months ago I was wearing these trousers," she says, holding them up in front of herself. They are at least four times as wide as she is.

She climbs inside one of the trouser legs and pulls them up to her miniscule waist. She throws her arms up in the air and the trousers drop to the ground.

"But I can wear this now," she says, doing another twirl.

I shovel more food into my mouth.

"I didn't have to give up any of the foods I love," she says, walking into an immaculately clean and tidy kitchen.

She waves her arms over various plates covering the worktop. The camera zooms in on a plate of colourful lettuce leaves, a bowl of chopped up celery, a plate of cucumber and tomato slices, a bowl of fruit salad, a bowl of ice cubes, and a bowl of what looks like sesame seeds.

"I could still eat three good meals a day while on the diet, so I never went hungry," she says, picking up a piece of celery, popping it into her mouth and winking.

A voiceover man tells me to call now for a free information pack. It contains everything I need to know about the diet, including an easy to follow step by step instruction booklet telling me how to get started. I should call today to ensure that I don't miss out on this great offer. All I need to do is pick up the phone now and call the number on my screen for a free information pack today, four-ninety-nine postage and packing. I scoop the last bit of mashed potato into my mouth and switch off the television.

I take my plate into the kitchen and put it on the side. I'll sort that out later. I wander back into my bedroom and pick up my phone. The Cyclops eye winks at me. I have one new message from Louise. Yep. I drop my phone down. I walk into my study and turn my computer on. I walk back into my bedroom and pick up my phone. I walk back into my study and sit down at my desk. I put my phone down next to my keyboard and I open MatesDates. I have one new message. I click on the pulsing envelope at the top of the screen. It's from Seth. I open it. Sorry, just quickly, here's my phone number, just in case you're running late or can't make it or whatever tomorrow. 077889151664. Seth.

I reply to the message and send him my phone number. So that's sorted. The Cyclops eye winks. I have one new message from an unknown number. I open the message. Hi just checking this is you, Seth. I reply. I think this is me, is that you? I send the message. I save his number. The Cyclops eye winks. I have one new message from Seth. This is indeed me. Have a good morning. I'll see you later. I put my phone down. I switch my computer off and go back into my bedroom. I can't settle. I sit on the edge of my bed. I notice the diary. I twist round and bring my feet up onto my bed. I shuffle myself back and lean up against the pillows. I move them around until I'm comfortable. I pick up the diary and open it.

I scan over what I read last night. Saturday 29th January ~ The sun shone on us today. It was frightfully cold but I was too excited for it to bother me. Ronald was already there, waiting for us outside. He stood under the canopy and waved us across the road. I could see from the glint in his eye that he was as excited as I was. Frank took the key from his pocket and unlocked the door. I walked in and gazed in awe at the ceiling as though I had never laid eyes upon it before. The sun shining outside made the inside look entirely different. Ronald ran up the stairs, two at a time. My heart was racing as I followed him up the stairs. He pulled the doors open at the top of the stairs and stood in the doorway. He thought it was wonderful, as did I. I don't think I will ever think differently about it. Ronald strode to the front and stood in front of the stage, his arms wide open. The stage?

I scan over the page. My eye is drawn to two words towards the end of the page. Talbot's Theatre. My heart races. My palms feel clammy. I wipe my hands on the duvet. I go back to where I left off. Ronald strode to the front and stood in front of the stage, his arms wide open. I walked towards him, touching the velvet fabric covering the seats as I went. I stood next to Ronald and looked at the stage, it was magnificent, more than I could ever have dreamed. I turned around and surveyed the rows and rows of seats. I closed my eyes and imagined the seats full of people. Now, dear diary, don't be fooled into thinking that the theatre is large, for it is not. It is, however, large enough for our plans. When I walked up the steps and stood in the centre of the stage I could envisage night after night of sold out performances. I walked backstage and found dressing rooms and storage for costumes, which reminds me, I need to collect the material from the haberdashery. I also need to speak to Frank to fix a day when I can measure up the dancers for their costumes. And we absolutely must find a pianist. Oh diary. Dear, dear diary, I am in love with Talbot's Theatre. We have so much to organise and so little time. Wish us luck.

I get off the bed and walk into my study. I pick up the phone and call my parents.

"Hello," my mum says.

"Dad there?" I ask.

"Hello Mum, how are you? Oh I'm fine, thanks for asking. If it wouldn't be too much trouble would you mind getting Dad for me, if you don't mind, please and thank you," Mum says.

"You ok?" I ask.

"It wouldn't hurt you to care," Mum says.

"I do care," I say. "I've just got some good news for

Dad."

"Oh, ok then," Mum says. "Tom, it's your daughter."

"Hello," Dad says.

"Nan wasn't a prostitute," I say.

"Well I knew that anyway," he says. "But what's made you so sure?"

"I read her diary," I say.

He doesn't say anything.

"Well, I've not read it all, just a few pages," I say.

"And?" he says.

"And, her and Granddad either bought or were given that Talbot Theatre, and they put on shows and things there," I say.

"So why did those people write such horrible letters to her?" Dad asks.

"I don't know," I say. "Perhaps the shows were a bit risqué or something."

"Perhaps," Dad says. "I'm still not sure you should be reading her diary though."

"Well I can't get rid of it, and I can't have a book in my house that I haven't read," I say.

"So what's your excuse with the piles of books in your study?" Dad asks.

"I can't help it when they're buy two get one free," I say. "It would be criminal not to buy them."

"Maybe if you read some of those books, you might get some inspiration for your own book," Dad says.

"I'm reading a book at the moment that's giving me a few new ideas," I say.

"Good, get that masterpiece written," he says. "I want to retire."

"You're already retired," I say.

The doorbell rings.

"I'm going to have to go," I say. "I think Louise is at the door."

"Have you got any of that shepherd's pie left?" Dad asks.

"Yeah, a bit," I say.
"Not for long," he says.
I laugh.
"See you soon," I say.
"Love you," Dad says.
"Love you too," I say.

I hang up the phone, put the diary in my desk drawer and walk to the door. Louise hurries past me to the bathroom.

"Sorry I'm early," she says, shutting the bathroom door behind her.

I walk into the kitchen and look at the clock on the microwave. It's eleven fifty. I hear the toilet flush. The door opens. Louise walks towards me and wipes her hands down my jeans.

"You really need towels in the bathroom," she says.

I look down at the wet patches on my thighs.

"Thanks," I say.

"Food?" Louise says.

"Leftover shepherd's pie in the fridge," I say.

She walks into the kitchen. I walk to the airing cupboard and pull out a pile of towels. I take them into the bathroom and hang them over the towel rail. I walk into the kitchen and Louise is eating a bar of chocolate. She's standing in front of the microwave, dropping her head from side to side as the timer counts down. The microwave beeps. Louise beeps along with it. She opens the door and takes out the plate.

"Are your hands made of asbestos?" I ask.

She laughs.

"I have to use an oven glove to take things out of the microwave," I say.

She puts her plate down on the table and looks at me with a sad face.

"Aww, is the platey watey too hotty wotty for your dewicate handy wandies," she says, patting me on the head.

I push her away and take the empty oven dish to the sink.

I turn on the tap and squirt out some washing liquid into the dish. I leave it to soak.

"So what's new with you?" I ask her.

She dumps the bin bag of my clean clothes onto the floor and sits down.

"Not much," she says, eating. "My boss has been sacked."

"Nice one," I say. "What happened?"

"I planted some drugs in her locker," she says.

"You did what?" I ask.

"Not really," she says. "But I wish I had."

"So what really happened?" I ask.

"She was caught flashing at a guy in a coma," she says.

"You're joking," I say.

"Nope," she says. "Apparently she's been doing it for a while. She would wait for the families to go and then she'd stand by the bed, pull the curtain around them and pull her top up."

"So how did she get caught?" I ask.

"Well she saw a family leave, so she went over to the guy's bed, pulled the curtain around them, pulled her top up and was dancing around when the guy's daughter came back because she couldn't find her car keys and thought they'd fallen out when she'd been visiting her dad," she says.

I laugh.

"It's not funny," Louise says, laughing. "They looked back over the security cameras and saw her loitering by the coma patients' beds with a mop or a cloth. She was pretending that she was cleaning, so no-one really paid attention to her. And when the visitors had gone, she'd pounce."

"So what's your new boss like?" I ask.

"Lovely," Louise says. "We're going out on Wednesday."

"Are you allowed to do that?" I ask.

"As long as I'm not flashing coma patients, they don't

really care what I do," Louise says.

"Fair enough," I say.

"How about you," Louise says. "What's new with you?"

"Nothing," I say, leaning my back against the sink.

"Stop being a grump," she says. "You've got a date in a bit."

"I know, but it's just a date, nothing serious, remember?" I say.

"Good girl," Louise says.

"Oh, and my nan wasn't a prostitute," I say.

"Aw, that's a shame," Louise says.

"Why?" I say.

"It could have made for an interesting book," Louise says. "Better than the tripe you're writing at the moment."

"Oi," I say. "And for your information, I've had a few new ideas for something else."

"And how many words have you written?" Louise asks.

"Well none yet," I say.

"I knew it," Louise says.

"It's just in the ideas stage at the moment," I say.

"Yuh-huh," Louise says.

"So why are you here so early?" I ask.

"Bored," Louise says.

She scrapes some meat from her plate onto the floor. Beryl licks around Louise's feet.

"Drink?" Louise says.

"You know where it is," I say.

I walk into the living room and sit down. I pick up a magazine and flick through the pages. Louise comes in with a glass of water.

"Your milk's out of date," she says.

"I'll get some later," I say.

"So you've not thrown that out yet," she says.

"What?" I ask.

"The painting," she says.

"I don't know what to do with it," I say.

"Hang it up," she says.

"I can't," I say.

"Why not?" she asks.

"You know I'd end up knocking half the house down if I tried to hammer a nail into a wall," I say.

"True," she says. "Well you can't leave it there."

"I know," I say. "But I've got to get dressed now."

"Make an effort," she says.

"I will," I say.

"But not too much," she says.

I walk into my bedroom and pick some clothes up off the floor. I sniff them. I drop a couple of tops back onto the floor. I pull on a pair of jeans and a white vest. I shove my arms into a pink cardigan and slip my feet into a pair of trainers. I bend down and tie up the laces. I walk into the living room. Louise is curled up on the sofa watching a DIY programme on the television. Beryl is curled up at her feet.

"Satisfactory?" I ask.

"Nope," Louise says. "But it'll do."

"Thanks," I say.

"Have fun," she says.

"I'll try," I say. "See you in a couple of hours."

"Or maybe longer," she says, craning her head back to wink at me.

"Don't eat all my food," I say.

"Bye," she says.

I open the front door and walk outside. I walk up to The Salmon Tree and sit on the wall in the car park. I check my phone. I'm early. A few people walk past. I smile politely. I keep my phone in my hand just in case he calls.

"Hi," a voice says.

I look up. It's Seth. He looks much better in person than in his photos.

"Sorry if I'm late," he says.

I smile at him.

"I'm always early," I say.

He laughs. I stand up.

"Shall we?" he says, gesturing towards the pub.

So far so good. A couple walk out of the pub. The man holds the door open for me. I take it from him.

"Thank you," I say, walking inside.

I walk to the bar. Seth stands next to me. I take my purse out of my handbag. The barman looks at me.

"Can I have a pint of lager please," I say.

"Which one?" he asks.

"Whichever one you're nearest to," I say, looking in my purse for a note.

"This one ok?" he asks.

"Yep," I say. "Fine."

I check the menu on the bar.

"And some cheesy wedges," I say.

The barman puts my pint in front of me. He looks at Seth.

"No, it's ok," he says. "I'll get my own."

The barman turns around and presses some buttons on the till. He turns back to me and hands me a wooden spoon with a number four on it. I hand him a ten pound note. He puts it in the till and hands me my change. I put it in my bag and take a sip of my pint. The barman looks at Seth.

"I'll have the same, thanks," he says.

"Is it alright if I put the food on the same spoon?" the barman asks.

Seth nods. The barman pulls his pint and puts it on the bar. Seth roots around in his wallet for the right change. He showers coins into the barman's hand.

"We'll be outside," I say to the barman.

"No worries," the barman says.

I pick up my pint and Seth picks up his. We walk through the pub to the back door and go into the beer garden. It's not too cold. I sit down at a picnic table. Seth sits opposite me. I put the wooden spoon into an empty pint glass that's sitting on the table. We drink. I'm not really in the mood to chat. He smiles at me.

"So?" he says.

"So," I laugh.

"Have you had a good day so far?" he asks.

"Yeah it's been pretty good," I say. "My friend Louise …"

"What have you been doing?" he asks.

"Well my friend Louise came round earlier," I say. "She's dogsitting for …"

"Have you known her long?" he asks.

"I don't even want to count the years," I say, laughing. "But we met at primary school."

"So you trust her with your dog?" he asks.

"I trust her with everything I have," I say. "She's like a sister to …"

"Have you got any sisters?" he asks.

"No, I haven't," I say. "I'm an only …"

"Any brothers?" he asks.

"No," I say. "No brothers."

"So you're an only child then?" he asks.

"Indeed I am," I say.

"Why's that?" he asks.

"I don't know," I say. "You'd need to talk to my parents."

"Are they alive?" he asks.

"Excuse me?" I say.

"Are your parents still alive?" he asks.

"They are," I say. "Last time I checked."

"What's your mum's name?" he asks.

"Karen," I say.

"What does she do?" he asks.

"She's retired," I say.

"What's your dad's name?" he asks.

"Tom," I say.

"What does he do?" he asks.

"He's also retired," I say.

"Don't they get bored?" he asks.

"Far from it," I say. "When I was round there on Friday, my dad was clearing out the loft and …"

"Have you got any cousins?" he asks.

"I have," I say.

"How many?" he asks.

I count on my fingers.

"Six," I say.

"Boys or girls?" he asks.

"Two boys, four girls," I say.

"What are their names?" he asks.

"Michael, Joshua, Natalie, Hannah, Andrea and Jordan," I say.

"That's three boys and three girls," he says.

"Jordan is a girl," I say.

"How old are they?" he asks.

"I have no idea," I say.

"Why not?" he asks.

"I don't always know how old I am," I say. "Let alone family members I don't speak to."

"Why don't you speak to them?" he asks.

"It's a really long story that I don't really want to go into," I say.

"What are your hobbies?" he asks.

"Well, I like loads of things," I say. "I like writing and reading and I sometimes knit and I used to bake a bit but I haven't done it for …"

"What sort of things do you write?" he asks.

"Bits of everything really," I say. "I used to write poetry but I don't do so much …"

"Who's your favourite poet?" he asks.

"I don't really have one," I say.

"What else do you write?" he asks.

I take a long sip of my beer.

"I've written short stories in the past," I say. "And the odd play but …"

"What are your short stories about?" he asks.

"Erm," I say. "I've written loads. I couldn't even begin to tell you what they're all about, but I mainly like to write about quirky people who …"

"When do you do most of your writing?" he asks.

"Whenever I get inspiration really," I say.

"And when is that?" he asks.

"I don't know," I say. "Inspiration can come whenever it wants. It doesn't care what you're doing."

"So do you normally get your inspiration in the morning or at night?" he asks.

"I don't know," I say. "When it comes, it comes. I don't tend to check the clock."

"But on average, when would you say you do most of your writing?" he asks. "In the morning or at night?"

"I couldn't even say," I say. "I just write when I write."

"Have you ever been published?" he asks.

"I haven't," I say. "But I'd like …"

"Why haven't you?" he asks.

"A few reasons," I say. "But mainly because I'm lazy."

I laugh. He doesn't crack a smile.

"Don't you want to be published?" he asks.

"I do want to be published," I say. "I'm just too lazy to get it done. One day I'll get it sorted."

The waitress comes over with two plates of cheesy wedges and some napkins. She puts them down on the table.

"Thank you," I say.

She smiles at me. She picks up the beer glass and wooden spoon, and walks away. I pick up a potato wedge. It's hot. I drop it back down. I wipe my fingers on a napkin.

"Have you ever been on holiday?" Seth asks.

"Yeah, a few times," I say.

"Where was your favourite place?" he asks.

"That would have to be Japan," I say.

"Do you like Japanese food?" he asks.

"I love it," I say. "We went to some amazing restaur …"

"Do you like Japanese music?" he asks.

"To be honest, I haven't really heard any," I say. "They listen to all sorts over …"

"Do you like Japanese people?" he asks.

"Well the ones I met were very lovely and welcoming," I say. "They were all impressed that I knew how to use chopsti …"

"Can you use chopsticks?" he asks.

I'm starting to feel irritated. I pick up the same potato wedge that I put down earlier. It's cooler. I blow on it and put it in my mouth.

"I haven't had these in a while," I say. "But they're as good as I remember."

I pick up another one and wrap a strand of melted cheese around it. I eat it.

"Can you use chopsticks?" he asks.

"Just about," I say. "I managed quite well when I was in Japan and they were happy to see me try."

"Why did you go to Japan?" he asks.

"I have a friend who lives there," I say. "And she invited me to visit."

"Where did you meet her?" he asks.

"At university," I say.

I drink some beer and eat some wedges.

"Is she Japanese?" he asks.

"No," I say. "She's Engli …"

"Where's she from then?" he asks.

"England," I say.

"Why does she live in Japan?" he asks.

"She works out there," I say. "I'm quite jealous actually. I wish I had the guts to pack up and go to anoth …"

"Do you drive?" he asks.

"I do," I say.

"Have you got your own house?" he asks.

"I do," I say. "Well it's a bungalow not a hou …"

"Have you got a garden?" he asks.

"It's more like a jungle at the moment," I say. "I did try to give it a haircut the other day but …"

"Why did you get a dog?" he asks.

"We always had dogs when I was little," I say. "And when I moved into my own house …"

"I thought you said it was a bungalow," he says.

At least he's paying attention to some of the things I'm saying.

"It is. And when I moved in, it felt empty and I was a bit lonely, so I got a dog to keep me company," I say.

"What sort of dog is it?" he asks.

Hasn't he even read my MatesDates profile?!

"She's a shi-tzu," I say.

"Is it a boy or a girl?" he asks.

"She's a she," I say. "Shes tend to be girls."

"What's it called?" he asks.

"She's called Beryl?" I say.

"Why did you call it Beryl?" he asks.

"My grandmother put it in her will," I say, smiling.

"That's a stupid thing to put in a will," he says.

I take a deep breath. I look around the garden. Couples and families and friends are sitting together, laughing and chatting and enjoying themselves. I pick up a couple of wedges and eat them. The more I eat, the more they lose their amazingness.

"My grandmother wasn't what you would call conventional," I say.

"What would you call her?" he asks.

"I don't know," I say. "She was just a bit different, a bit eccentric."

"How so?" he asks.

"Well firstly she put in her will that I name one of my children Beryl," I say.

"Have you got children?" he asks.

"No," I say.

"Do you want children?" he asks.

"I don't know," I say. "I haven't really thought about it."

"Do you like children?" he asks.

"I do like children," I say. "But I can never manage to eat a whole one."

I laugh. He doesn't. I drink. I laugh. Beer comes out of my nose. I cough. He just looks at me. I wipe my mouth with a napkin. I laugh. I eat a potato wedge and cover my mouth with my hand. I can't stop laughing. I pick up my glass and swallow down the liquid.

"I've just got to go to the toilet," I say. "Do you want anything?"

"No," he says.

I laugh.

"I mean, do you want anything from the bar?" I say. "Not from the toilet."

I giggle. I'm drunk. He doesn't say anything. I pick up my bag and stand up. I wobble. I really need to go to the toilet. I hurry inside and walk straight for the toilet. My eyes blur. I push the door open and walk straight for a cubicle. I pull the lock across. It's broken. Typical. I hurry into the next cubicle. I'm going to wet myself. I pull the lock across. It locks. I drop my bag to the floor and fumble with the buttons on my jeans. I manage to get my clothes sorted before wetting myself. I sit down. I drop my head into my hands. I laugh. I can't stay here. I don't have the energy to answer any more questions. I might just steal something. The interrogation from the police will be a lot less stressful than this date. I laugh. I bring my bag up to my knees and open it. I pull out my phone and press a button to wake up the screen. The screen doesn't wake up. I press another button. Nothing happens. I pull the back off my phone and pop out the battery. I put it back in and clip the cover back on. I turn the phone over and press a button. Nothing happens. I press all the buttons. Nothing happens. I put the phone to my ear.

"Louise," I say. "I need you."

I laugh and sob at the same time. I stand up, pull my jeans up and flush the toilet. I hold my bag, unlock the cubicle door and walk to the sink. I turn the tap on and rinse my hands. I turn off the tap and put my hands under the hand dryer. It doesn't work. I drop my head and laugh. I press the button on the front of the dryer. It whirs into action and blows hot air out onto my hands. It lasts a few seconds. I wipe my hands down the front of my jeans. I walk into the pub and make my way over to the bar. I perch on a bar stool and lean my elbows on the bar.

"What can I get you?" the barman asks.

"Pint," I say. "Please."

"The same as before?" he asks.

"That'll do," I say.

"Going well, eh?" he asks.

"Excuse me," I say.

"Your date," he says.

I laugh.

"Sorry," the barman says. "I don't mean to be rude, but I've been watching you through the window and you really don't look like you're enjoying yourself."

I stand up. I laugh. The barman puts the pint down in front of me.

"First dates are never supposed to be brilliant," I say.

"True," the barman says. "But have you ever had a worse first date than this?"

I laugh.

"No, I haven't," I say.

I open my purse and dig out some coins. I give them to the barman. He walks over to the till. I take a sip of my drink. He walks towards me and gives me my change.

"Thank you," I say.

I pick up my drink.

"Er," the barman says.

"Yes?" I say.

"I don't know if this is inappropriate, considering that

you're on a date and everything," he says.

I put my drink back on the bar.

"But could I get your number?" he asks.

I laugh. Typical. I've been waiting at the bus stop for years with no sign of a bus and this is like the tenth bus to come along in the past couple of weeks.

"I'm sorry," he says. "I shouldn't have asked."

"No, honestly, it's fine," I say.

I put my bag on the bar and pull out my phone. I press a button to wake up the screen.

"Gah," I say.

"What's up?" the barman asks.

"Dead battery," I say.

"So you can't even text a friend to be your get out call?" he asks.

I drop my head forward and laugh.

"No!" I say.

The barman laughs. I sigh.

"I can't give you my number," I say. "Because I don't know what it is."

I laugh.

"It's ok," he says, picking up a beer mat.

He gets a pen from under the bar and writes his number on the beer mat. He passes it to me.

"Thank you," I say, sitting back down.

"I can promise you that you won't spend more time talking to the barman when you're on a date with me," he says.

I laugh. I put the beermat in my bag.

"I'm Zac, by the way," he says.

"Nice to meet you Zac Bytheway," I say. "I'm Lexa."

"That's an interesting name," he says.

"I'm really called Alexana," I say. "But I shorten it."

"That's still an interesting name," he says.

"Well, yeah," I say. "My parents like to be a bit different."

"I shorten my name too," he says.

"Zachary?" I ask.

"People assume that," he says. "But my name is Isaac."

"I like that name," I say.

"Really?" he asks.

"Yeah," I say. "It's distinguished."

"And what's your date's name?" he asks.

"Seth," I say.

Zac doesn't say anything. I look at him, waiting for him to speak.

"My date!" I say, getting off the stool.

"You should really get back to him," he says.

"I don't want to," I whimper.

"Seriously, though," he says. "Give me a call."

"Will do," I say.

I smile, pick up my bag and my drink, and walk to the back door.

32

I make my way to Seth and sit down opposite him.
"I thought you'd done a runner," he says.
I laugh.
"There was just a problem at the bar," I lie. "A barrel needed changing or something."
I'm too fed up and drunk to care about the lie. I'm bored. I want to go back inside and talk to Zac.
"What was the last thing you bought?" Seth asks.
"Eh?" I say.
"What was the last thing you bought?" he asks again.
"This pint," I say, holding up my drink.
"I mean, something that isn't food or drink," he says.
"Oh," I say. "That would be a pregnancy test."
"Why did you buy that?" he asks.
"I couldn't be bothered to do any washing up and I needed something to stir my tea," I say.
I laugh. He doesn't.
"My friend thought she was pregnant," I say. "She wasn't."
"How do you know she wasn't?" he asks.
"She took a test," I say. "It was negative."

"Those tests aren't a hundred per cent accurate," he says.
"Well I guess we'll just have to wait and see," I say.
He sips his drink.
"How about you?" I say.
"What about me?" he asks.
"Well you've asked me about a hundred questions about me but you've not said anything about you," I say.
"You haven't asked me anything," he says.
"You haven't given me the chance to ask anything," I say.
"Now's your chance," he says, staring at me.
My mind goes blank.
"Er," I say. "So where do you work?"
"All over," he says.
"Oh right, how come?" I ask.
"I'm an electrician," he says.
I remember now from his profile.
"Do you like it?" I ask.
"No," he says.
"Oh," I say. "What would you rather do?"
"I don't know," he says.
I sip my drink. He looks at me.
"So," I say. "Did you enjoy looking after your nephew last night?"
"I always do," he says.
"What did you get up to?" I ask.
"Not much," he says.
"Did he like the cat videos?" I ask.
"Yes," he says.
"Sometimes I lose half a day watching those things," I say. "And the dog ones too."
I laugh. He doesn't.
"I saw one the other day," I say, laughing. "And I had to watch it on repeat. There was a dog sitting on a chair at the dinner table wearing a sweatshirt, and a guy had put his arms through the arms of the sweatshirt, and he was cutting up

food and feeding it into the dog's mouth."

I giggle.

"It was so funny," I say. "If you ignored that they were people hands, it looked like the dog was feeding himself."

I laugh. He doesn't.

"Haven't you seen that one?" I ask.

"No," he says.

"At one point, the dog's wearing a pair of glasses and reading a magazine," I say, laughing.

He stares at me. I stop laughing. I drink most of my pint, leaving about an inch of the liquid in the bottom of the glass.

"Well I really should go now," I say. "My friend is dogsitting and I don't want to leave them for too long."

"Ok," he says.

We walk through the beer garden and into the pub. Zac is wiping down the bar. He looks at me and smiles. I smile back.

"Thank you," he says to us.

"Thank you," I say back.

He winks at me. I laugh. I walk through the front door into the car park. Seth walks over to a car.

"Do you want a lift home?" he asks.

"No thanks," I say. "I don't live far from here. And the walk might do me good. I'm a bit tipsy."

"Ok," he says. "Bye."

He turns around and gets in his car.

"Bye," I say.

I walk out of the car park and make my way home.

I push my front door open and slam it closed. Beryl runs out of my study towards me. I pick her up and walk into the study.

"How was it?" Louise asks.

I glare at her.

"Good, eh?" she says.

I put Beryl on the armchair by the window. I walk into my bedroom and drop my bag on my bed. I take out my phone and plug it in to charge.

"I wondered why you didn't reply," Louise says, standing in the doorway.

"I needed you," I say. "I needed you to call me to get me out of there, but I had no battery."

I sit down on my bed and drop backwards. Beryl jumps up next to me.

"He wouldn't stop asking questions," I say.

Louise laughs.

"Question after question after question," I whine. "And he kept cutting me off mid-sentence. And then when I tried to ask him questions, he gave me one word answers."

I feign crying. Louise sits on the bed and strokes my hair. My phone beeps. Louise leans over me and picks up my phone.

"You have two new messages," she says. "One from someone called Louise. How's it going? Aw, she seems nice."

I look at her. She smiles.

"And one from Seth," she says.

I sit up.

"Is this your interrogator?" she asks.

"Yep," I say. "What does he say?"

"Thanks for this afternoon, I had a really nice time. Let me know if you want to do it again sometime," she reads.

"It doesn't say that," I say.

"It does," she says, shoving the phone in my face.

"I don't believe it," I say, reading the text.

"I take it you don't want to do it again sometime," she says.

"Not in a million years," I say.

I drop my head back down and close my eyes.

"Who's Zac?" she asks.

I open an eye. She waves the beer mat at me.

"Stop going through my bag," I say.

"I didn't," she says. "It fell out."
"Uh-huh," I say.
"Soooooo?" she says.
"So nothing," I say.
She looks at me.
"He's a barman at The Salmon Tree," I say.
She laughs.
"And he gave you his number when you were on a date with someone else?" she says. "Smooth."
"He could see that I wasn't enjoying myself," I say.
"Such a gentleman," she says.
"Give it back," I say.
She drops the beer mat onto my face. I put it back in my bag.
"Have you had a good afternoon?" I ask.
"Yeah it was ok," she says.
"What did you two get up to?" I ask.
Louise laughs.
"What did you do?" I ask, sitting up.
"We didn't do anything, did we Beryl?" Louise says.
I look at her.
"Apart from organise another date for you," she squeals, clapping her hands.
"You did what?" I ask.
"We got bored, didn't we Beryl?" Louise says. "So we thought we'd have a little look at your MatesDates profile and send out a few more messages to a few more people, and we didn't expect anyone to reply but we got one reply pretty much straight away. And you're meeting him for a drink tomorrow."
I glare at her.
"You can thank me later," she says.
I sigh and sit up.
"Show me what he's like," I say.
I get up and walk into my study. Louise follows me. I sit down on my desk chair and Louise leans over my shoulder.

She moves the mouse and opens my MatesDates profile. She clicks through my messages and opens EverythingYouWant's profile.

"He's gorgeous," I say.

"I thought you'd approve," she says.

"And he wants to meet me?" I ask.

"Apparently so," she says.

"What did you say to him?" I ask.

"The same as I sent to those guys the other day," she says.

"He's seen my picture, right?" I ask.

"Yes," she says.

"And he wants to meet me?" I ask.

"Indeed he does," she says.

I smile. I look into his smouldering eyes staring at me from the screen.

"This can't really be him," I say. "Someone who looks like this can't be looking for a girlfriend on a dating site. He must have women throwing themselves at him all the time."

"I asked him that," she says. "Well, you did. And he said that he doesn't get asked out at all, and if he tries to chat someone up in a bar, the girls think he's doing it for a bet or a laugh with his friends or only after one thing. So he uses dating sites as a way of getting to know people."

"I see," I say. "I think."

"He's only interested in dating too, so you haven't got to take it too seriously," she says.

"Well it can't be much worse than today's date," I say.

"There you go," she says. "That's the attitude."

"What's his name?" I ask.

"Luc," she says.

"Luke?" I ask.

"No, Luc," she says. "He's half French."

"Ooh," I say.

"I know!" Louise says.

"So where are we going?" I ask.

Louise leans over me again and opens a message from Luc. I scan over the message. Are you free tomorrow (Tuesday) afternoon for a quick coffee? I'm working all day but can nip out for an hour or so. So shall we say 11am at Greenley's? We can share some carrot cake! My number 07365854541 if you need to contact me before then. Until tomorrow, Luc.

"He's very well spoken," I say. "Or written."

"And at least you know you've only got to spend an hour with him," she says.

"True," I say. "Did you give him my number?"

"I did," she says.

I grin. I'm excited.

"Did you get any milk?" she asks.

"I forgot," I say.

"I'll bring some round tomorrow," she says.

"You're coming round tomorrow?" I ask.

"To dogsit, silly," she says.

"Don't you have to work?" I ask.

"I've got my new boss wrapped around my little finger," she says, waggling her little finger at me.

"Are you sure?" I ask.

"Yep," she says. "I've got to work tomorrow morning, so I'll just have to leave an hour or two early to make sure I'm here on time."

"Is there any point you going in?" I ask.

"Not really," she says. "But I will anyway."

"Ok," I say.

"I'm going home now," she says.

"Ok," I say. "Thanks for looking after Beryl."

"No worries," she says.

"But you're not getting any thanks for sending a message to Seth," I say.

"But I will get some thanks tomorrow for sending a message to Luc," she says, winking at me.

"We'll see," I say. "It's only a date, nothing serious, remember?"

"Exactly," she says. "See you tomorrow."

Louise walks into the hall. I hear the front door slam shut. I look at Luc's pictures. He's very good looking. Not my usual type, but it's just a date, nothing serious. I open my desk drawer and take out the plastic wallet. I slide out the photos and the papers. My hand finds the newspaper article. I hadn't noticed before, but the picture on the article is the most recent photo of Talbot's Theatre. I look at the headline. FIRE DESTROYS TALBOT'S THEATRE. I read the article.

Flames swept through the prestigious Talbot's Theatre last night, completely destroying the building. Police and fire fighters believe that the blaze was started by teenagers who were using the building as a site for an illegal dance party. In the late 1940s and early 1950s the theatre was infamous for staging progressive and risqué shows. Ever since the opening of the long running *Dressed As A Girl* in 1949, the theatre's popularity and notoriety grew. A victim of the recession, the Talbot Theatre closed in 1986, and was much mourned by the avant-garde from all areas of the arts. The owners, Frank Wright and his wife Evelyn, are devastated by the fire. "It's terrible," said Mr. Wright, sadly. "We were one of the first theatres to stand up to prejudice, showing a drag act chorus line. I know we had quite a bit of opposition at first, and there were a lot of people happy to see us close, but all in all most people grew to love us and came time and again to see our glamorous productions." His wife, the former Evelyn Bell, continued, "This theatre was a large part of our lives, and even when we moved away from the area, leaving Ronald Noble at the helm, we always kept in touch and often visited. We are proud of what we achieved here and the barriers that we helped to break down. I just can't believe that all of our hard work has been burnt to the ground. But our memories will never be lost. It was a beautiful place, and it will remain that way in our hearts. It will be sadly missed." There are no immediate plans for the future of this site.

It makes sense. Kind of. But how come Dad doesn't know anything about it? Surely he must have been there or heard his parents talking about it. What was with all the secrecy? I'm too tired to think about it now. I turn my computer off and put the papers and photos back into the drawer.

I walk into the kitchen, open the back door and Beryl runs out. She quickly does her business and comes back inside. I lock the back door and pull the curtain across. I pick up a mug and get a drink of water. I notice the bin bag on the floor and drag it through the kitchen, through the hall and into my bedroom. I put the mug on the windowsill and pick up the bag. I shake the clothes onto my bed. They are crumpled and creased and balled up and tangled. I pick up each item of clothing and shake it, then hang it on a hanger and squish it between other things in my wardrobe. No need for ironing there. The creases will drop out. I take the bin bag back into the kitchen and put it in a drawer.

I go back into my bedroom, close the curtains and get undressed. I put on my pyjamas and get into bed. I yawn. I'm more tired than I thought. I stare at the ceiling. Is that how you made all of your money, Nan? With the theatre? Why didn't you tell me about it? What were you hiding?

***

The doorbell rings. Beryl barks. My eyes won't open. I'm still asleep. I roll over. The doorbell rings again. Beryl jumps on my head. I pull myself up and drag myself to the door. I open the door and pull it towards me. A bottle of milk greets me.

"Take your time, why don't you?" Louise says.

"Ok," I say.

I yawn and stretch. I take the milk and walk into the

kitchen. I put the bottle on the side. The front door slams closed. I open the back door and Beryl runs out. Louise walks into the kitchen.

"Feed yourself," I say.

"Charming," she says.

"Shower," I say.

I walk into the bathroom, close the door and do my business. I wrap a towel around myself and go into my bedroom. I pull on the jeans I wore yesterday and a black and white top from the wardrobe. I pick up a black cardigan off the floor and slip my feet into a pair of flip flops. I brush my hair and then tousle it. I walk into the living room.

"You look better than you did yesterday," Louise says.

"Thanks," I say.

"Have fun," she says.

"I'll try," I say.

I get my bag, open the front door and make my way into town.

33

I walk up to Greenley's. No-one is waiting outside. I'm early. I walk along the road and have a look in some shop windows. I take my phone out of my bag and switch it off silent. I check the time. It's ten fifty. I walk to the end of the road, turn around and walk back. I check the time. It's ten fifty-four. I sit on a bench near the coffee shop. A woman is struggling with a baby and a toddler. The baby won't stop crying and the toddler keeps crouching down, pulling chewing gum from the underside of the bench and putting it in its mouth. The woman frantically bounces the baby until it looks like its head is going to fall off, and pulls the toddler up every time it crouches down.

"Dirty," the woman says. "No Shelby. Dirty."

I check the time. It's ten fifty-seven. I open a new text message. Hey, I'm a bit early. Sitting outside on a bench next to an incompetent mother. I send it to Luc. I look at my phone for a reply. Nothing. I look around to see if I can see him. It's not too busy but no-one looks familiar. Shelby continues to put dirty things into her mouth. His mouth. Her mouth. I can't tell what flavour child it is. I look at Shelby's chubby face in the hope of noticing something masculine or feminine in his or her expression. Nothing. The orange tracksuit also does nothing in determining the sex of this child. The mother looks at me. I awkwardly smile.

"What are you looking at?" she asks.

"Nothing, sorry," I say.

I stand up for fear of being brandished a paedophile and walk over to Greenley's. I look through the window but can't see Luc in there. I look at my phone. No new messages. I wander along the street again, stopping longer at the shop windows. My phone beeps. I have one new message from Luc. I thought you looked pretty rough in your profile picture but wanted to see if you were better looking in real life. You're not. Hopefully I won't see you later.

I close my eyes. A tear rolls down my cheek. I feel like I've been punched in the stomach. My chest tightens. I can't breathe. I gasp for air. I put my phone in my bag and walk back through town. Everyone is looking at me. Everyone is laughing at me. They know. They all know. They're in on it. They've all been in on it. My legs feel heavy. I walk. I bump into people. I don't say sorry. I say it in my head. I turn into a quiet road and stop. I look up at the sky and let myself cry. A postman walks past. I feel stupid. I speed up my pace and walk home. I slam my front door open. I walk in. Louise leans her head out of the kitchen.

"That was quick," she says.

I kick the front door closed, throw my bag down and walk into my study. I sit down at my desk and turn on my computer. I stand up and walk into the bathroom. I pull the end of the toilet roll up to my face and blow my nose. I drop down and sit on the closed toilet seat. Beryl comes in and jumps on my lap. Louise stands in the doorway eating some cheese.

"What happened this time?" she asks.

"I think you mean 'what didn't happen?'" I say.

"What didn't happen?" she asks.

"The date," I say. "The date didn't happen."

"Why not?" she asks. "Was he nothing like his photos in real life? Did you do a runner?"

"The other way around," I say.

"What?" she says.

I stand up, Beryl jumps off my lap, and I walk back into the hall. I pick up my bag and take out my phone. I find Luc's message and pass my phone to Louise. I walk into my study and sit down. I open my MatesDates profile. I click to edit my profile. I scroll down to the bottom of the screen and click the Delete Profile button. The screen goes blank for a second then returns to the home page. It's as though I never existed. I close MatesDates and turn my computer off.

"I can't do it," I say. "I can't look for something when there's nothing there to find."

Louise puts my phone down on my desk.

"People are cruel," she says. "Do you want me and Safa to beat him up?"

I laugh.

"We'll do it you know," she says.

I sigh.

"Smash in his oh so attractive face," she says, punching the air. "Then he'll know what it's like to be ugly."

I cry.

"I give up," I say.

"You can't let one idiot make you feel that way," she says, wrapping her arms around me. "What about that Zac? And don't forget William wants to talk to you when he's back. You can't give up on that. You don't know what will happen."

"I don't want to know what will happen," I say.

"Not now you don't, but sleep on it and you'll feel better when you wake up," she says.

"It's only half eleven," I say.

"I bet you could still have a sleep," she says.

"You're right," I say. "I'm not in the mood to do anything."

"I know," Louise says.

I stand up and walk into my bedroom. I pull off my clothes and pull on my pyjamas. I get into bed and Beryl jumps up beside me. Louise comes in and walks over to the television. She turns it on and puts a DVD in.

"Something to try and cheer you up," she says.

"What is it?" I ask.

"Stand-up comedy," she says.

I smile. My head sinks into the pillow.

"Thank you," I say.

"Any time," Louise says.

I shut my eyes.

***

The DVD's menu music loops. I reach my hand out for the remote control and switch off the television. I turn over. I'm awake. I rub my eyes. Beryl climbs onto my chest and stretches out. I scratch her back. She lets out a smelly yawn and jumps off me. I get out of bed and stretch. I walk to the kitchen and open the back door. Beryl runs out. I'm hungry. I look at the clock on the microwave. It's seven minutes past four. I make some microwave porridge and stand by the back door. Beryl runs around the garden. I feel empty.

I sit on the doorstep. The grass is short. Did Louise cut the grass? When did she do that? I smile. Beryl runs. I eat. I finish my porridge, stand up and put my bowl in the sink. I'll sort that out later. I walk into the hall and pick up Beryl's ball. I stand at the back door and throw the ball outside. Beryl chases it. She carries it in her mouth and walks towards me. I take it out of her mouth and throw it. She jumps up in excitement and chases the ball. She kicks it and pushes it with her nose, then picks it up in her mouth and brings it to me. I take it and throw it. She chases it and brings it back. To be as happy as a dog with a ball. At this moment in time, the ball is her world. Nothing else exists for her but the ball. I'm jealous.

It starts to rain. I stand up and walk inside. Beryl follows me. I shut the back door, lock it and pull the curtain across. I open the dishwasher and load in plates and bowls and mugs and cutlery. I put a plastic soap bubble into the slot on the inside of the dishwasher door. I snap the slot closed and then close the dishwasher door. I press some buttons on the front and it starts up. I wander into the hall. Beryl drops her ball and starts a fight with Cheryl. I walk into the living room and pull the sheet off the canvas. I sit on the floor in front of it.

I know I'm not a supermodel but I'm not ugly. Some supermodels are ugly, but if they call themselves edgy, they're no longer ugly. William doesn't think I'm ugly. Well, he didn't think so when he painted this. I don't know what he thinks now. I stand up and walk into my study. I take my phone off my desk and press a button to wake up the screen. I have no new messages. I want a new message. I want a new message from William. I sit down on my desk chair and spin myself around. I stop myself and open my desk drawer. I pick up Nan's diary and open it to a random page.

Saturday 19th February ~ I am extremely tired today as we have been so busy. I don't know what time I went to bed last night, but I finally finished sewing all of the sequins on the dress last night. If I never see another shiny bead again, it will be far too soon. Frank woke up early and went to the theatre to check the lights and the staging and I met him there a few hours later, once I had tidied up the hem of the dress and stitched the feathers into a fan. When I arrived at the theatre Ronald was rehearsing a dance on the stage and Harry was playing the most fabulous tune on the piano. I ran down to the stage and sat in the middle of the front row and watched as Ronald danced to the microphone and started singing. His voice gave me goosebumps, I'd never heard him sing before. He will be the star of the show, I just know it. When he finished, he took a bow and I gave the loudest round of applause that I could. Ronald came down and sat next to me. I passed him the box and when he opened it, he could not control his smile. He stood up, holding the dress in front of him. He disappeared backstage and I went to talk to Harry. Ronald came back out a short while later wearing my sequined creation. I passed him the fan and he held it in front of his face. He twirled and did a few dance steps across the stage. I asked him if it was too tight or too restricting and he continued to dance. He held the fan up and kicked his leg out, he looked incredible. Once I have bought his wig and shoes, he will be complete. Frank has spoken to a few more people who are interested in performing, but I will need some help with the sewing. I must ask Harry if he can speak with his tailor. Frank wants to open at the beginning of April. I am too excited for words.

I laugh. I put the diary down on my desk and take the photos out of my desk drawer. I lay the photo of the suited man and the woman in the burlesque dress side by side on my keyboard.

"You must be Ronald," I say to the suited man. "And you must be Ronald," I say to the woman.

I pick up the phone and call my parents.

"Hello," Dad says.

"Hello," I say.

"How are you?" Dad asks.

"Fine," I say. "You know Nan?"

"Have you read some more of her diary?" he asks.

"Only a page," I say.

"Do I want to know what you've read?" he asks.

"I think you will," I say.

"Go on," he says.

"Well," I say. "The shows that were put on at Talbot's Theatre were drag shows."

"What?" Dad says.

"Drag shows," I say. "Men dressing up as women."

"I know what a drag show is," Dad says.

"It would appear, and I am just making assumptions here, but it looks like the man in the suit and the woman in the burlesque dress are in fact the same person," I say.

"How did you work that out?" he asks.

"Well they look uncannily familiar," I say. "And from what Nan was saying about a guy called Ronald ..."

"Ronald?" Dad says, surprised.

"Do you know him?" I ask.

"Yeah, he worked with my dad," he says.

"I think that's him," I say. "The man in the suit, and the woman in the dress."

"No," he says. "That's not Ronald in the photos."

"Are you sure?" I ask.

"Yes," he says. "I remember he used to come and visit us, a couple of times a year at least. He was a blonde man, from what I can recall. And he wore glasses. No, it's definitely not him in the photos. I don't remember his wife though."

"Maybe he wasn't married," I say. "Maybe he liked the men."

"He had children," he says. "They were a bit younger than myself and Alan. We didn't like them much."

"The plot thickens. I'll keep digging," I say. "This is getting interesting."

"Anything too interesting, and you keep it to yourself," Dad says.

"Ok," I say.

"Although, you could use some of this as inspiration for your book," he says. "You know, if you've got a bit of writers' block or anything."

"I was thinking exactly the same thing," I say. "By the way, how's the sculpture coming along?"

"I haven't started it yet," he says.

"Oh?" I say. "Why not?"

"I can't decide what I want to do," he says.

"But I thought it was more enjoyable to walk an unknown path than go to the shops, or something like that," I say.

"Indeed it is," he says. "But even if you walk an unknown path, you have to start somewhere, and there are too many places to start."

"Well I'll let you get back to it," I say.

"Ok," he says. "Take care."

"You too," I say.

"Love you," he says.

"Love you too," I say.

"Bye," he says.

"Bye," I say.

"Bye," he says.

"You already said that," I say.

"Ok," he says. "Sorry. Bye."

"Hang up the phone," I say.

"Bye, bye, bye," he says.

"Bye," I say, hanging up the phone.

I turn on my computer and put the photos back in the plastic wallet. I find the newspaper article. I forgot to tell him about that. I'll call him back later. I open a new document and start typing. I write about a young woman in the nineteen fifties, just recently married, who is discontented with the humdrum of normality. She's a housewife and she doesn't mind it but she wants something more. She goes to the theatre and to the cinema and she looks at pictures of women in magazines, looking glamorous. One day her husband tells her that he's managed to buy an old theatre, just for her. I don't know where he got the money from just yet. Maybe someone died and left him a lot of money in the will or maybe, maybe, I don't know yet. I can sort that bit out later. They go to the theatre and it's very small, and very hidden, but it's also very beautiful. The outside is a bit shabby, but they can clean that up with a lick of paint, but the inside is immaculate. Maybe the theatre had to close down because of the war and no-one opened it back up. Maybe that's why it was cheap enough to buy. Maybe the previous owner was too old or too ill or injured during the war, and couldn't manage to run it. Or maybe he died and his wife sold it or gave it away. I don't know. But she loves it. She loves the idea of putting on shows and being involved with the production and the magic of the theatre. She wants to make costumes and paint scenery.

They fix up the theatre and involve their friends and members of the community, but more men than women are interested in being a part of their theatre, so some of the men have to wear dresses. There is uproar in the community, especially from the strict churchgoers who maintain that it is sinful. They boycott the theatre, insisting that the woman and her husband are working for the devil.

I write and write and write. My phone beeps. It makes me jump. I save what I have written under the title of better book and pick up my phone. I have one new message from William. I take a breath in. I open it. I got back home this morning and have to go to the job centre tomorrow, oh joy. I won't ask you to meet me there again. But we could meet in the park afterwards. William.

I reply. Hope you had a nice time away. Tomorrow is fine. What time? I look at the clock on the wall. It's nearly ten past eleven. I look at the time on my computer screen. It's eleven fourteen. The clock on the wall is not far wrong. I close down my computer and walk into my bedroom. My phone beeps again. I have one new message from William. Time away was great thanks. Really needed a break. Meeting is at 9:30 so should be out by 10. William.

I reply. I'll see you tomorrow in the park at ten-ish then. Just to warn you, I'll be bringing Beryl, so you may need to wear knee pads. I send the message, turn my phone on silent and get into bed. Beryl jumps up next to me. I set my radio alarm for eight o'clock in the morning. I lie down and close my eyes.

***

An incessant hissing and crackling drills its way into my ears. I sit up quickly. I feel sick and dizzy. My eyes fill with black splotches that fade away. I turn the tuning dial on the radio ever so slightly. A clear voice sings something about love. I don't want to listen to that. I get up and open the curtains. Beryl doesn't move. I walk into the kitchen and open the back door. Beryl runs outside and does her business. She comes back inside. I close and lock the back door. I open a tin of dog food and dollop half the tin into her bowl. I stir in a couple of handfuls of biscuits, put the bowl on the floor and Beryl eats.

I walk into the bathroom and turn on the shower. The room starts to steam up. I throw my pyjamas into a pile in the corner and climb into the shower.

I wrap a towel around myself and another around my hair. I walk into my bedroom and find my hair dryer. I put my hair dryer on my bed and flick my head down. I unravel the towel and rub it over my hair. I switch my hairdryer on and blast shots of hot air through my hair. It takes forever to dry. I walk into the kitchen and open the fridge. I close the fridge and open a cupboard. I close that cupboard and open another. I'm not hungry. I'm too nervous to eat. I open the fridge and take out a bar of chocolate. I eat it in two bites.

I walk back into my bedroom. I look out of the window. It doesn't look like it's going to rain but it doesn't look warm. I pull on a pair of black tights, a red and white dress, and a black cardigan. My feet find their way into a pair of red trainers. I give my hair one more going over with the hair dryer. My hair doesn't dry. I pull it back and twist an elastic hair band around it. That'll do for now.

I pick up my phone and put it in my handbag. I put Beryl's collar on her and clip her lead to it. I put on my jacket, unlock the front door and walk outside.

34

Beryl and I walk into the park. It's quite quiet. Beryl chases some pigeons. I take my phone out of my bag. I press a button to wake up the screen. I check the time. It's nine thirty-two. I walk around the park. An old man is shuffling along mumbling to himself. I walk past him.

"They're watching," he says. "They know where you are and what you're doing. Mark my words. They're watching."

Nutter. I carry on walking. I look over my shoulder. He's not wearing a tin foil hat. I walk towards the bench I sat on when I first met William. No-one is sitting there. It must be a sign. It's not a sign. No-one is sitting on the other benches either. I sit down. Beryl plays with a stone at my feet. I take my phone out of my bag. I check the time. It's nine thirty-eight. I call Louise.

"What?" Louise says.

"I'm meeting William," I say.

"What?" Louise says.

"I'm in the park now," I say. "He sent me a text me to say that he'd give me a chance to explain everything. We're meeting at ten."

"The only ten I care about right now is the buh-TEN I press to end this call so I can go back to sleep," Louise says.

"I'm really nervous," I say.

"It'll be fine," she says.

"You don't know for a fact that it's going to be fine," I say. "You can't see into the future."

"Hmm, sounds familiar," Louise says. "Didn't a wise woman once say that, not too long ago?"

"I feel sick," I say.

"Do you like him?" she asks.

"Yeah," I say. "I do."

"More than the other one?" she asks.

"Gregory," I say. "And yeah I do. He didn't even bother to get in contact with me."

"Just don't do anything stupid," Louise says.

"Like what?" I say.

"I don't know," Louise says. "Just don't be too much of your normal self."

"Louise," I say.

"I'm sorry," she says. "Just say what you have to say and let him make up his mind if he wants you or not. Don't scare him away."

Beryl pulls away, yanking my arm. I drop my phone. I pull Beryl back with one arm and pick up my phone with the other hand.

"Beryl!" I shout.

I look up. William walks towards me with Beryl walking at his heel.

"Got to go," I whisper. "He's here."

I press the button to end the call and put my phone in my bag.

"Hi," I say.

"Hi," William says.

William sits down next to me.

"This is the bench we sat on when Beryl tried to kill me," he says.

"Is it?" I lie. "I hadn't noticed."

I had noticed and he had noticed. This had to mean something. Beryl jumps up on the bench and climbs on William's lap.

"Sorry about her," I say, pulling Beryl away.

"It's ok," he says. "I don't mind."

I smile and look down.

"How was the job centre?" I ask.

"Same as usual," he says. "If you don't mind, can we please not talk about that? I'm not in the mood to punch my fist through a brick wall."

"Noted," I say.

I look down again.

"I'm sorry," I say.

I look at him. He smiles at me.

"Can I explain?" I ask.

"Well that's what we're here for," he says.

I feel awkward. I don't know where to start.

"I don't know where to start," I say.

"I tend to go for the beginning," he says. "You might like to try that."

"Now there's a plan," I say, laughing nervously. "Ok, so, well, my friend Louise has been on this dating site for absolutely ages, and she kept insisting that I sign up and go out with people, but I never really fancied it to be honest with you. I know it's silly but I like the idea of meeting someone in real life, like bumping shopping trolleys in the supermarket or both reaching for the same book at the library or …"

"Or having their dog almost kill them in the park?" he asks.

"Exactly," I say. "So I didn't think you could really meet anyone decent on a dating site. And then one day, I don't know why, I signed up. I got a message from Gregory or I sent him a message, I can't really remember now, and we arranged to meet up, which we did, one evening, for a drink, but he had to cut the date short and promised to make it up to me. That was the day before I met you. I'd left Beryl with my parents that night, so the next morning I went to pick her up and we thought we'd walk home through the park, and then some idiot thought it would be a good idea to tangle his legs up in her lead."

I stop talking and take a breath. I feel like crying. I look at him. He's looking at me.

"And then you said about going to see the band, and he said about going to see the band, and I'd had a really lovely second date with Gregory, but I also liked you and as I'd only been out with Gregory a couple of times I didn't think there was anything wrong with going out with you. But then I couldn't go to see the band with you because William would have been there and that would have been awkward but I didn't know that you were related. Well I thought you were when you both spoke about Nana Bertie, and then I thought you were brothers, which is a lot worse than cousins as you should never go out with brothers at the same time. Not that it's ok to go out with two people at the same time, but going out with brothers at the same time is really bad and …"

"Breathe," he says.

"I'm sorry," I say. "I just don't know how to explain this. What happened is so unlike me."

"Just take your time," he says. "I'm here because I wanted to let you explain yourself. You don't have to make it more complicated than it is."

"Ok," I say.

Beryl curls up on the bench. She rests her head on my thigh.

"I went out with Gregory and he was telling me about his sister and he said that he had no brothers, so I knew then that you weren't brothers. I was hoping it had been a coincidence about Nana Bertie, but deep down I knew it wasn't. You had to be cousins. And I went out with

Gregory, and I liked him, and he was nice. And I went out with you, and I liked you, and you were really nice. And then you went and did that picture of me, and no-one has ever done anything like that for me before, apart from my dad, but that doesn't count. And I was going to make a decision before it got too serious and before anyone could get hurt, but I waited too long."

"Who would you have chosen?" he asks.

"Don't ask that," I say.

"I'm just curious," he says.

"You," I say.

"Are you just saying that because I'm here?" he asks.

"No," I say. "But I don't expect you to believe me."

He doesn't say anything.

"And then when I was at yours and Gregory came round, and it all kicked off, I didn't know what to do or say to make things better, and I didn't know who to talk to and I know I probably handled it all wrong and made all the wrong decisions, but it's happened and there's nothing I can do about it now. But I am sorry. I didn't mean for any of this to happen."

He smiles at me.

"And I didn't think it would end like this," I say. "I mean, I'd only been out with both of you a couple of times. I didn't expect for you both to turn so funny with me."

"I can probably explain that one," he says.

"Oh?" I say.

"This was years ago, and I'm not proud of it, but it happened, and it's not who I am anymore," he says.

"Ok," I say.

"Gregory had been going out with a girl for a while, not long, maybe a couple of months, and I don't know why I did it. Maybe I just wanted to see if I could. I don't know. But anyway. One night I was out with some friends and I saw Gregory's girlfriend. She was out with her friends. So I went up to her and said hi and bought her a drink and then one thing led to another, and I regret it, and we were extremely drunk, and I know that's no excuse, but we ended up in bed together, and because she really liked Gregory, she didn't want to lie to him, so she told him the next morning."

I don't say anything. I look at him. He's looking down at his hands.

"What happened?" I say.

"He beat me up," he says. "I deserved it. I know that. But it put a strain on our relationship."

"I can imagine," I say.

"And then when he found you at my house, he thought the same things was happening again," he says. "When you came back to mine and I was on the phone, it was Gregory filling my ears with abuse. He wouldn't believe that I'd met you independently and that I hadn't known you'd been out with him. I probably shouldn't have slammed the door in your face, but I just didn't want to deal with everything. I didn't want him in one ear and you in the other."

I feel terrible. I had never meant to hurt Gregory but I wasn't to know what had happened between him and William.

"He must have forgiven you, though, for the girl you slept with," I say.

"I don't think he'll ever forgive me," he says.

"Then why was he at your house?" I ask.

"His mum doesn't know what happened. I don't know why he never told her, but Gregory had come round to pick up some things I'd borrowed from his mum," he says.

"Right," I say. "It's a bit of a mess, isn't it?"

"You can say that again," he says.

"It's a bit of a mess, isn't it?" I say.

He looks at me and smiles. It starts to rain.

"I know you probably won't want to," I say. "But do you want to come back to mine, for a drink, or some lunch?"

"You don't know what I probably do or don't want to do," he says.

"I know," I say. "I'm sorry."
"But I probably will want to," he says.
I smile. I try to hold it down but my mouth won't let me.
"Are you sure?" I ask.
"Yes," he says. "Now move. I don't know if you've noticed, but it's raining."

I stand up. Beryl jumps off the bench. William stands up and we all walk out of the park.

I run up to the front door and pull my keys out of my bag. I unlock the door and push it open. Beryl runs in. William and I follow. It's so cold. I push the door closed and drop my bag onto the floor. I unclip Beryl's lead and unbuckle her collar. I walk into the kitchen and take her towel off the radiator. I rub her dry.

"You kept it then?" William says.
"What?" I say.
"My painting," he says.

I walk out of the kitchen into the hall. He is standing in the doorway to the living room. I feel embarrassed.

"Yeah," I say. "I couldn't get rid of it."
"Why not?" he asks.
"I really like it," I say.
"Narcissist much?" he asks.

I laugh.

"If I was a narcissist, I would have hung it up and not left it in the living room and covered it with a sheet," I say.
"So what's the real reason for not hanging it up?" he asks.
"I don't know how to do it," I say.
"Do you want me to do it?" he asks.
"You don't have to," I say.
"I don't like the thought of one of my paintings just being sat on the floor under a sheet," he says.
"What about all those things in your conservatory?" I ask.
"They're unfinished," he says.
"Hmm," I say. "Ok."

"And where would you like this masterpiece to go?" he asks.

"I was going to originally hang it in my bedroom," I say.

"So where would you like it now?" he asks.

"In my bedroom," I say.

I laugh and blush. He laughs.

"Hammer? X hooks? Nails?" he asks.

"Er," I say. "My dad said there was a toolbox in the shed."

He laughs. I walk into the kitchen and unlock the back door.

"But be careful," I say. "A family of inner-ear eating spiders live in there."

"Thanks for the warning," he says.

He stands in front of me.

"Oh," he says. "I forgot something."

"What?" I ask.

He puts one arm around my waist and the other hand on my neck. He pulls me close to him and kisses me. My insides explode. I wrap my arms around him and put my hands on his back. I pull him close to me. I don't want the kiss to end. I step back.

"I forgot something too," I say.

"Oh?" he says.

"You go and battle the spiders and I've just got to tidy up a bit in my bedroom," I say.

He laughs.

"Ok," he says. "I think we've both got a challenge on our hands."

I laugh. He walks towards the shed. I walk into my bedroom. I pick up Louise's pro/con list and rip it up. I stuff the paper into a boot in my wardrobe. I'll definitely get rid of that later. I scoop up all the dirty and clean clothes off the floor and carry them into my study. I dump them on the armchair by the window. Most of them fall on the floor. I turn around and something on my desk catches my eye. I hold my 'to do' list and reread Louise's suggestions. 4) Reply to your MatesDates messages. I pick up a pencil and tick that off. 5) Go on lots of dates. I sigh and tick that one off. 6) Meet your Prince Charming. I look over my shoulder. I hear William in the kitchen talking to Beryl. I tick that one off. 7) Fall in love. I smile and tick that one off.

"Done," I say.

Acknowledgements

This book would have never been written without the support of my parents, Carol and Tony Giltrow, and of course my dog, Lily (my very own Karen, Tom, and Beryl). Thank you Dad for checking my grammar and spelling. Thank you Mum for noticing plot holes and inconsistencies in the story. I wouldn't have made much sense without you. Your red pen skills were very much appreciated.

Thank you to Suzan Collins for reading my drafts and pointing out all of my mistakes, and to Di Humphrey for giving me support and encouragement at Lowestoft Library Writers' Group. Your blue pen skills were very much appreciated.

A big thank you to my facebook friends for liking and commenting on my word count status updates.

Mohammed H. Alghamdi, Kim Armon, Aino Bergh, Peter Buckley, Gemma Bulbul, Tess Caney, Kyang-Yu Chen, Jane Chu, Mel Cole, Alison Davies, Carla Dodd, Lucy Dodd, Lee Ann Dorr, Rebecca Giltrow, Charlotte Jane Glover, Caroline Hossack, Lea Haynes, Clare Hooper, Patricia Husband, Liz Mills, Rebecka Ottosson, Emily Robertshaw, Anita Sheldenkar, Holly Elizabeth Smith, Michelle Webb, Viki Webb, Kelly White, Joe Wilson, Millie Wilson, Liana Vava.

You all thought that you were just liking my status updates, but in fact you were giving me the encouragement to write so much more and finish my first novel.

Although every effort has been made to eradicate any errors in the text you have just read, some ninja mistakes may have slipped through. If you happen to spot something not quite right, please let me know: rgiltrow@gmail.com

Printed in Great Britain
by Amazon